RASPUTIN™

THE ROAD TO THE WINTER PALACE

CREATED BY

ALEX GRECIAN & RILEY ROSSMO

image

BOLSHOE SPASIBO
TO OUR FRIEND
ROBERT SALLIN

Image Comics, Inc.

Robert Kirkman — Chief Operating Officer
Erik Larsen — Chief Financial Officer
Todd McFarlane — President
Marc Silvestri — Chief Executive Officer
Jim Valentino — Vice President

Eric Stephenson — Publisher
Kat Salazar — Director of PR & Marketing
Emily Miller — Director of Operations
Corey Murphy — Director of Retail Sales
Jeremy Sullivan — Director of Digital Sales
Randy Okamura — Marketing Production Designer
Branwyn Bigglestone — Senior Accounts Manager
Sarah Mello — Accounts Manager
David Brothers — Content Manager
Jonathan Chan — Production Manager
Drew Gill — Art Director
Meredith Wallace — Print Manager
Addison Duke — Production Artist
Vincent Kukua — Production Artist
Sasha Head — Production Artist
Tricia Ramos — Production Artist
Emilio Bautista — Sales Assistant
Jessica Ambriz — Administrative Assistant

www.imagecomics.com

RASPUTIN, VOL. 1: THE ROAD TO THE WINTER PALACE
ISBN: 978-1-63215-267-1
First Printing

RASPUTIN™

THE ROAD TO THE WINTER PALACE

WRITER
ALEX GRECIAN

ARTIST
RILEY ROSSMO

COLORIST
IVAN PLASCENCIA

LETTERER
THOMAS MAUER

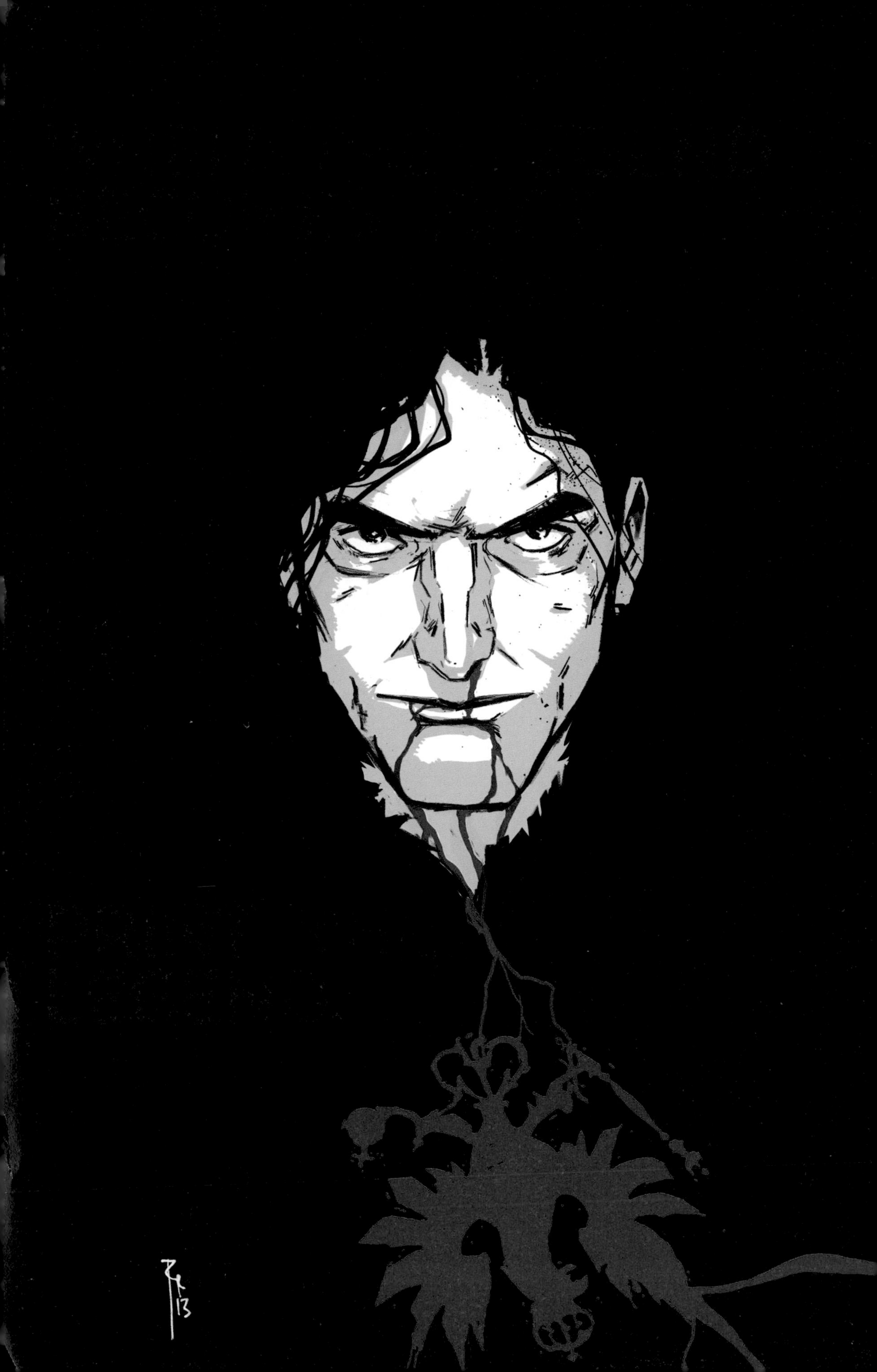

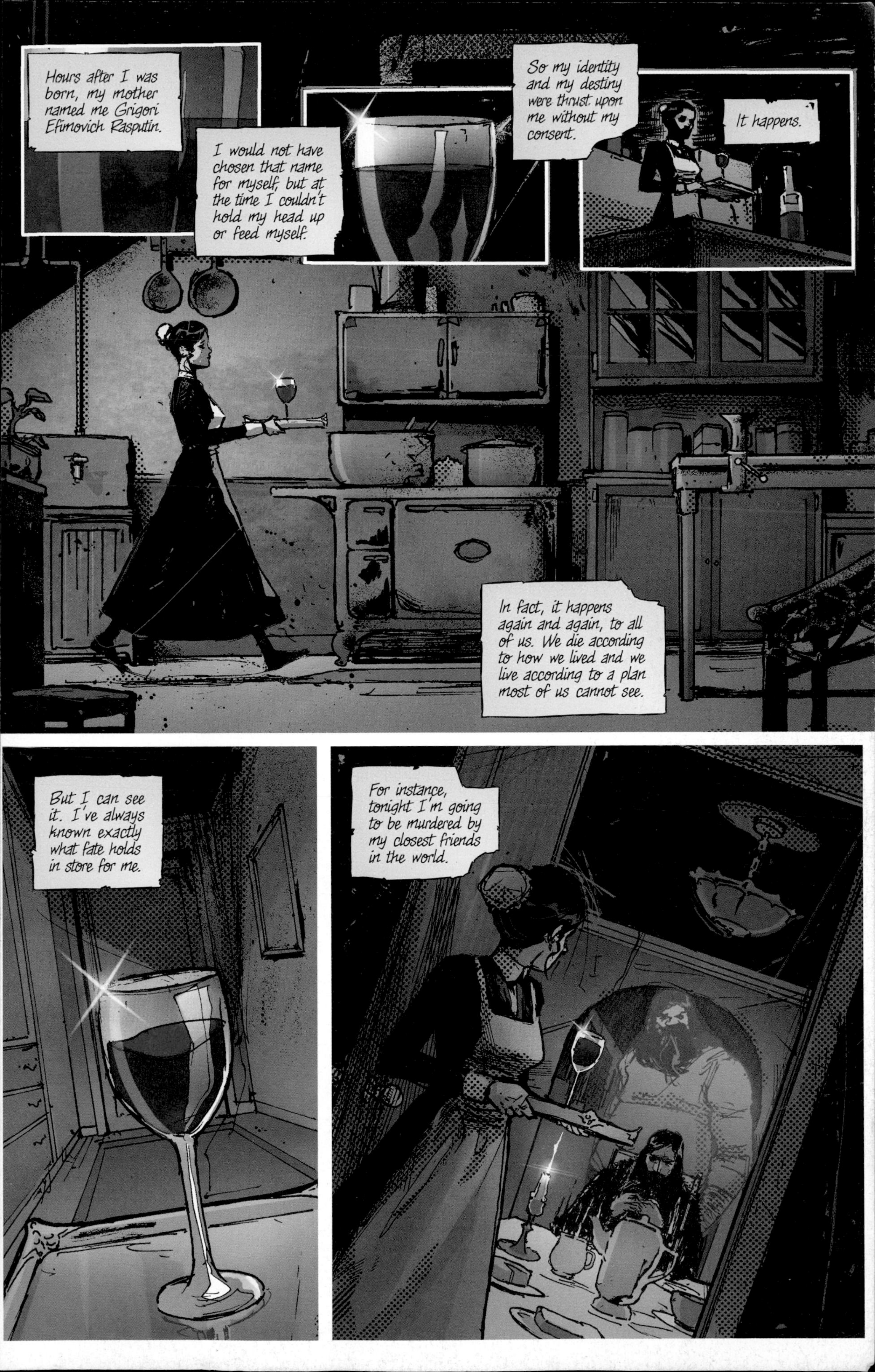
Hours after I was born, my mother named me Grigori Efimovich Rasputin.
I would not have chosen that name for myself, but at the time I couldn't hold my head up or feed myself.
So my identity and my destiny were thrust upon me without my consent.
It happens.
In fact, it happens again and again, to all of us. We die according to how we lived and we live according to a plan most of us cannot see.
But I can see it. I've always known exactly what fate holds in store for me.
For instance, tonight I'm going to be murdered by my closest friends in the world.

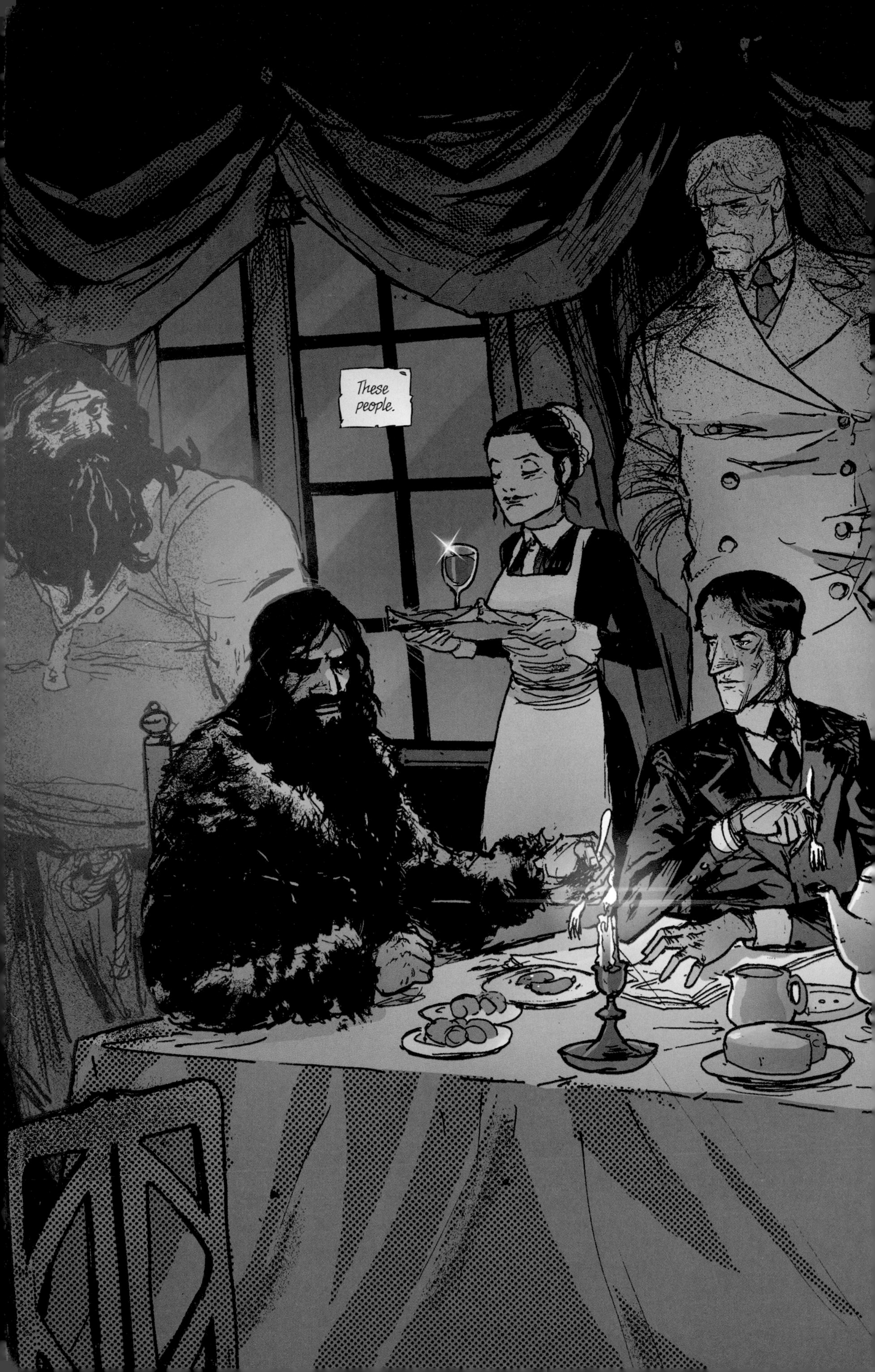
These people.

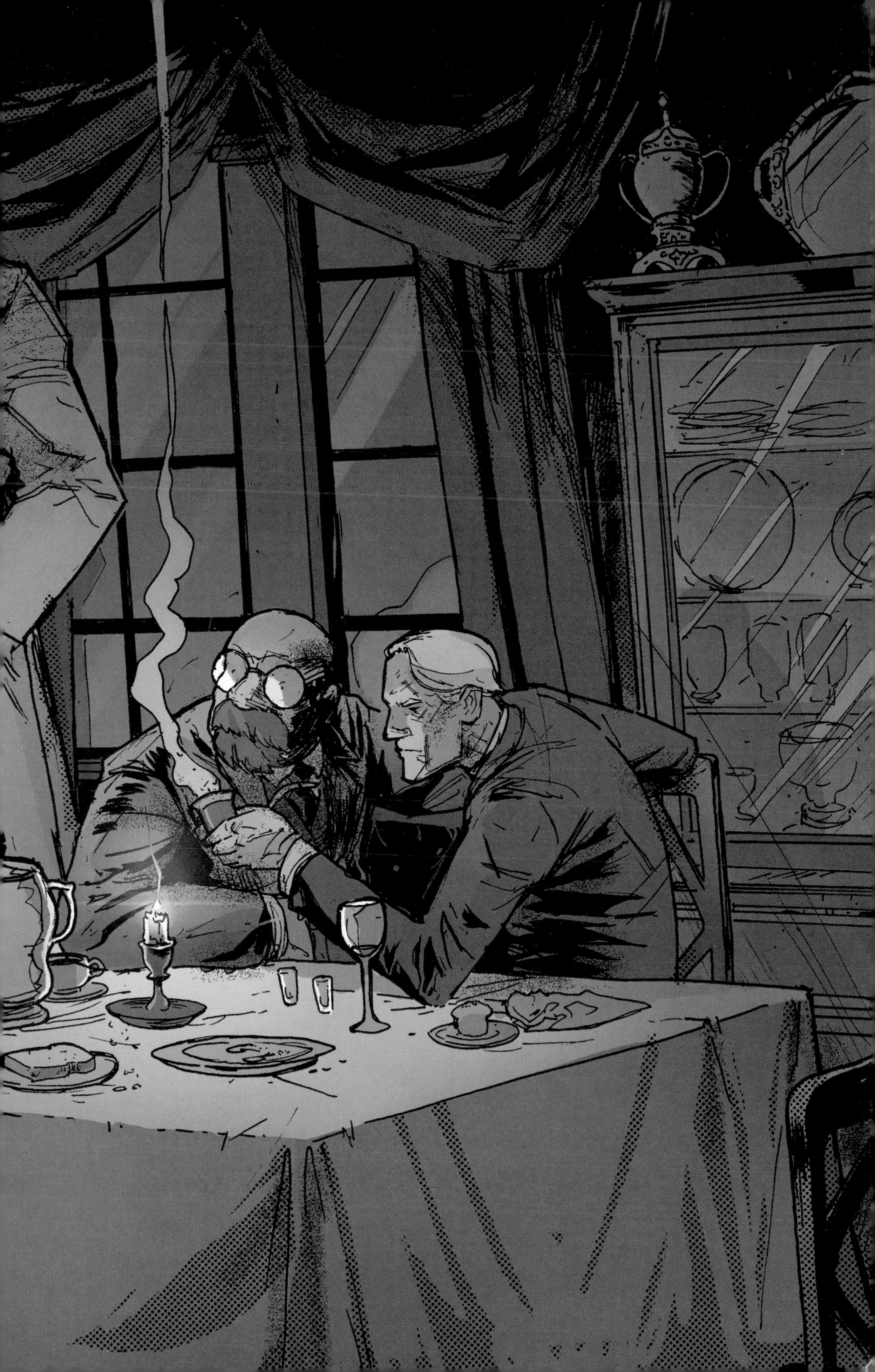

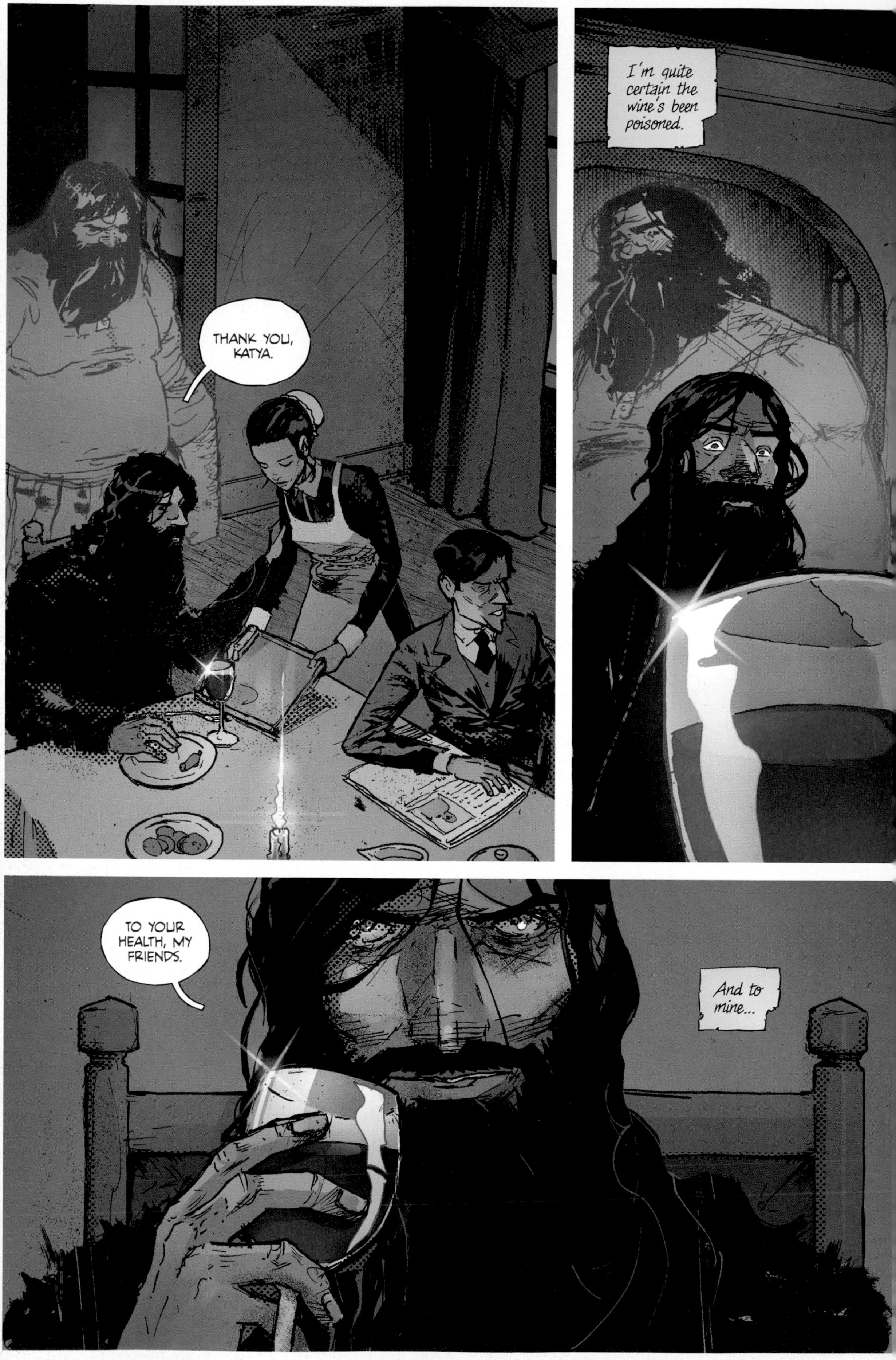
THANK YOU, KATYA.
I'm quite certain the wine's been poisoned.
TO YOUR HEALTH, MY FRIENDS.
And to mine...

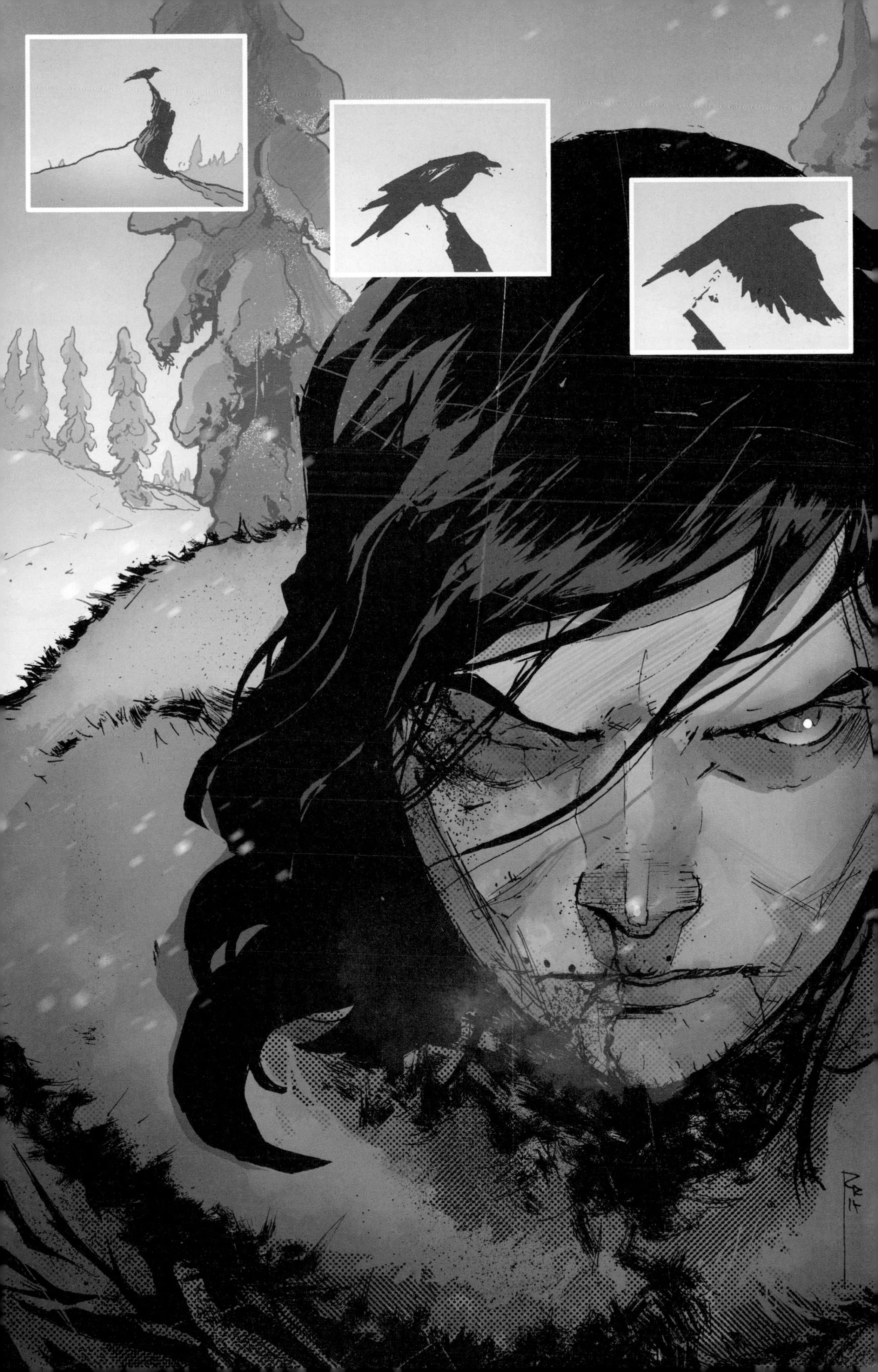

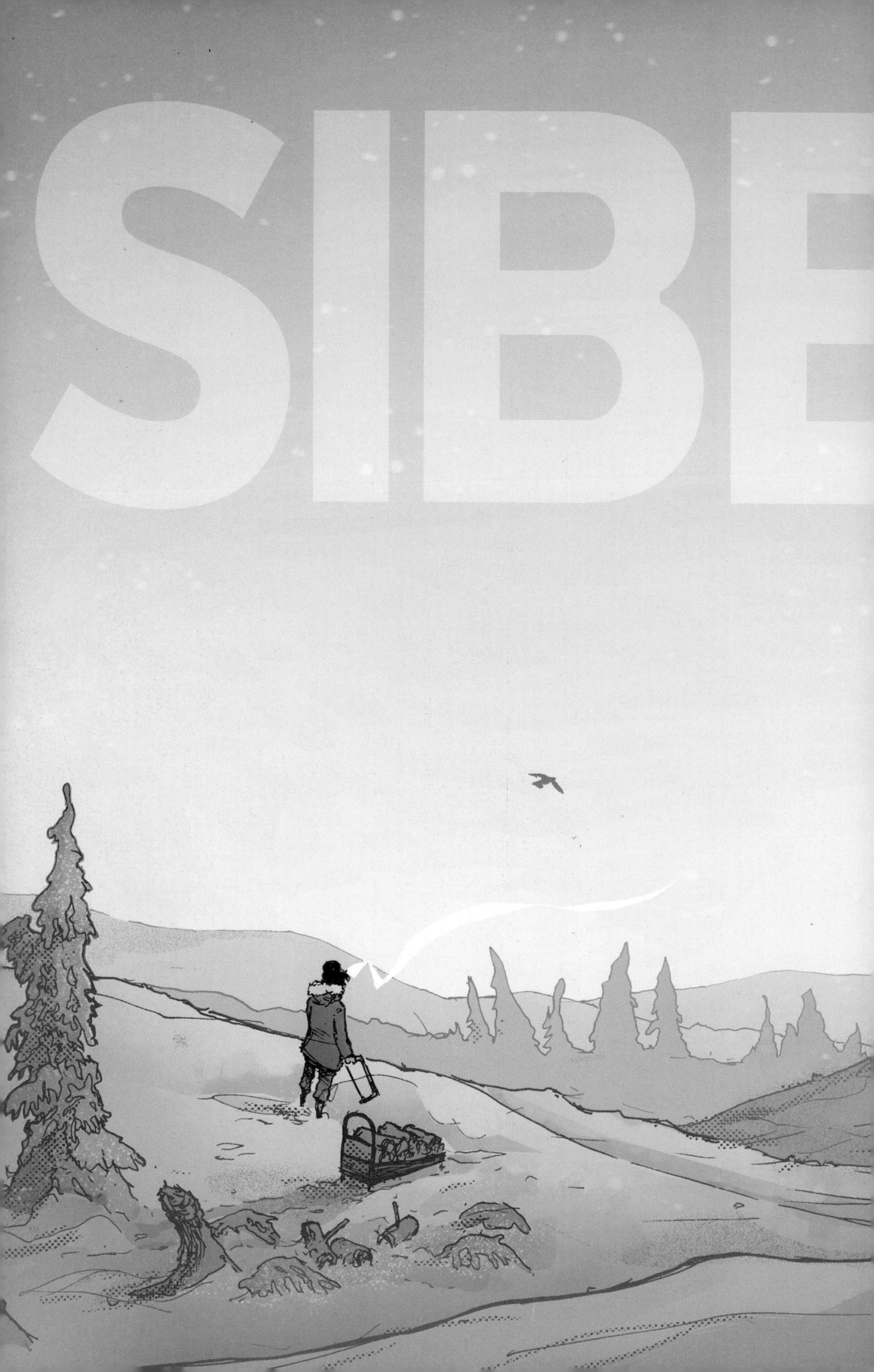

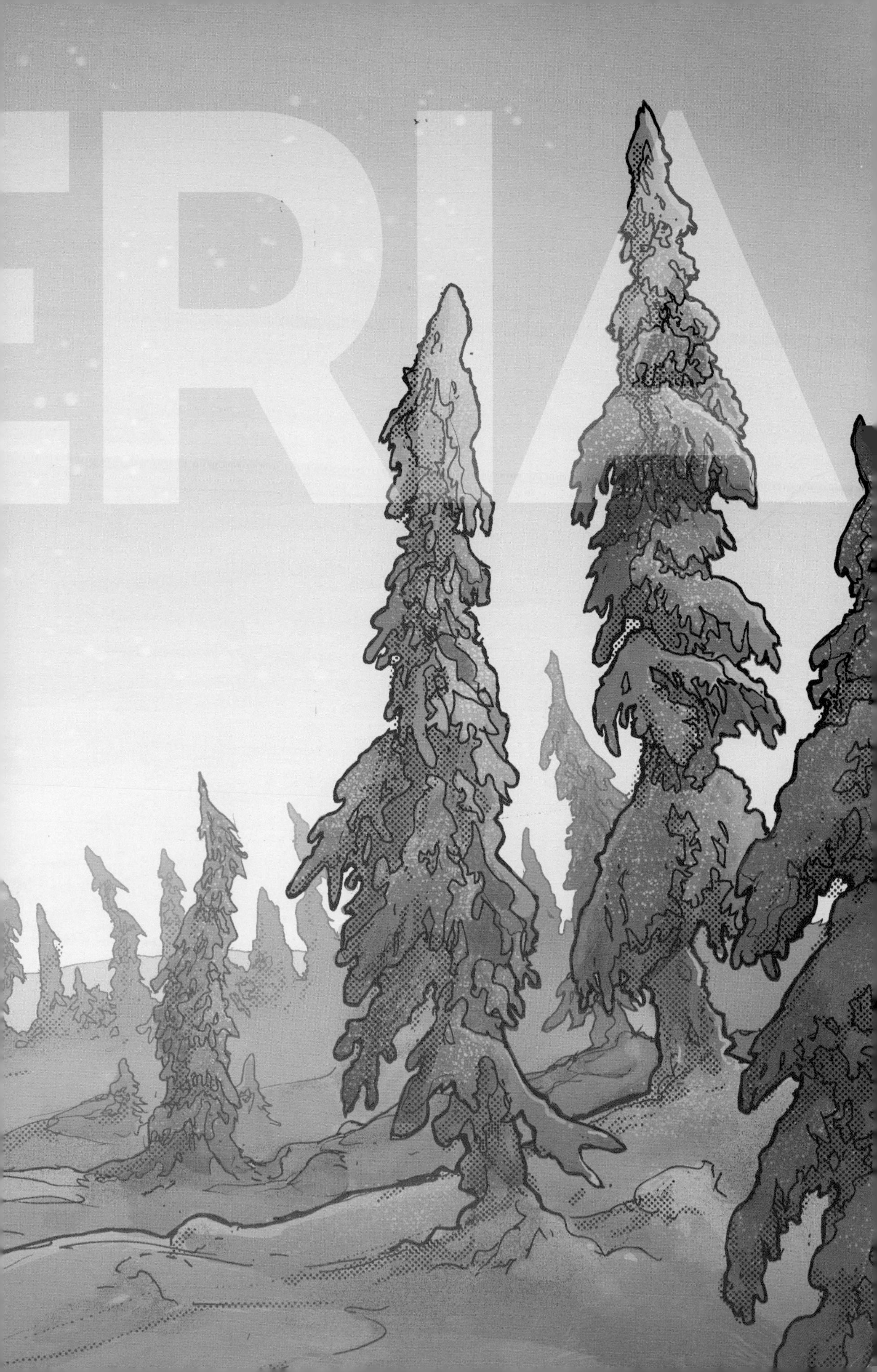

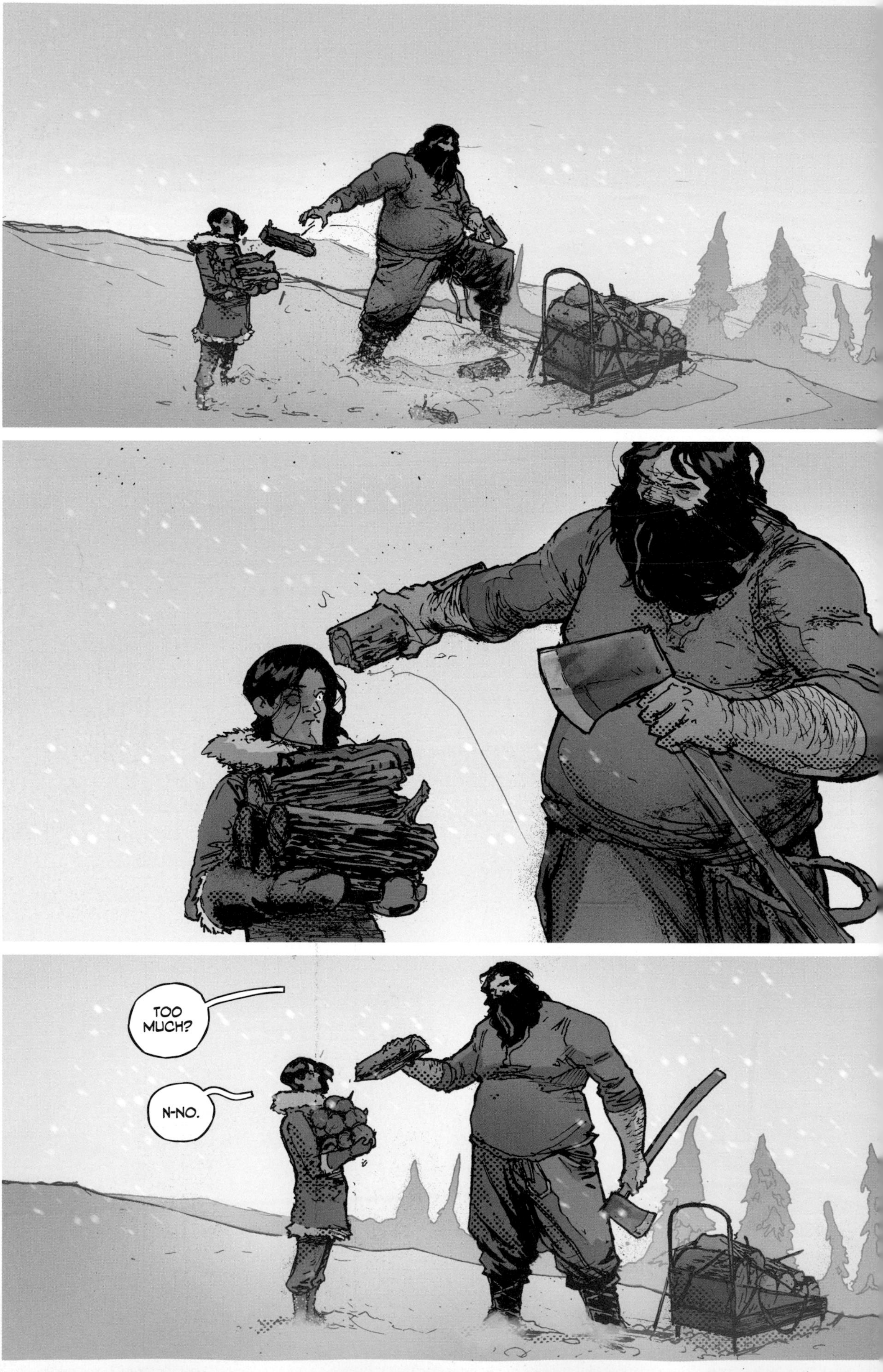
TOO MUCH?
N-NO.

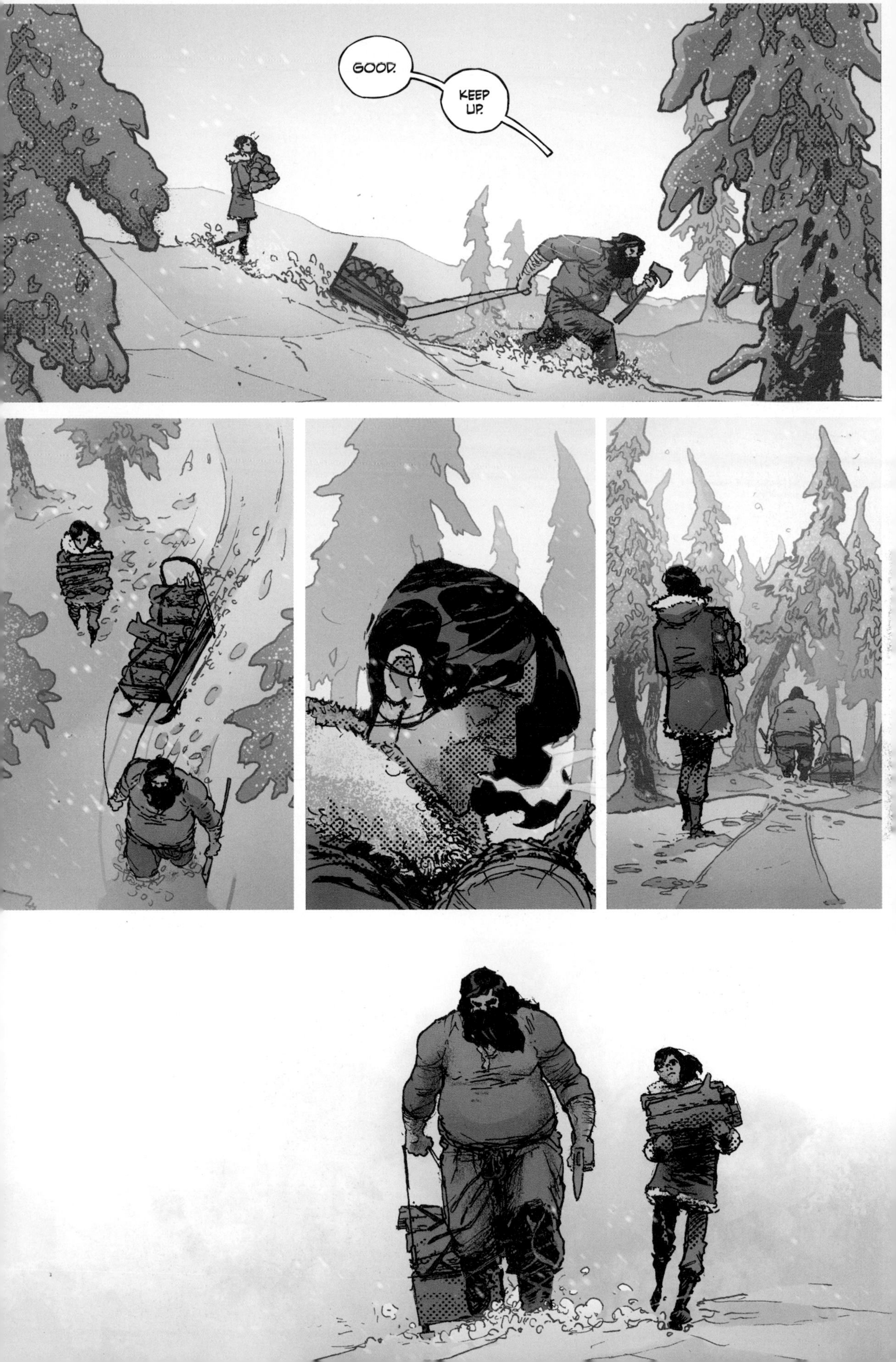
GOOD.
KEEP UP.

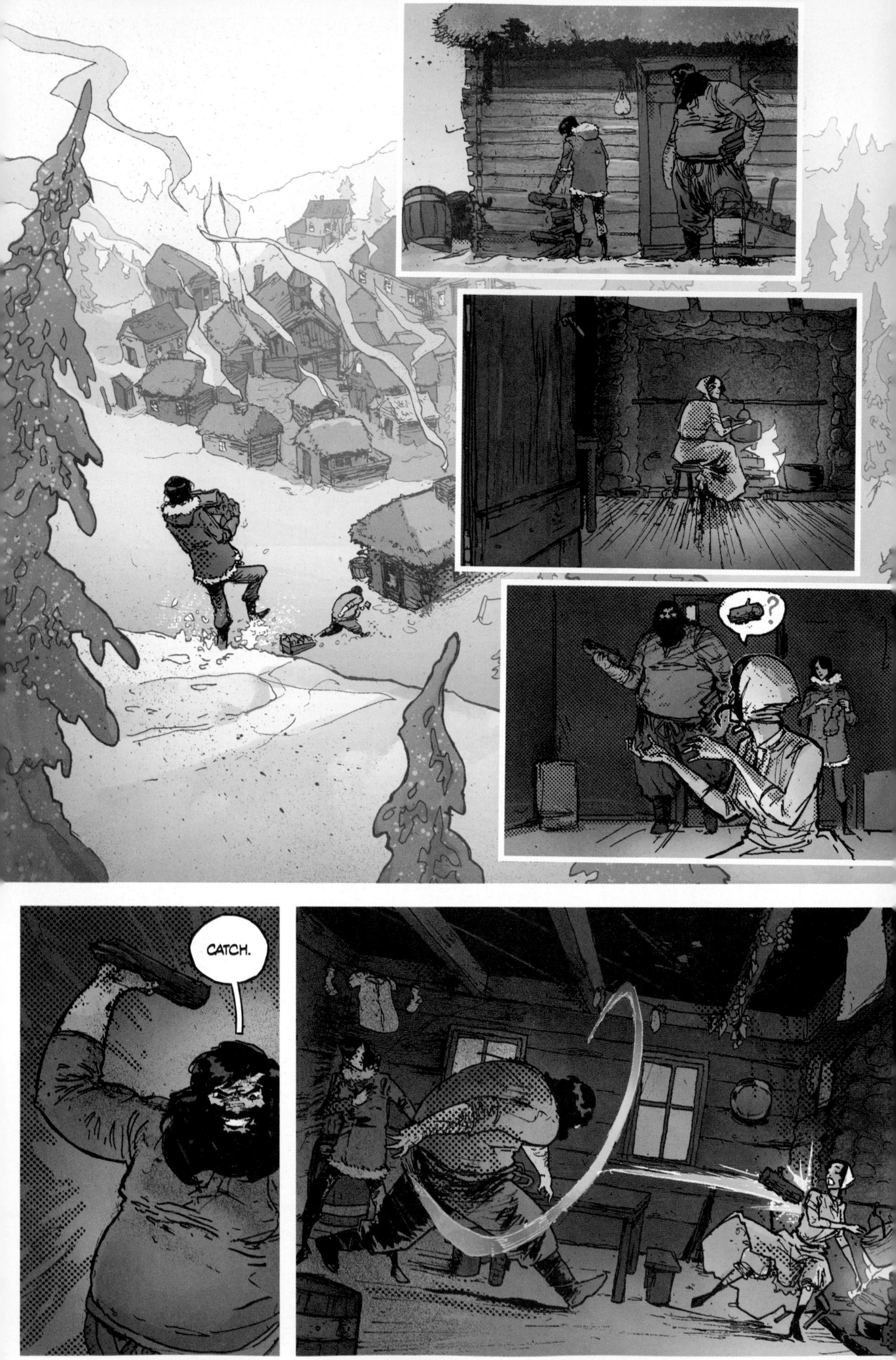
?
CATCH.

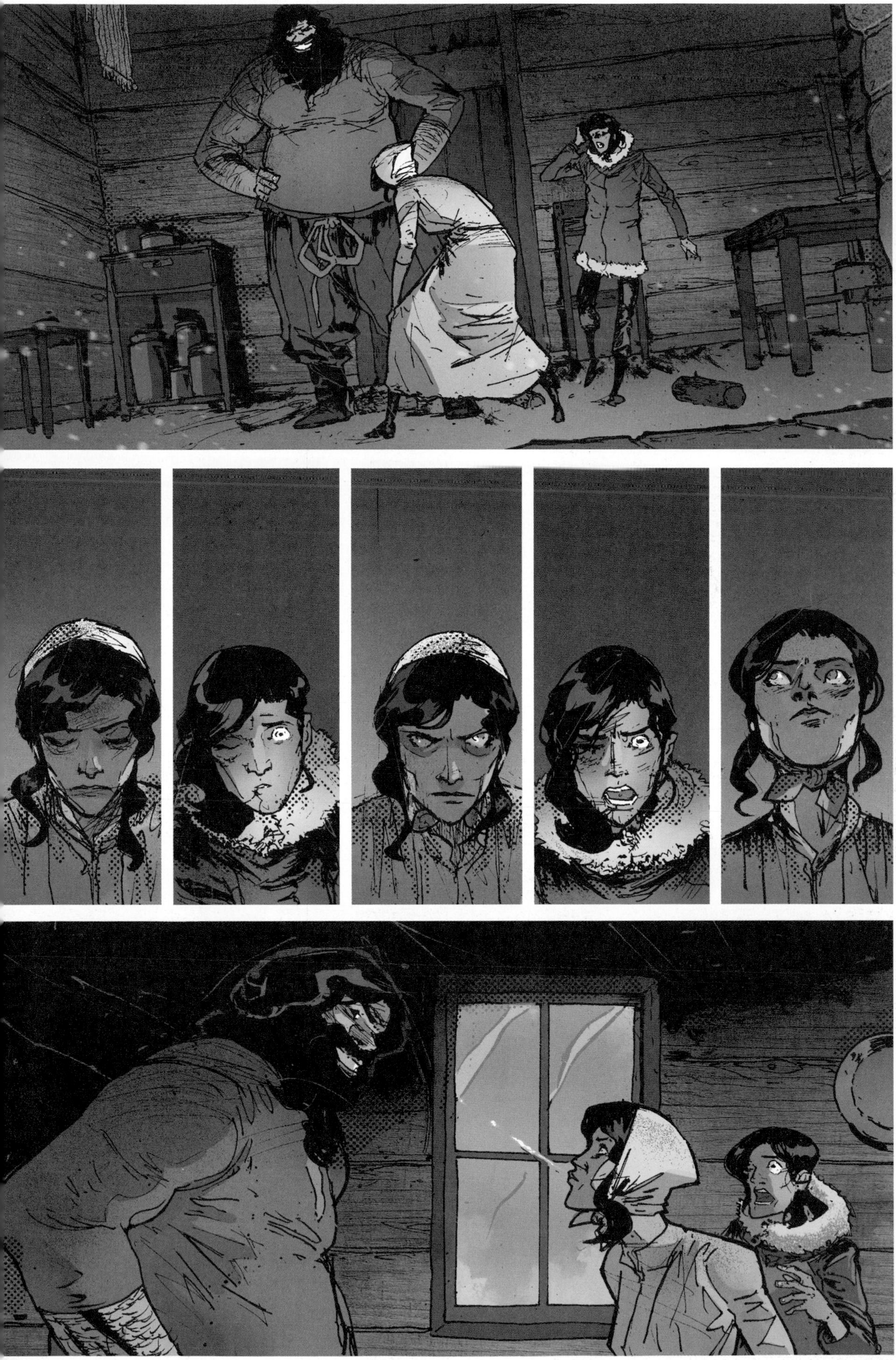

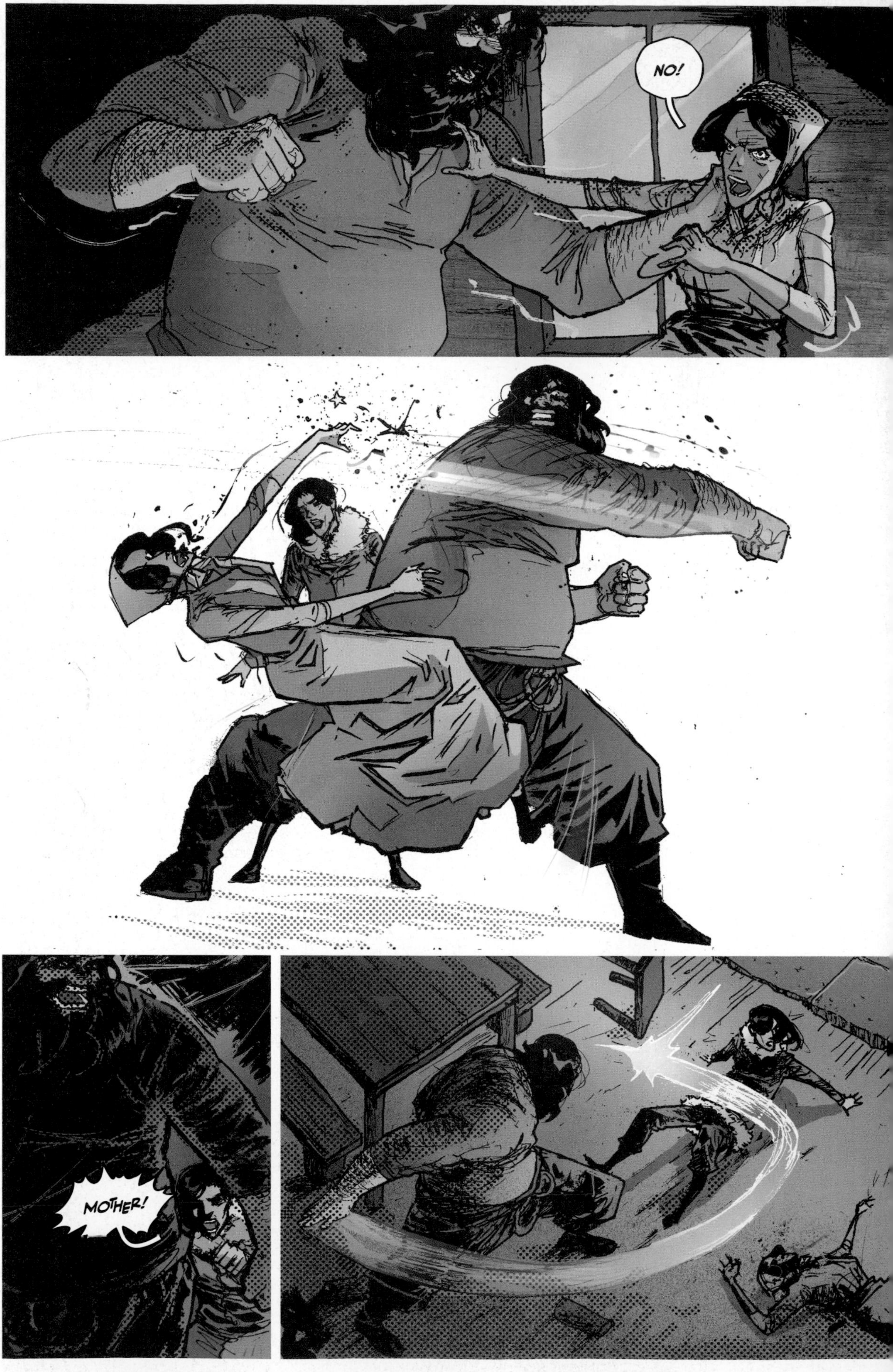
NO!
MOTHER!

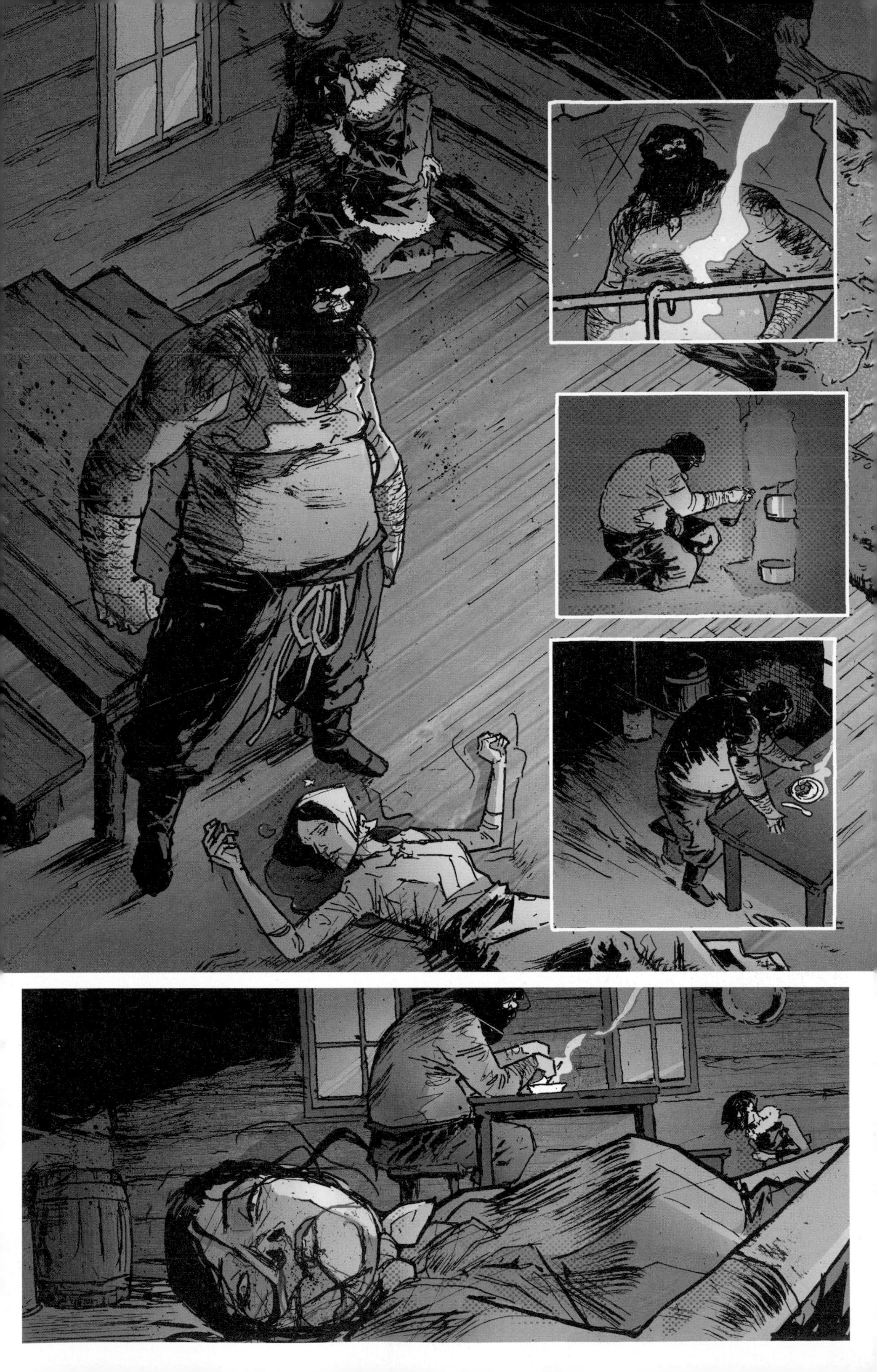

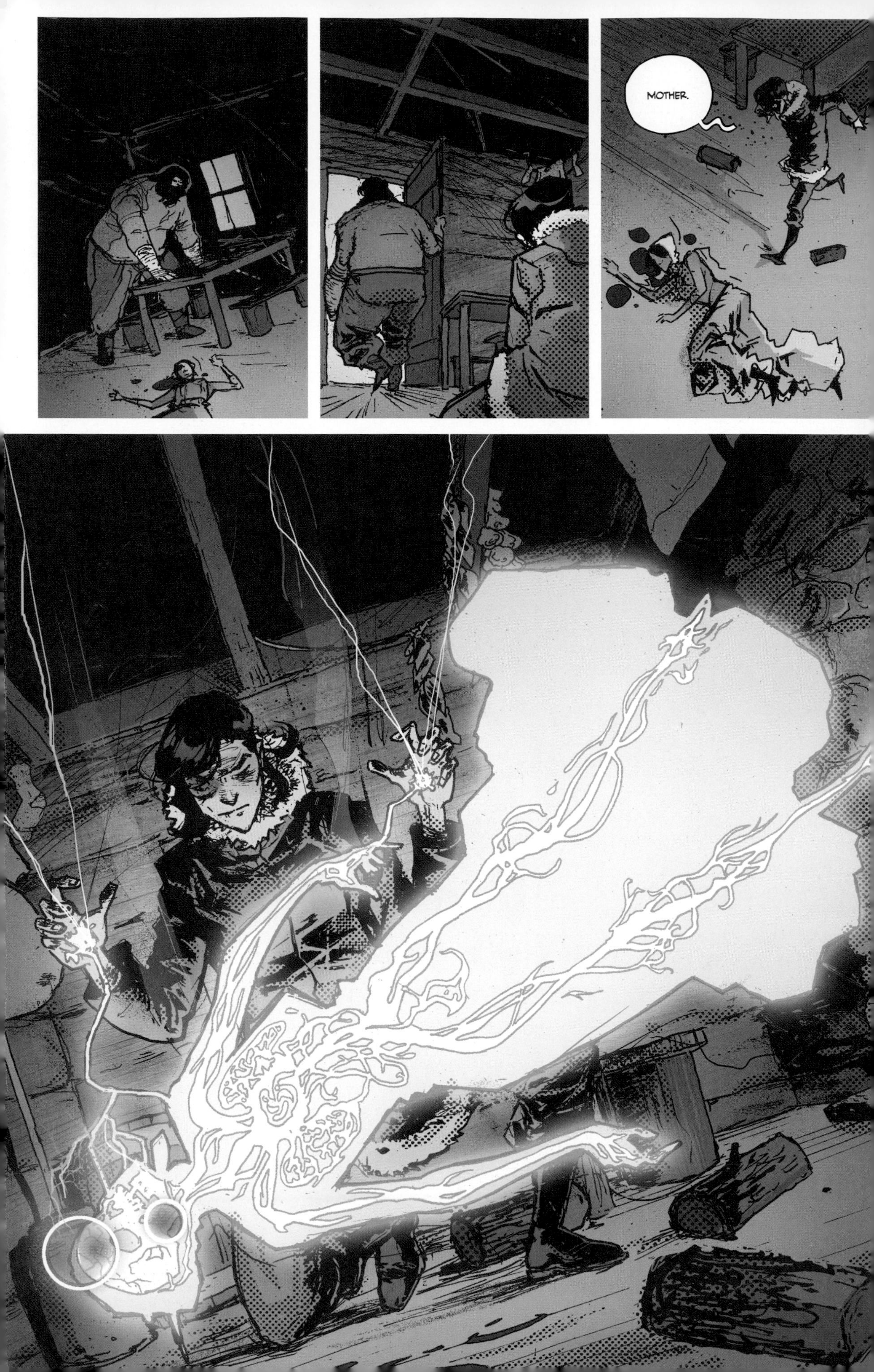
MOTHER.

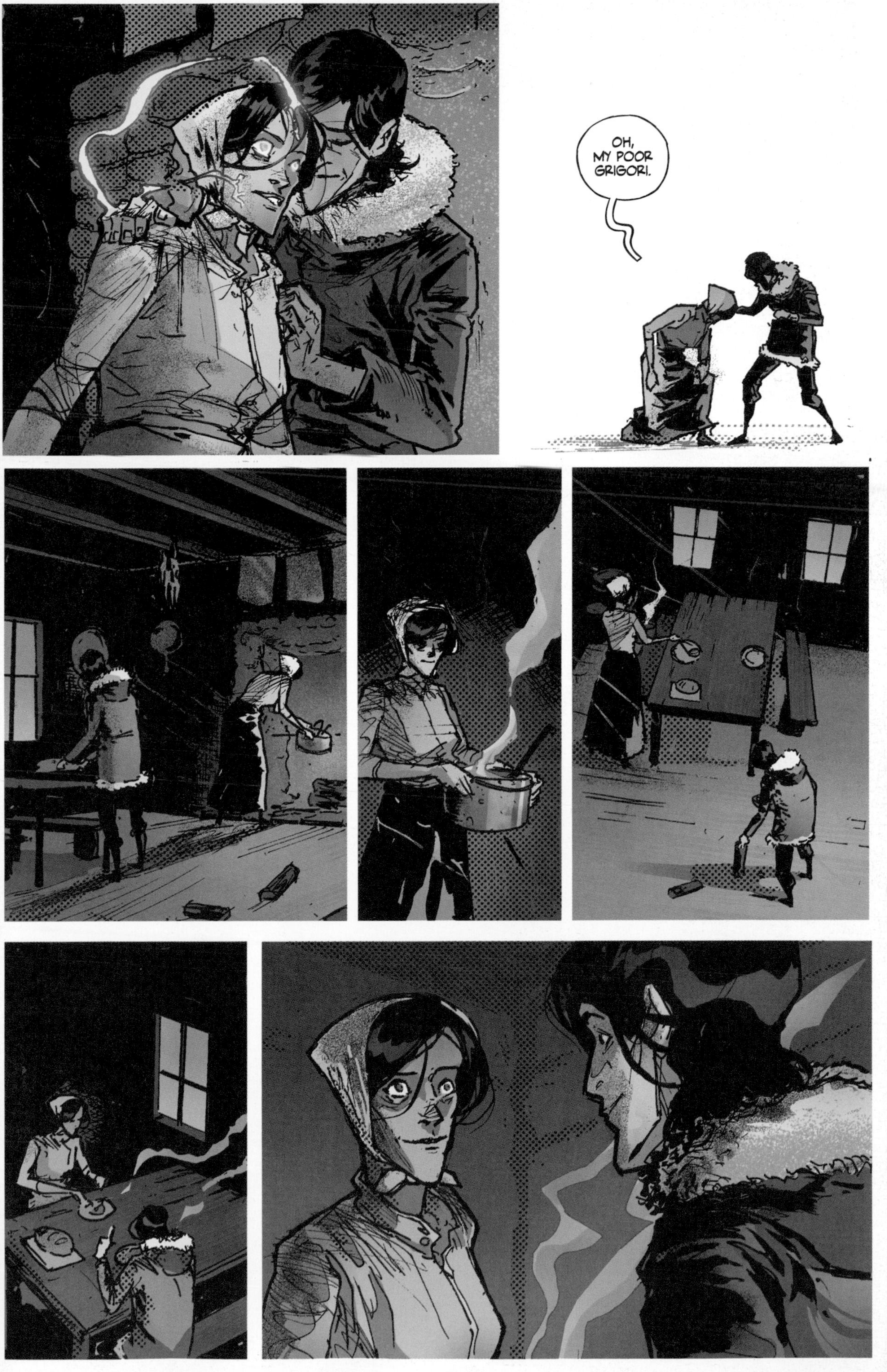
OH, MY POOR GRIGORI.

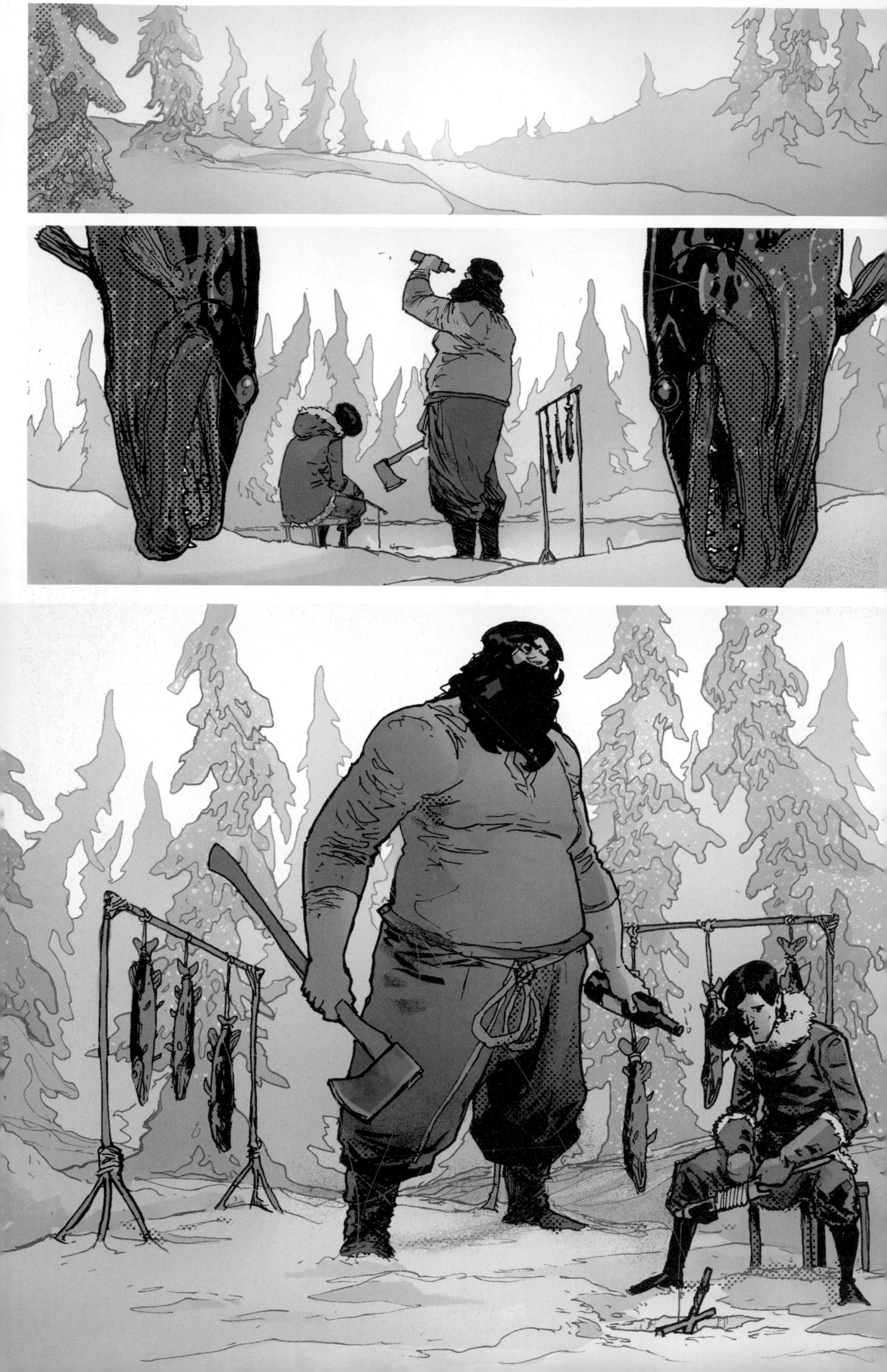

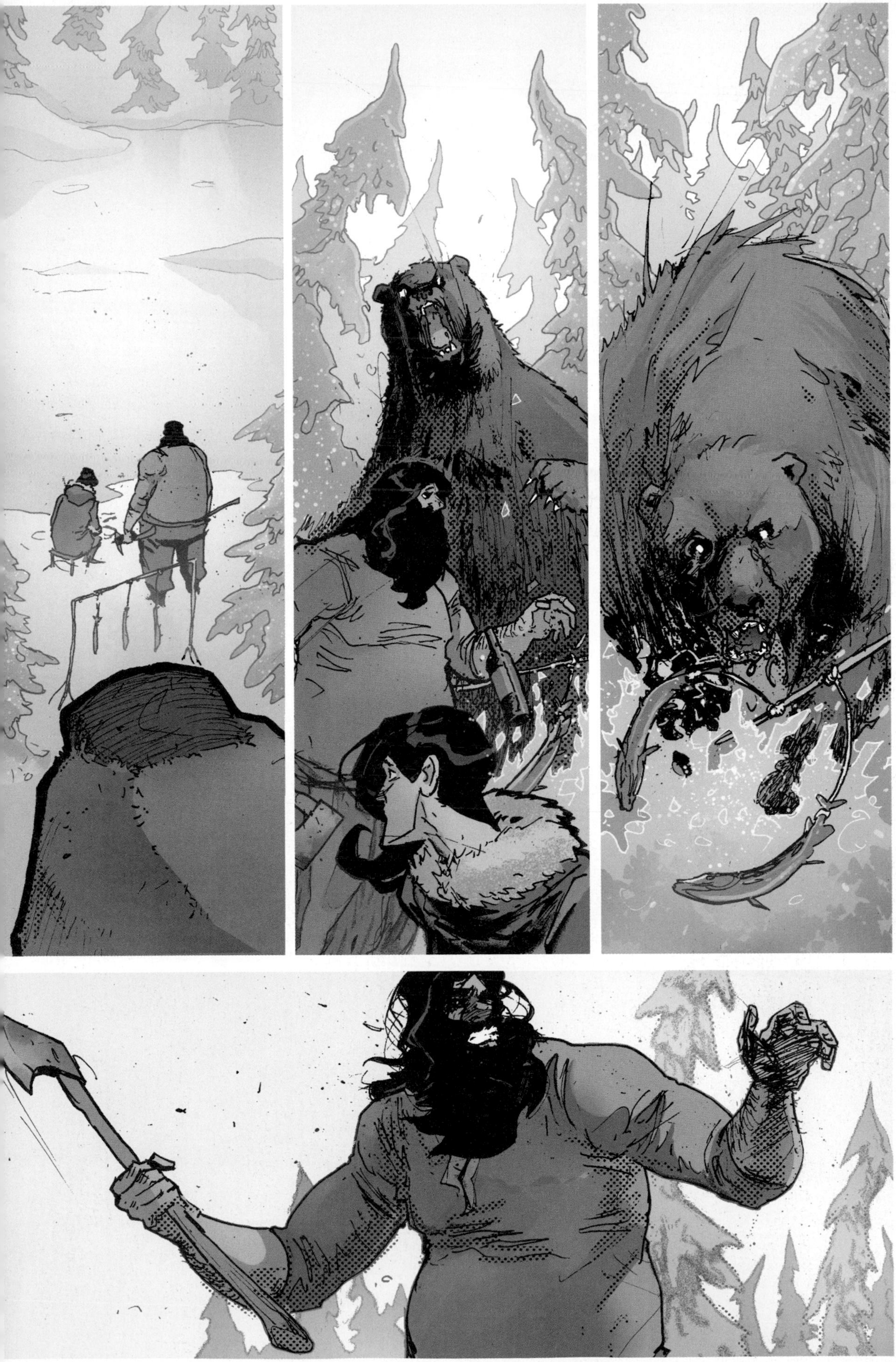

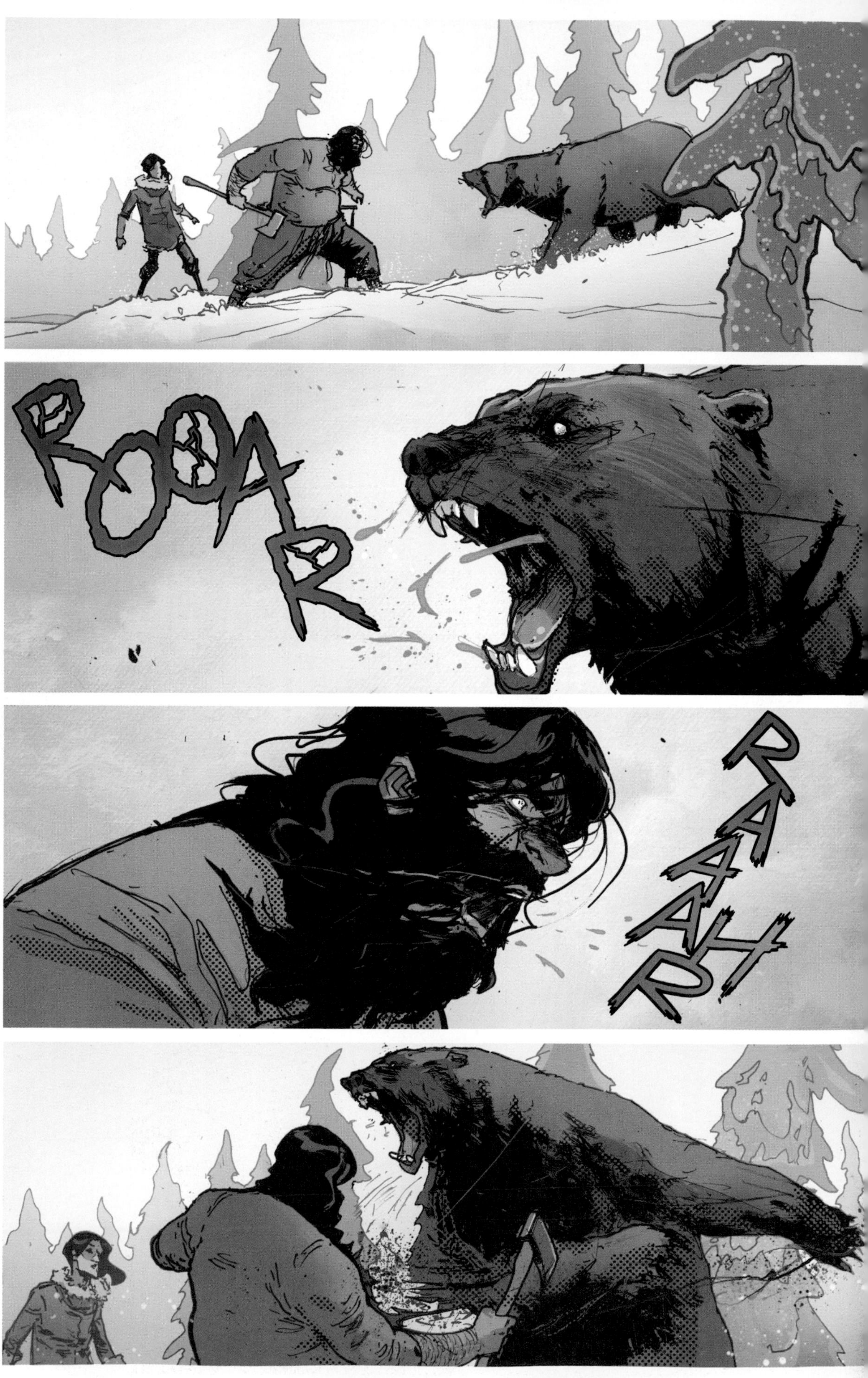
ROOAR
RAAAHR!

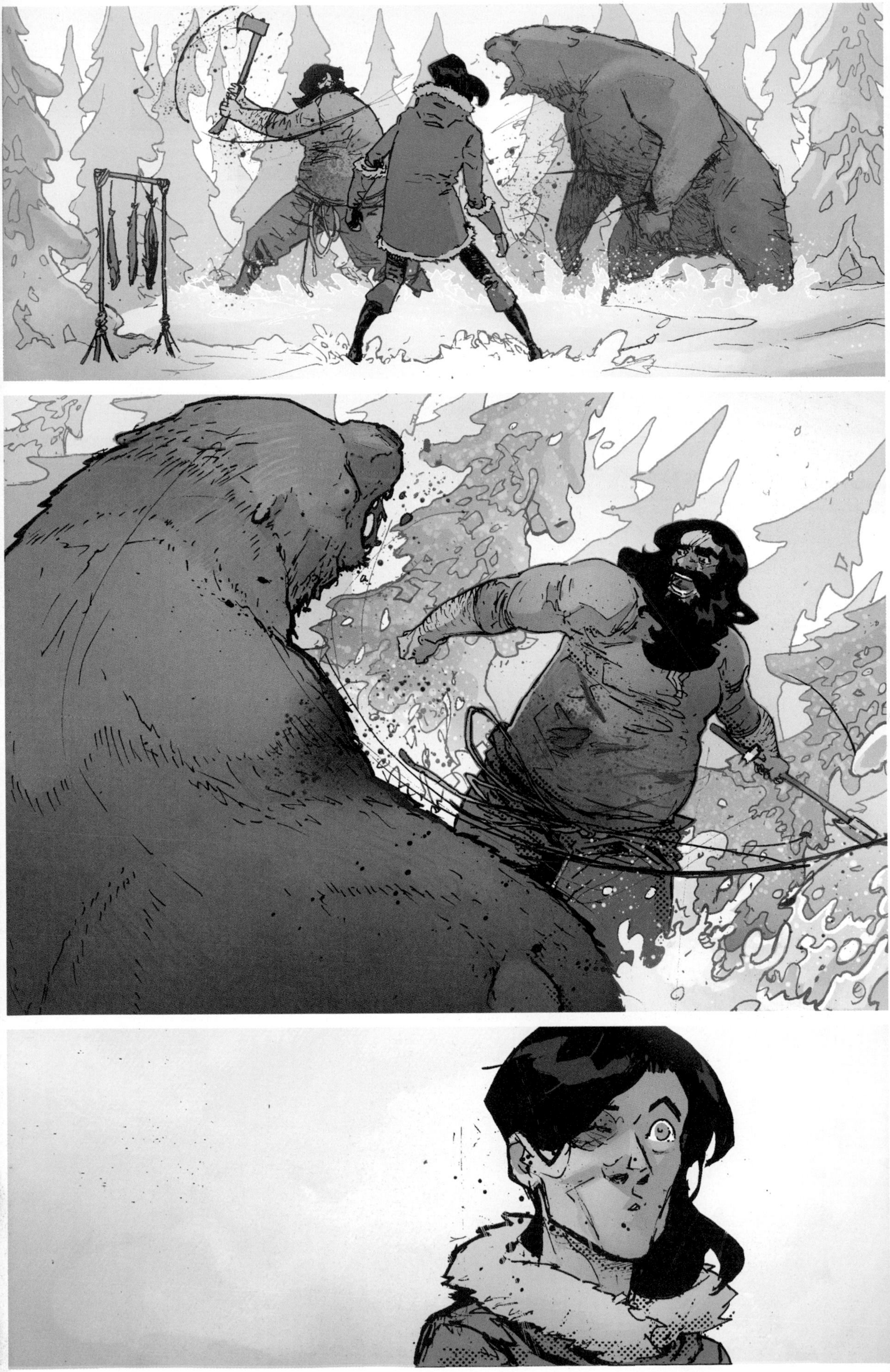

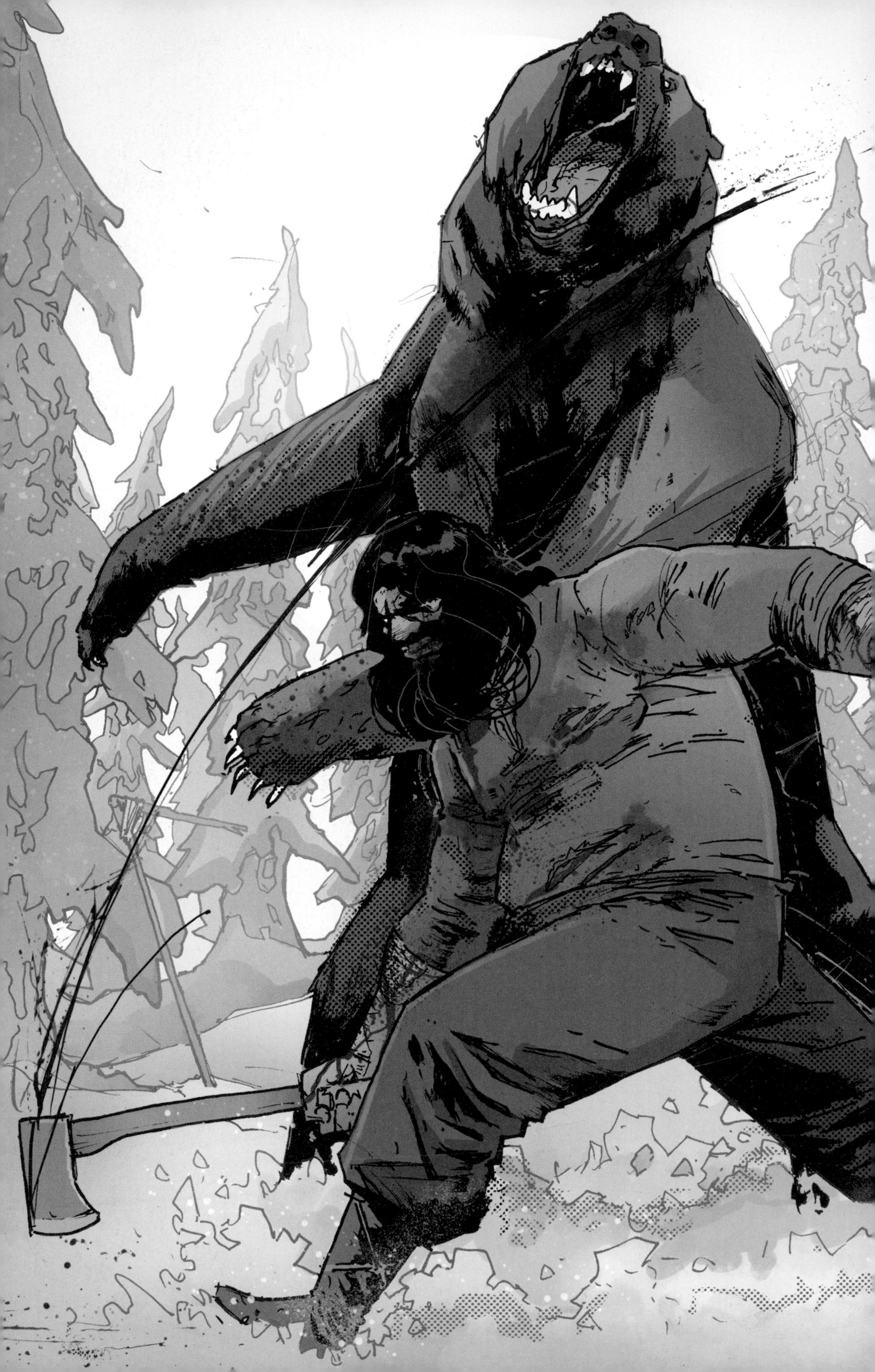

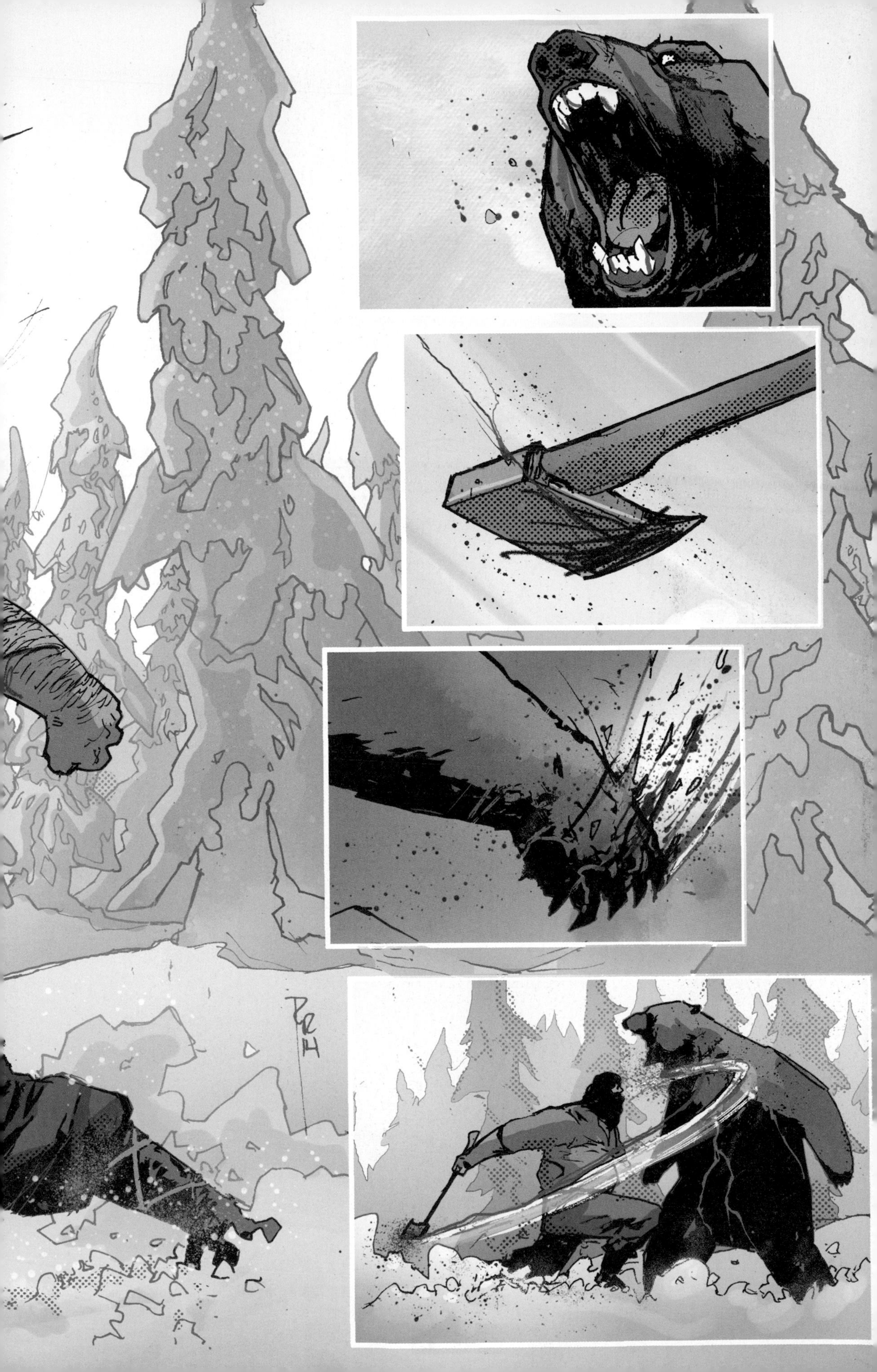

GRIGOR!?

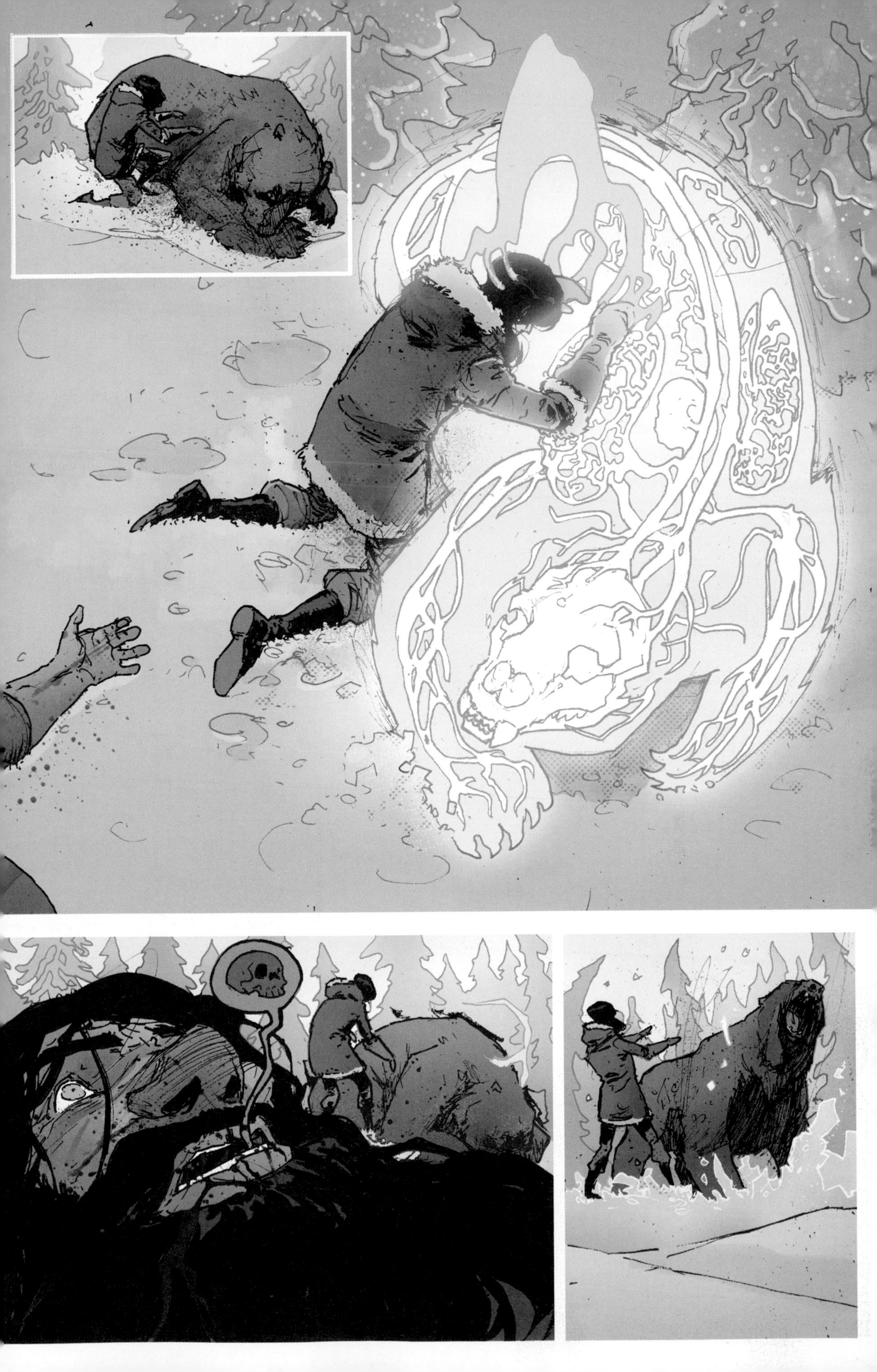

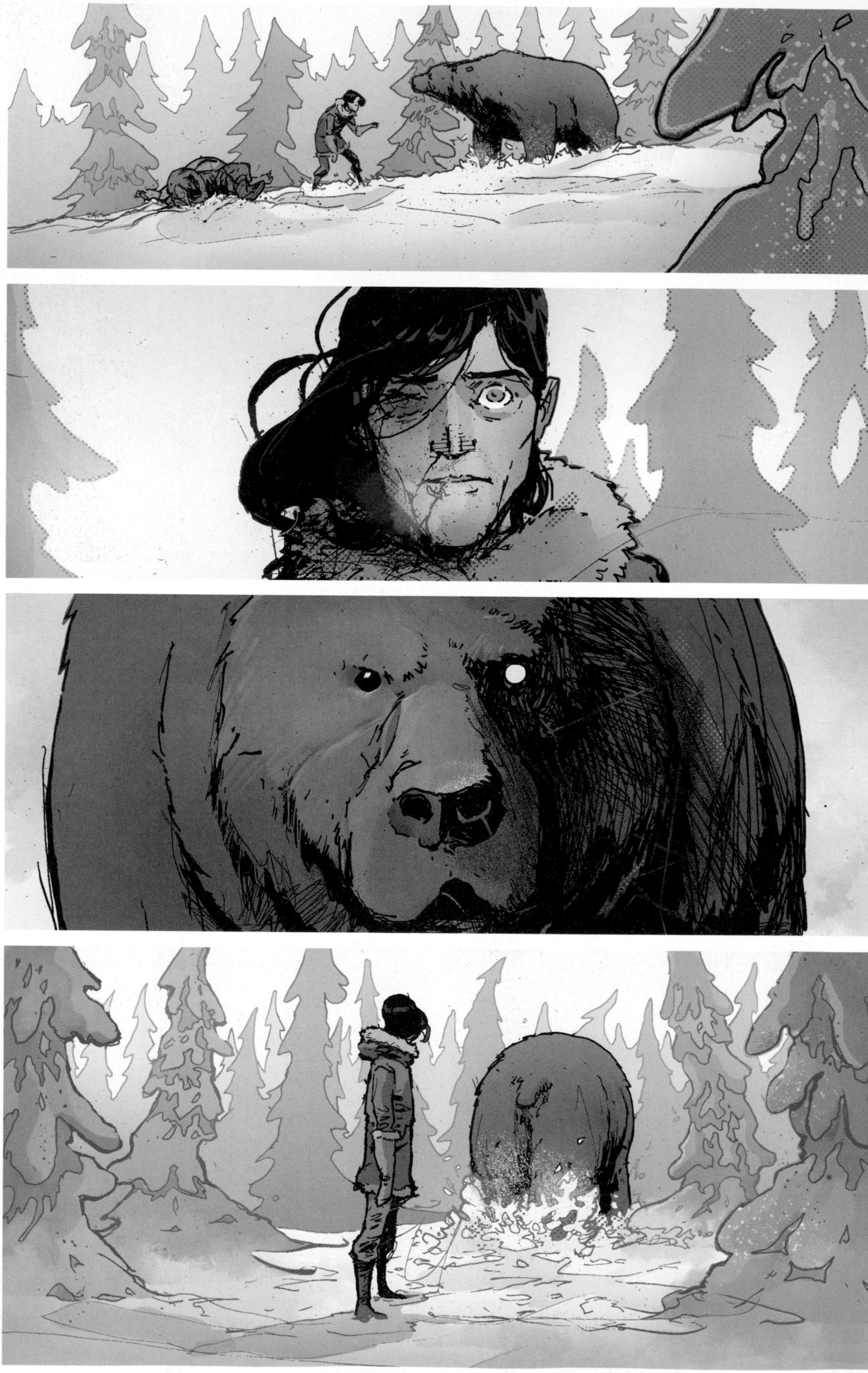

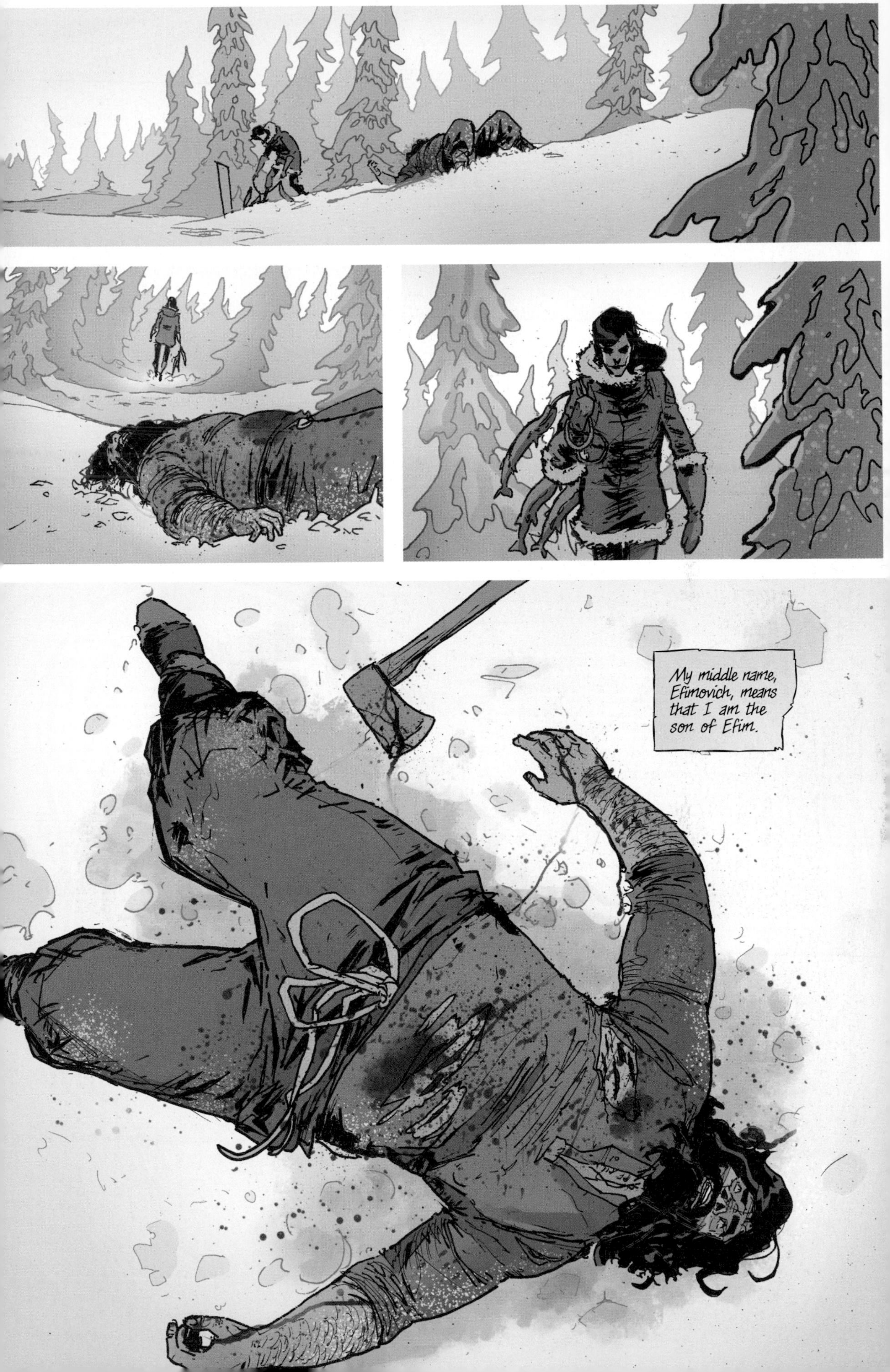
My middle name, Efimovich, means that I am the son of Efim.

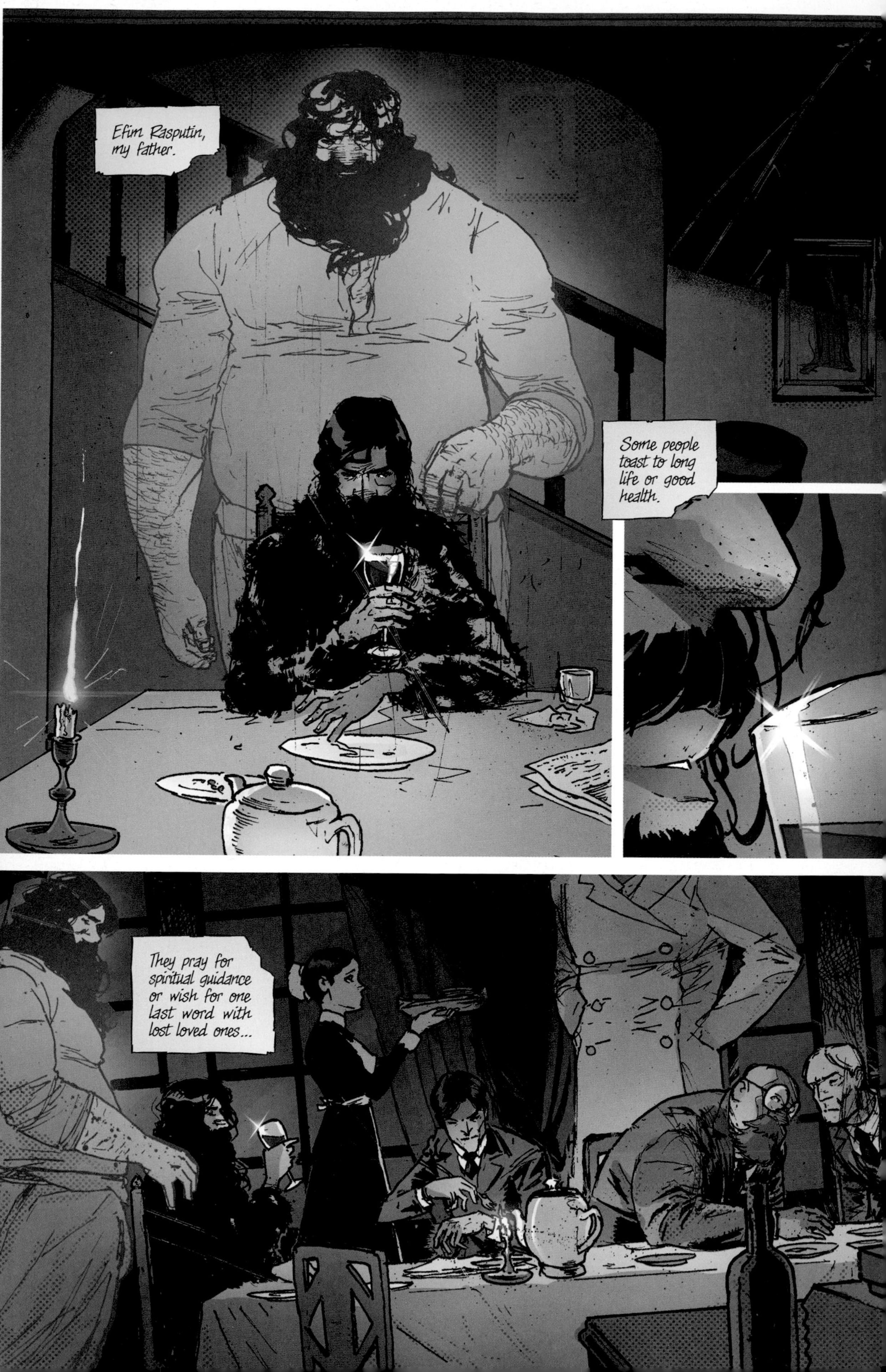
Efim Rasputin, my father.
Some people toast to long life or good health.
They pray for spiritual guidance or wish for one last word with lost loved ones...

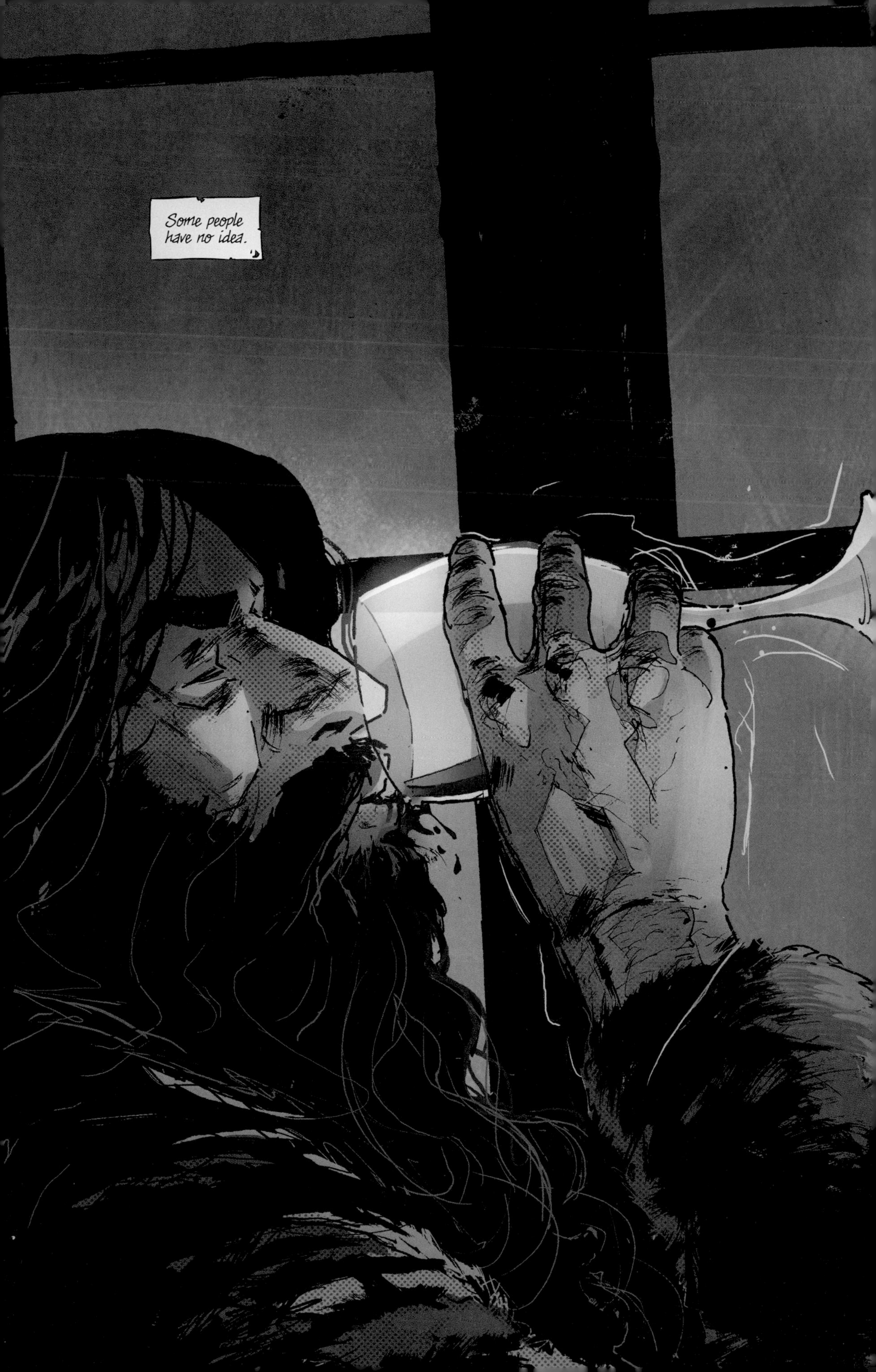
Some people have no idea.

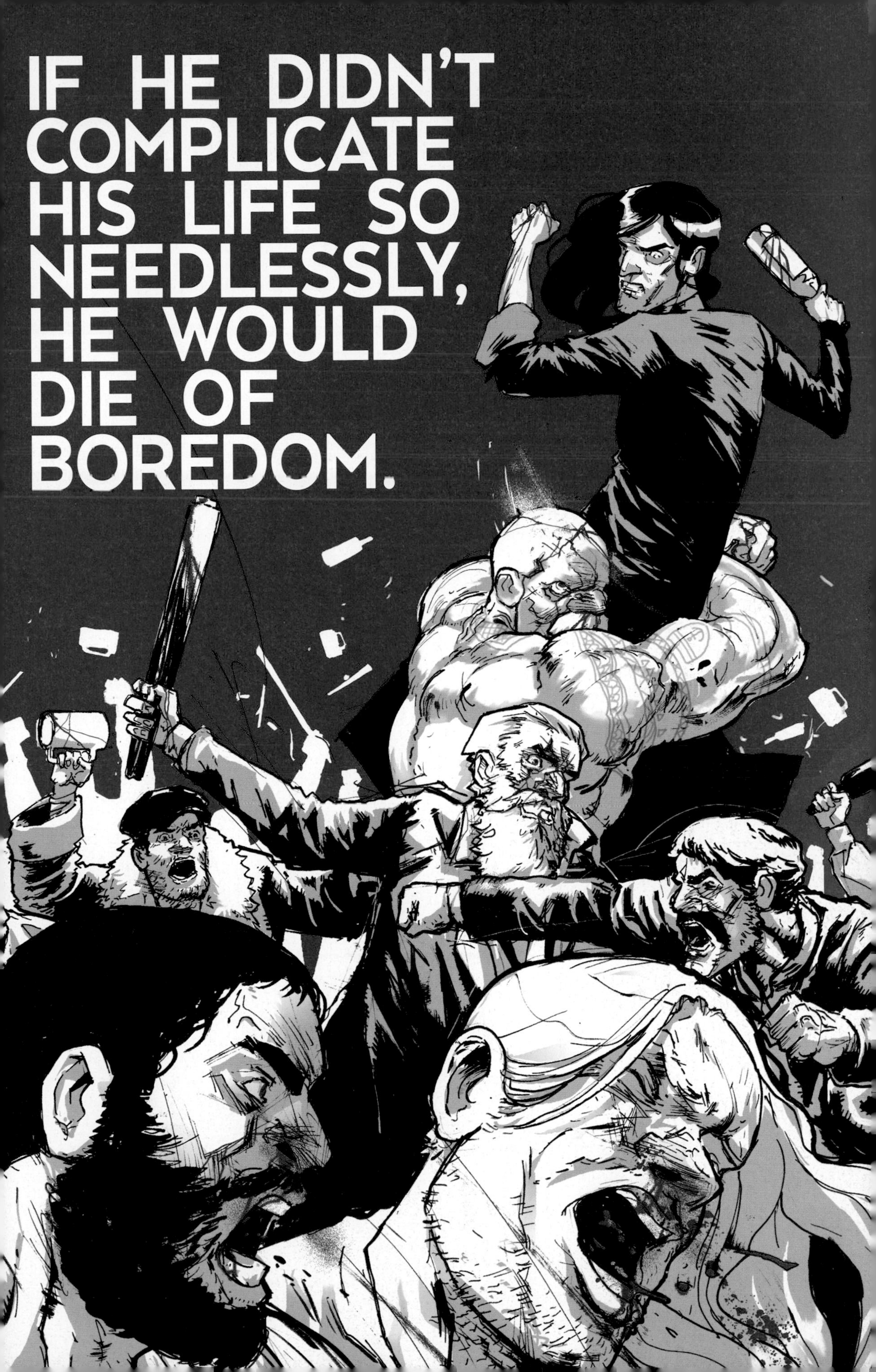
IF HE DIDN'T COMPLICATE HIS LIFE SO NEEDLESSLY, HE WOULD DIE OF BOREDOM.

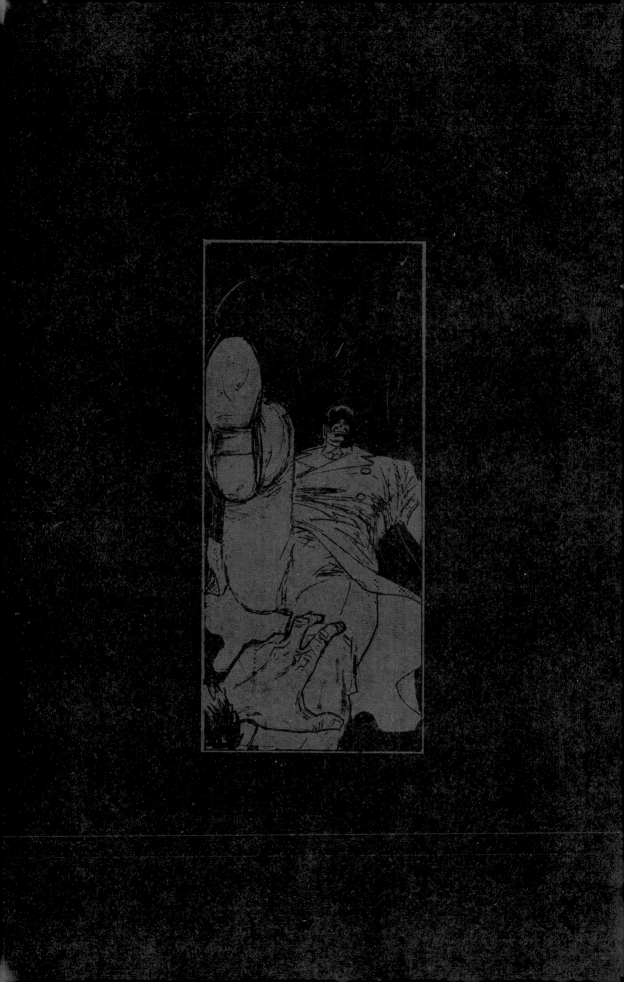

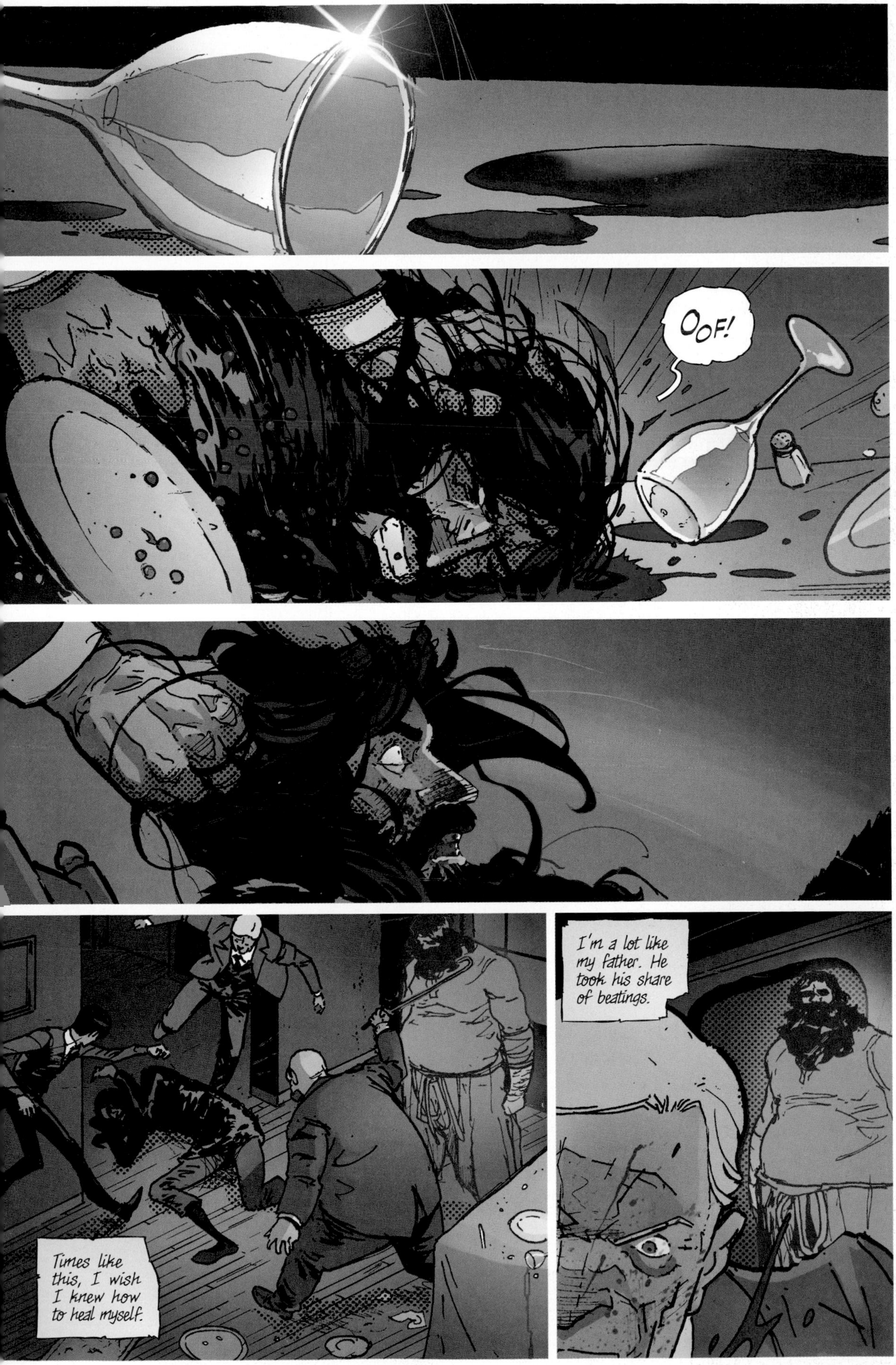
OOF!
Times like this, I wish I knew how to heal myself.
I'm a lot like my father. He took his share of beatings.

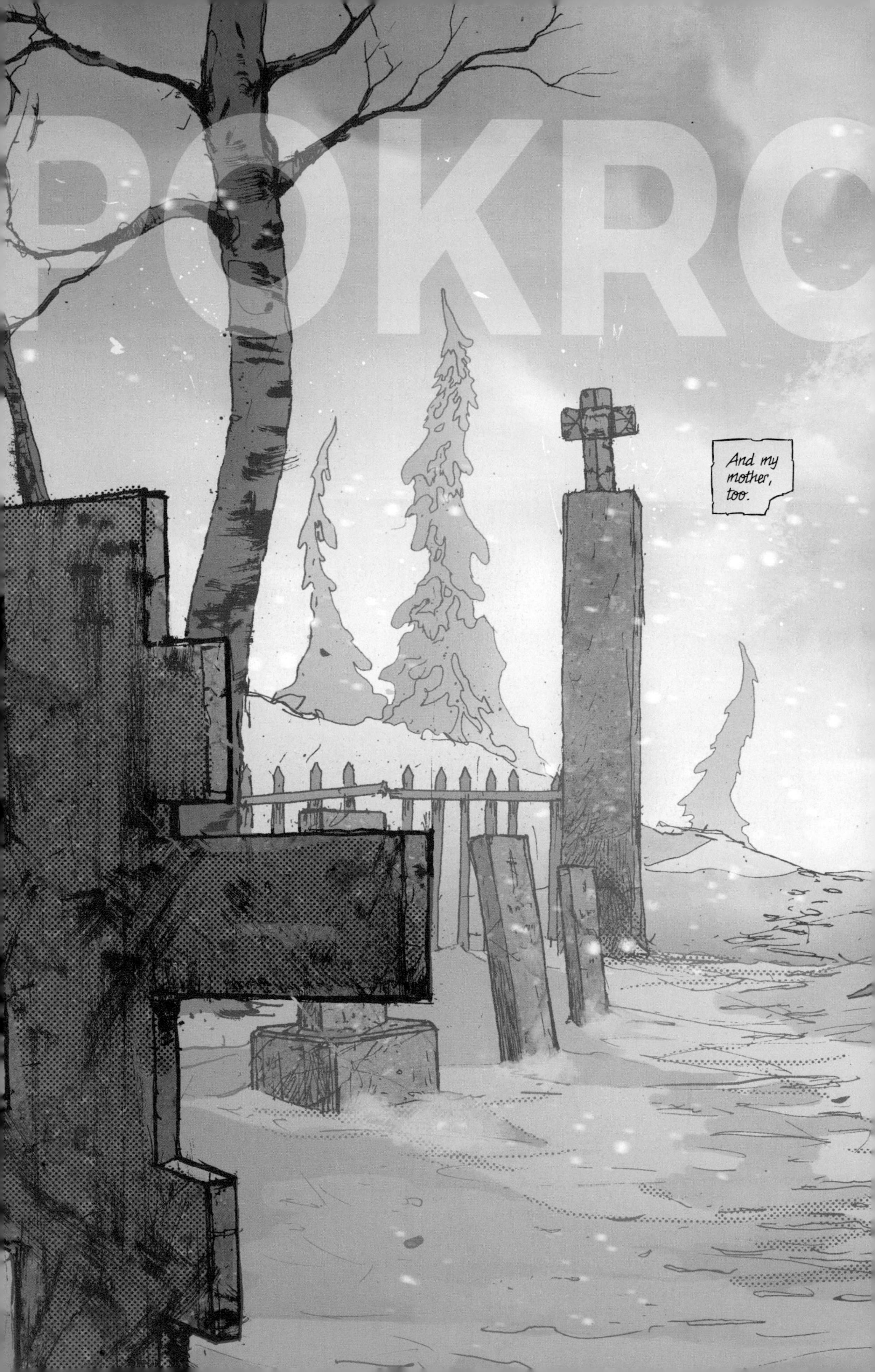
POKRO
And my mother, too.

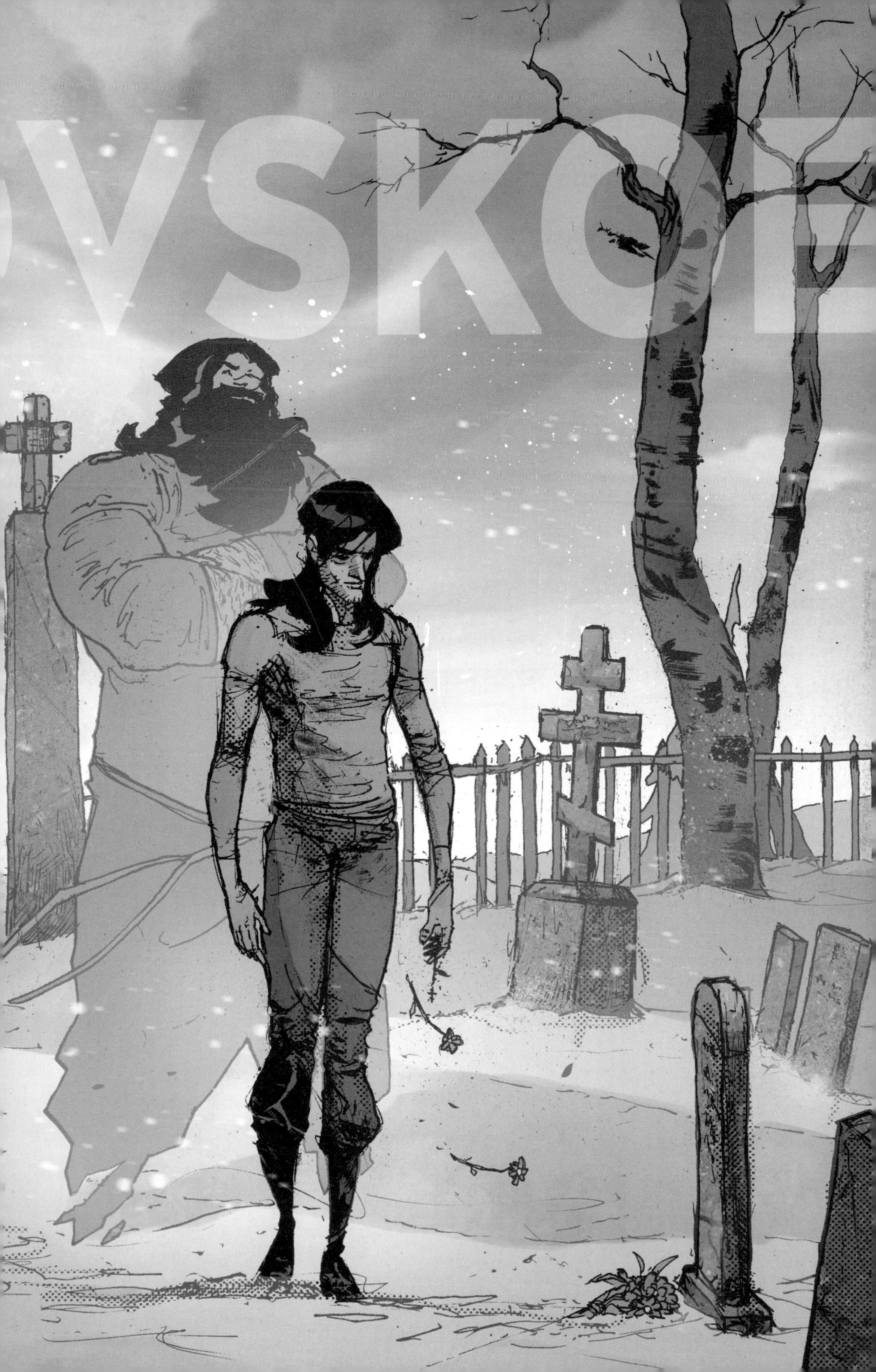
VSKOE

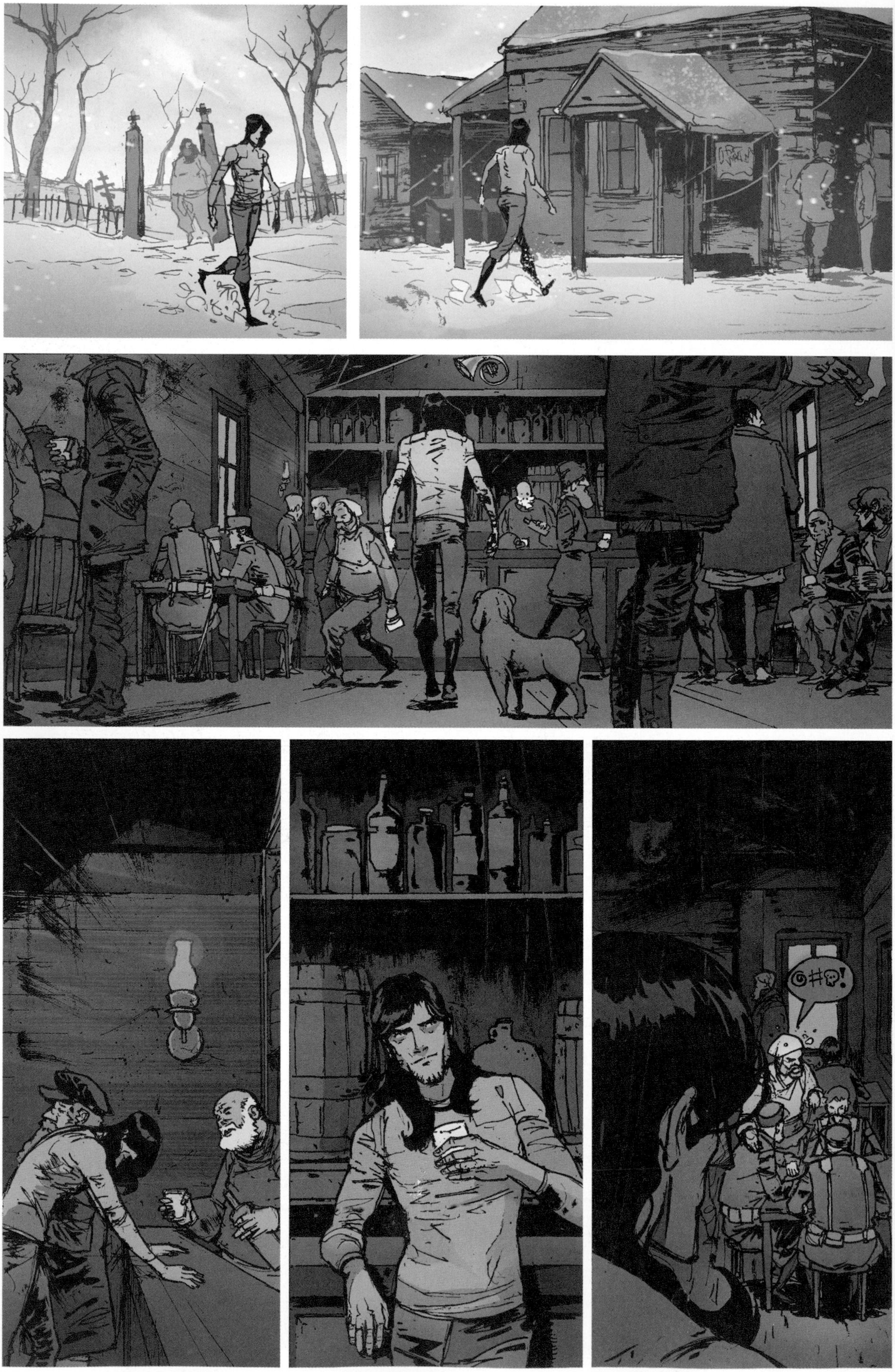

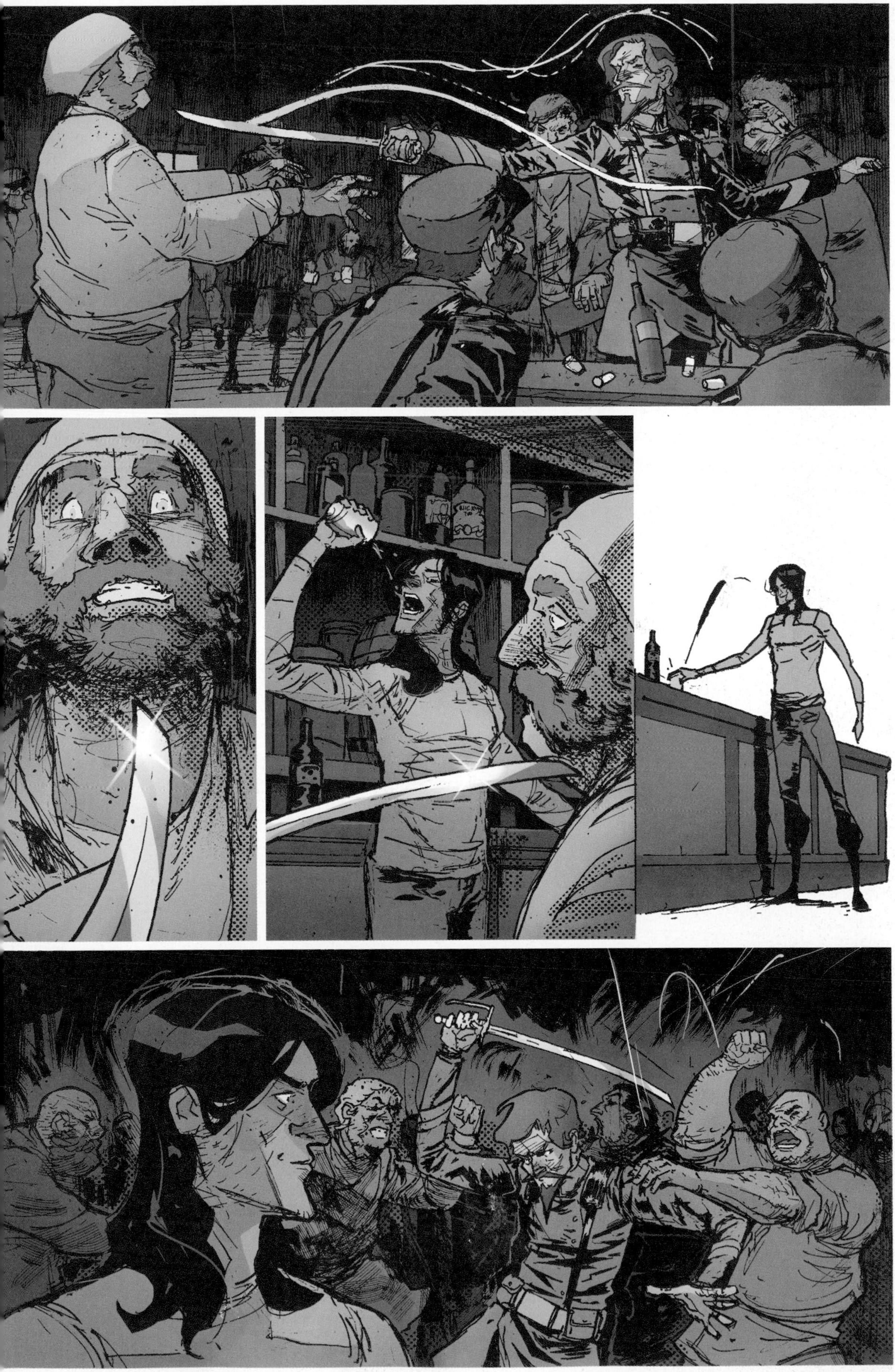

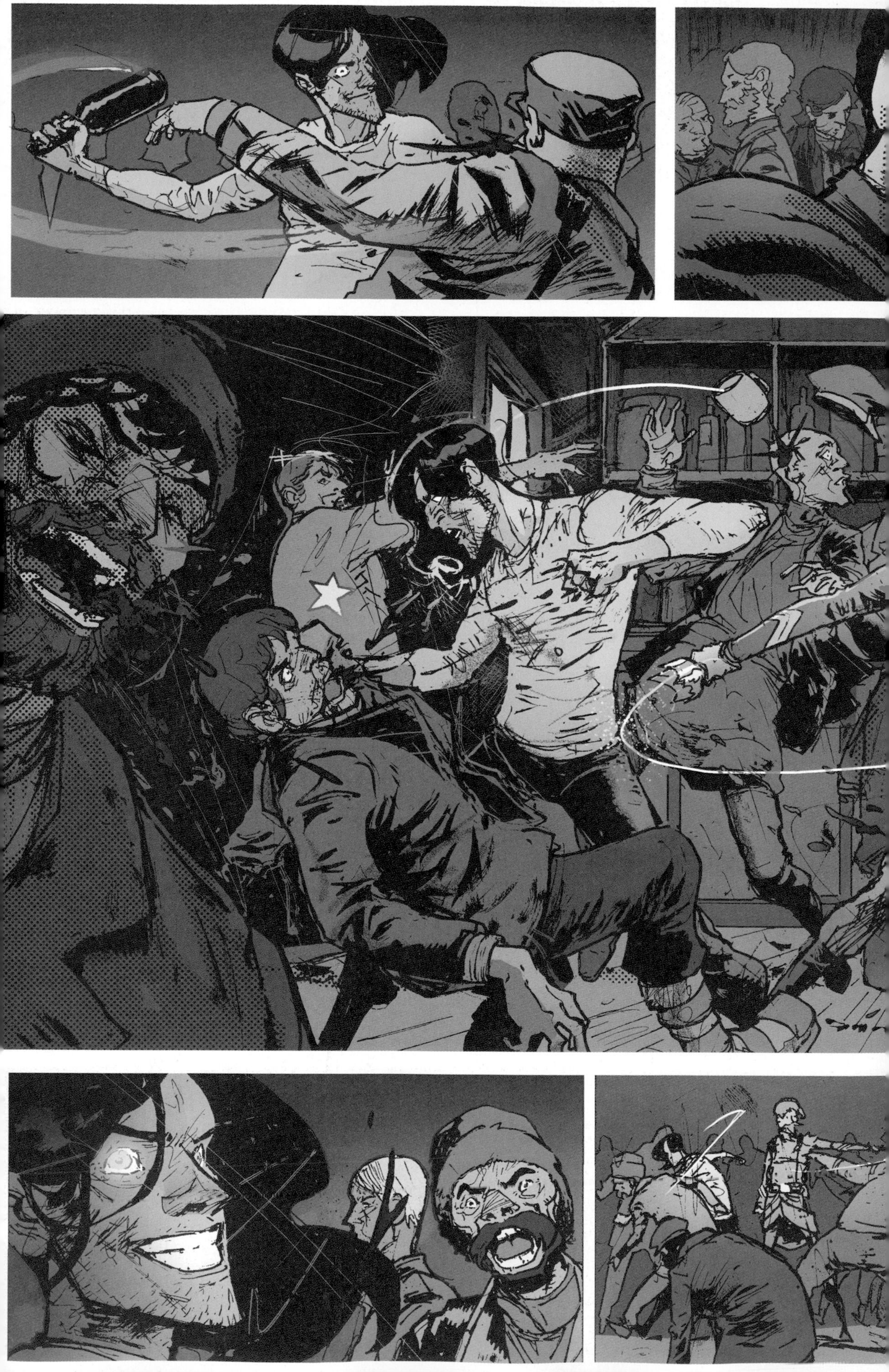

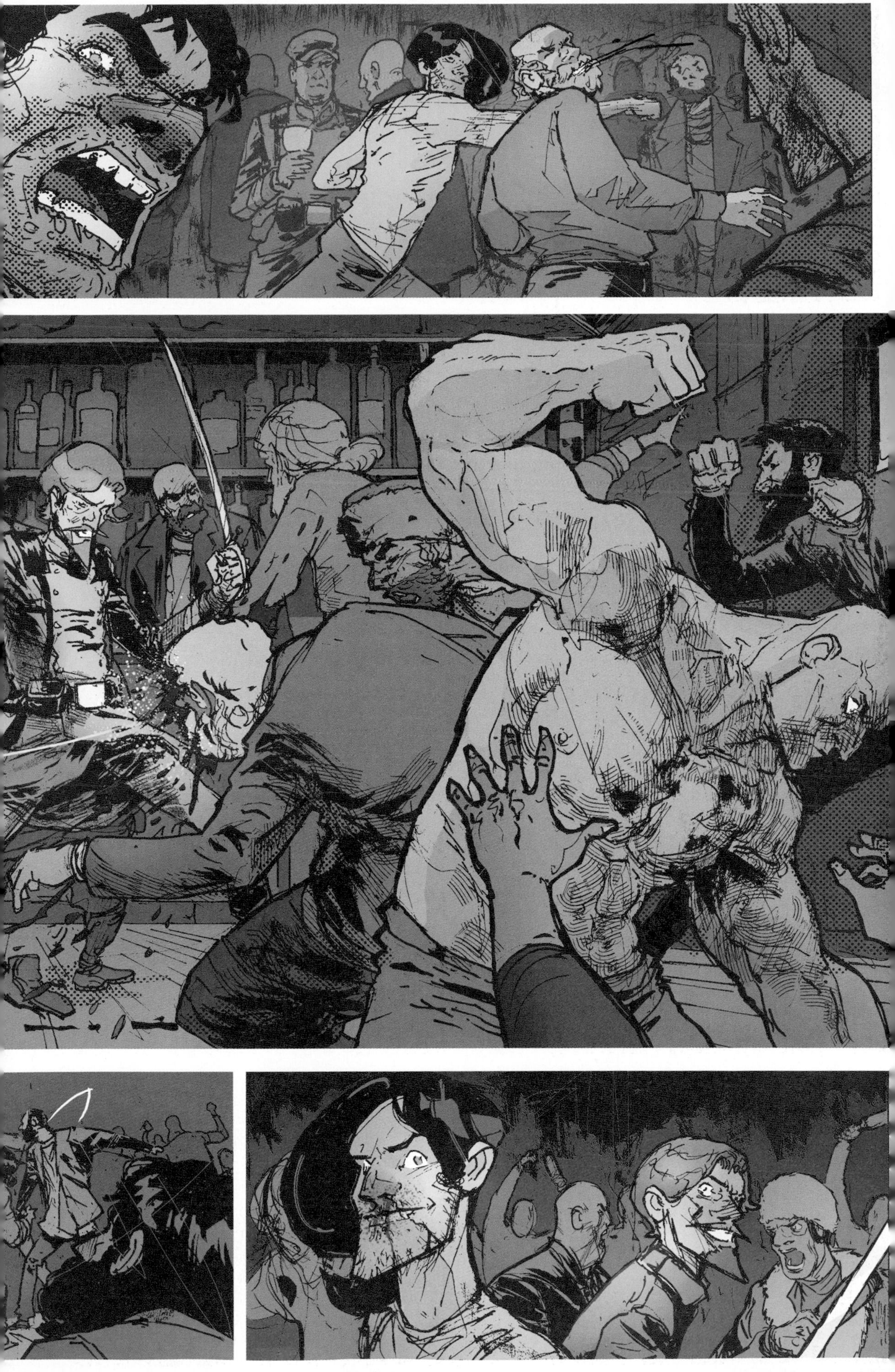

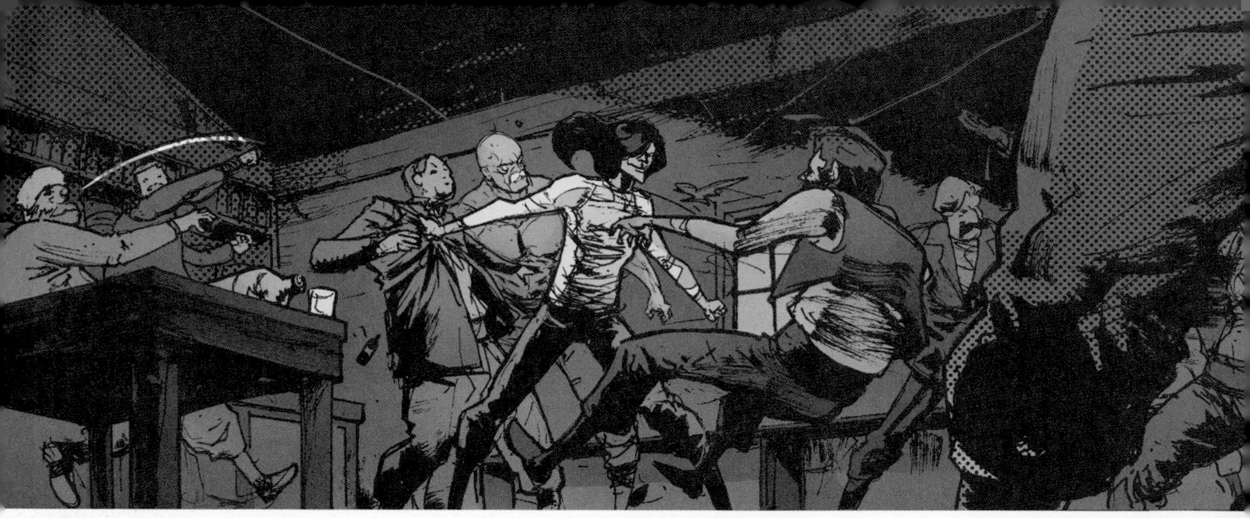
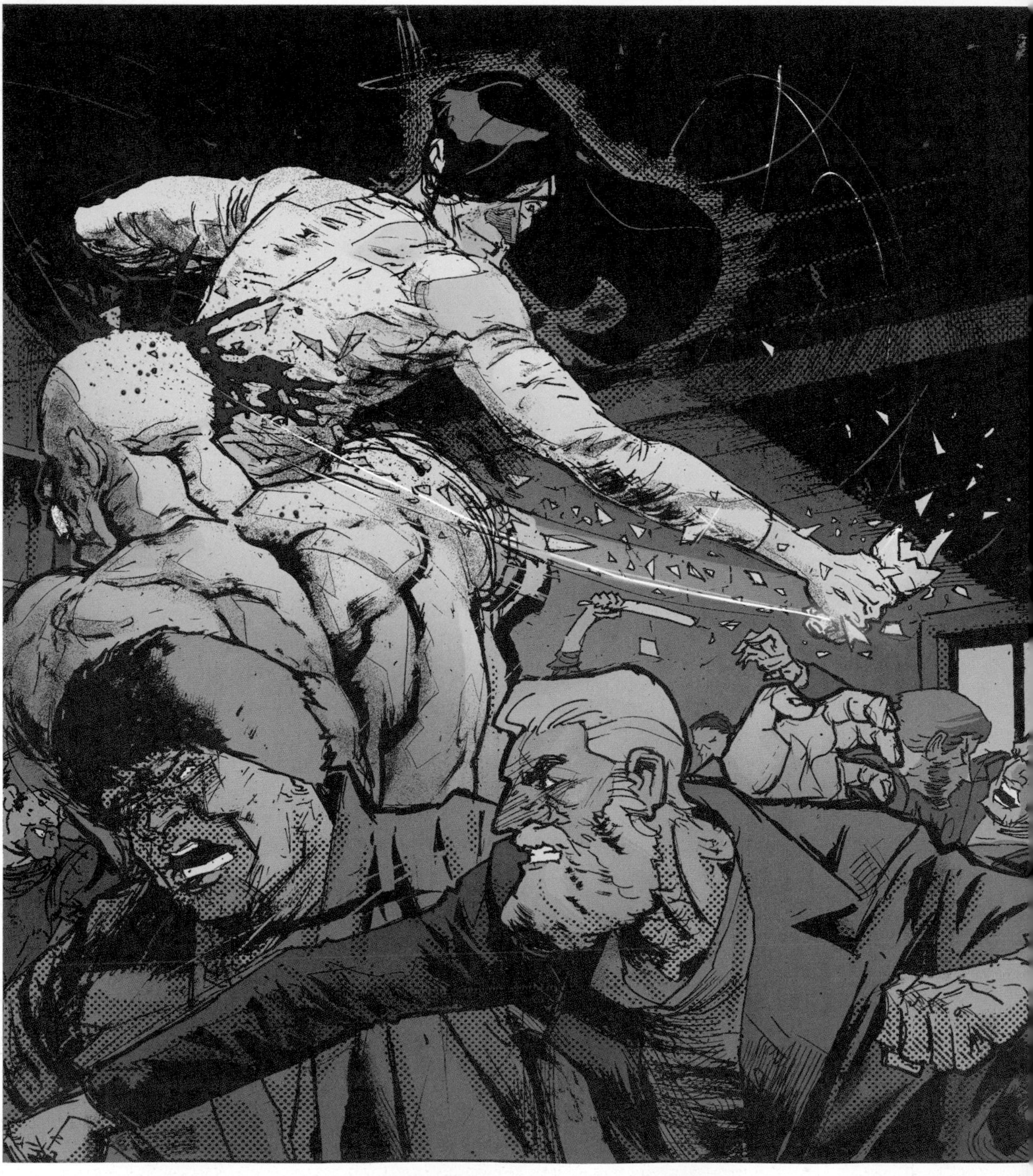

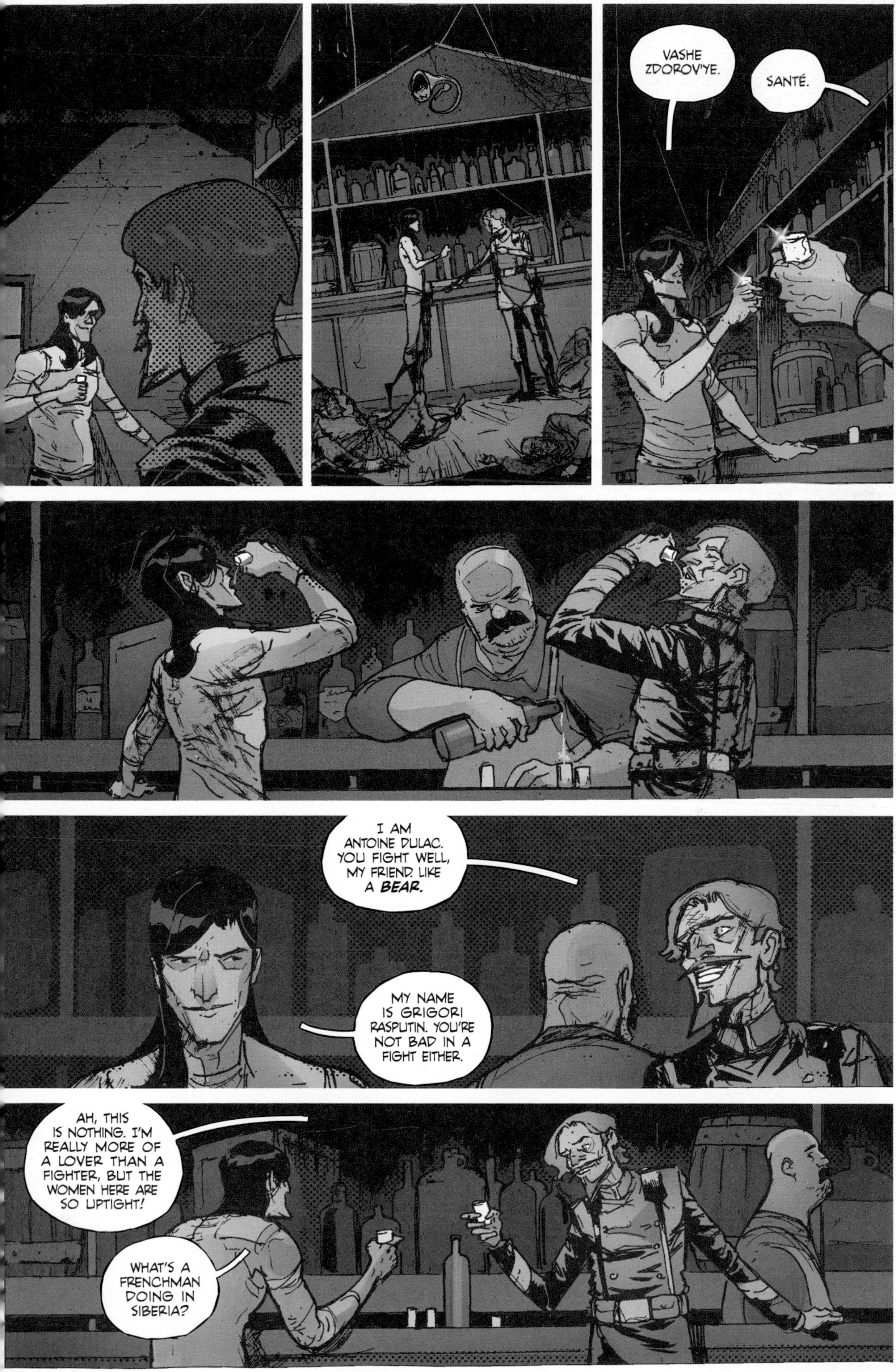
VASHE ZDOROV'YE.
SANTÉ.
I AM ANTOINE DULAC. YOU FIGHT WELL, MY FRIEND. LIKE A **BEAR.**
MY NAME IS GRIGORI RASPUTIN. YOU'RE NOT BAD IN A FIGHT EITHER.
AH, THIS IS NOTHING. I'M REALLY MORE OF A LOVER THAN A FIGHTER, BUT THE WOMEN HERE ARE SO UPTIGHT!
WHAT'S A FRENCHMAN DOING IN SIBERIA?

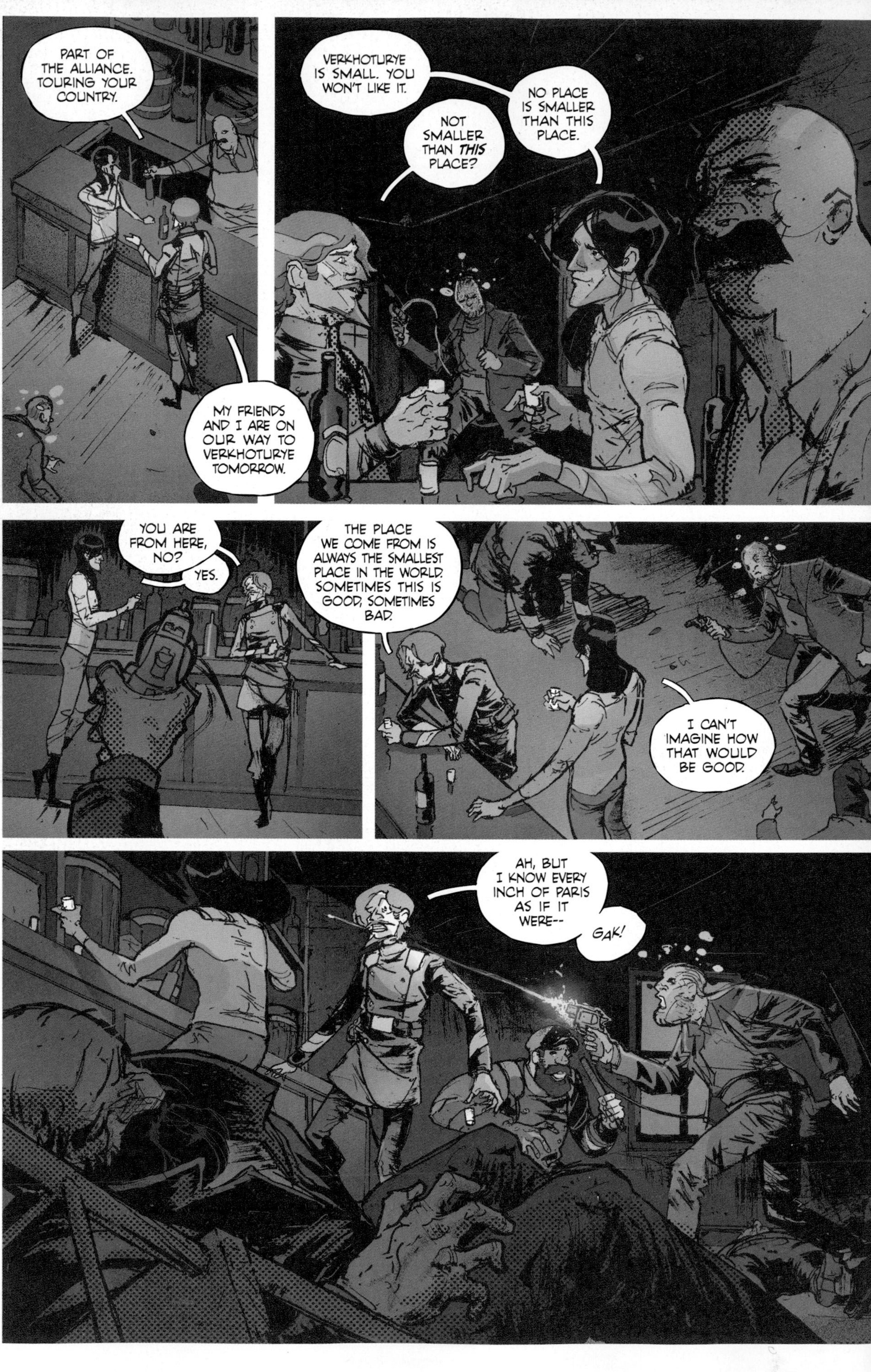
PART OF THE ALLIANCE. TOURING YOUR COUNTRY.
MY FRIENDS AND I ARE ON OUR WAY TO VERKHOTURYE TOMORROW.
VERKHOTURYE IS SMALL. YOU WON'T LIKE IT.
NOT SMALLER THAN *THIS* PLACE?
NO PLACE IS SMALLER THAN THIS PLACE.
YOU ARE FROM HERE, NO?
YES.
THE PLACE WE COME FROM IS ALWAYS THE SMALLEST PLACE IN THE WORLD. SOMETIMES THIS IS GOOD, SOMETIMES BAD.
I CAN'T IMAGINE HOW THAT WOULD BE GOOD.
AH, BUT I KNOW EVERY INCH OF PARIS AS IF IT WERE--
GAK!

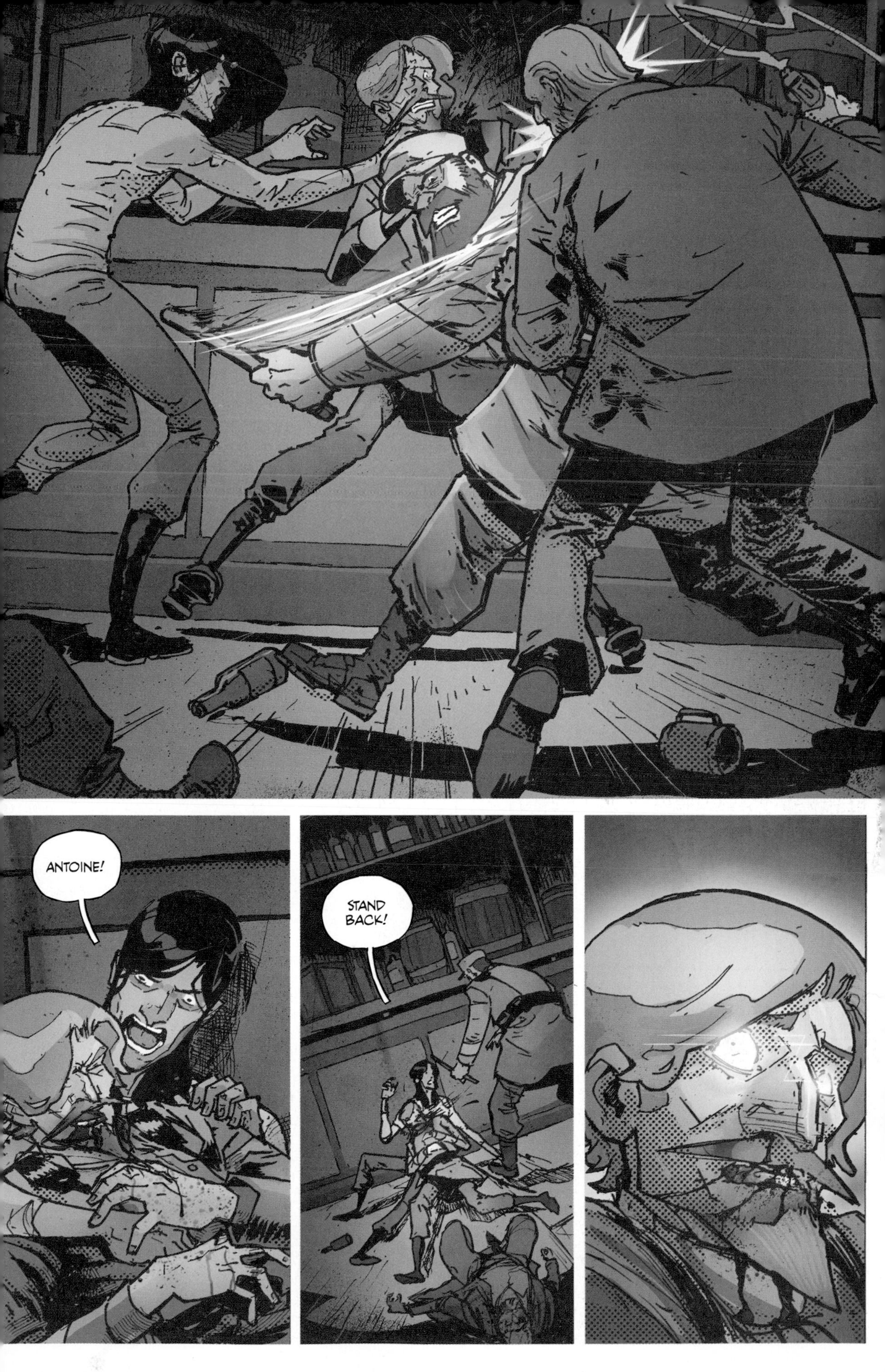
ANTOINE!
STAND BACK!

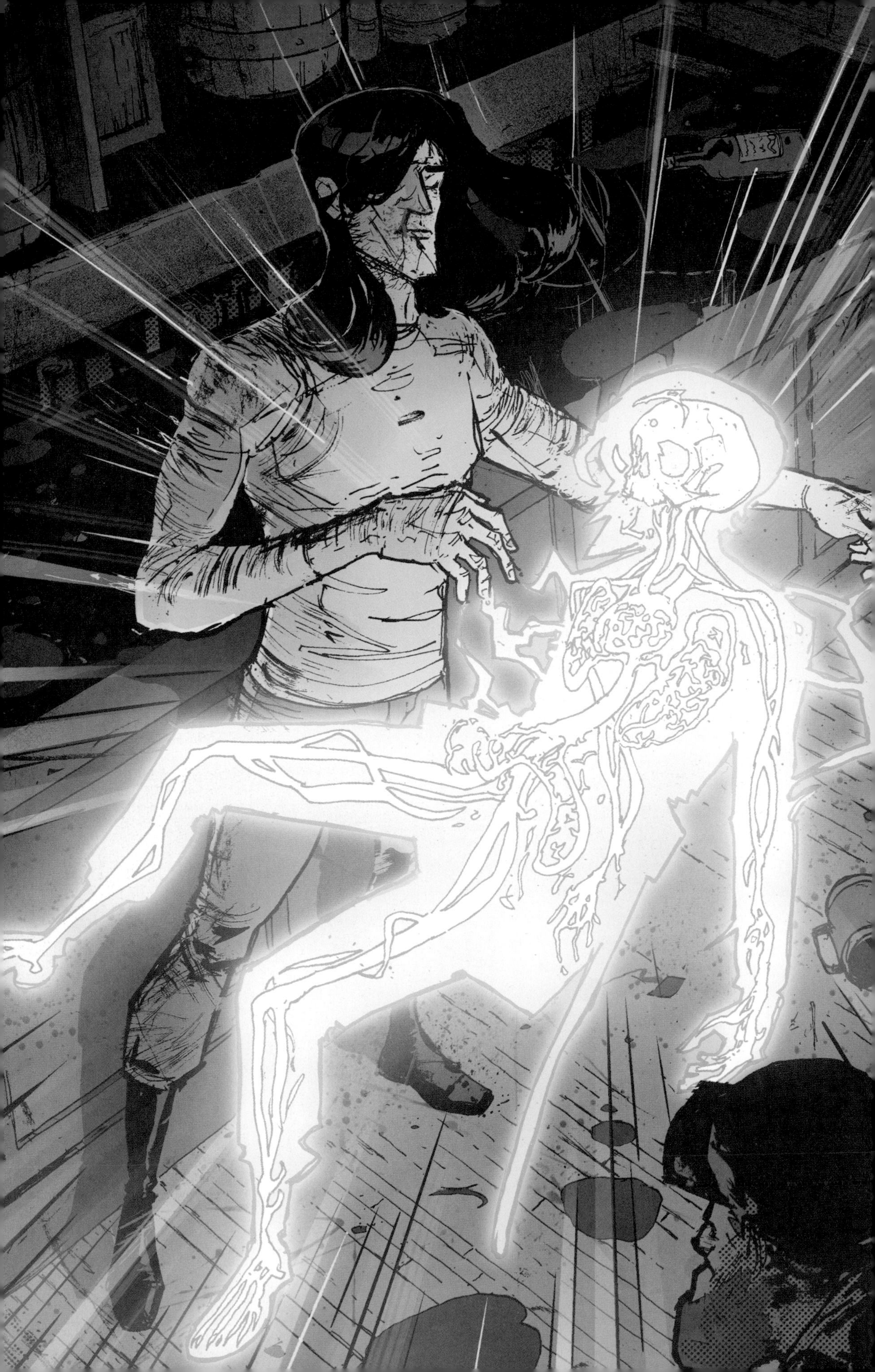

WHAT JUST--?

HOW?

YOU'LL SEE PARIS AGAIN, MY FRIEND.

BUT NOW YOU SHOULD REST.

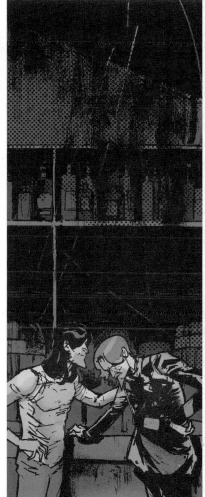

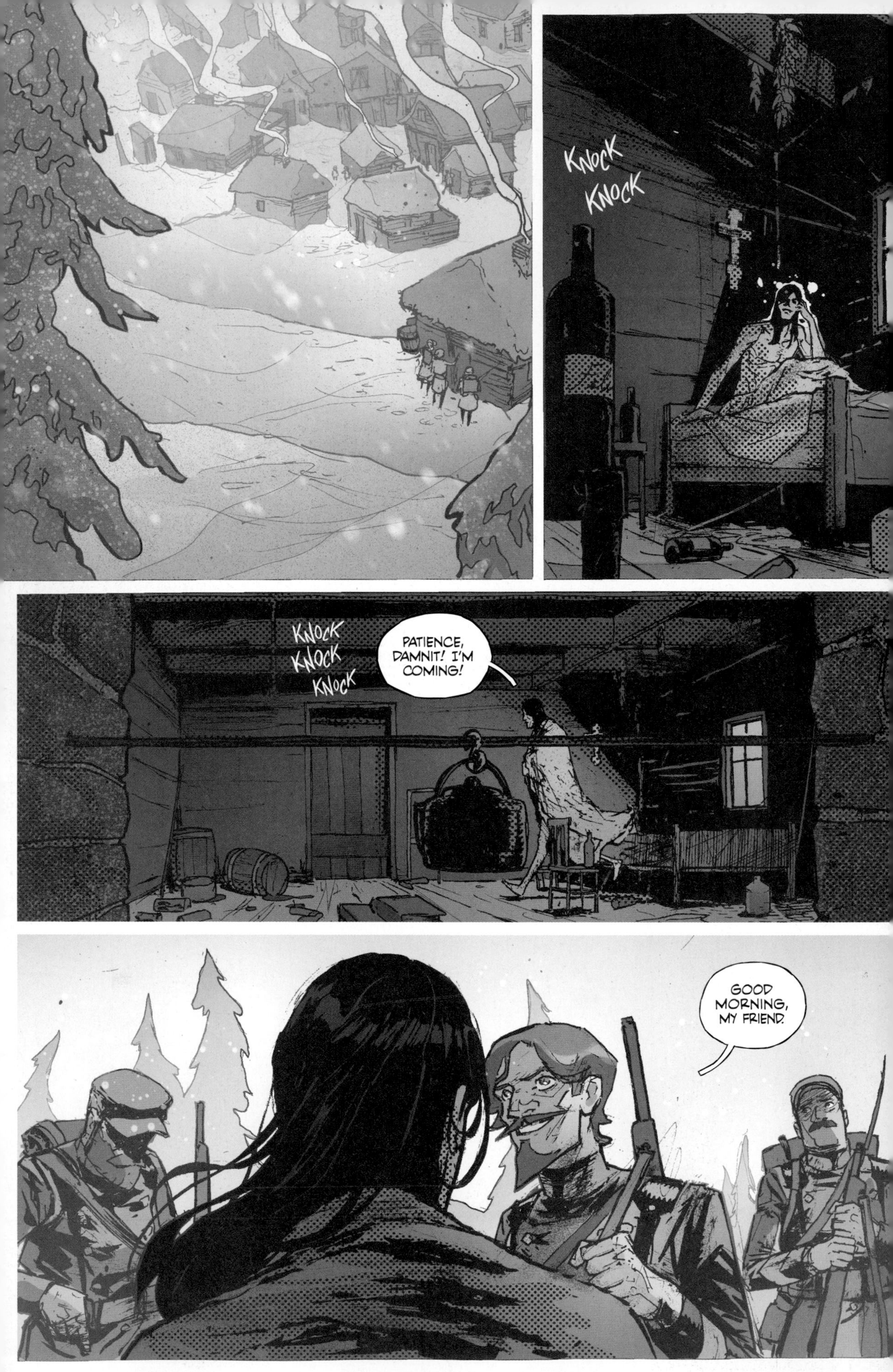
KNOCK
KNOCK
KNOCK
KNOCK
KNOCK
PATIENCE, DAMNIT! I'M COMING!
GOOD MORNING, MY FRIEND.

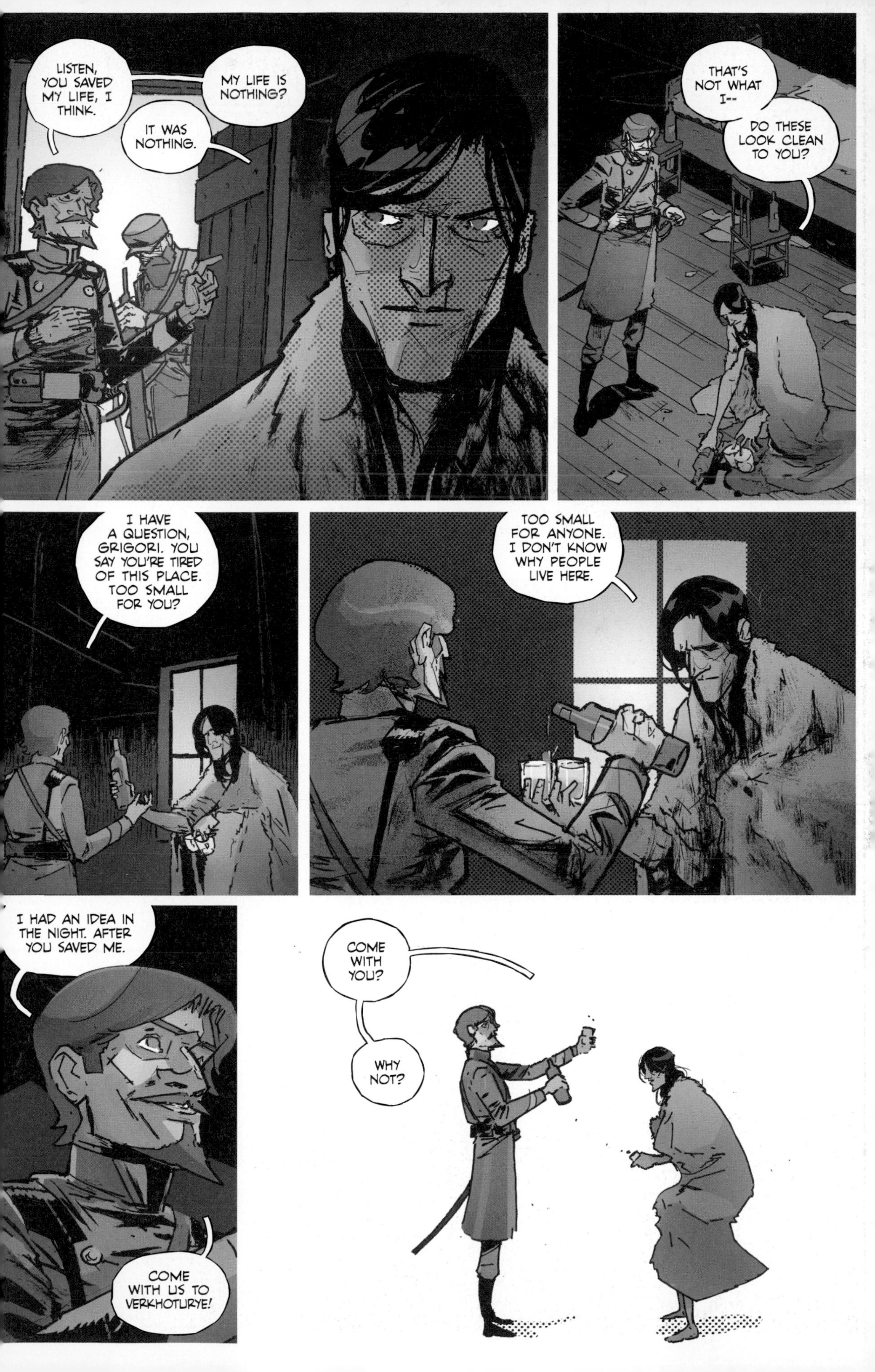
LISTEN, YOU SAVED MY LIFE, I THINK.
IT WAS NOTHING.
MY LIFE IS NOTHING?
THAT'S NOT WHAT I--
DO THESE LOOK CLEAN TO YOU?
I HAVE A QUESTION, GRIGORI. YOU SAY YOU'RE TIRED OF THIS PLACE. TOO SMALL FOR YOU?
TOO SMALL FOR ANYONE. I DON'T KNOW WHY PEOPLE LIVE HERE.
I HAD AN IDEA IN THE NIGHT. AFTER YOU SAVED ME.
COME WITH US TO VERKHOTURYE!
COME WITH YOU?
WHY NOT?

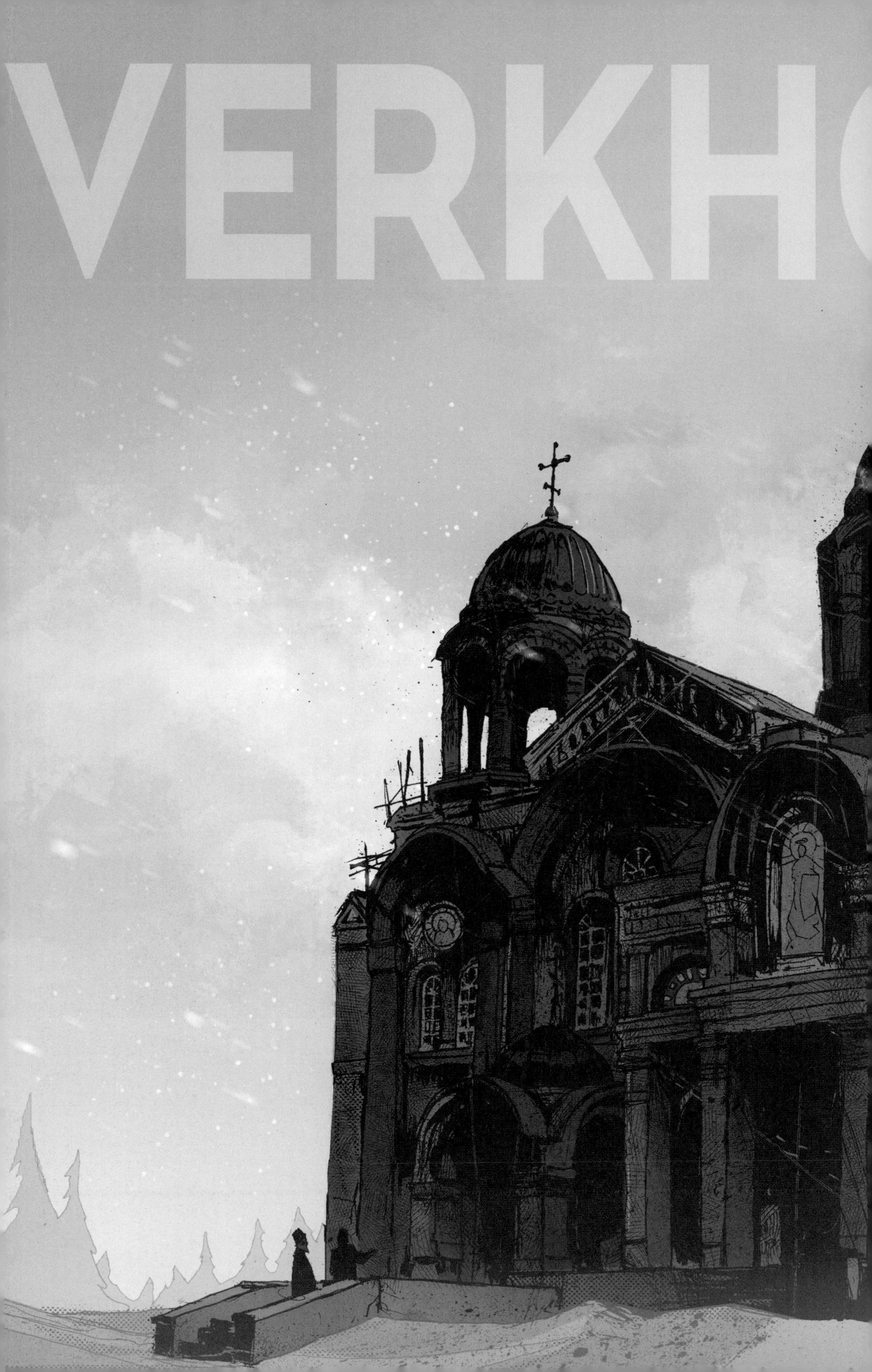
VERKHO

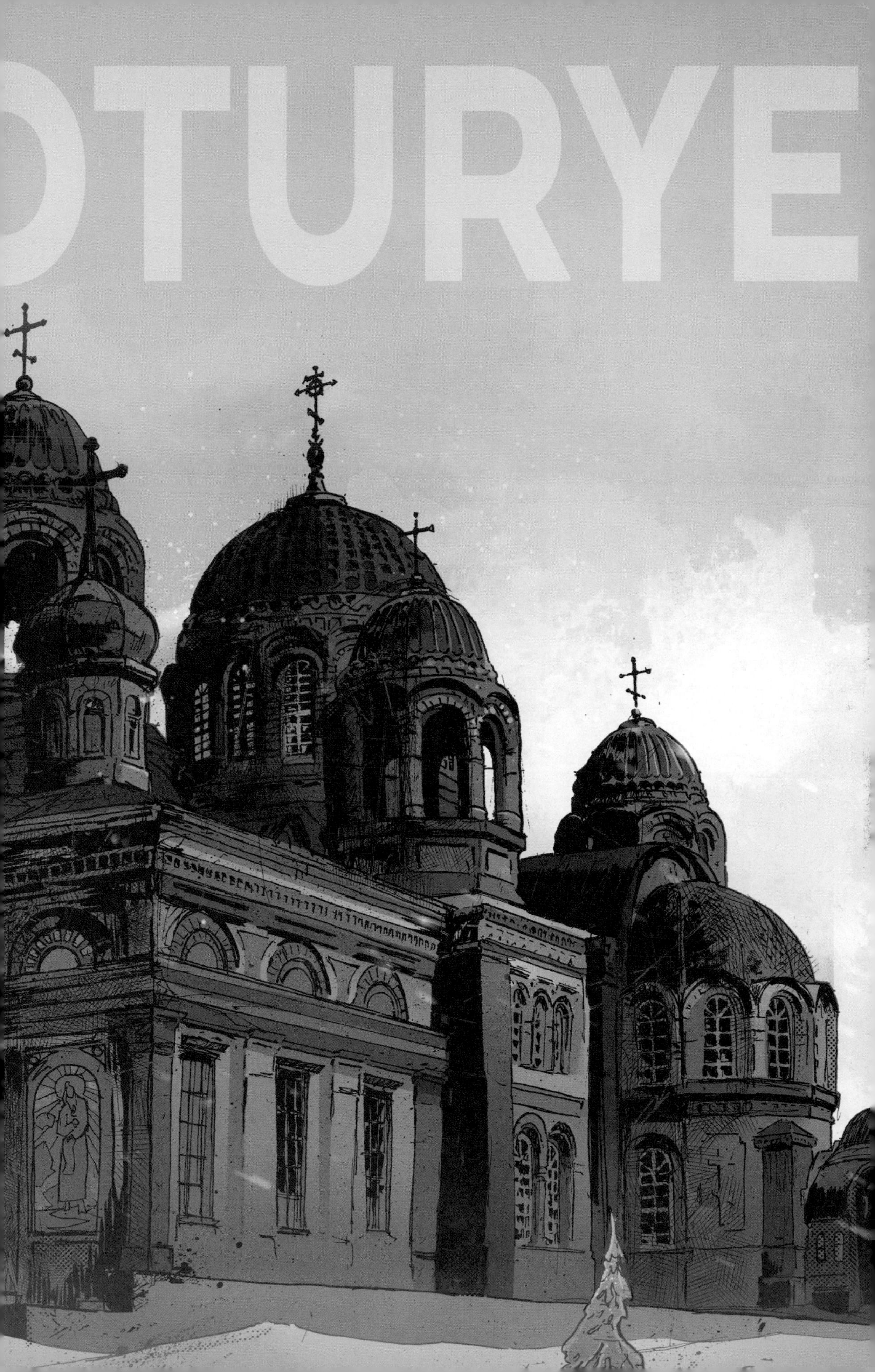
OTURYE

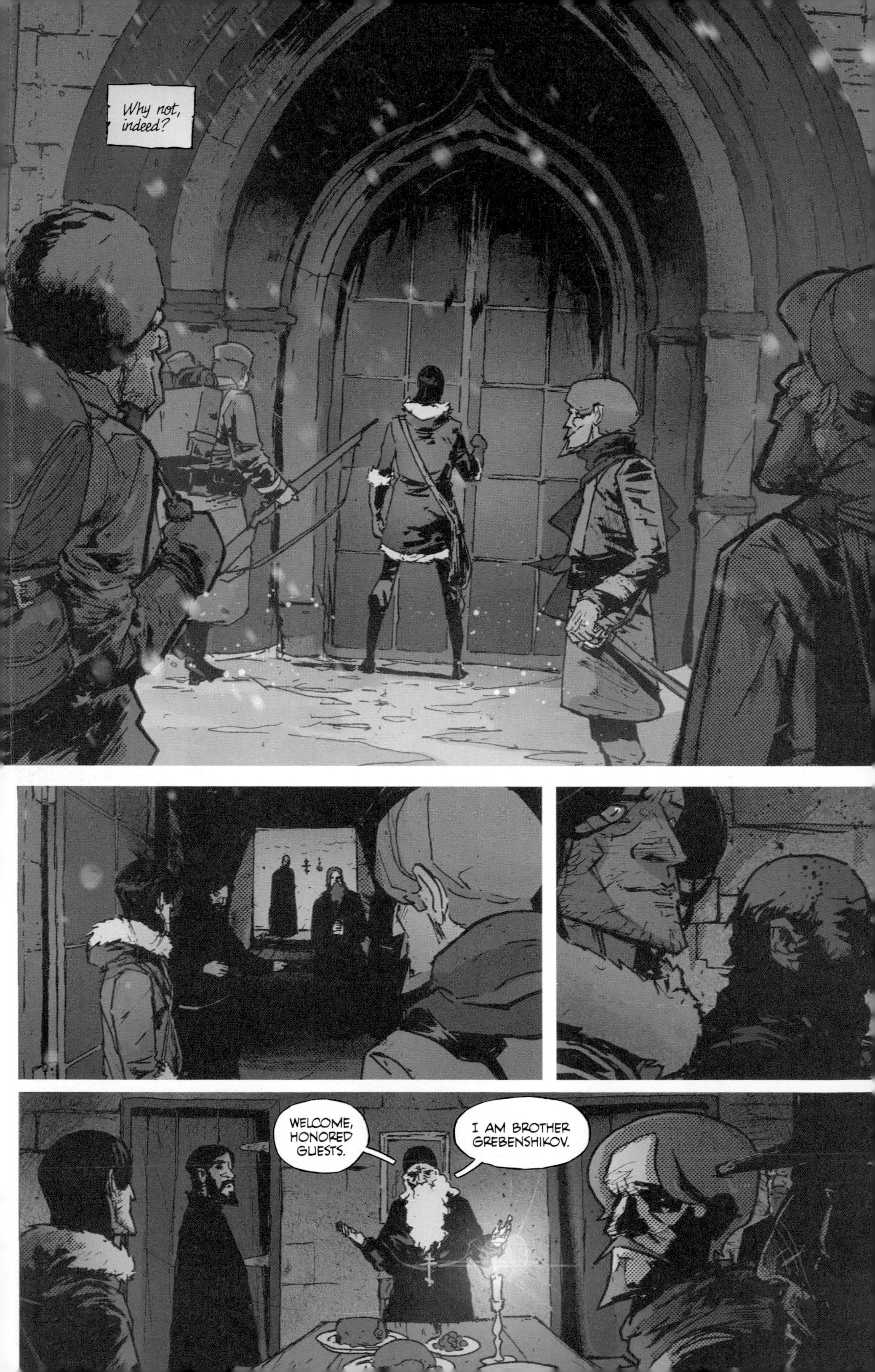
Why not, indeed?
WELCOME, HONORED GUESTS.
I AM BROTHER GREBENSHIKOV.

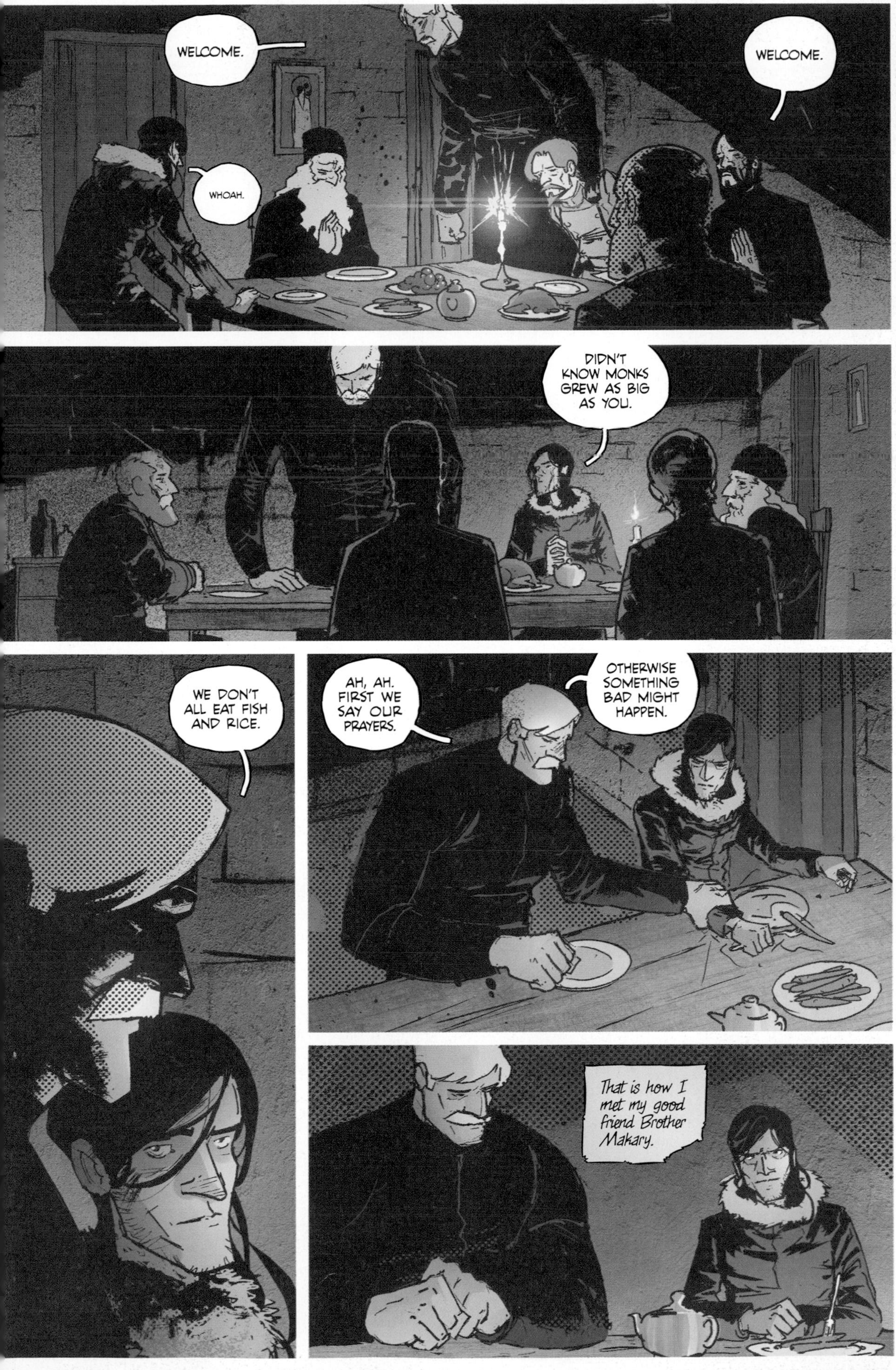
WELCOME.
WELCOME.
WHOAH.
DIDN'T KNOW MONKS GREW AS BIG AS YOU.
WE DON'T ALL EAT FISH AND RICE.
AH, AH. FIRST WE SAY OUR PRAYERS.
OTHERWISE SOMETHING BAD MIGHT HAPPEN.
That is how I met my good friend Brother Makary.

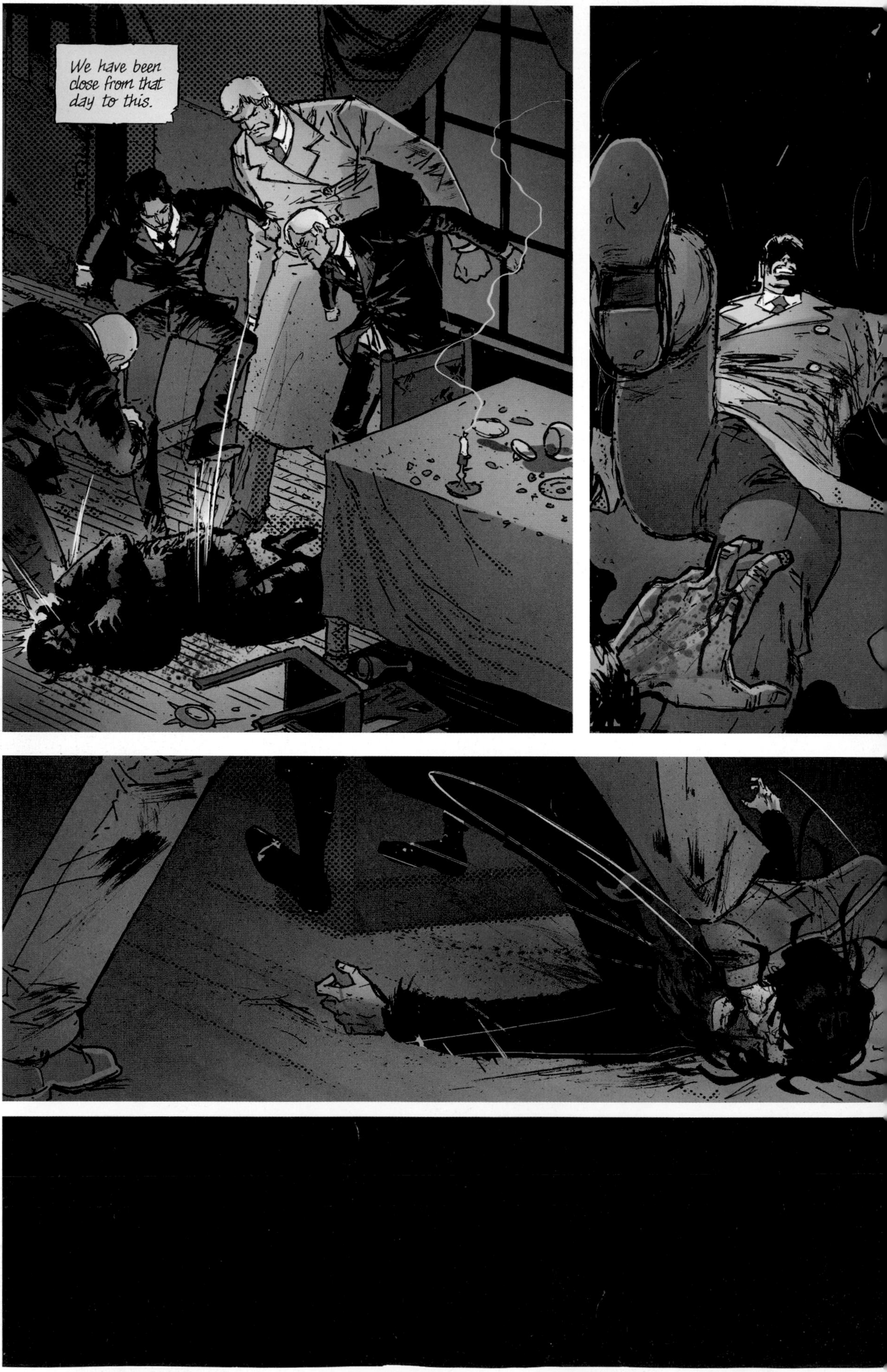
We have been close from that day to this.

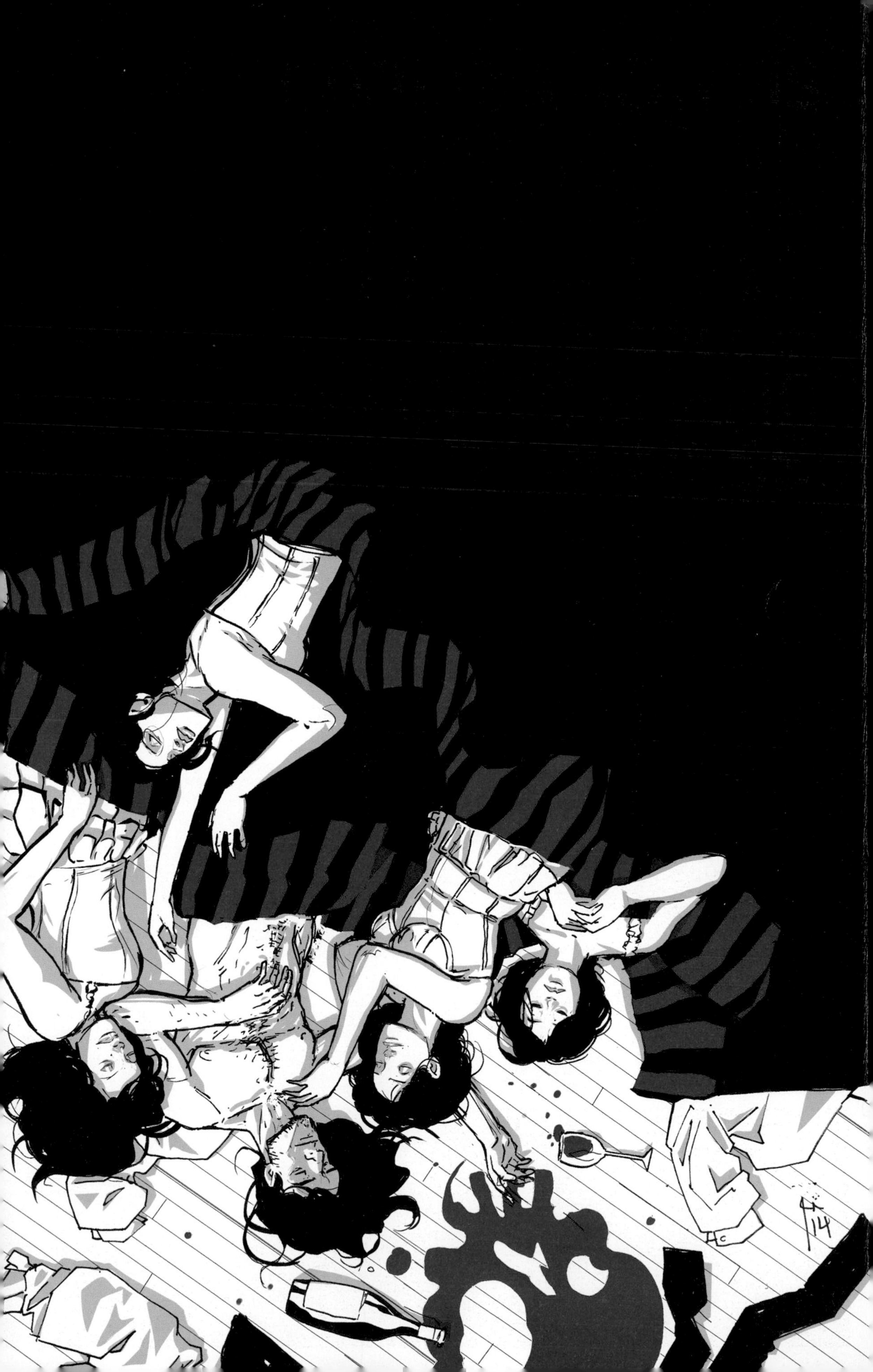

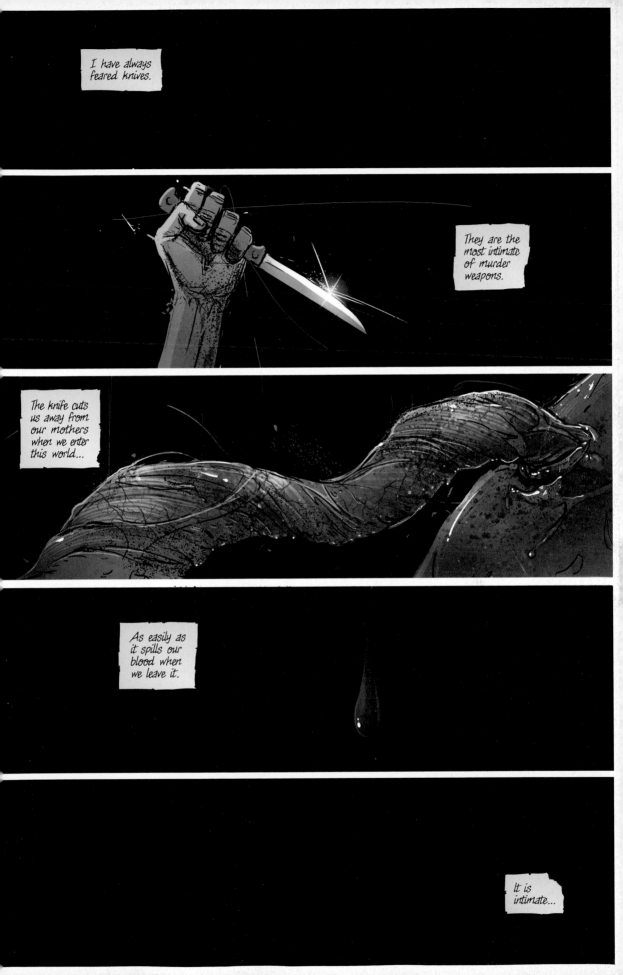

I have always
feared knives.

They are the
most intimate
of murder
weapons.

The knife cuts
us away from
our mothers
when we enter
this world...

As easily as
it spills our
blood when
we leave it.

It is
intimate...

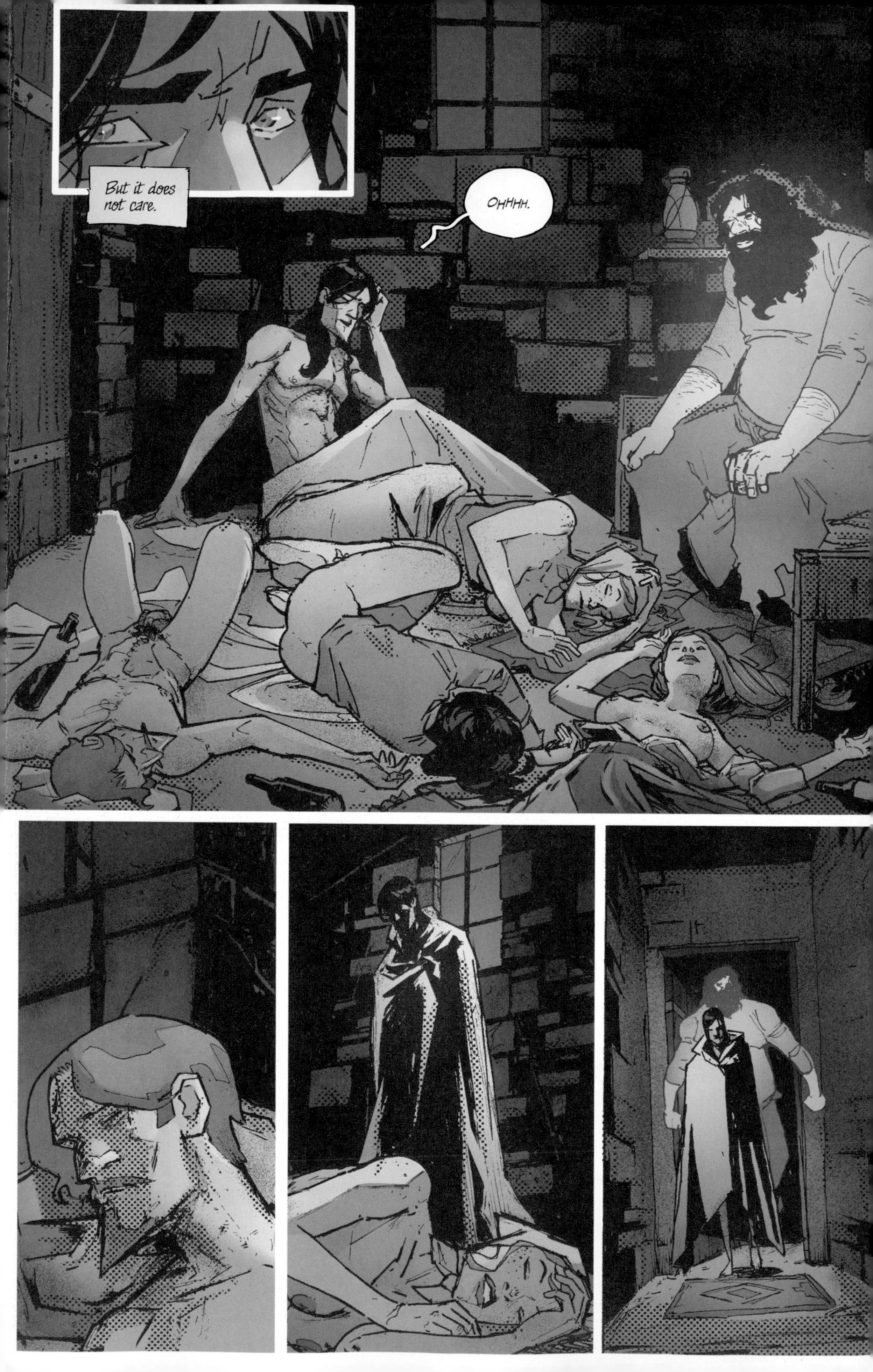
But it does not care.
OHHHH.

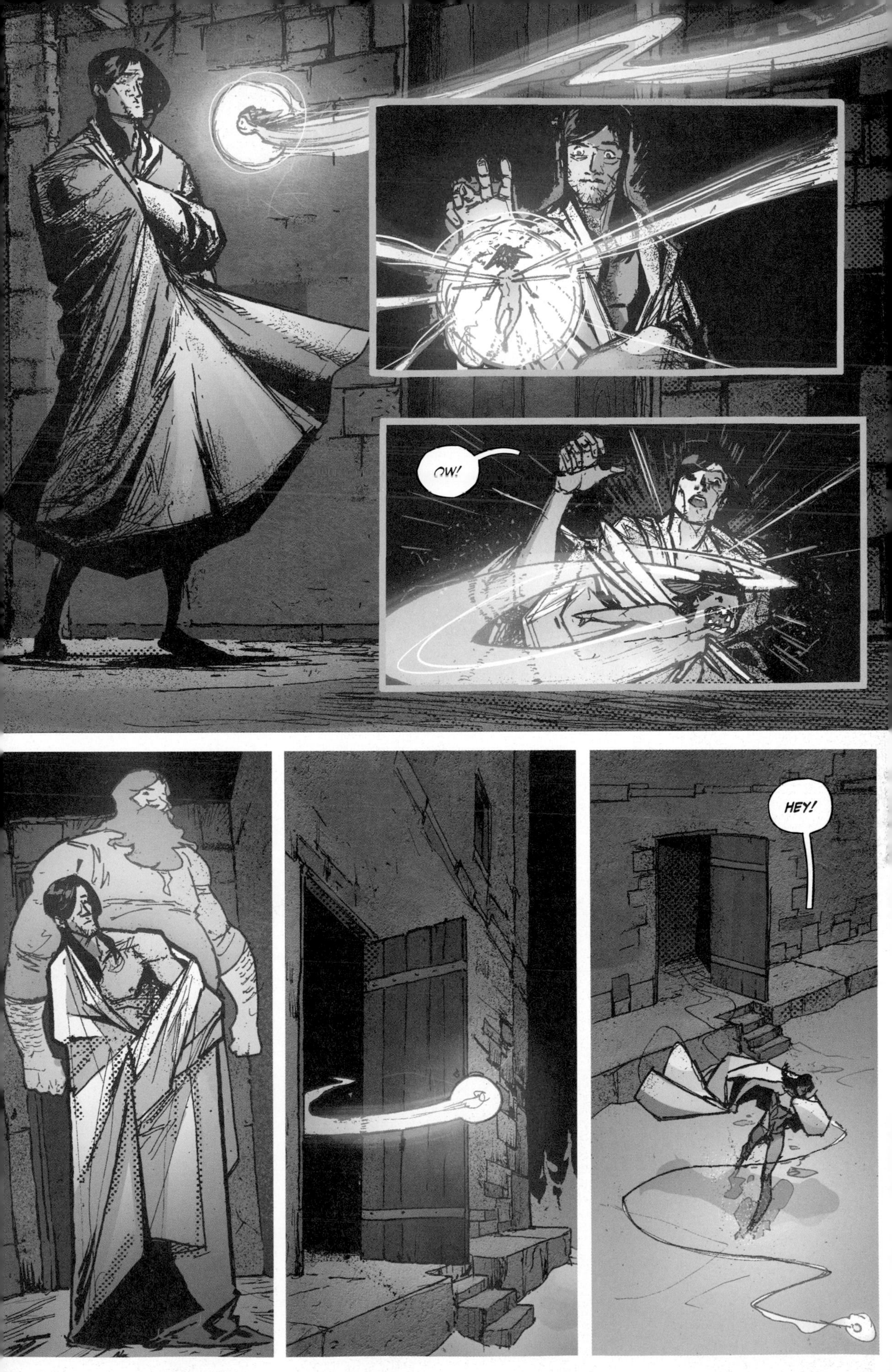
OW!
HEY!

WOW.

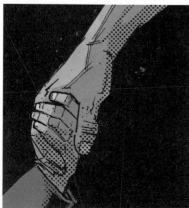

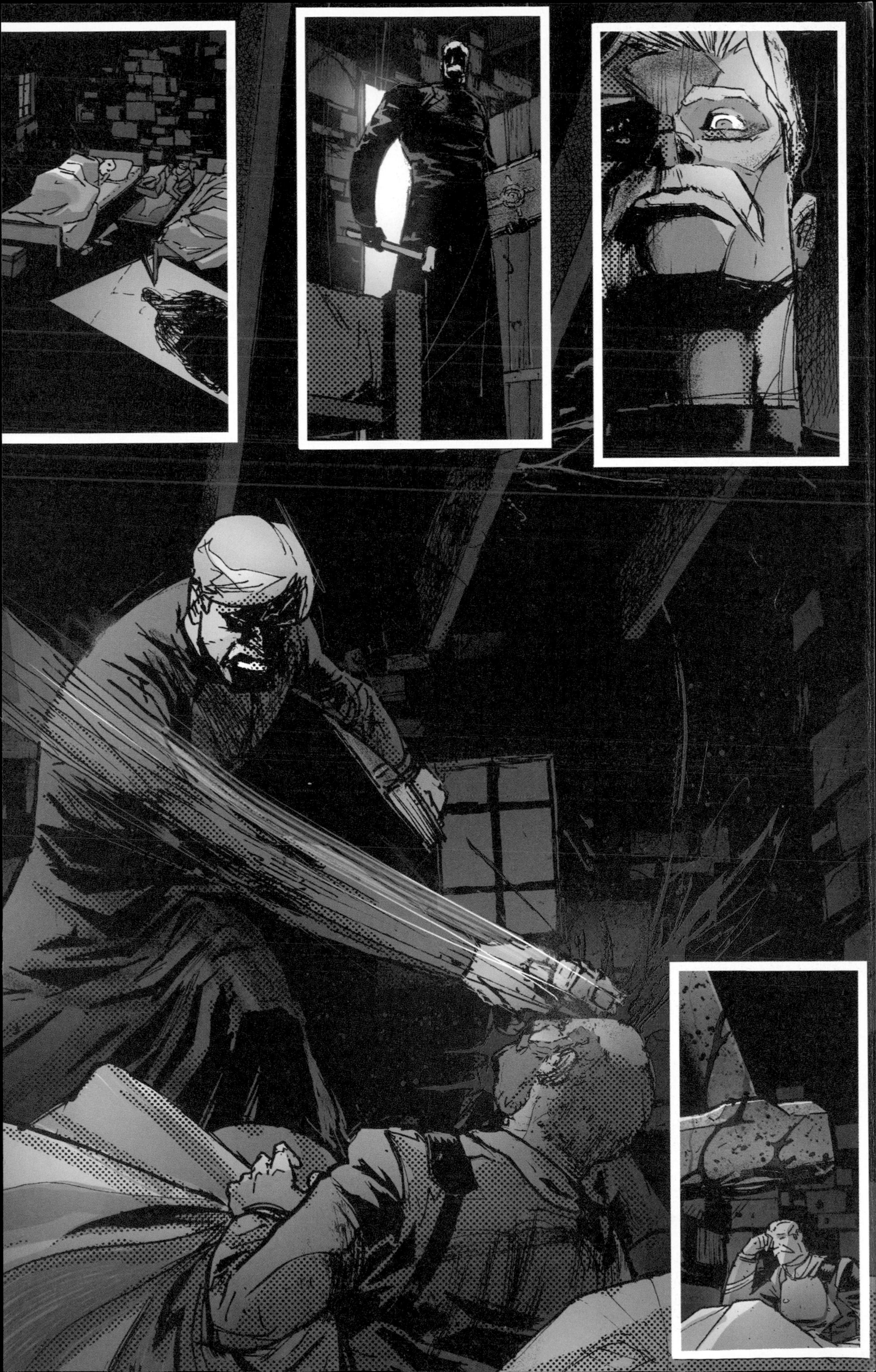

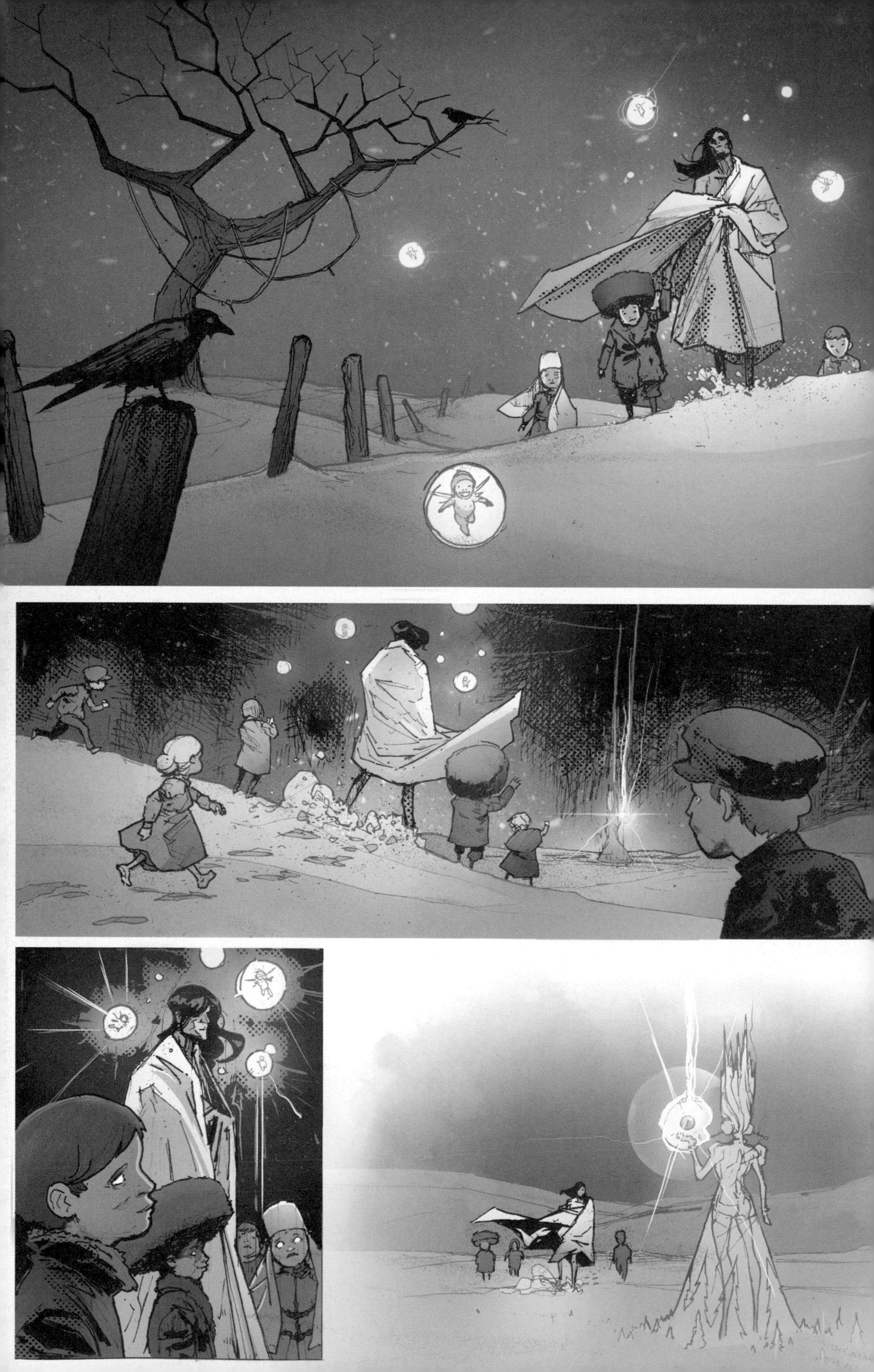

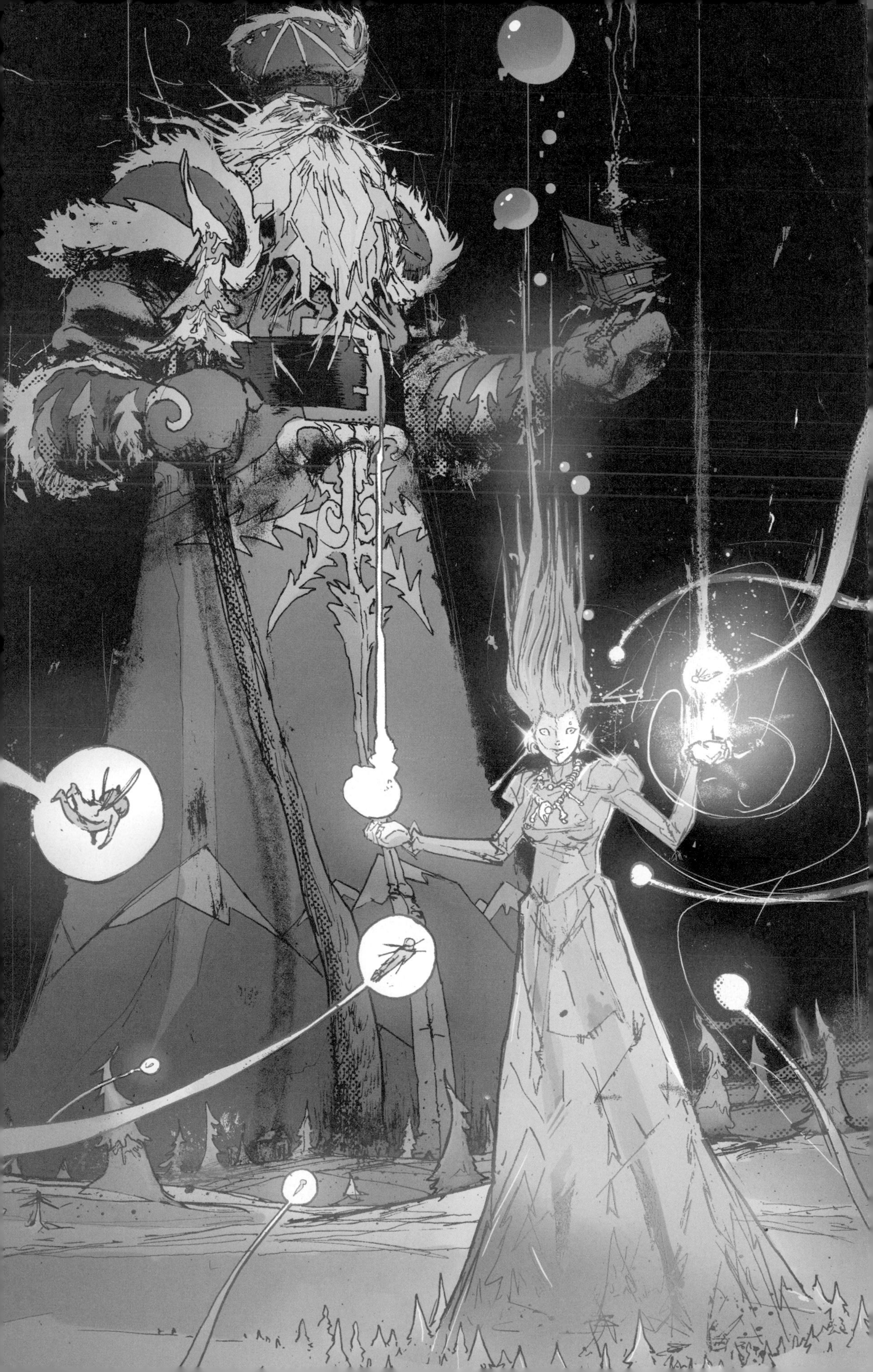

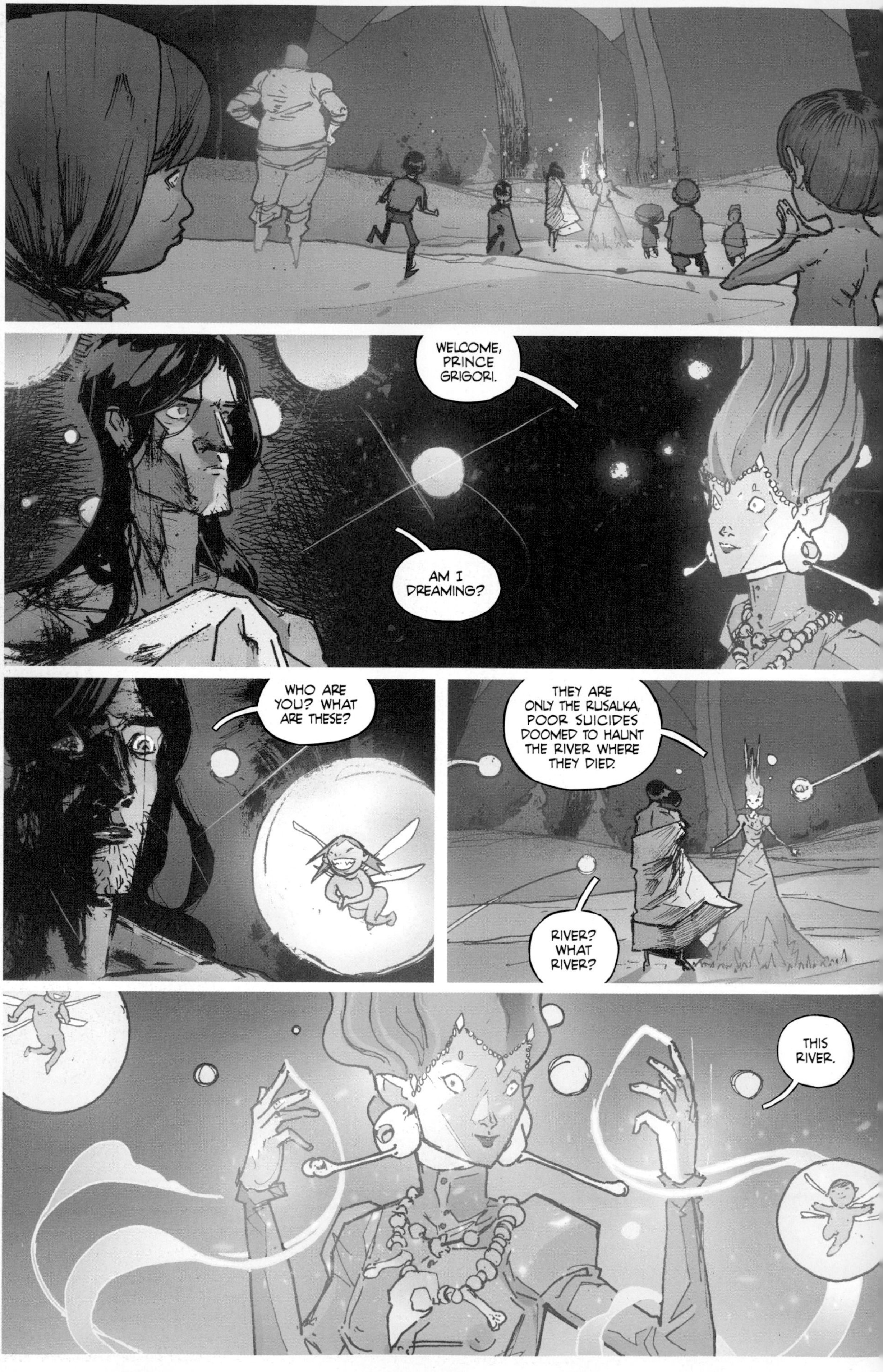
WELCOME, PRINCE GRIGORI.
AM I DREAMING?
WHO ARE YOU? WHAT ARE THESE?
THEY ARE ONLY THE RUSALKA, POOR SUICIDES DOOMED TO HAUNT THE RIVER WHERE THEY DIED.
RIVER? WHAT RIVER?
THIS RIVER.

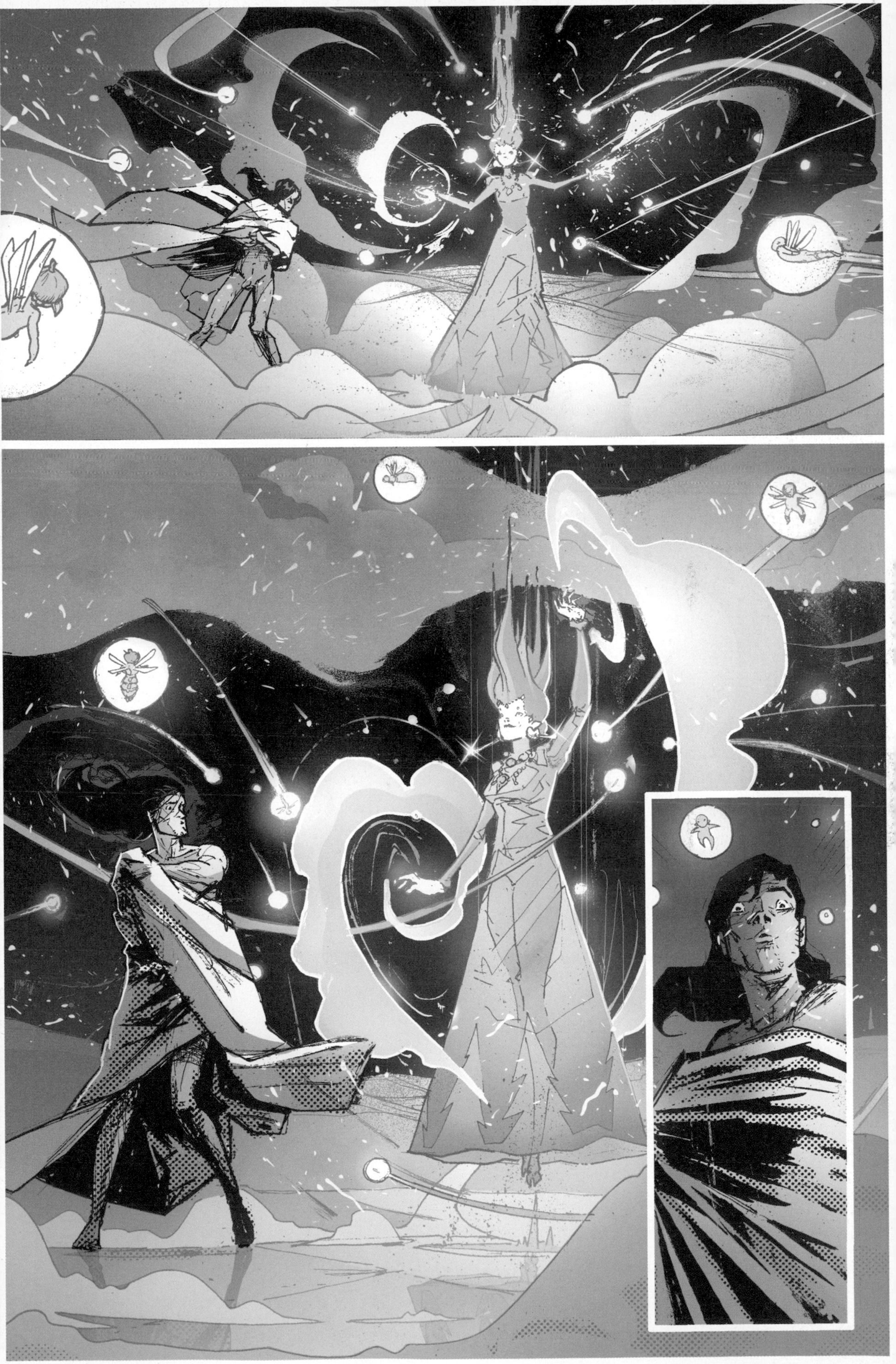

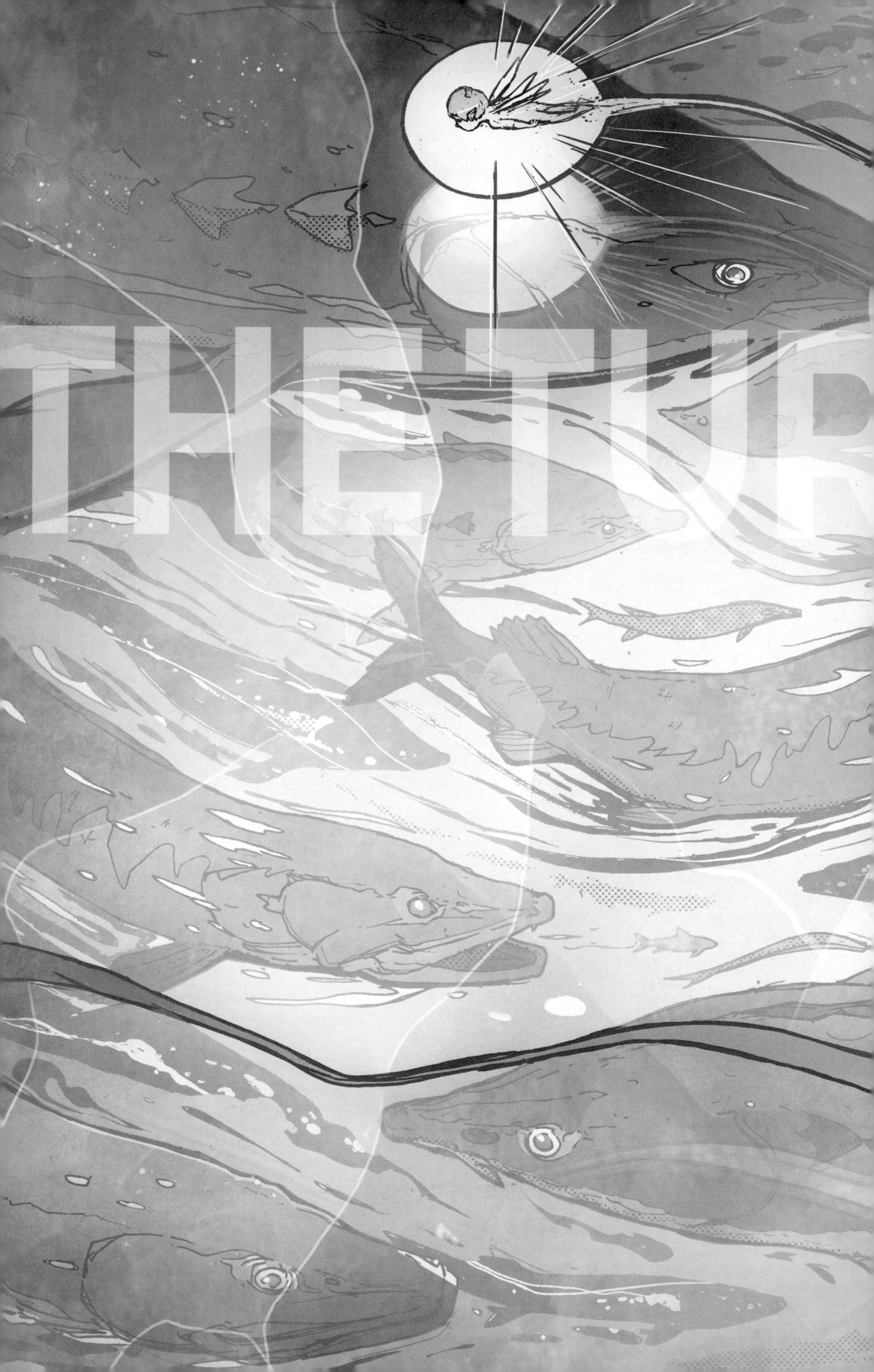
THE TUR

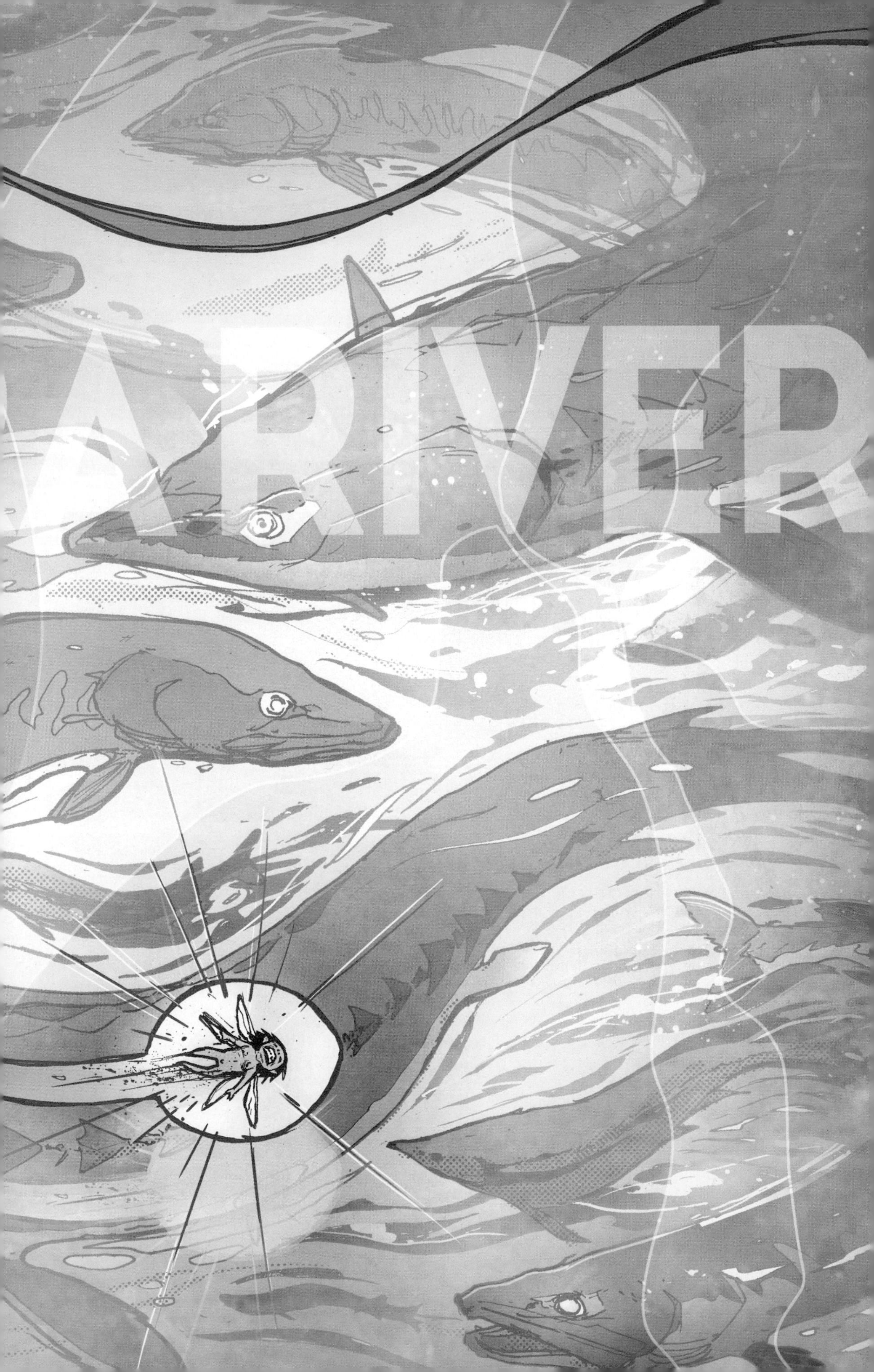
RIVER

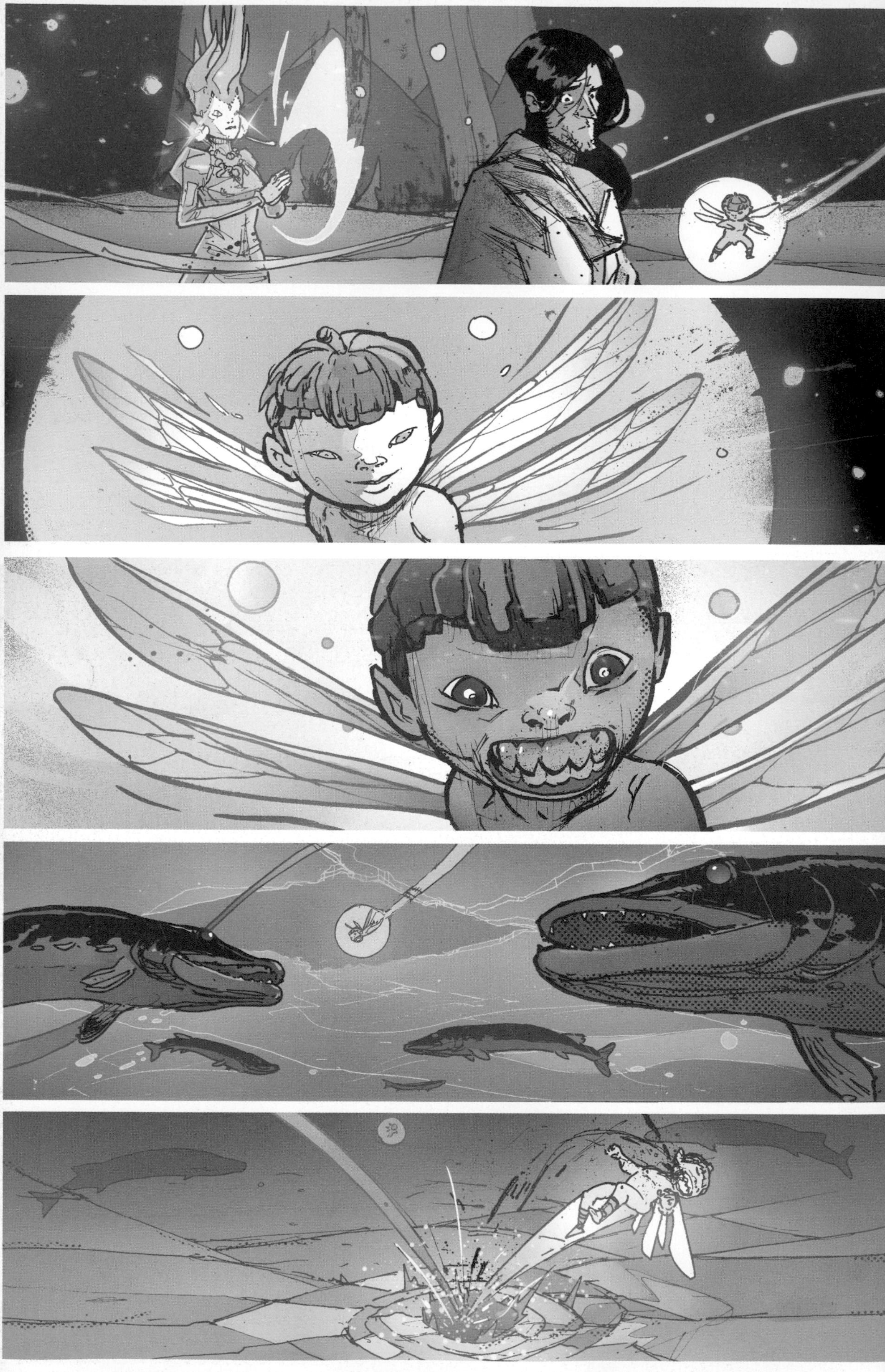

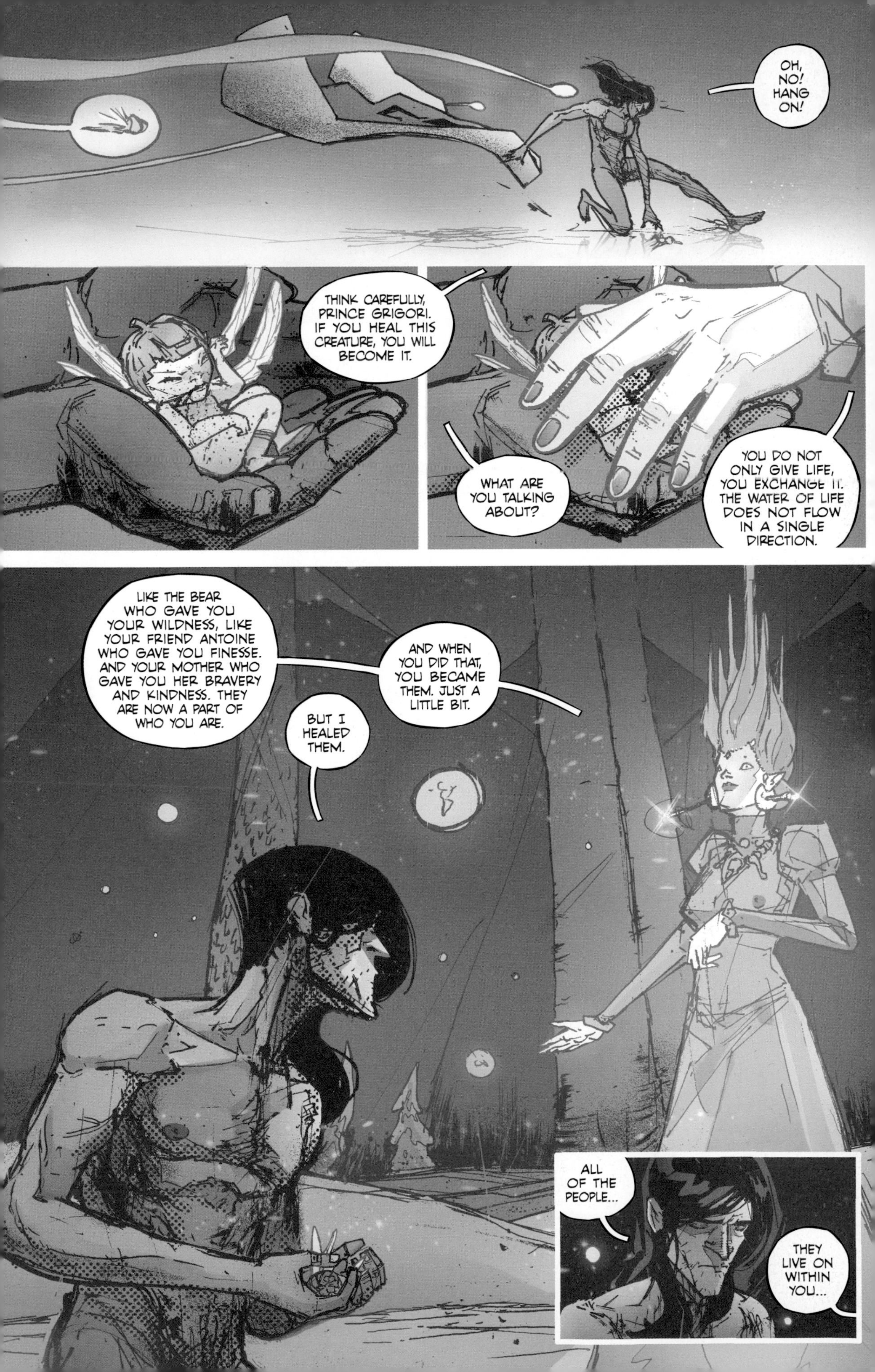
OH, NO! HANG ON!
THINK CAREFULLY, PRINCE GRIGORI. IF YOU HEAL THIS CREATURE, YOU WILL BECOME IT.
WHAT ARE YOU TALKING ABOUT?
YOU DO NOT ONLY GIVE LIFE, YOU EXCHANGE IT. THE WATER OF LIFE DOES NOT FLOW IN A SINGLE DIRECTION.
LIKE THE BEAR WHO GAVE YOU YOUR WILDNESS, LIKE YOUR FRIEND ANTOINE WHO GAVE YOU FINESSE. AND YOUR MOTHER WHO GAVE YOU HER BRAVERY AND KINDNESS. THEY ARE NOW A PART OF WHO YOU ARE.
BUT I HEALED THEM.
AND WHEN YOU DID THAT, YOU BECAME THEM. JUST A LITTLE BIT.
ALL OF THE PEOPLE...
THEY LIVE ON WITHIN YOU...

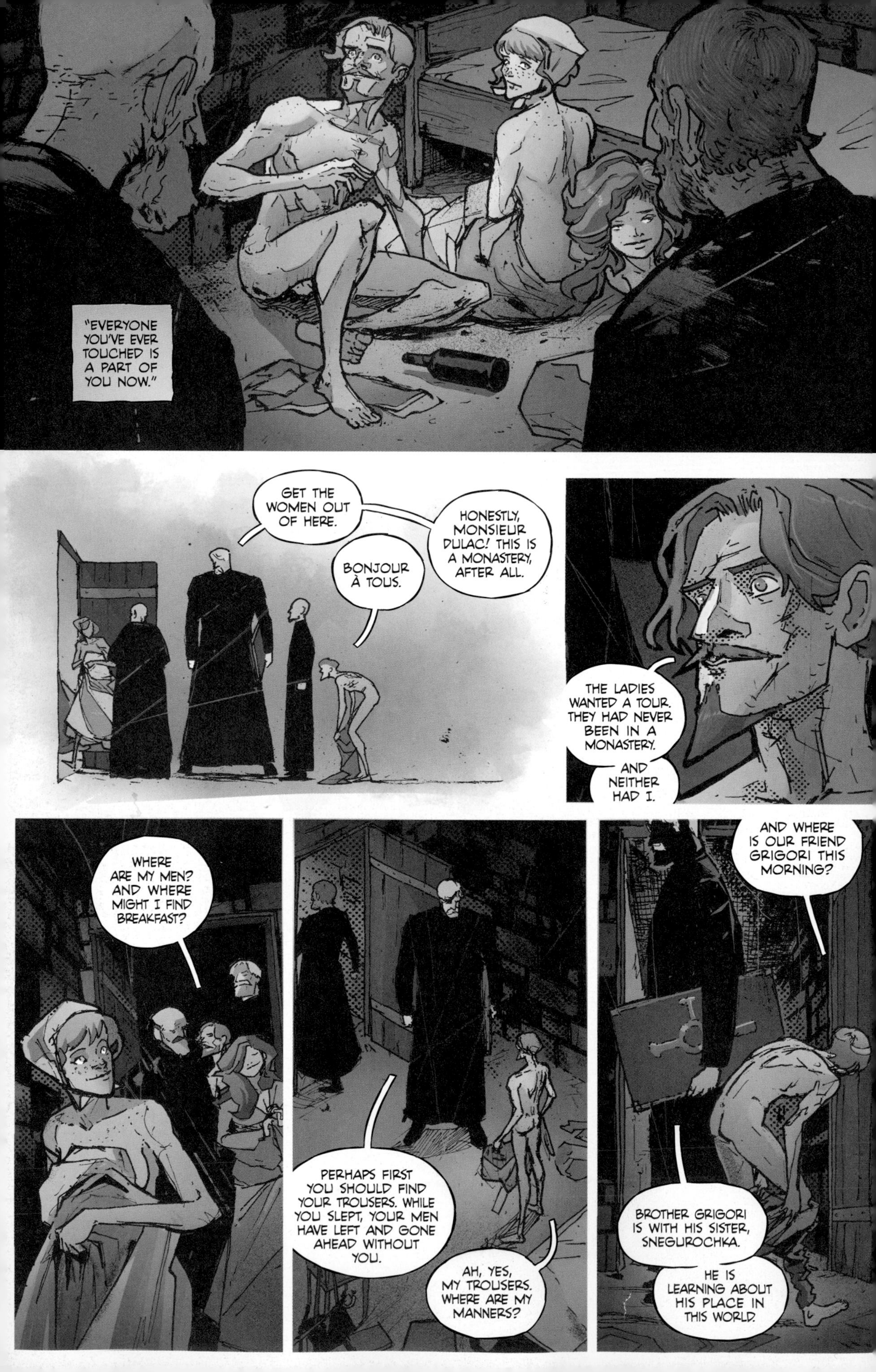
"EVERYONE YOU'VE EVER TOUCHED IS A PART OF YOU NOW."
GET THE WOMEN OUT OF HERE.
HONESTLY, MONSIEUR DULAC! THIS IS A MONASTERY, AFTER ALL.
BONJOUR À TOUS.
THE LADIES WANTED A TOUR. THEY HAD NEVER BEEN IN A MONASTERY.
AND NEITHER HAD I.
WHERE ARE MY MEN? AND WHERE MIGHT I FIND BREAKFAST?
PERHAPS FIRST YOU SHOULD FIND YOUR TROUSERS. WHILE YOU SLEPT, YOUR MEN HAVE LEFT AND GONE AHEAD WITHOUT YOU.
AH, YES, MY TROUSERS. WHERE ARE MY MANNERS?
AND WHERE IS OUR FRIEND GRIGORI THIS MORNING?
BROTHER GRIGORI IS WITH HIS SISTER, SNEGUROCHKA.
HE IS LEARNING ABOUT HIS PLACE IN THIS WORLD.

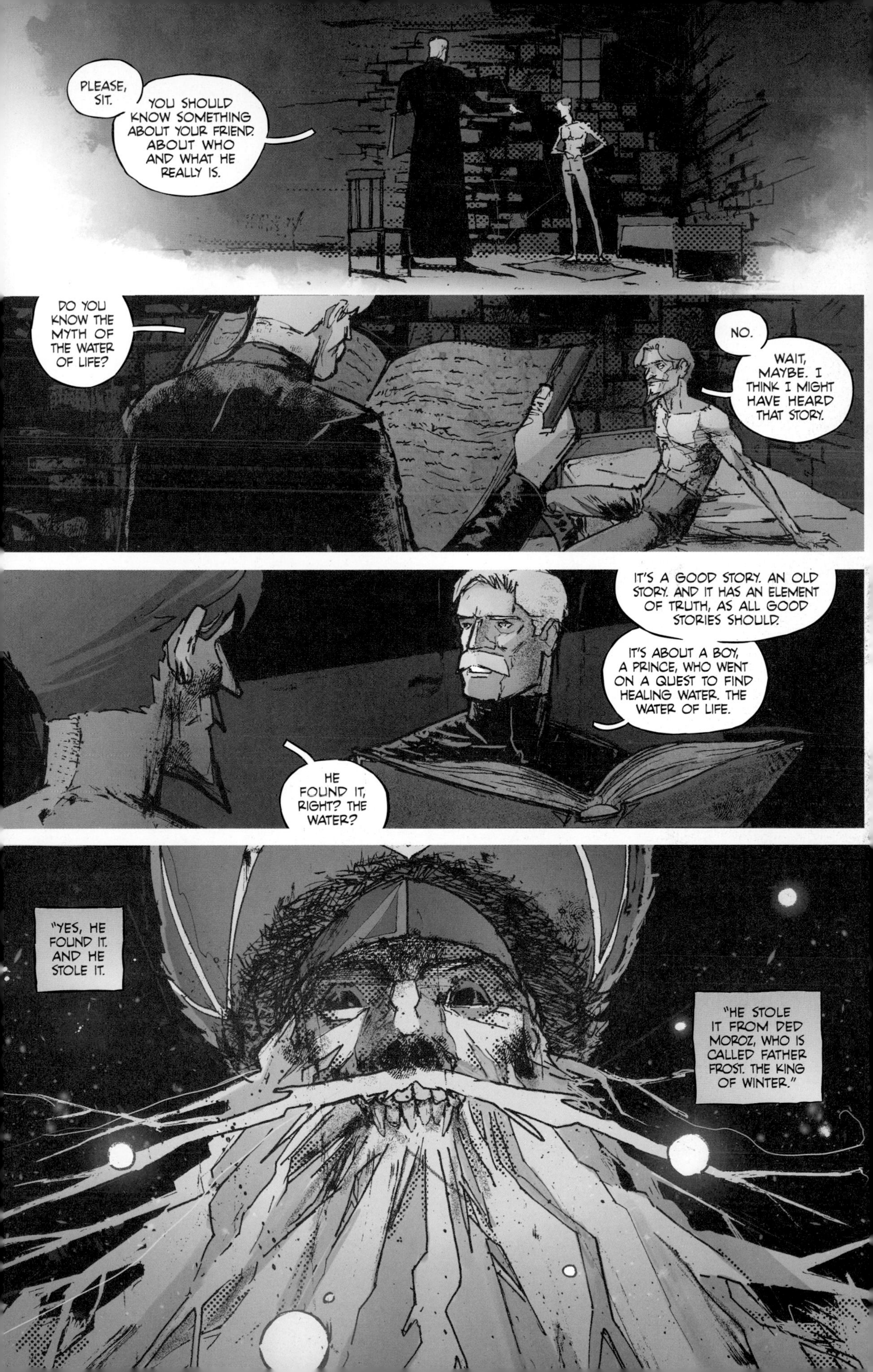
PLEASE, SIT.
YOU SHOULD KNOW SOMETHING ABOUT YOUR FRIEND. ABOUT WHO AND WHAT HE REALLY IS.
DO YOU KNOW THE MYTH OF THE WATER OF LIFE?
NO.
WAIT, MAYBE. I THINK I MIGHT HAVE HEARD THAT STORY.
IT'S A GOOD STORY. AN OLD STORY. AND IT HAS AN ELEMENT OF TRUTH, AS ALL GOOD STORIES SHOULD.
IT'S ABOUT A BOY, A PRINCE, WHO WENT ON A QUEST TO FIND HEALING WATER. THE WATER OF LIFE.
HE FOUND IT, RIGHT? THE WATER?
"YES, HE FOUND IT. AND HE STOLE IT.
"HE STOLE IT FROM DED MOROZ, WHO IS CALLED FATHER FROST. THE KING OF WINTER."

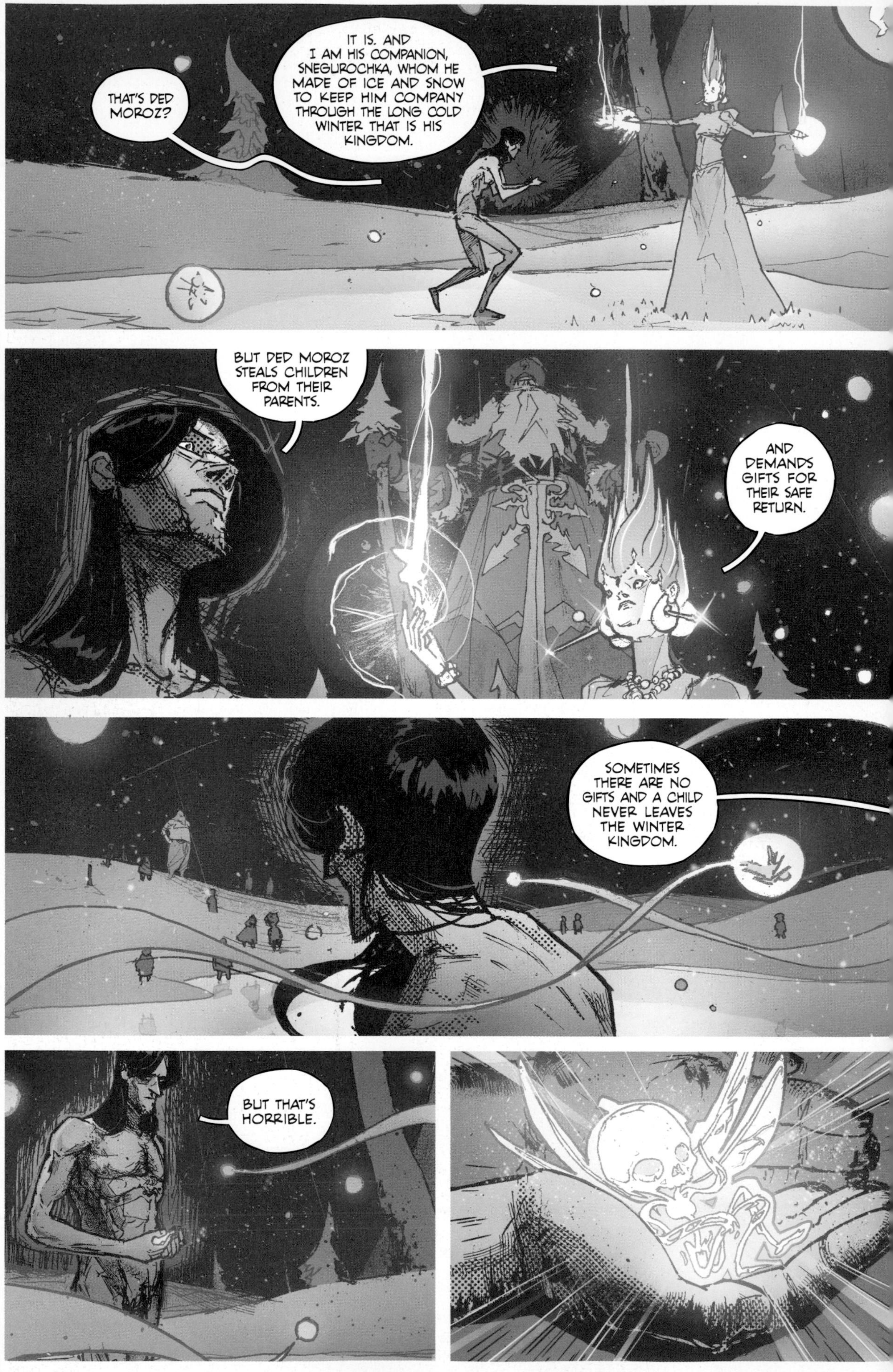
THAT'S DED MOROZ?
IT IS. AND I AM HIS COMPANION, SNEGUROCHKA, WHOM HE MADE OF ICE AND SNOW TO KEEP HIM COMPANY THROUGH THE LONG COLD WINTER THAT IS HIS KINGDOM.
BUT DED MOROZ STEALS CHILDREN FROM THEIR PARENTS.
AND DEMANDS GIFTS FOR THEIR SAFE RETURN.
SOMETIMES THERE ARE NO GIFTS AND A CHILD NEVER LEAVES THE WINTER KINGDOM.
BUT THAT'S HORRIBLE.

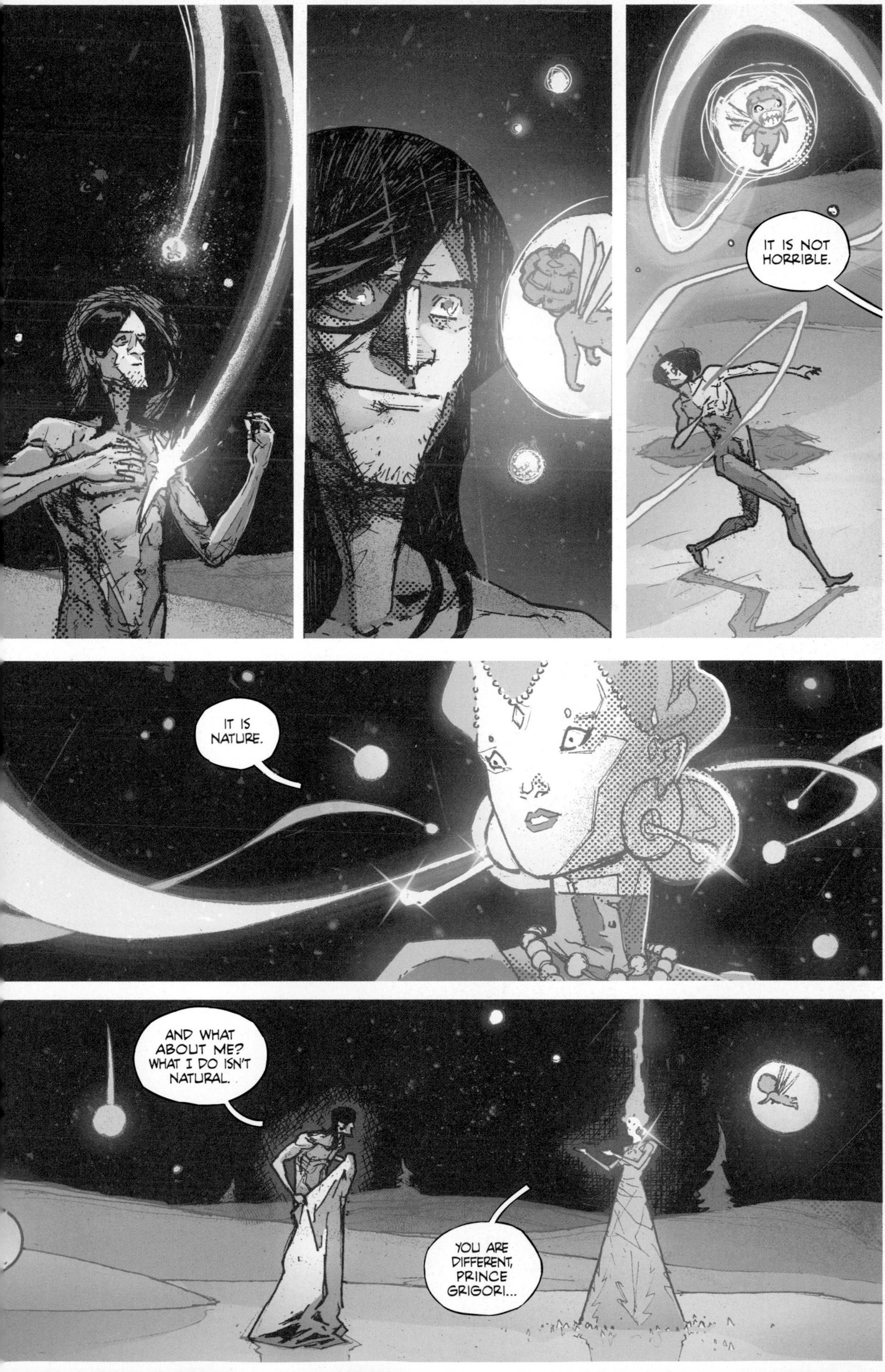
IT IS NOT HORRIBLE.
IT IS NATURE.
AND WHAT ABOUT ME? WHAT I DO ISN'T NATURAL.
YOU ARE DIFFERENT, PRINCE GRIGORI...

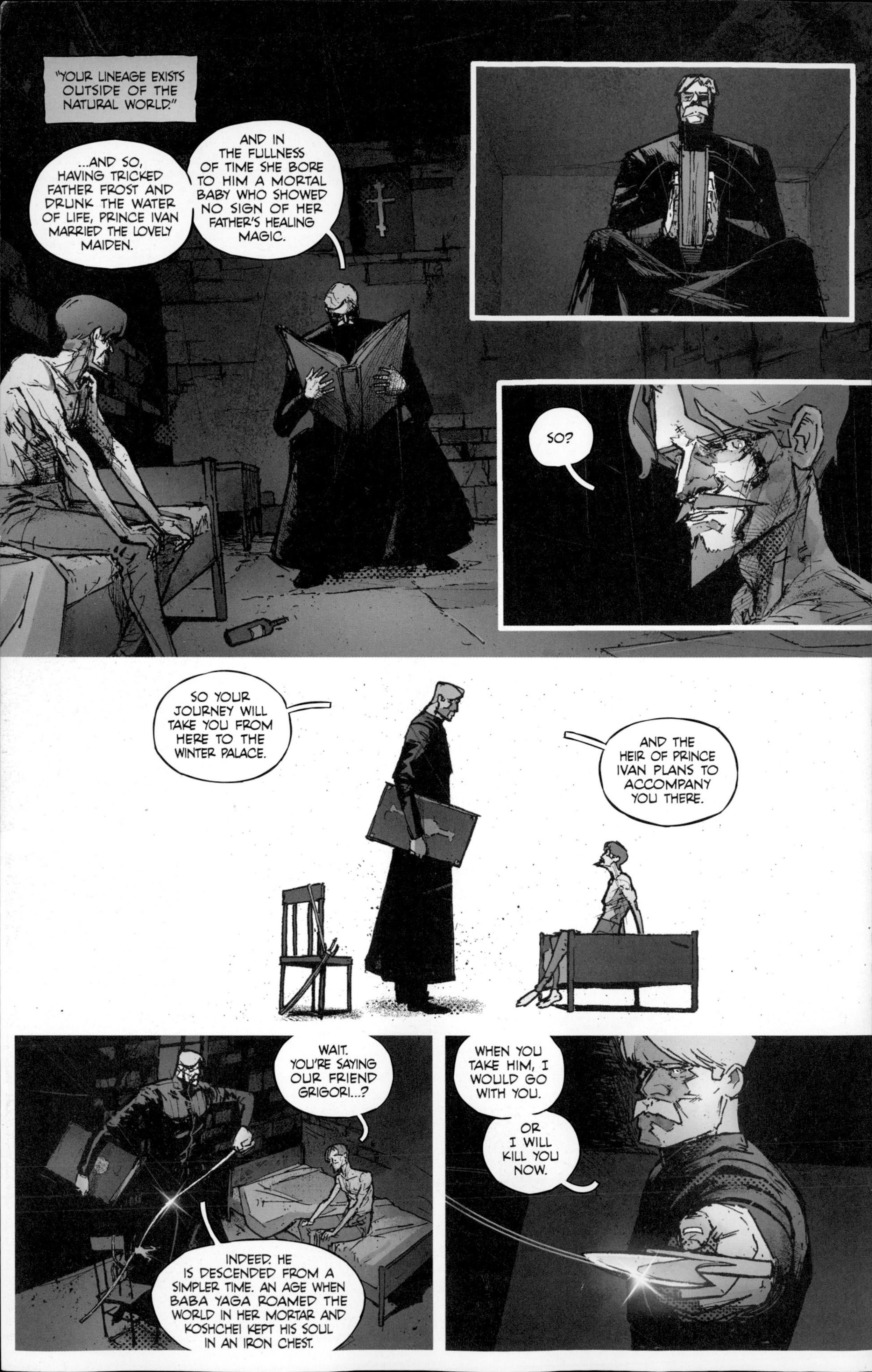
"YOUR LINEAGE EXISTS OUTSIDE OF THE NATURAL WORLD."
...AND SO, HAVING TRICKED FATHER FROST AND DRUNK THE WATER OF LIFE, PRINCE IVAN MARRIED THE LOVELY MAIDEN.
AND IN THE FULLNESS OF TIME SHE BORE TO HIM A MORTAL BABY WHO SHOWED NO SIGN OF HER FATHER'S HEALING MAGIC.
SO?
SO YOUR JOURNEY WILL TAKE YOU FROM HERE TO THE WINTER PALACE.
AND THE HEIR OF PRINCE IVAN PLANS TO ACCOMPANY YOU THERE.
WAIT. YOU'RE SAYING OUR FRIEND GRIGORI...?
INDEED. HE IS DESCENDED FROM A SIMPLER TIME. AN AGE WHEN BABA YAGA ROAMED THE WORLD IN HER MORTAR AND KOSHCHEI KEPT HIS SOUL IN AN IRON CHEST.
WHEN YOU TAKE HIM, I WOULD GO WITH YOU.
OR I WILL KILL YOU NOW.

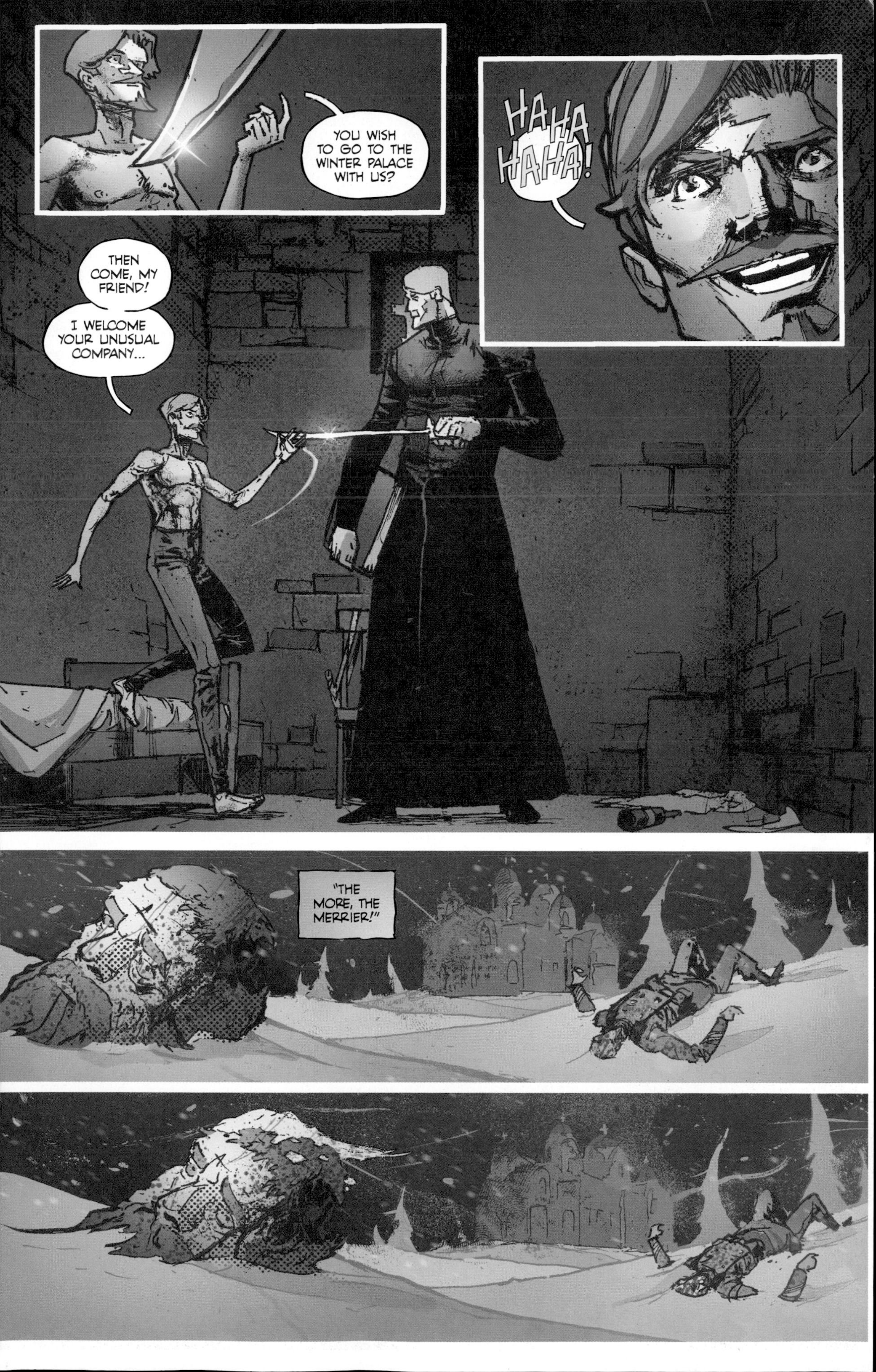
YOU WISH TO GO TO THE WINTER PALACE WITH US?
HAHA HAHA!
THEN COME, MY FRIEND!
I WELCOME YOUR UNUSUAL COMPANY...
"THE MORE, THE MERRIER!"

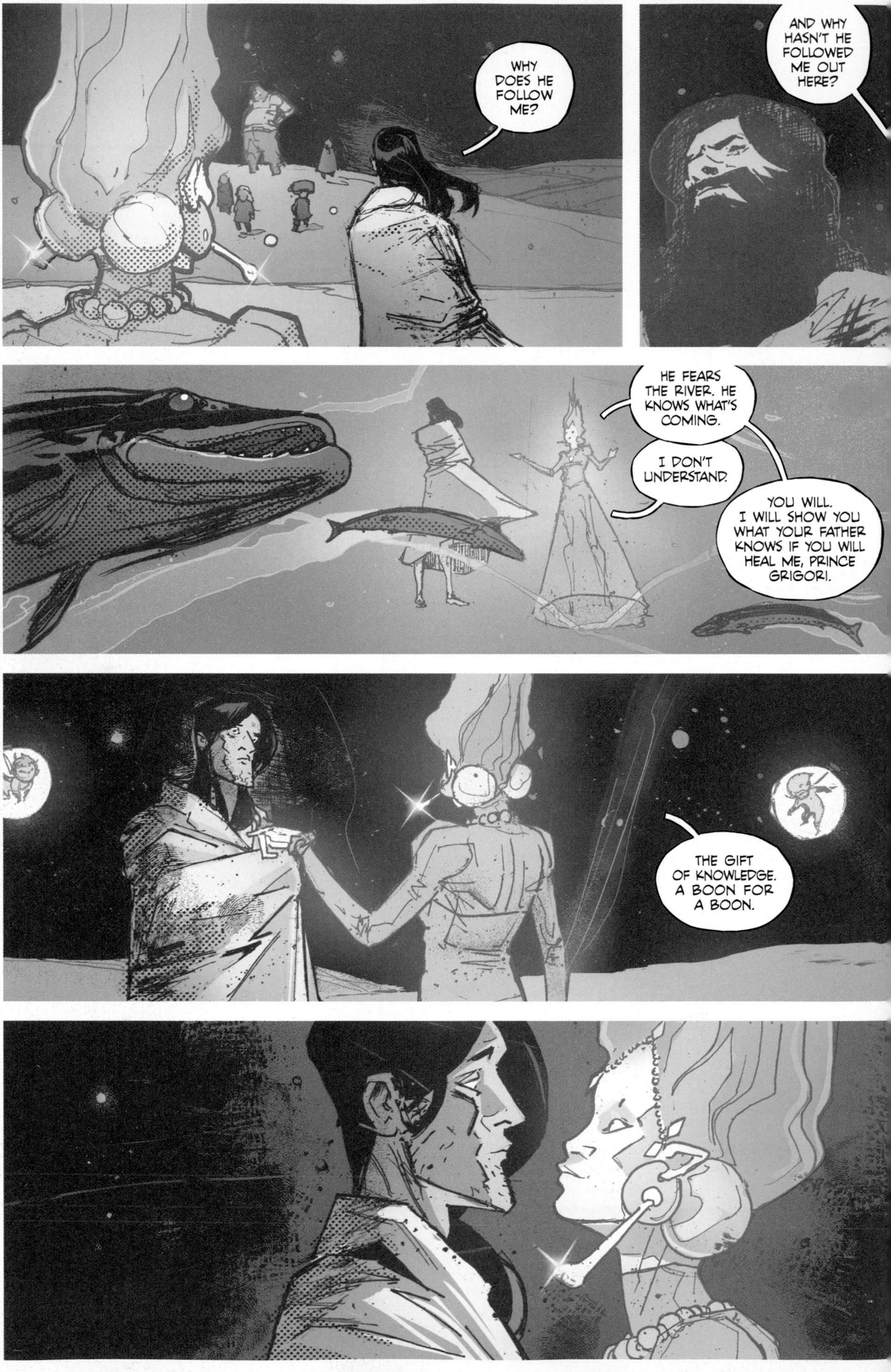
WHY DOES HE FOLLOW ME?
AND WHY HASN'T HE FOLLOWED ME OUT HERE?
HE FEARS THE RIVER. HE KNOWS WHAT'S COMING.
I DON'T UNDERSTAND.
YOU WILL. I WILL SHOW YOU WHAT YOUR FATHER KNOWS IF YOU WILL HEAL ME, PRINCE GRIGORI.
THE GIFT OF KNOWLEDGE. A BOON FOR A BOON.

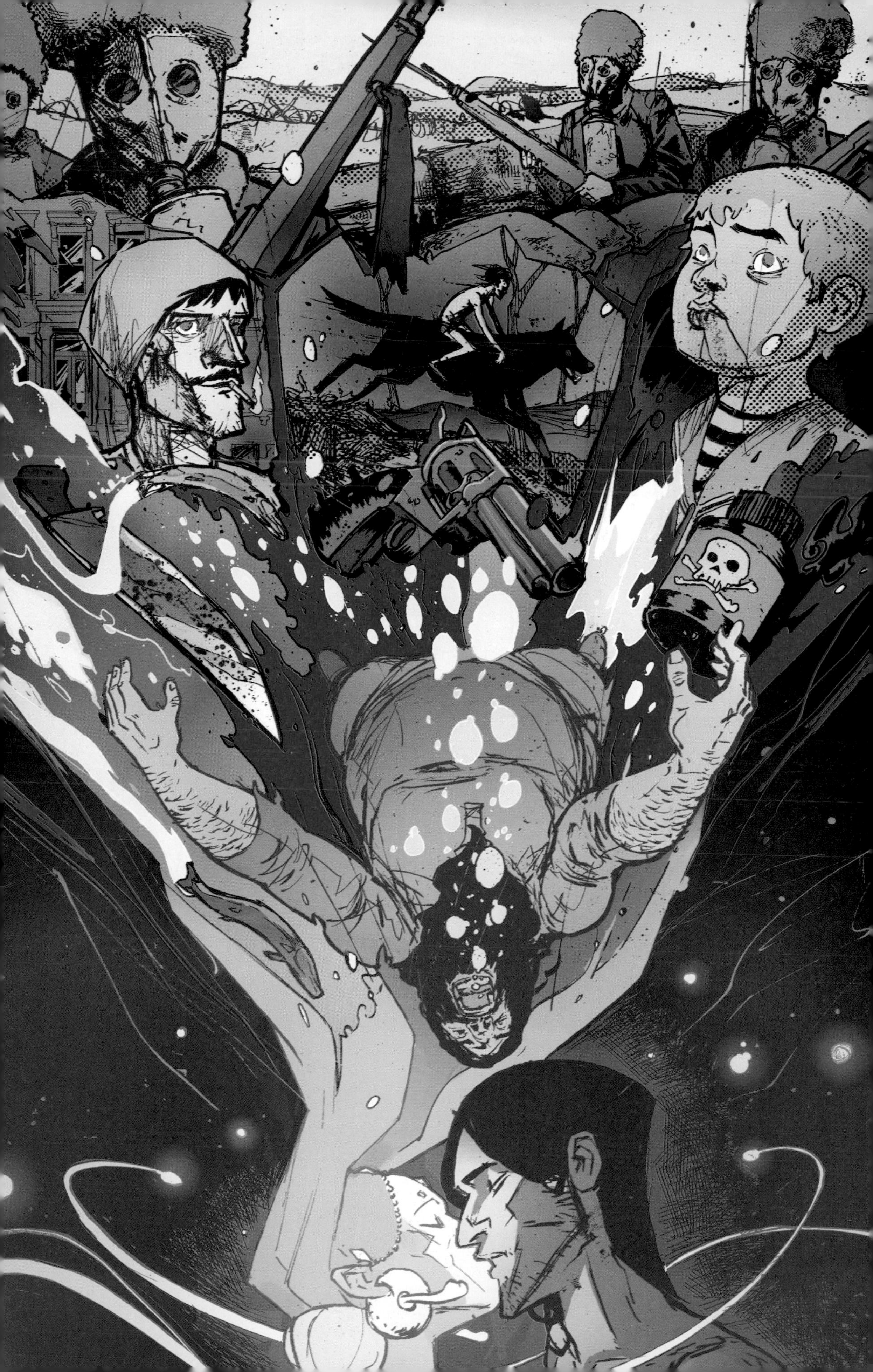

A BOON FOR A BOON. HEALING FOR KNOWLEDGE.

I RETURN TO THE ICE AND SNOW FROM WHICH I WAS FORMED.

AT LAST, I AM FREE.

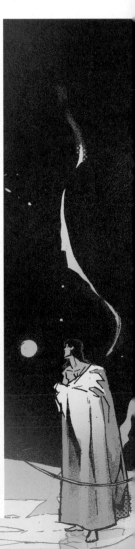

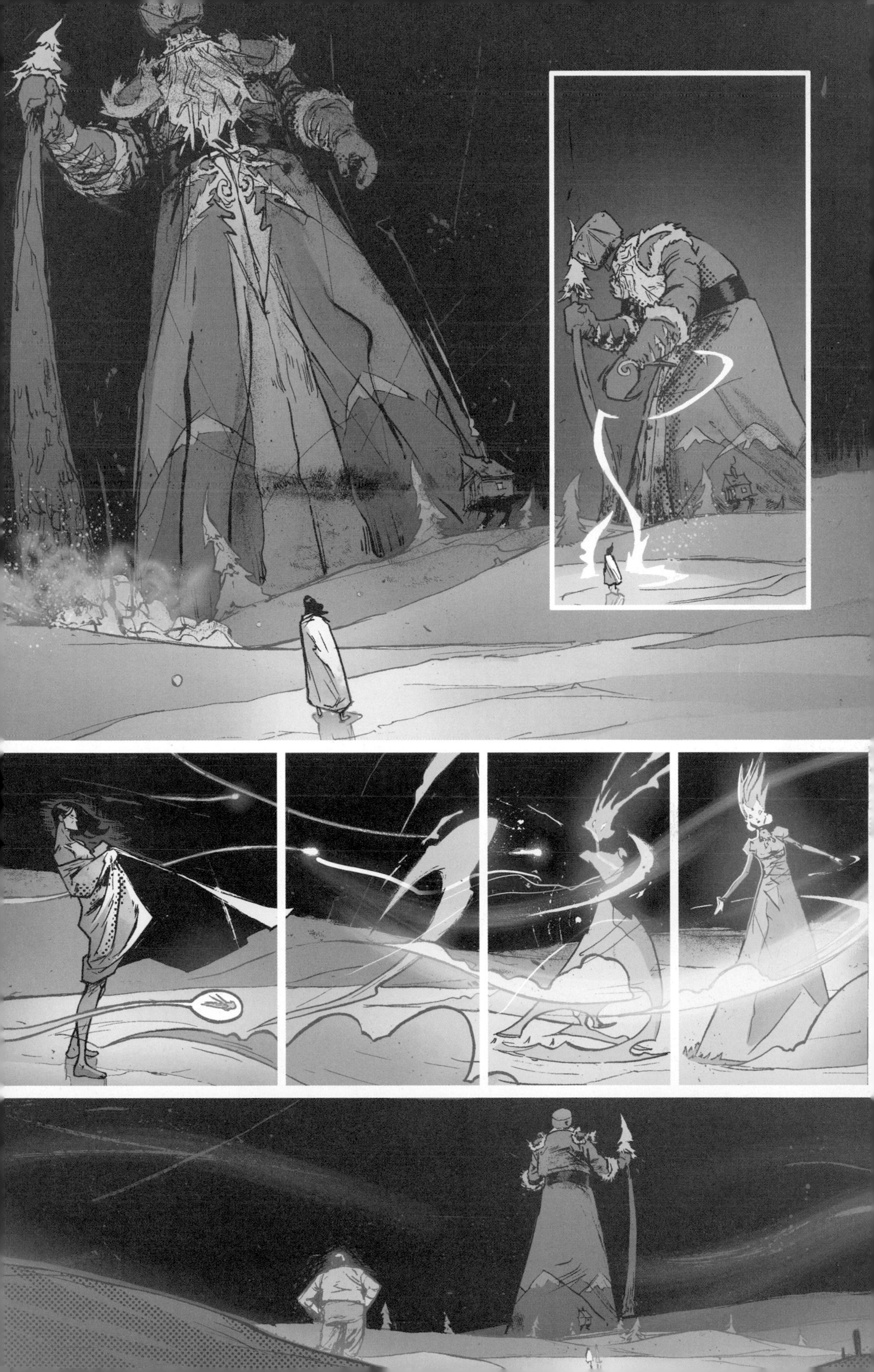

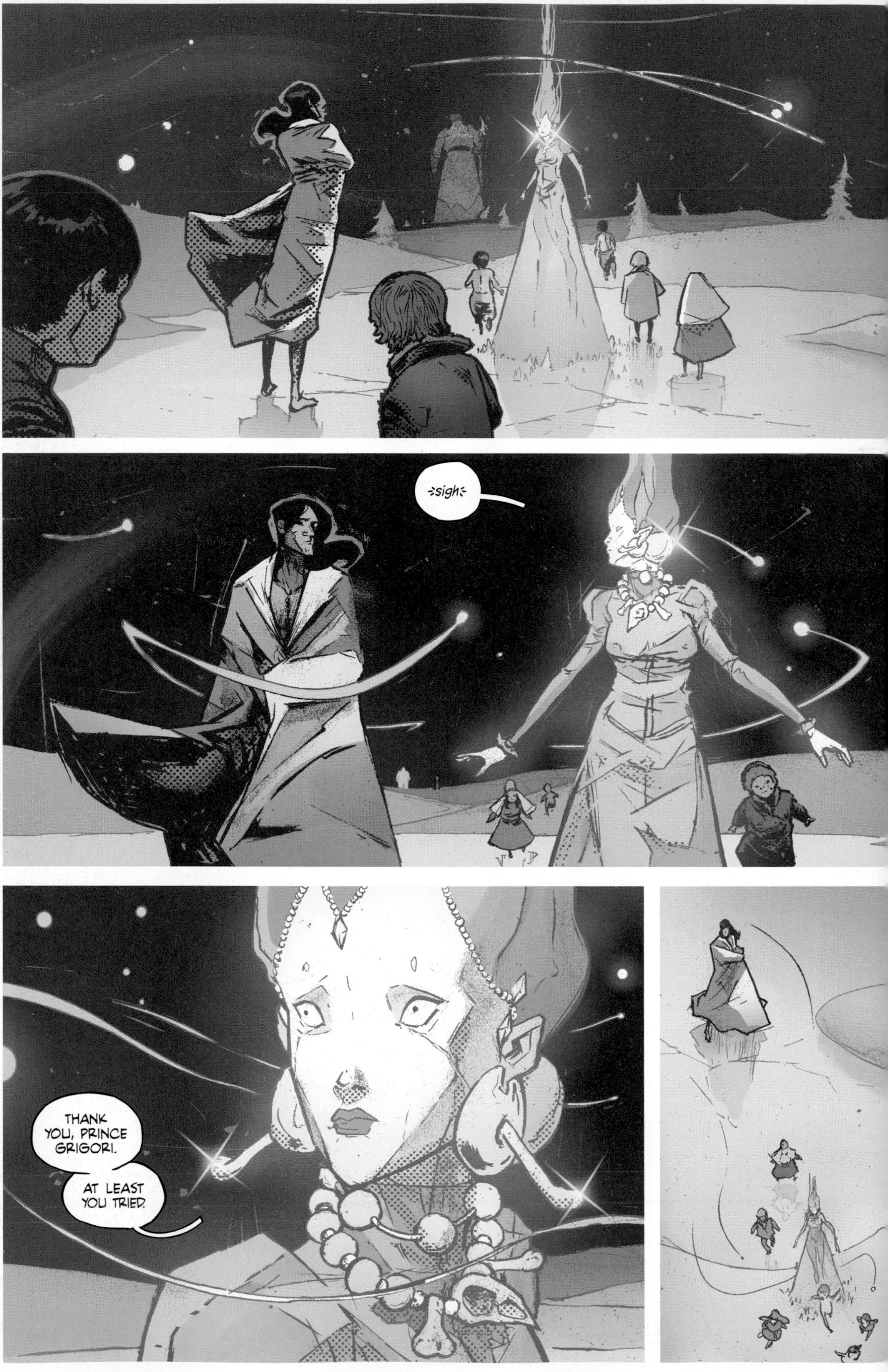

-sigh-
THANK YOU, PRINCE GRIGORI.
AT LEAST YOU TRIED.

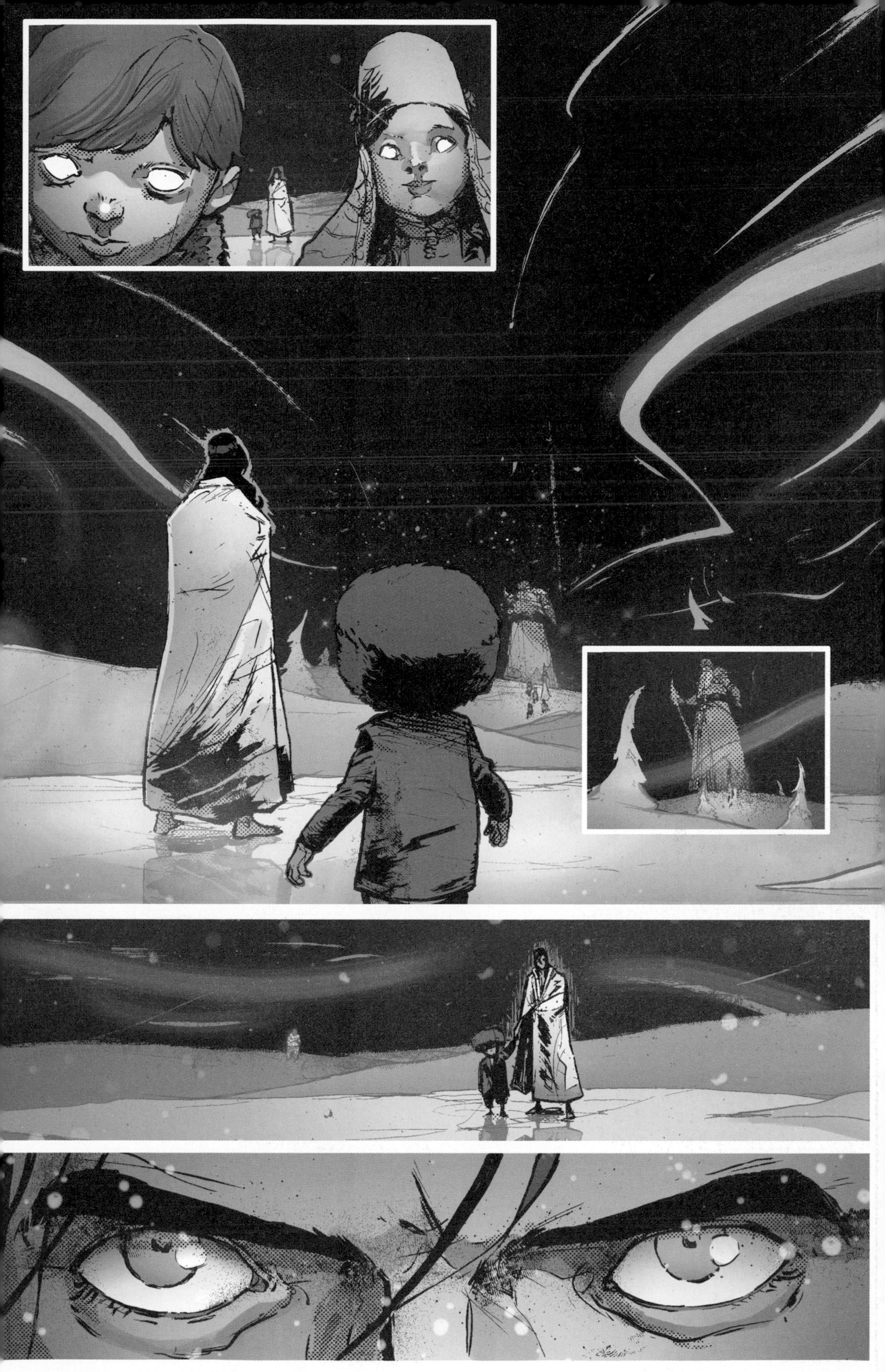

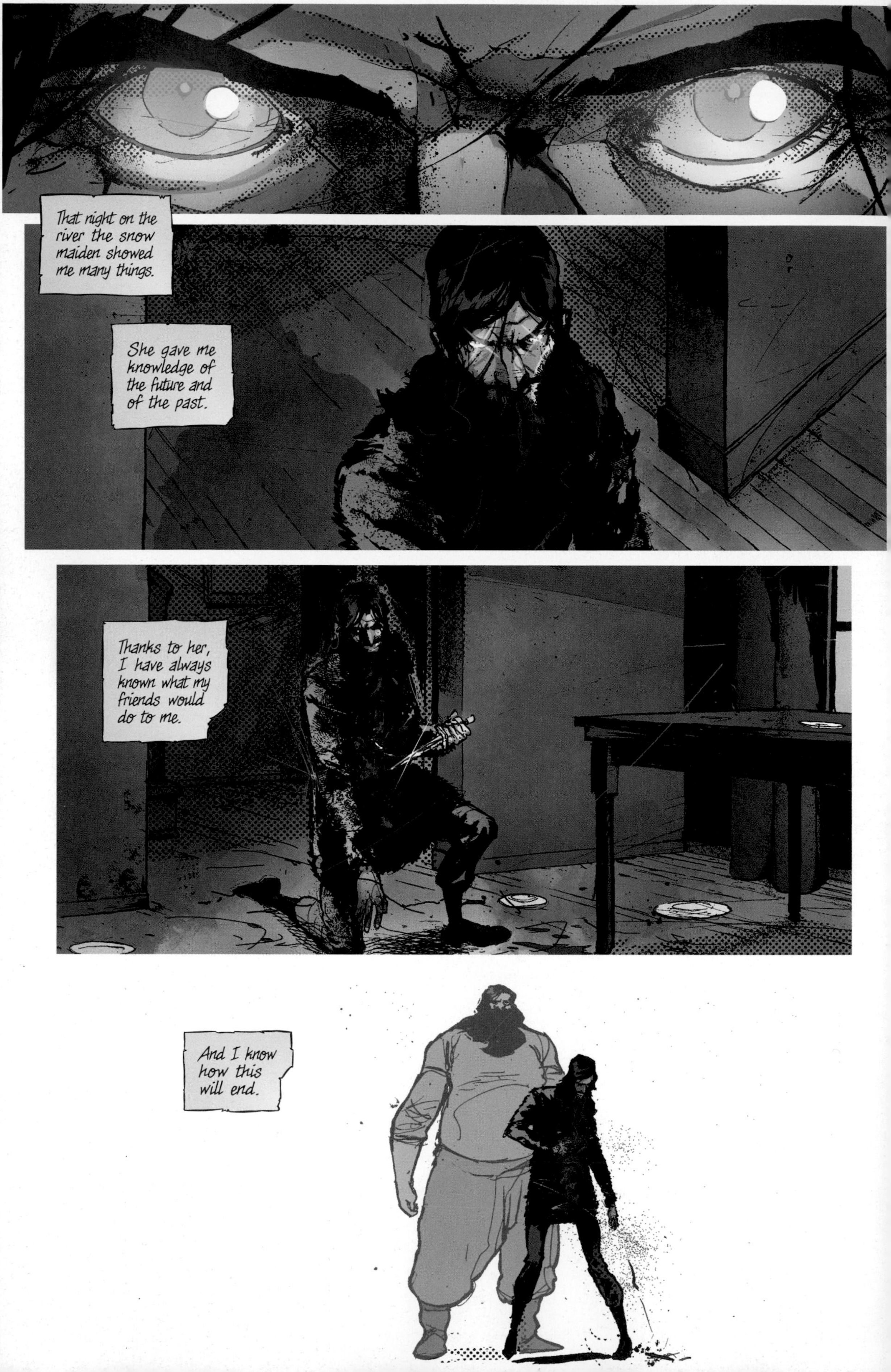
That night on the river the snow maiden showed me many things.
She gave me knowledge of the future and of the past.
Thanks to her, I have always known what my friends would do to me.
And I know how this will end.

NOT EVERYTHING HAS A NAME.
SOME THINGS LEAD US INTO A REALM BEYOND WORDS.

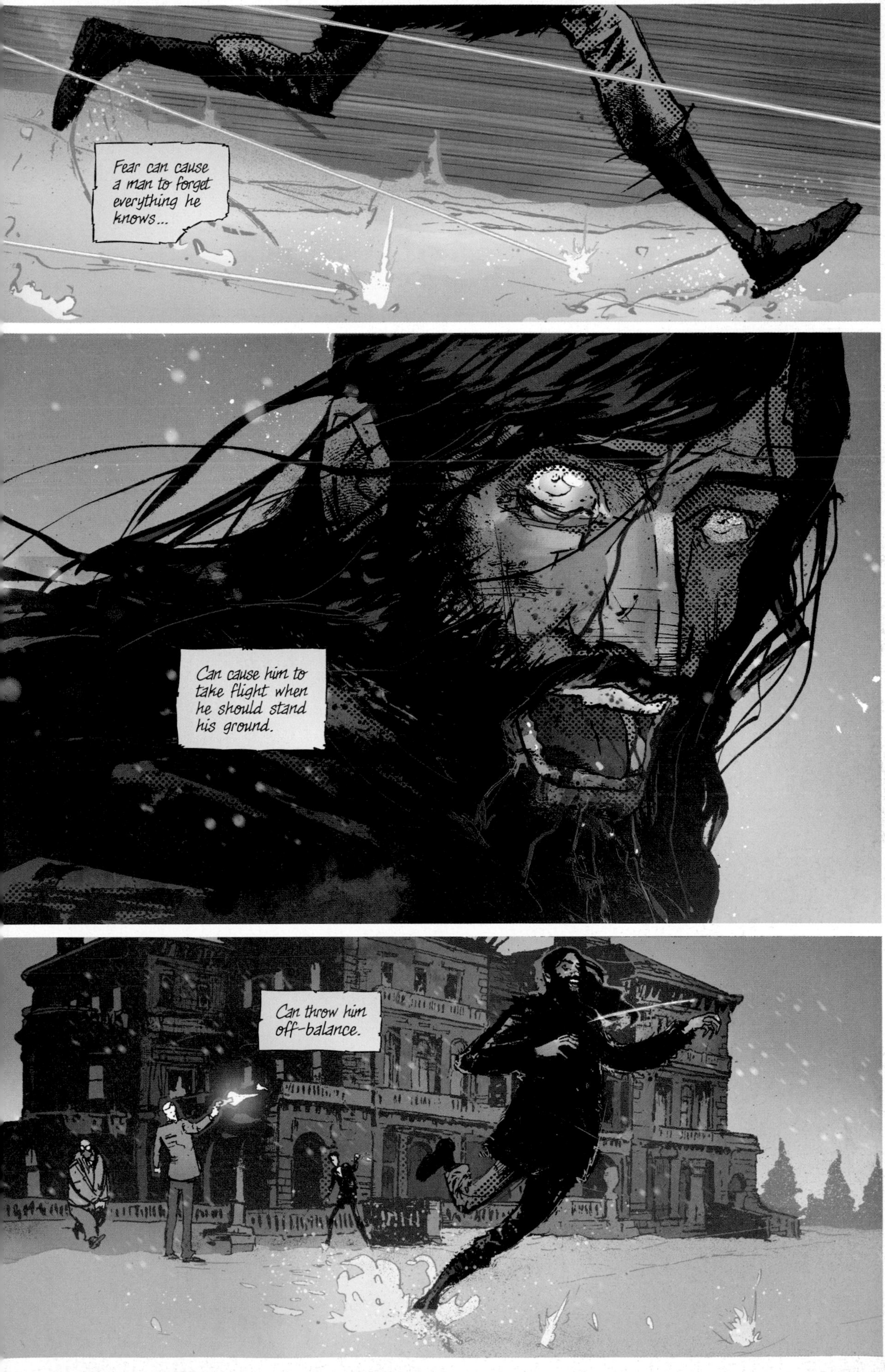
Fear can cause a man to forget everything he knows...
Can cause him to take flight when he should stand his ground.
Can throw him off-balance.

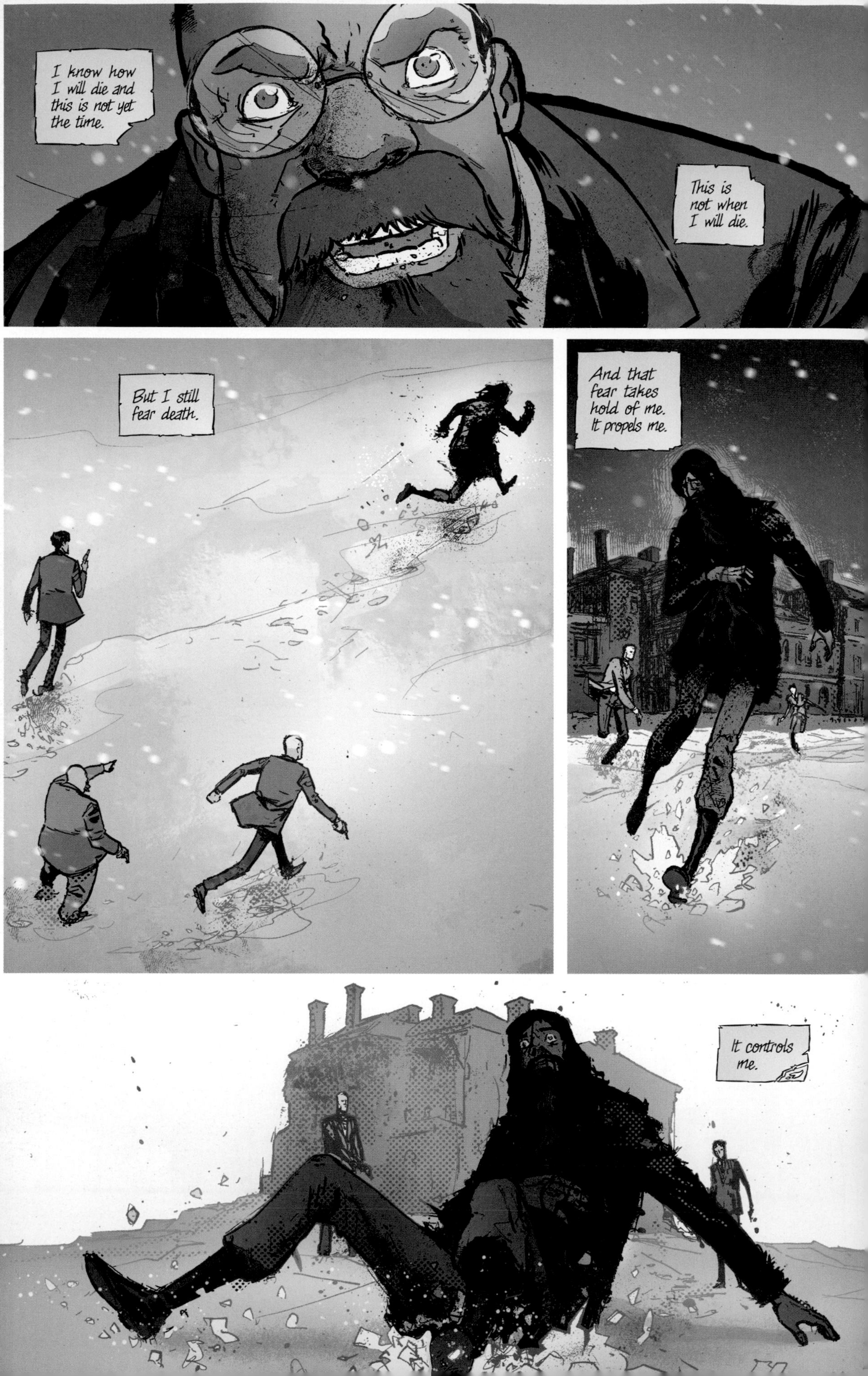
I know how I will die and this is not yet the time.
This is not when I will die.
But I still fear death.
And that fear takes hold of me. It propels me.
It controls me.

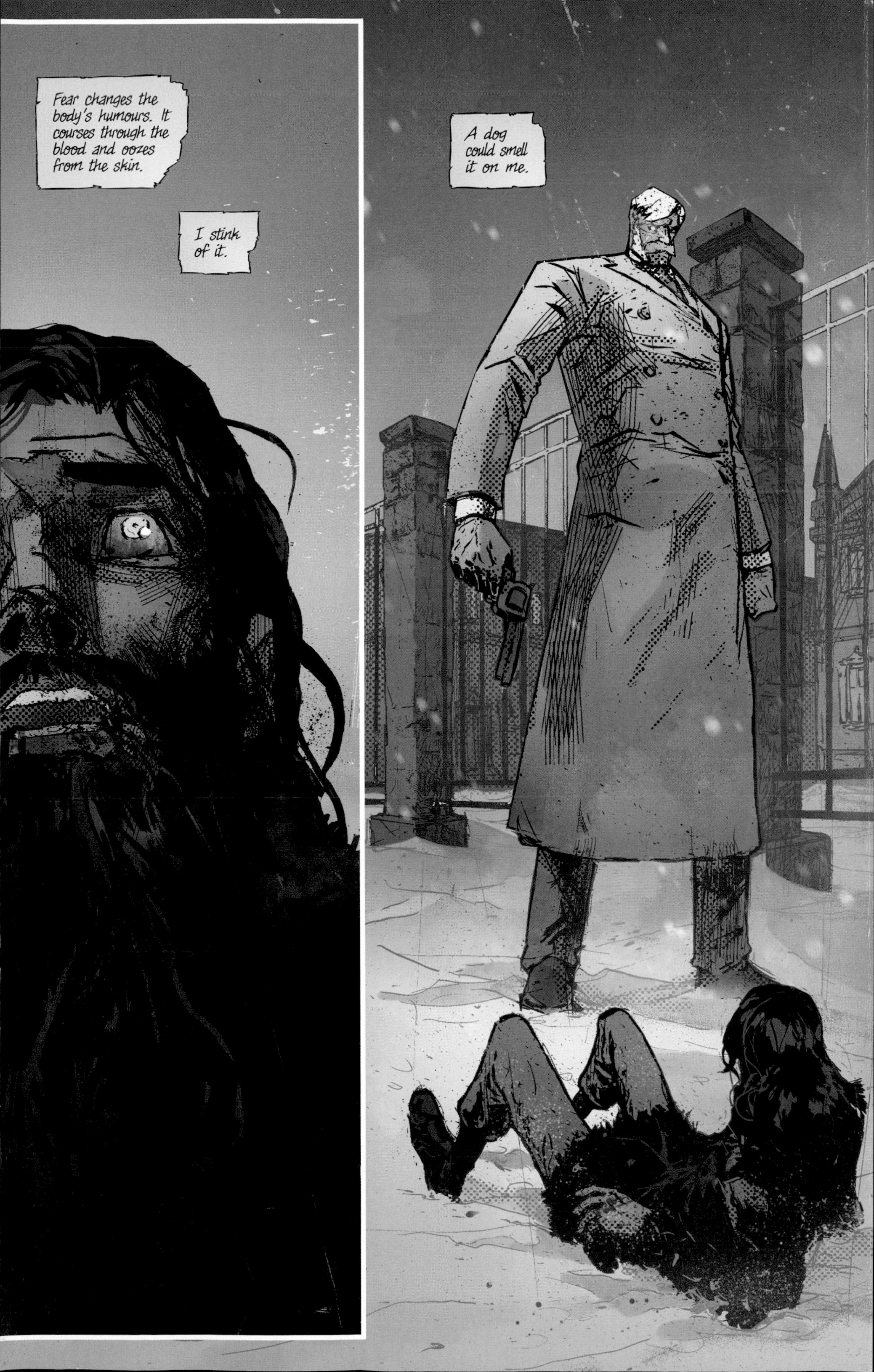
Fear changes the body's humours. It courses through the blood and oozes from the skin.
I stink of it.
A dog could smell it on me.

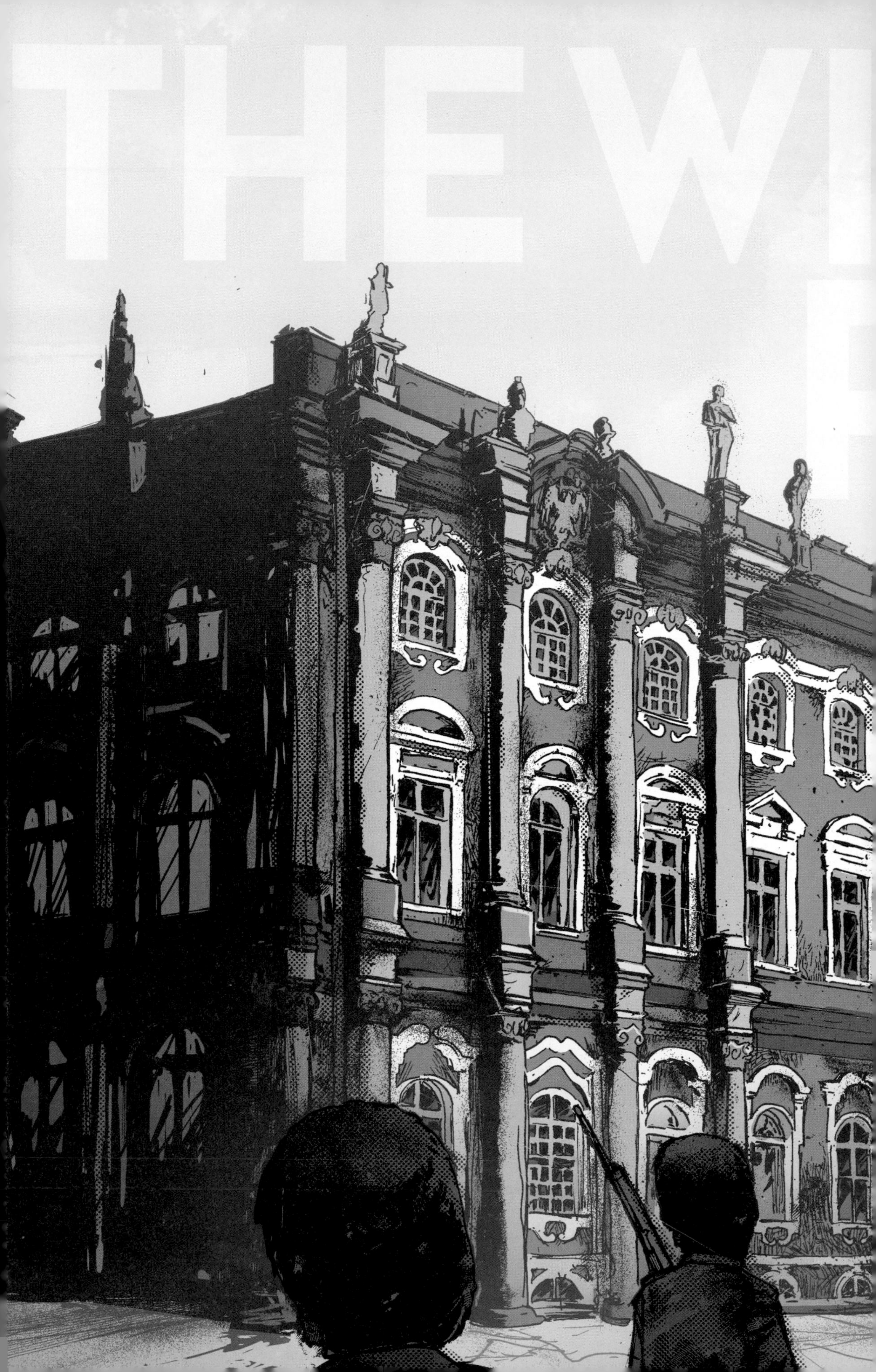
THE W

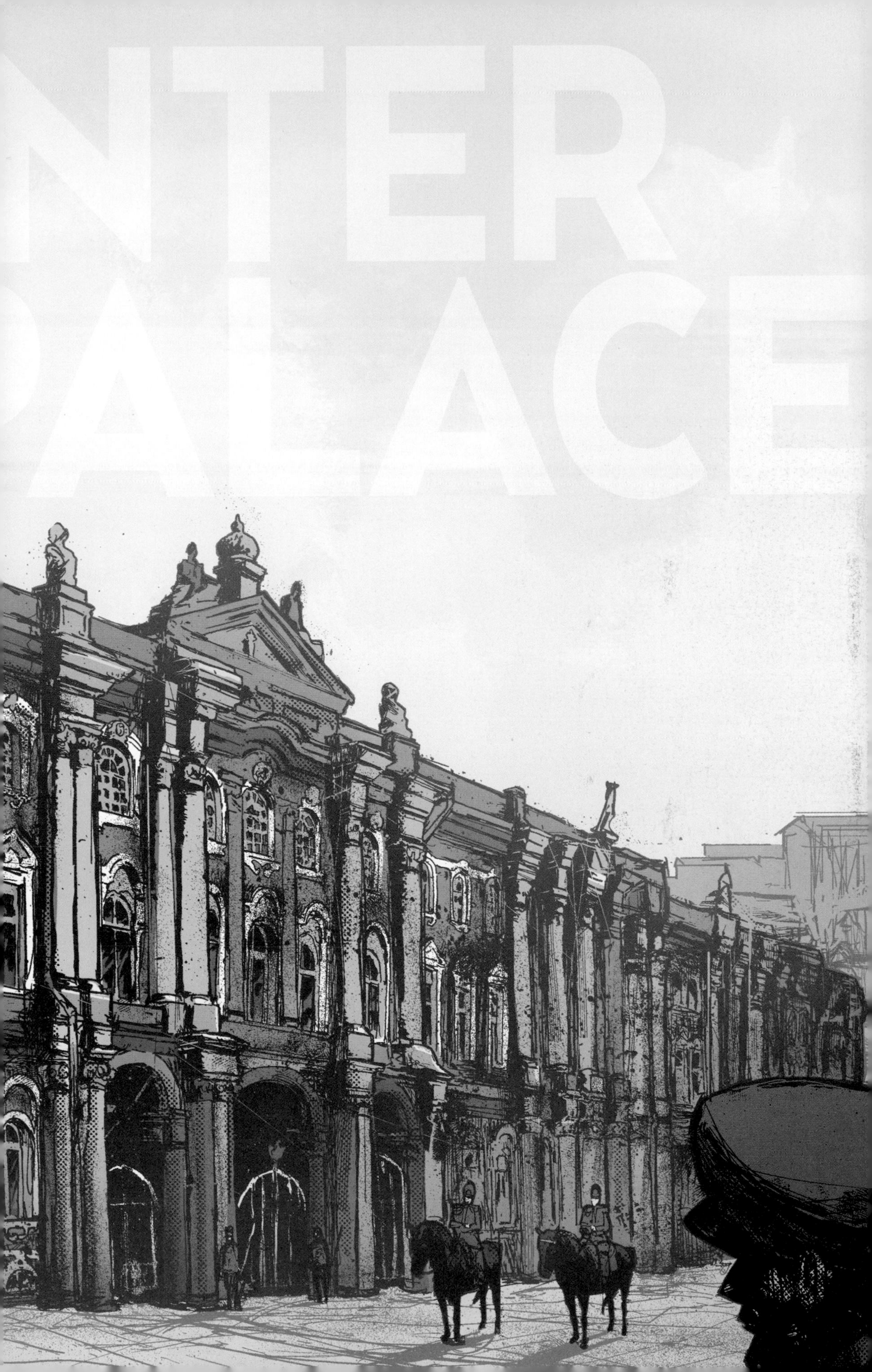
NTER
PALACE

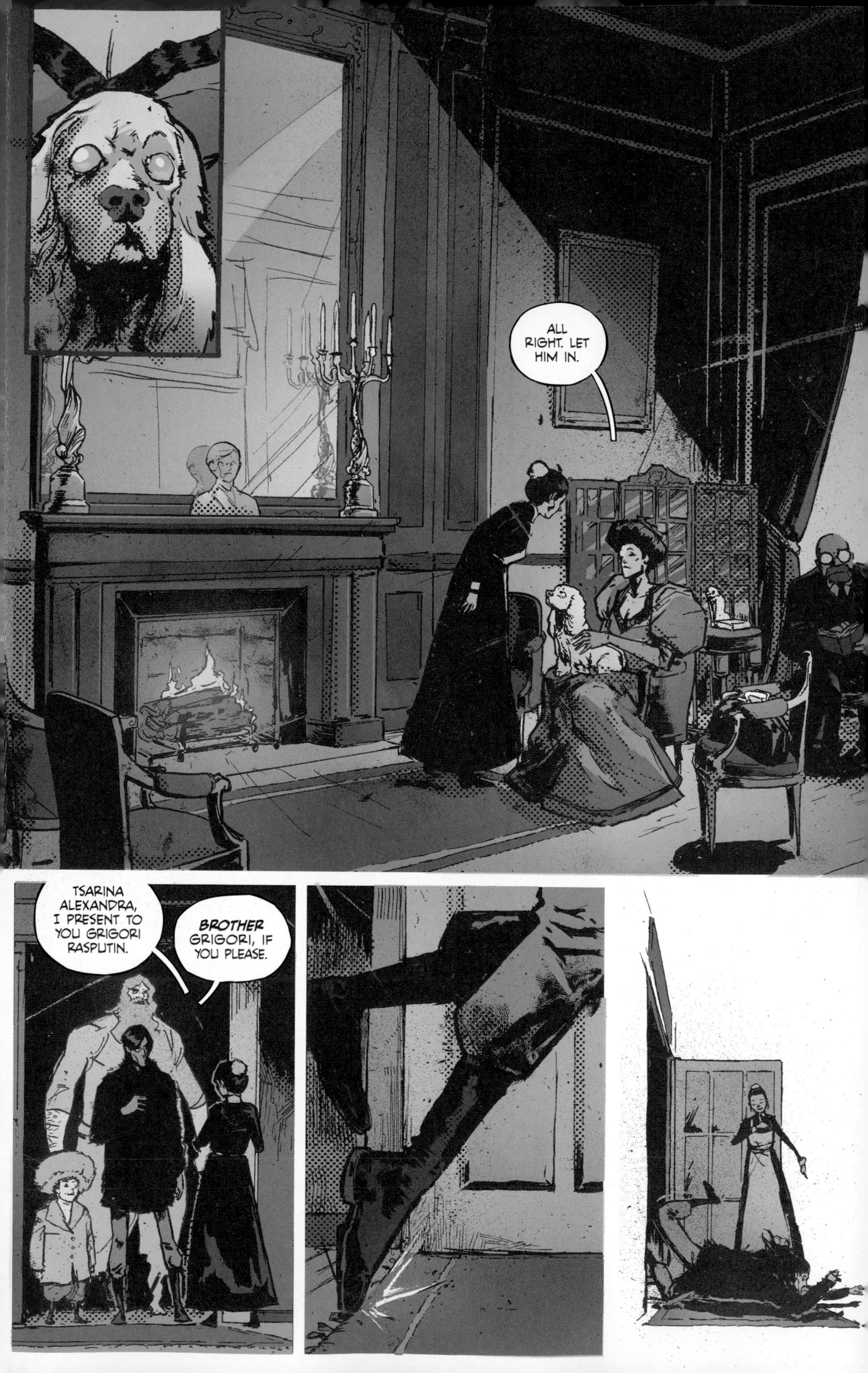
ALL RIGHT. LET HIM IN.
TSARINA ALEXANDRA, I PRESENT TO YOU GRIGORI RASPUTIN.
BROTHER GRIGORI, IF YOU PLEASE.

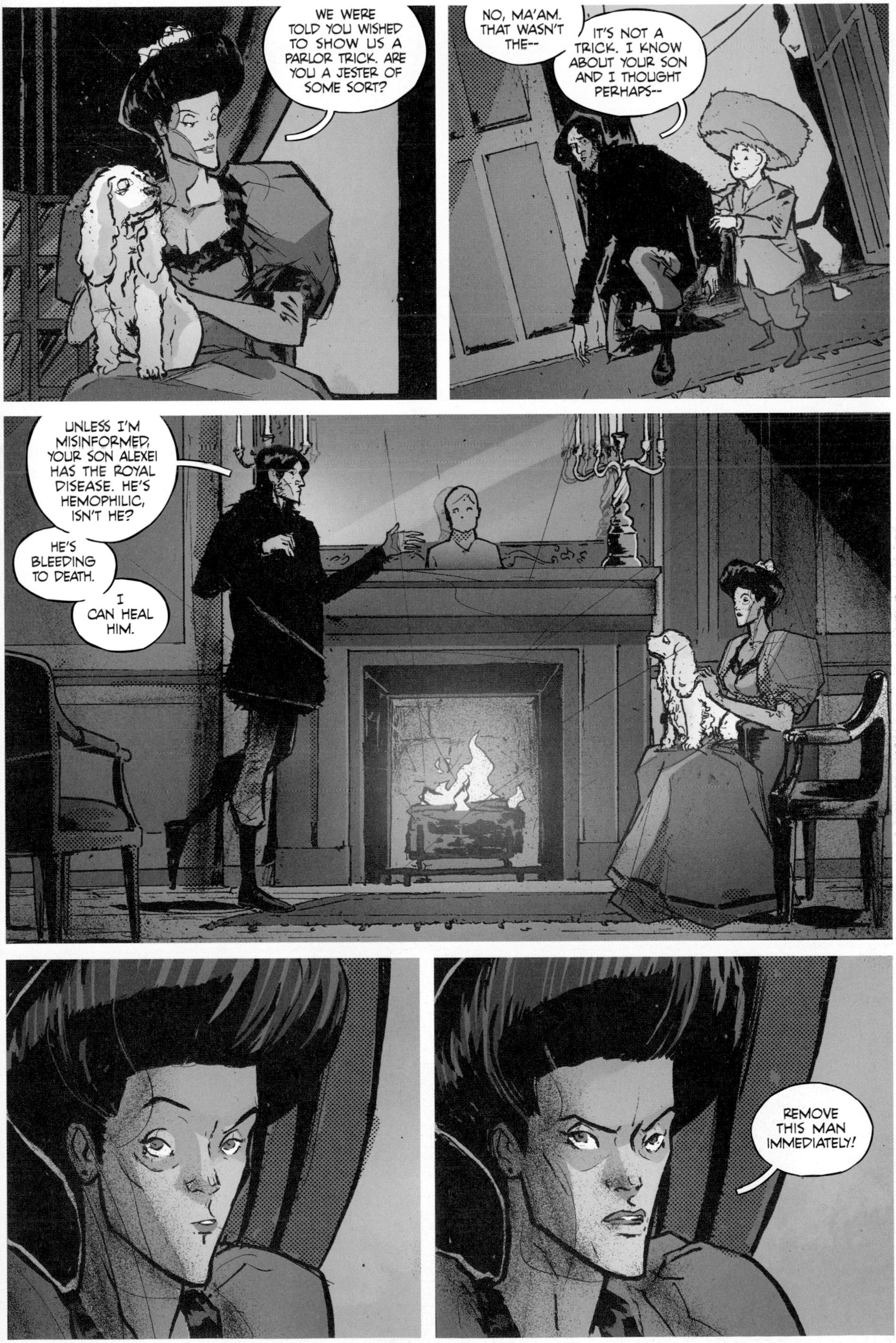
WE WERE TOLD YOU WISHED TO SHOW US A PARLOR TRICK. ARE YOU A JESTER OF SOME SORT?
NO, MA'AM. THAT WASN'T THE--
IT'S NOT A TRICK. I KNOW ABOUT YOUR SON AND I THOUGHT PERHAPS--
UNLESS I'M MISINFORMED, YOUR SON ALEXEI HAS THE ROYAL DISEASE. HE'S HEMOPHILIC, ISN'T HE?
HE'S BLEEDING TO DEATH.
I CAN HEAL HIM.
REMOVE THIS MAN IMMEDIATELY!

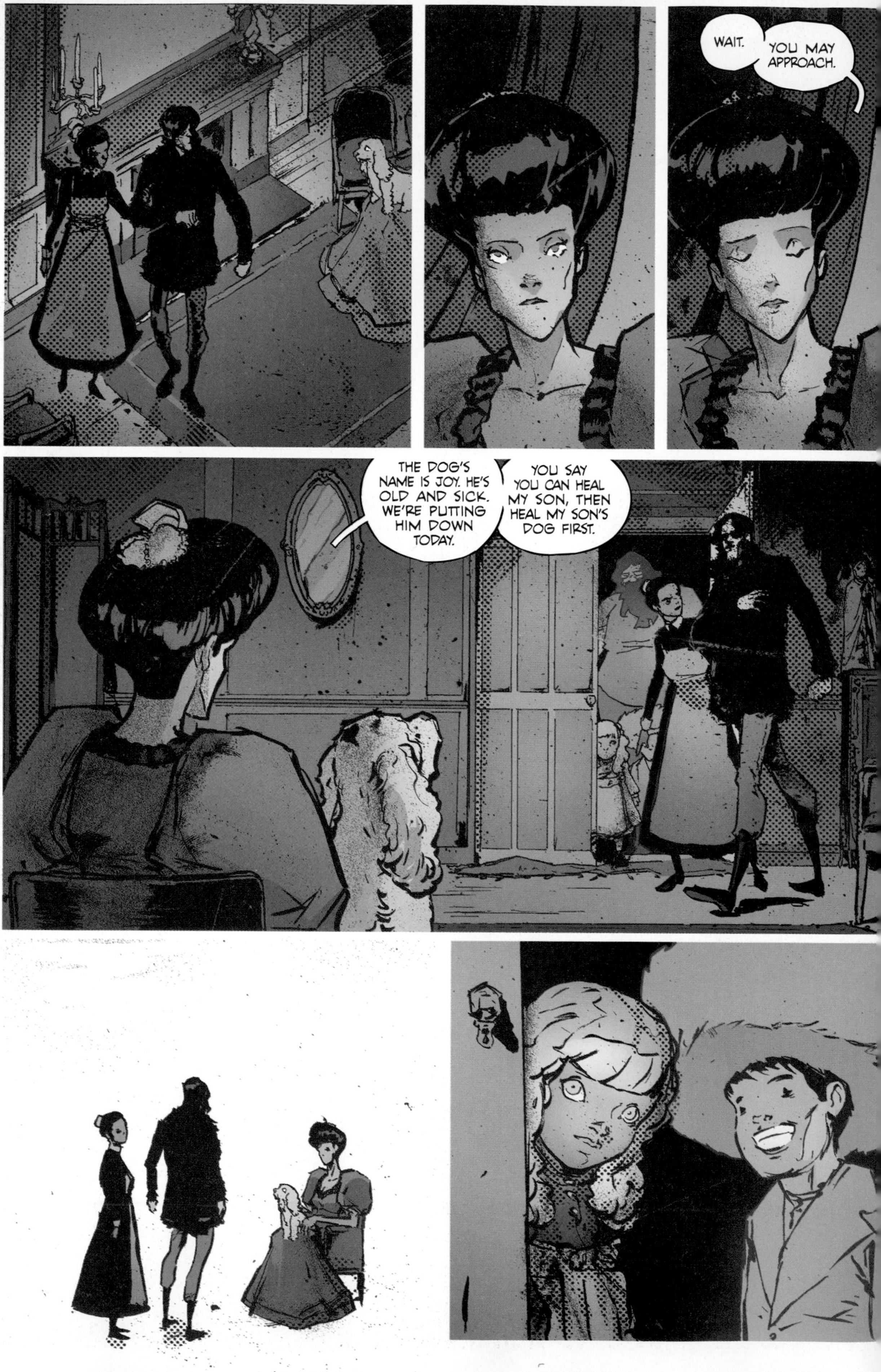
WAIT.
YOU MAY APPROACH.
THE DOG'S NAME IS JOY. HE'S OLD AND SICK. WE'RE PUTTING HIM DOWN TODAY.
YOU SAY YOU CAN HEAL MY SON, THEN HEAL MY SON'S DOG FIRST.

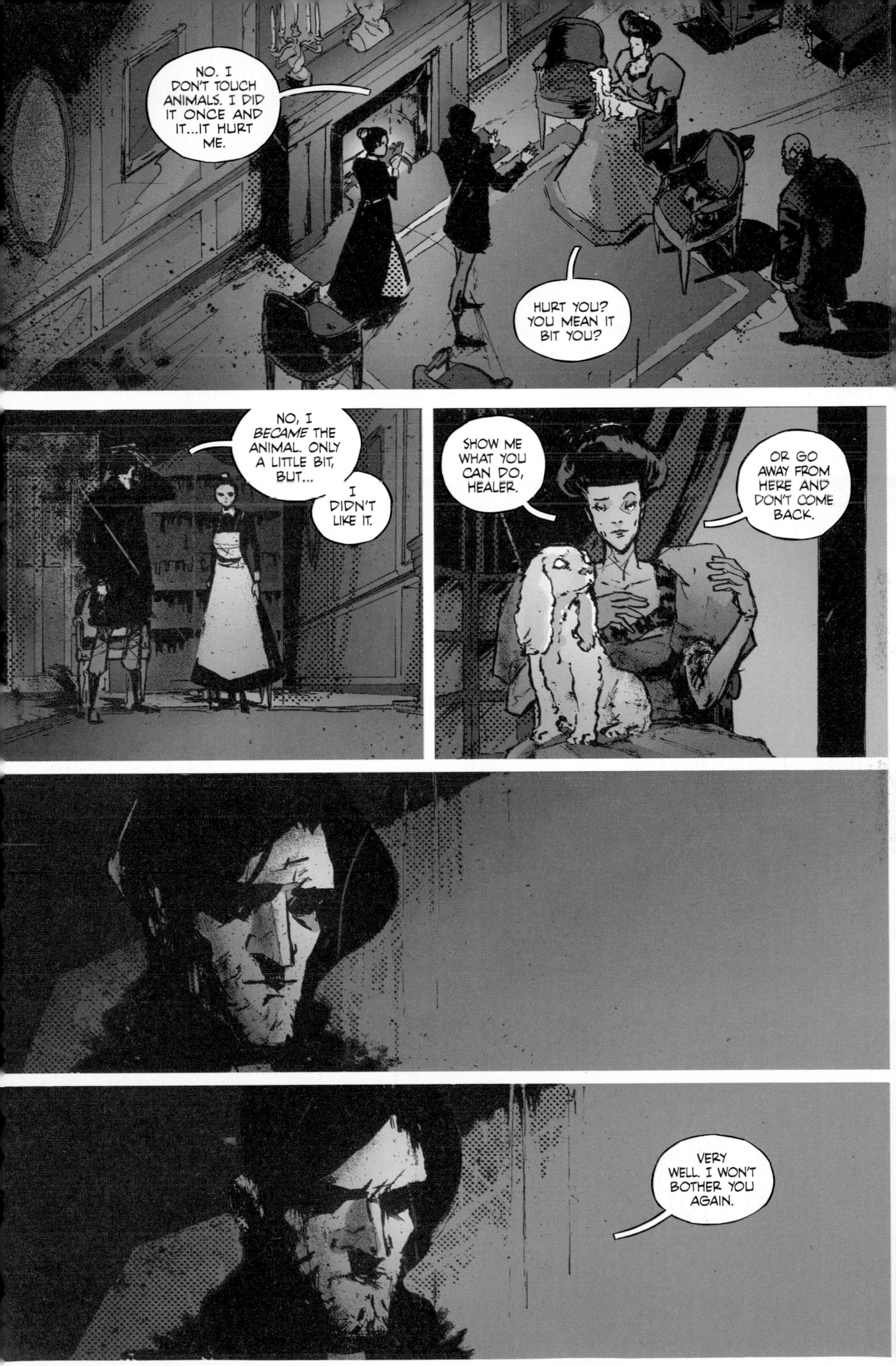
NO. I DON'T TOUCH ANIMALS. I DID IT ONCE AND IT...IT HURT ME.
HURT YOU? YOU MEAN IT BIT YOU?
NO, I *BECAME* THE ANIMAL. ONLY A LITTLE BIT, BUT...
I DIDN'T LIKE IT.
SHOW ME WHAT YOU CAN DO, HEALER.
OR GO AWAY FROM HERE AND DON'T COME BACK.
VERY WELL. I WON'T BOTHER YOU AGAIN.

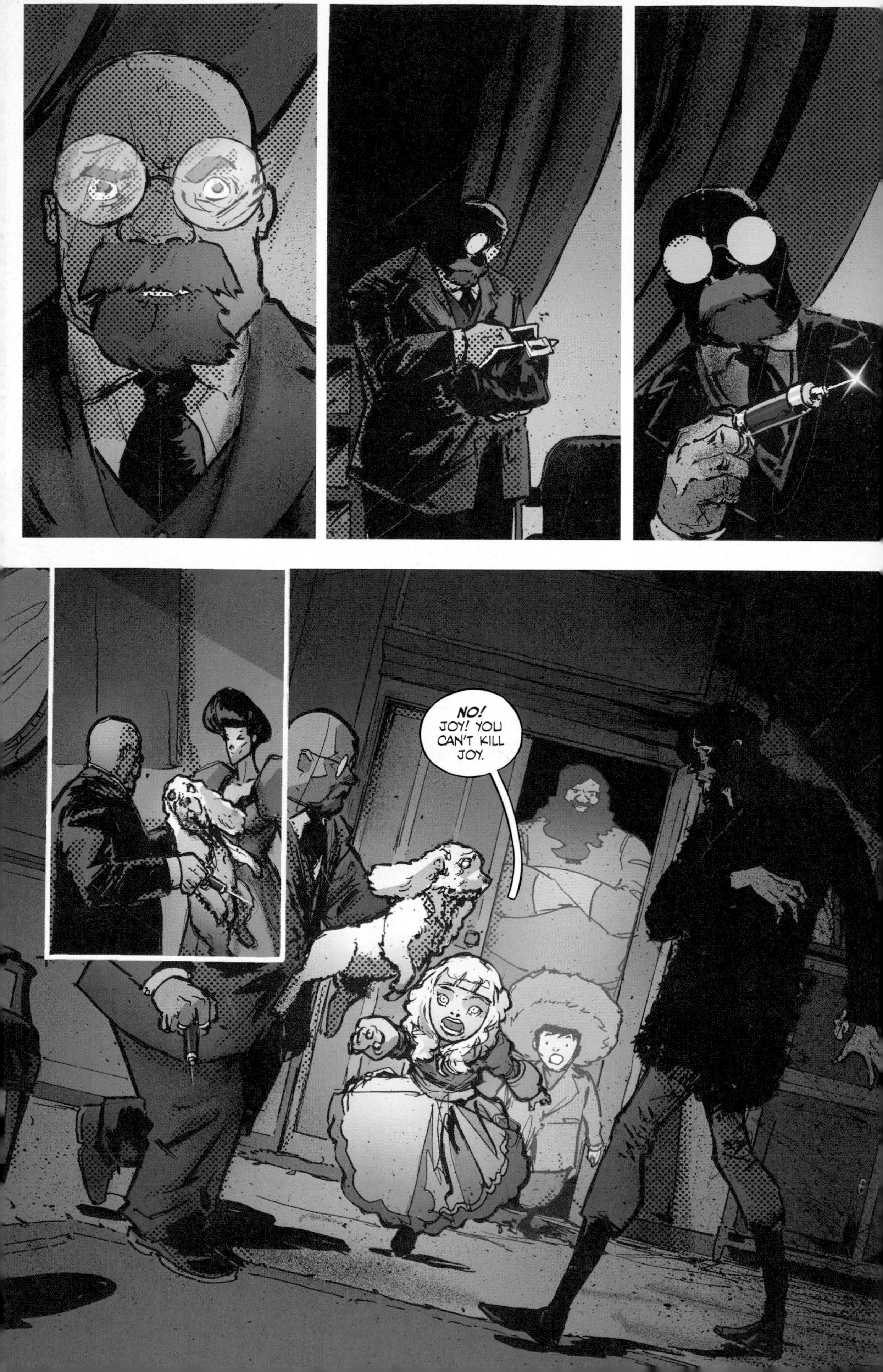
NO! JOY! YOU CAN'T KILL JOY.

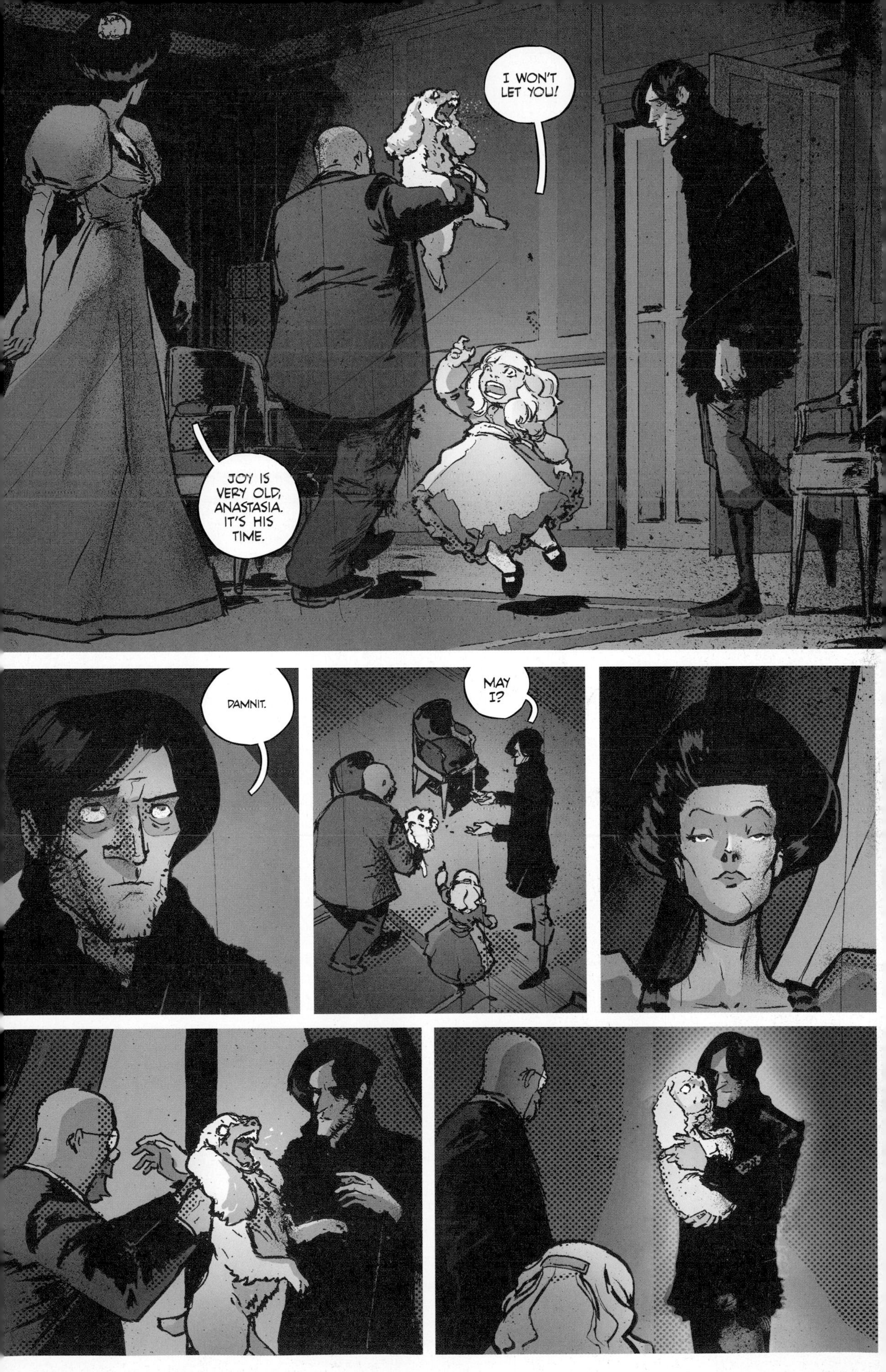
I WON'T LET YOU!
JOY IS VERY OLD, ANASTASIA. IT'S HIS TIME.
DAMNIT.
MAY I?

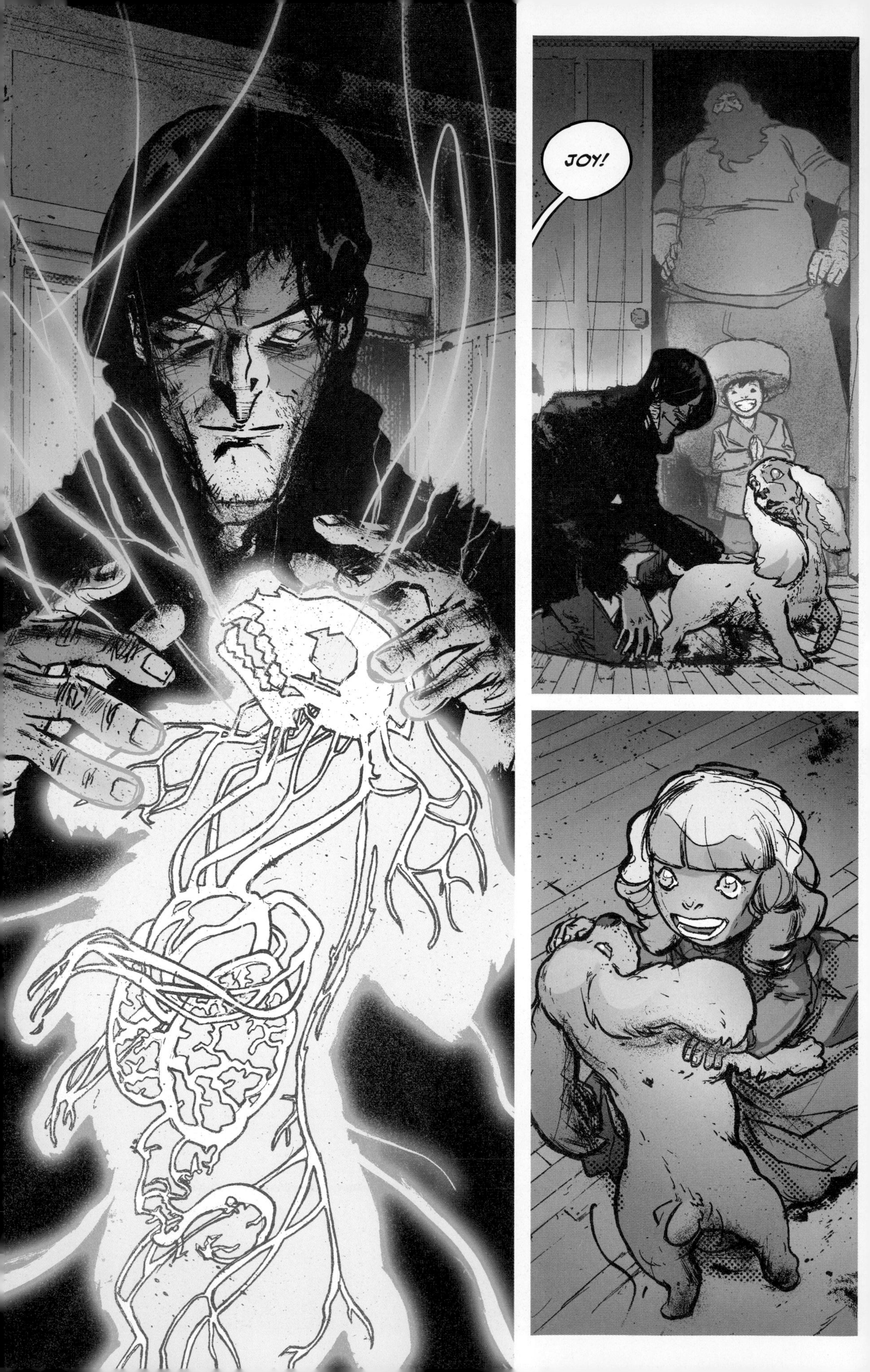
JOY!

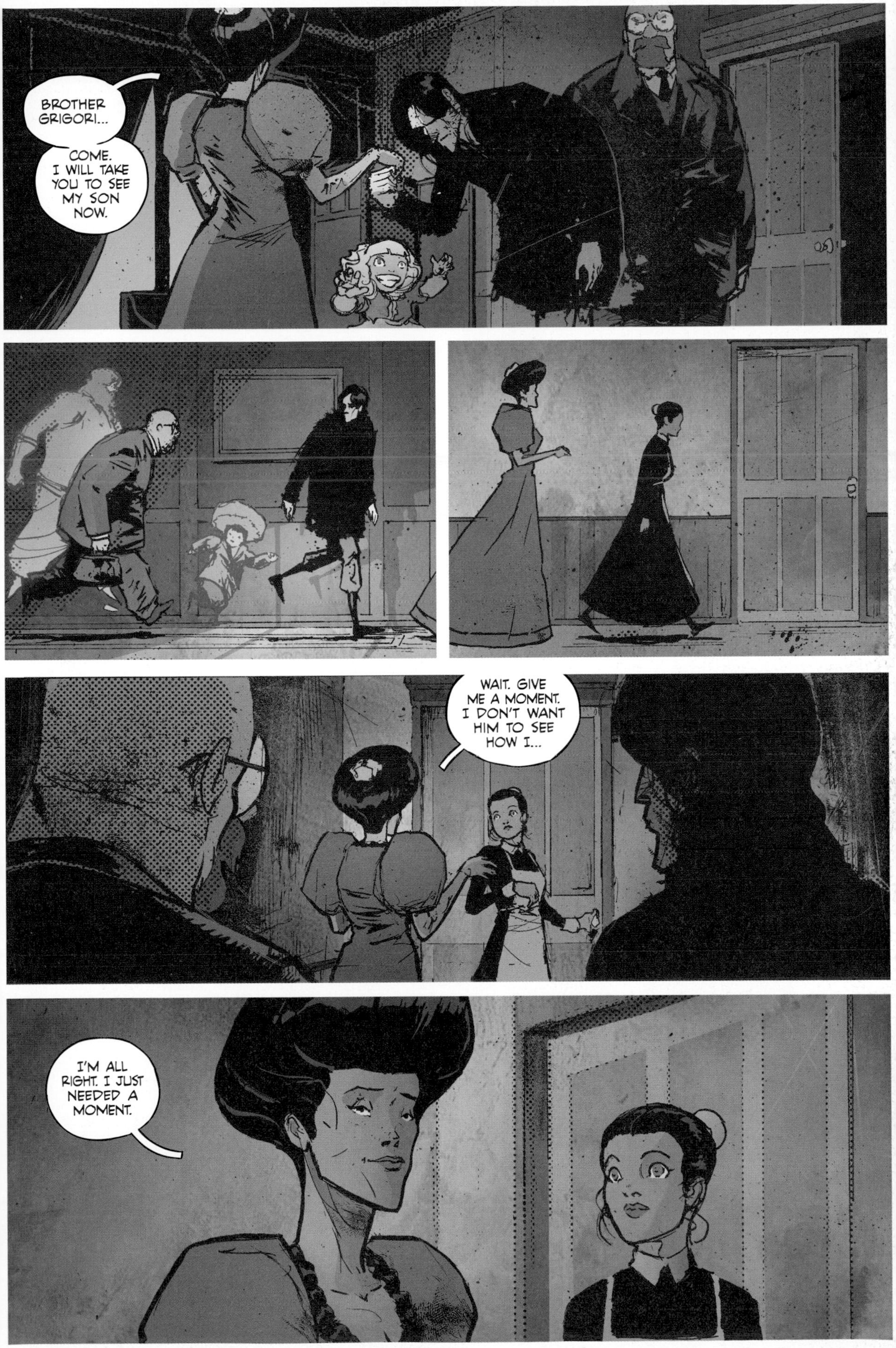
BROTHER GRIGORI...
COME. I WILL TAKE YOU TO SEE MY SON NOW.
WAIT. GIVE ME A MOMENT. I DON'T WANT HIM TO SEE HOW I...
I'M ALL RIGHT. I JUST NEEDED A MOMENT.

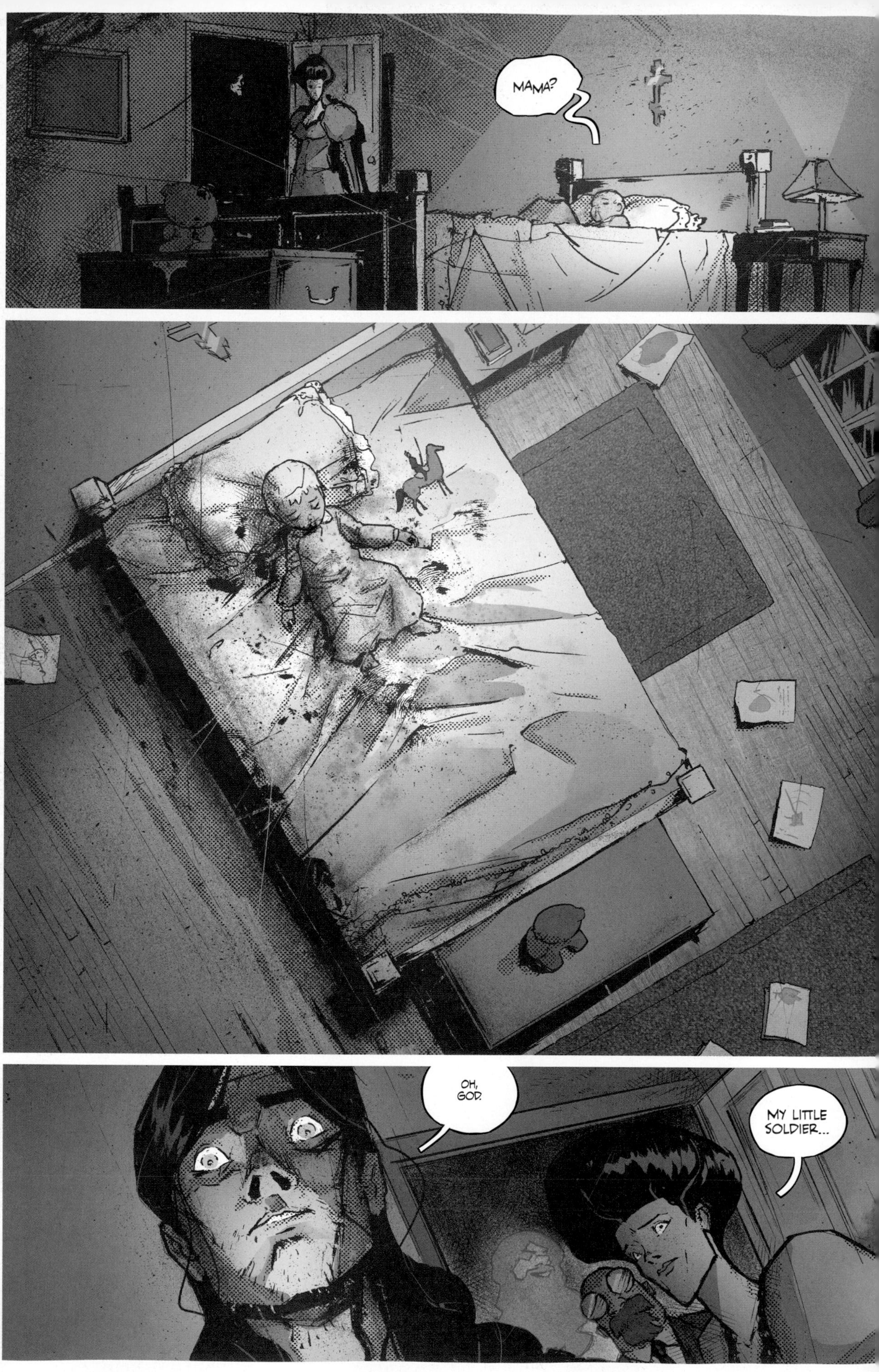
MAMA?
OH, GOD.
MY LITTLE SOLDIER...

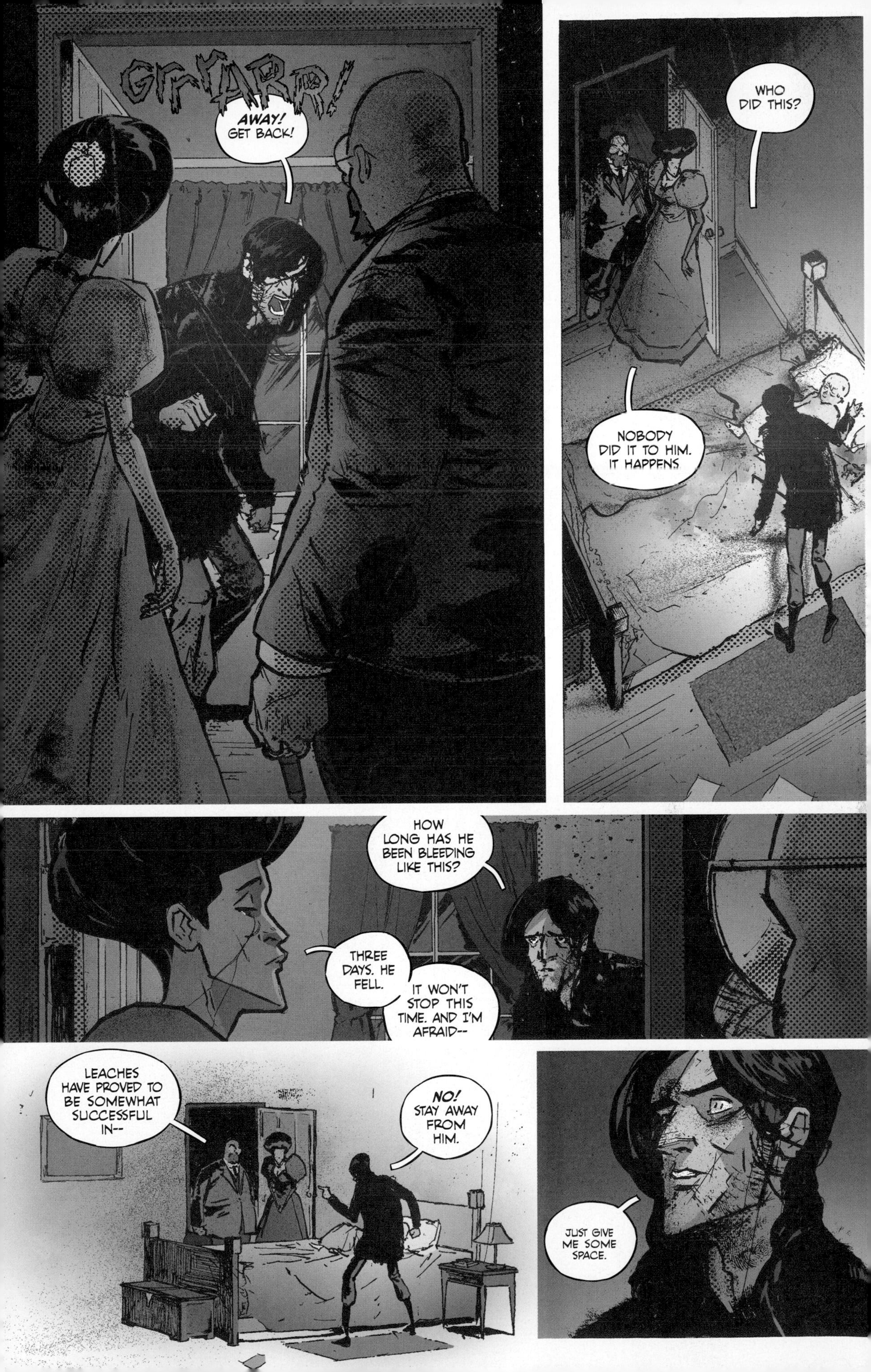
GRRYARR!
AWAY! GET BACK!
WHO DID THIS?
NOBODY DID IT TO HIM. IT HAPPENS.
HOW LONG HAS HE BEEN BLEEDING LIKE THIS?
THREE DAYS. HE FELL.
IT WON'T STOP THIS TIME. AND I'M AFRAID--
LEACHES HAVE PROVED TO BE SOMEWHAT SUCCESSFUL IN--
NO! STAY AWAY FROM HIM.
JUST GIVE ME SOME SPACE.

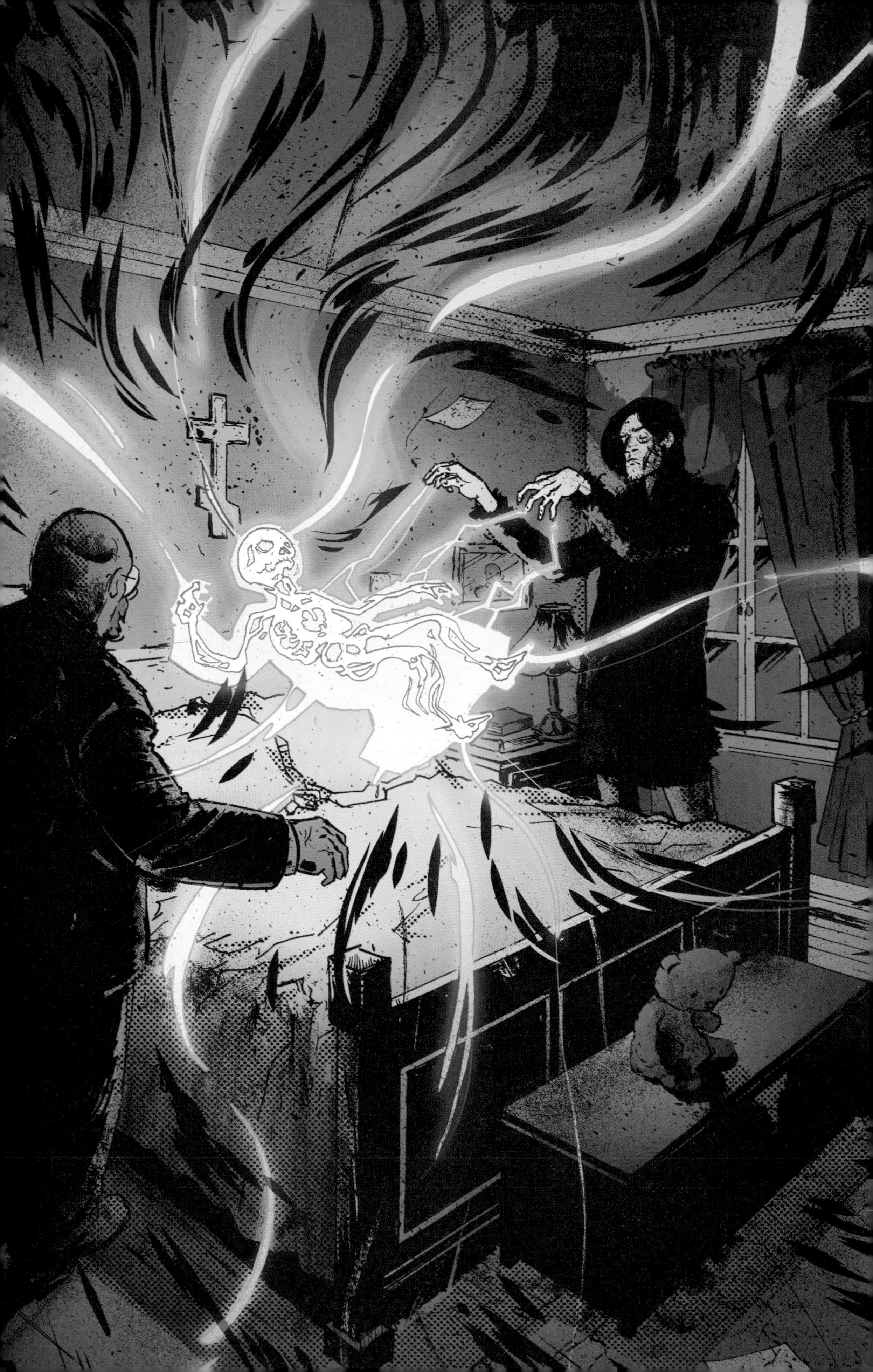

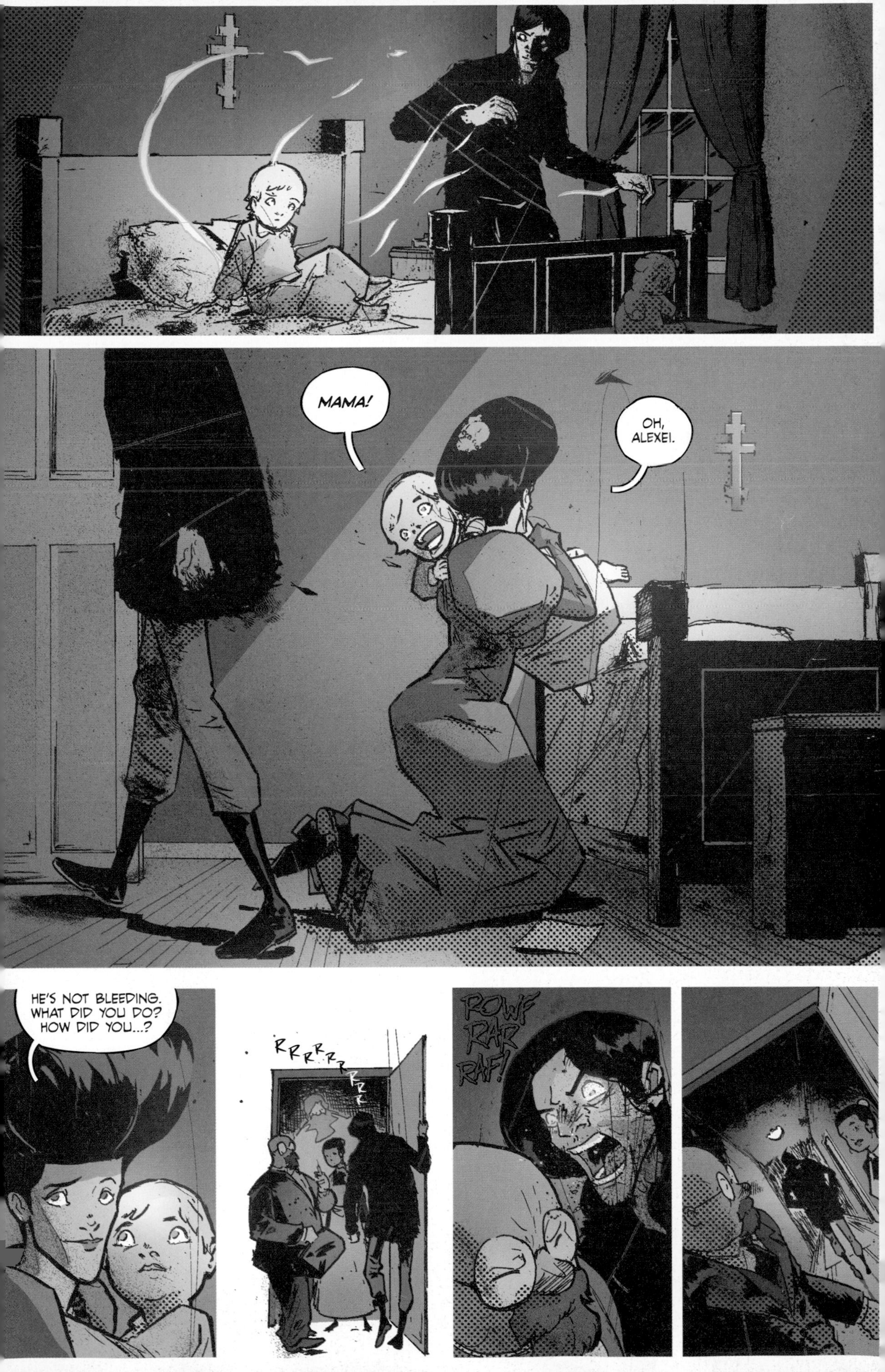
MAMA!
OH, ALEXEI.
HE'S NOT BLEEDING. WHAT DID YOU DO? HOW DID YOU...?
RRRRRRRRRR
ROWF RAR RAF!

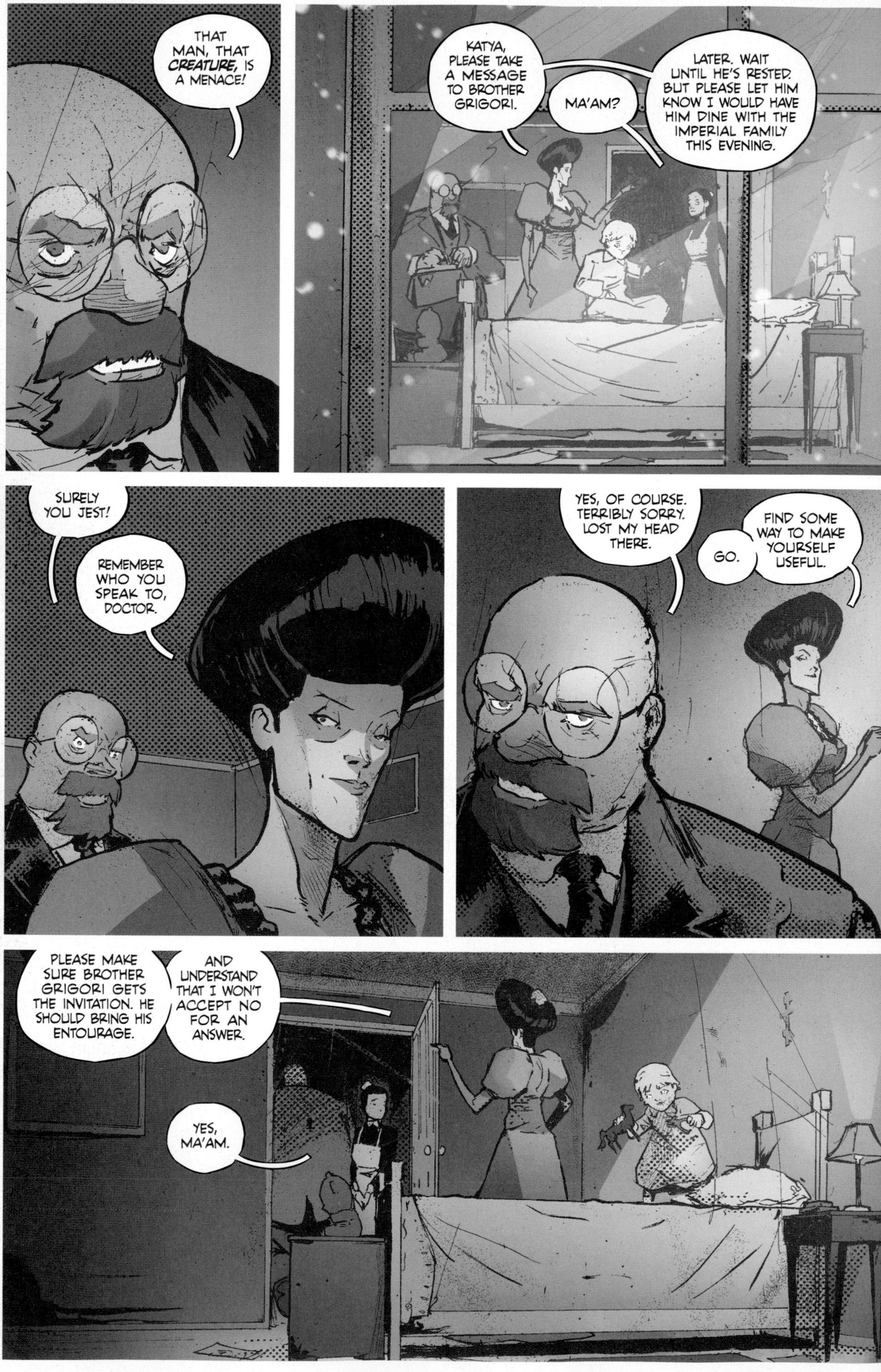
THAT MAN, THAT *CREATURE,* IS A MENACE!
KATYA, PLEASE TAKE A MESSAGE TO BROTHER GRIGORI.
MA'AM?
LATER. WAIT UNTIL HE'S RESTED. BUT PLEASE LET HIM KNOW I WOULD HAVE HIM DINE WITH THE IMPERIAL FAMILY THIS EVENING.
SURELY YOU JEST!
REMEMBER WHO YOU SPEAK TO, DOCTOR.
YES, OF COURSE. TERRIBLY SORRY. LOST MY HEAD THERE.
GO.
FIND SOME WAY TO MAKE YOURSELF USEFUL.
PLEASE MAKE SURE BROTHER GRIGORI GETS THE INVITATION. HE SHOULD BRING HIS ENTOURAGE.
AND UNDERSTAND THAT I WON'T ACCEPT NO FOR AN ANSWER.
YES, MA'AM.

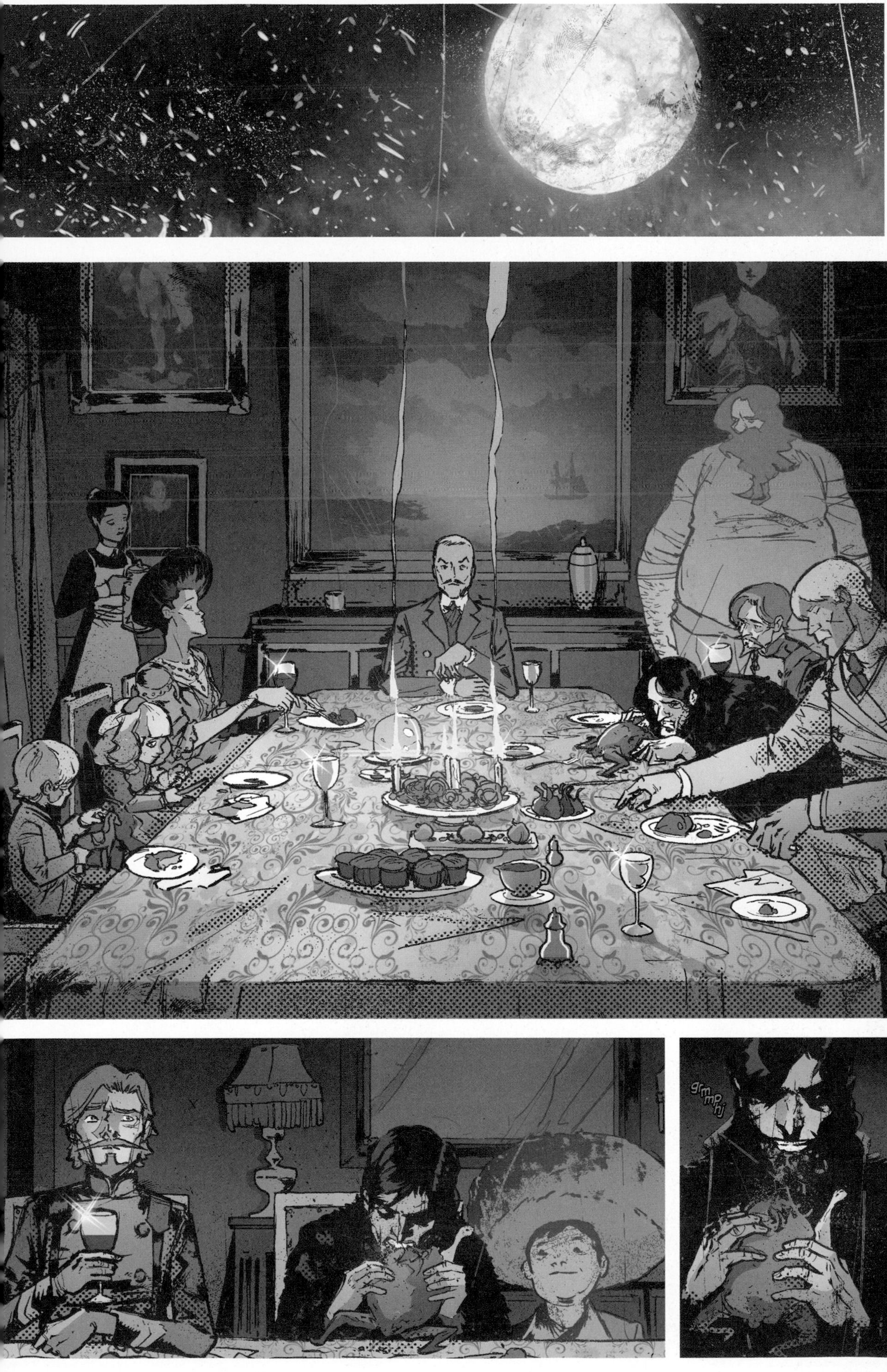
grmmphj

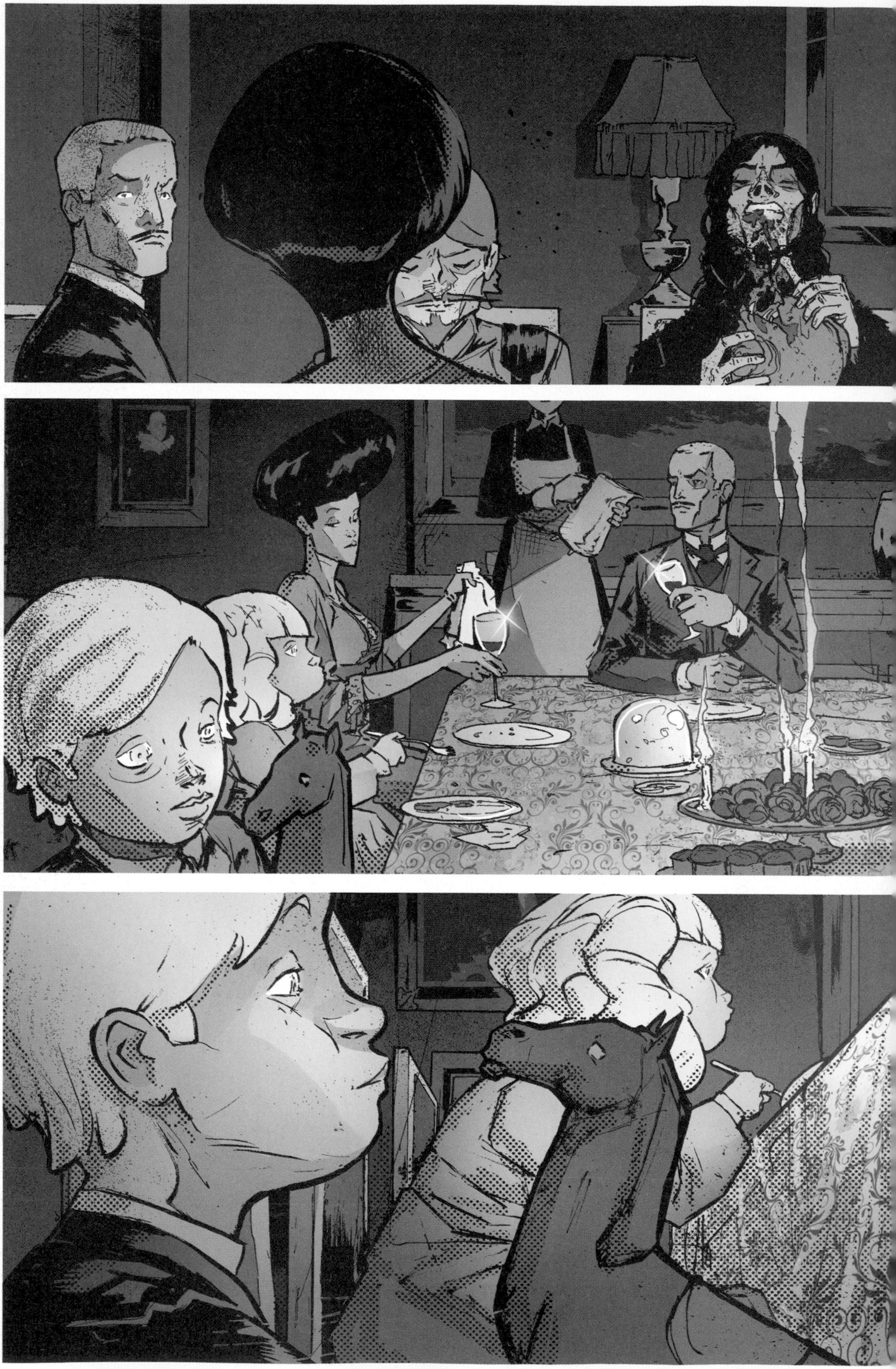

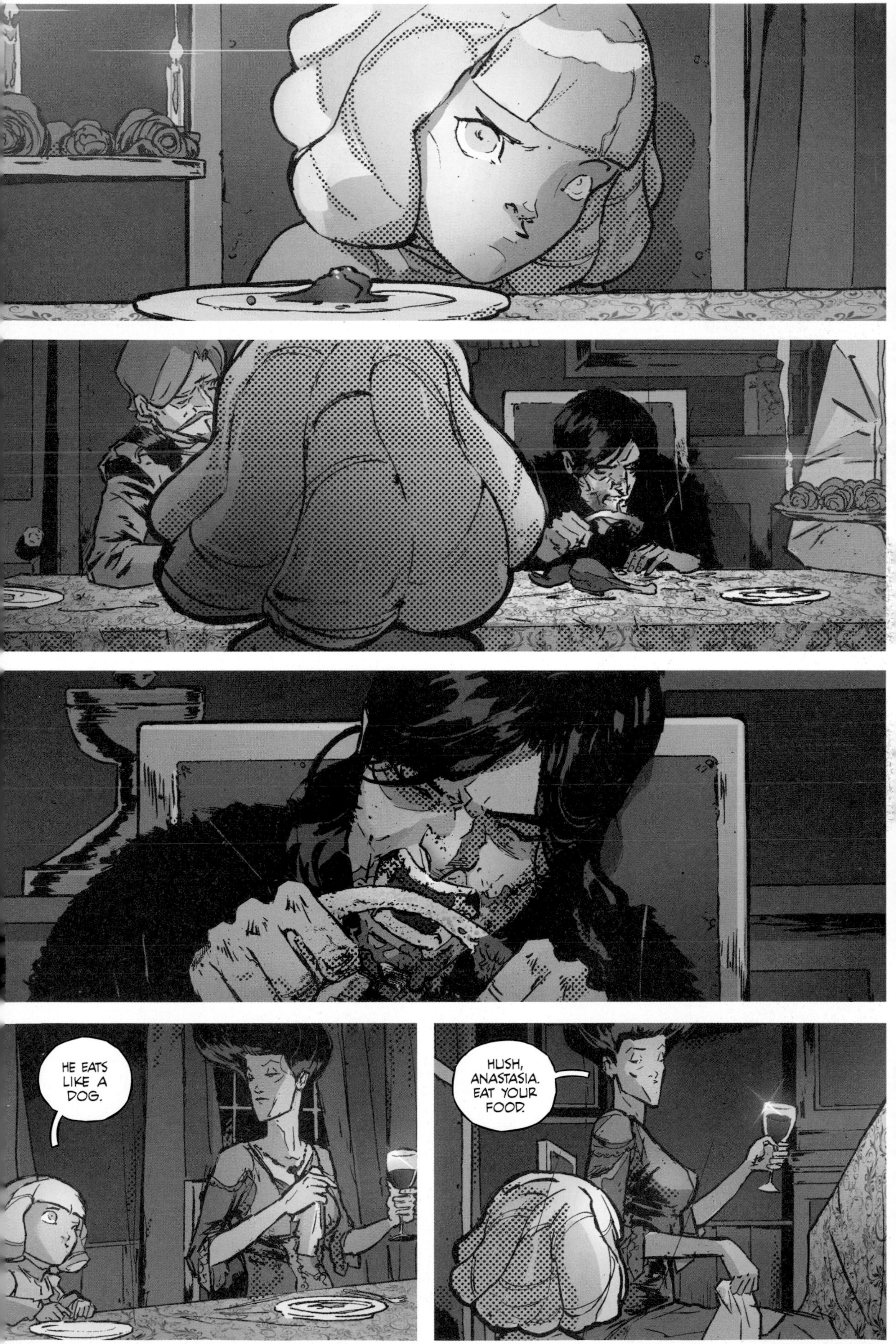
HE EATS LIKE A DOG.
HUSH, ANASTASIA. EAT YOUR FOOD.

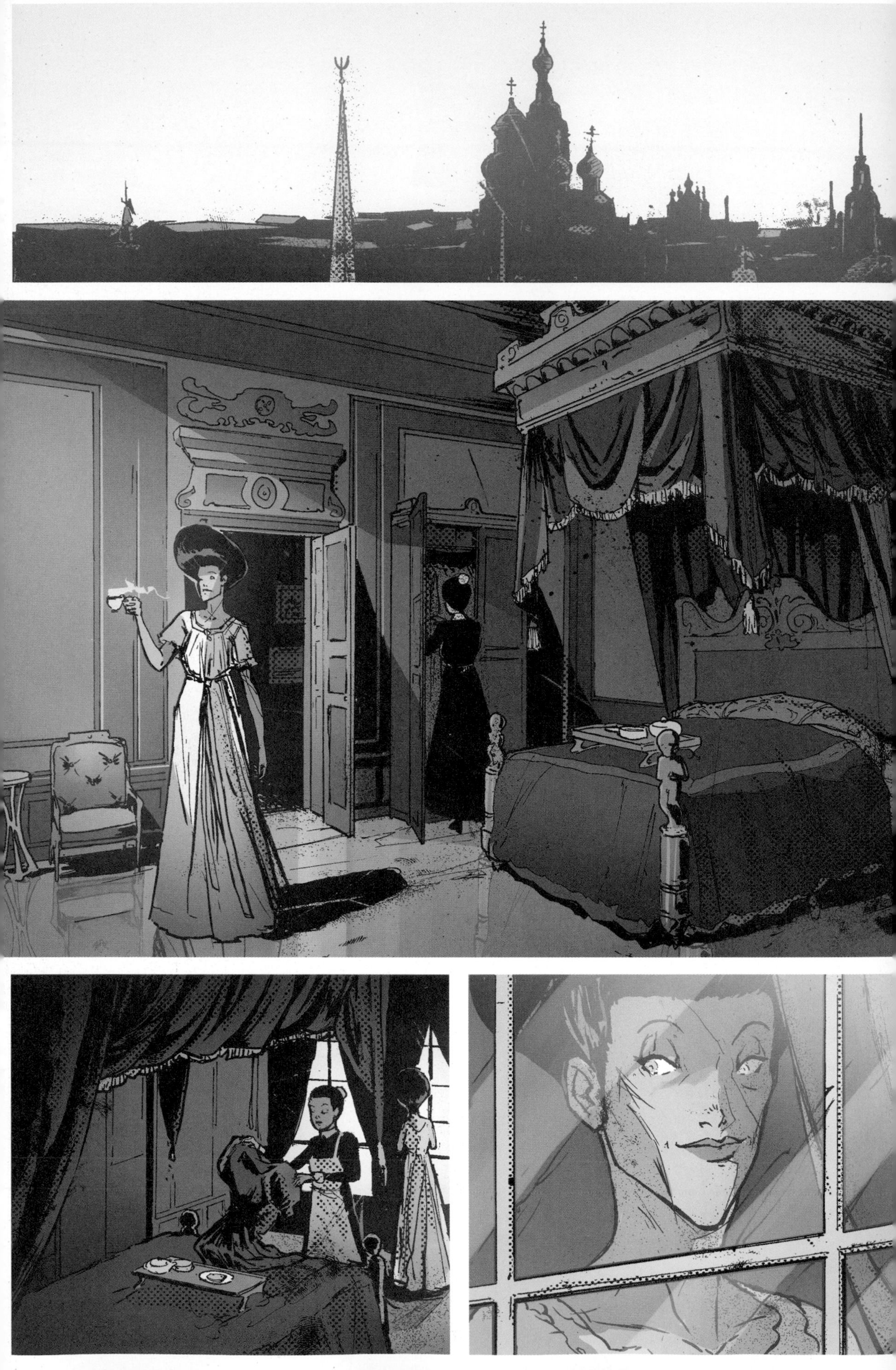

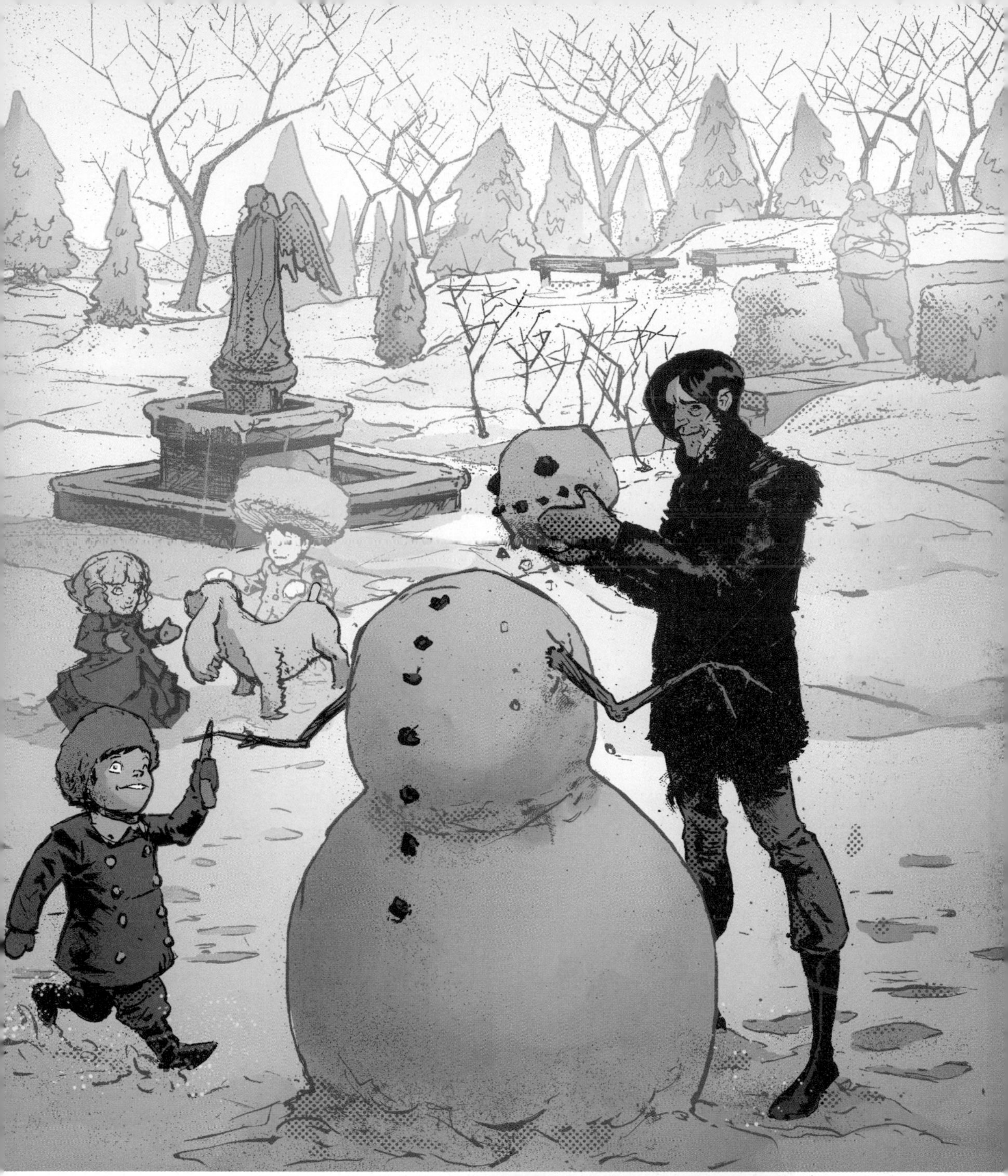

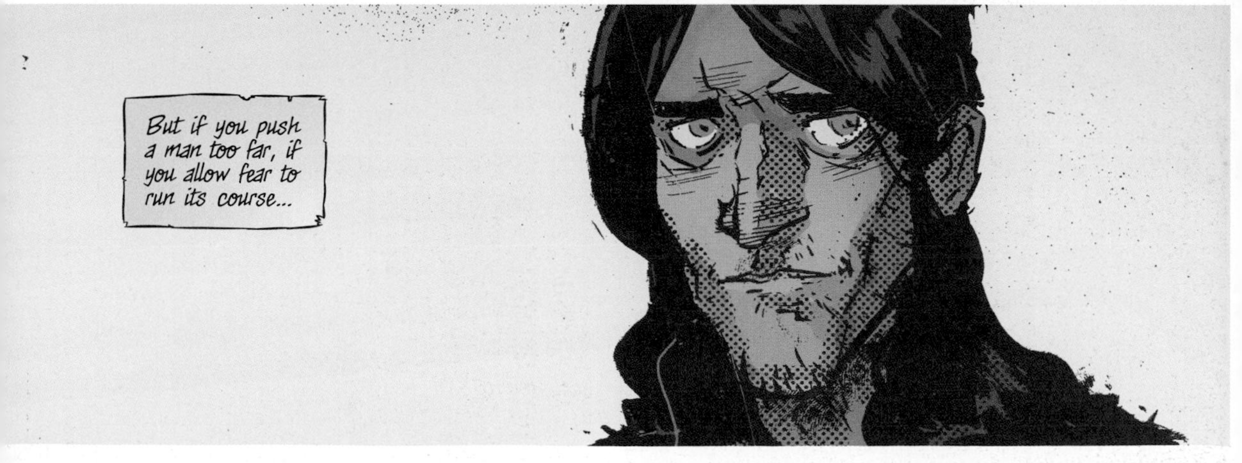
But if you push a man too far, if you allow fear to run its course...

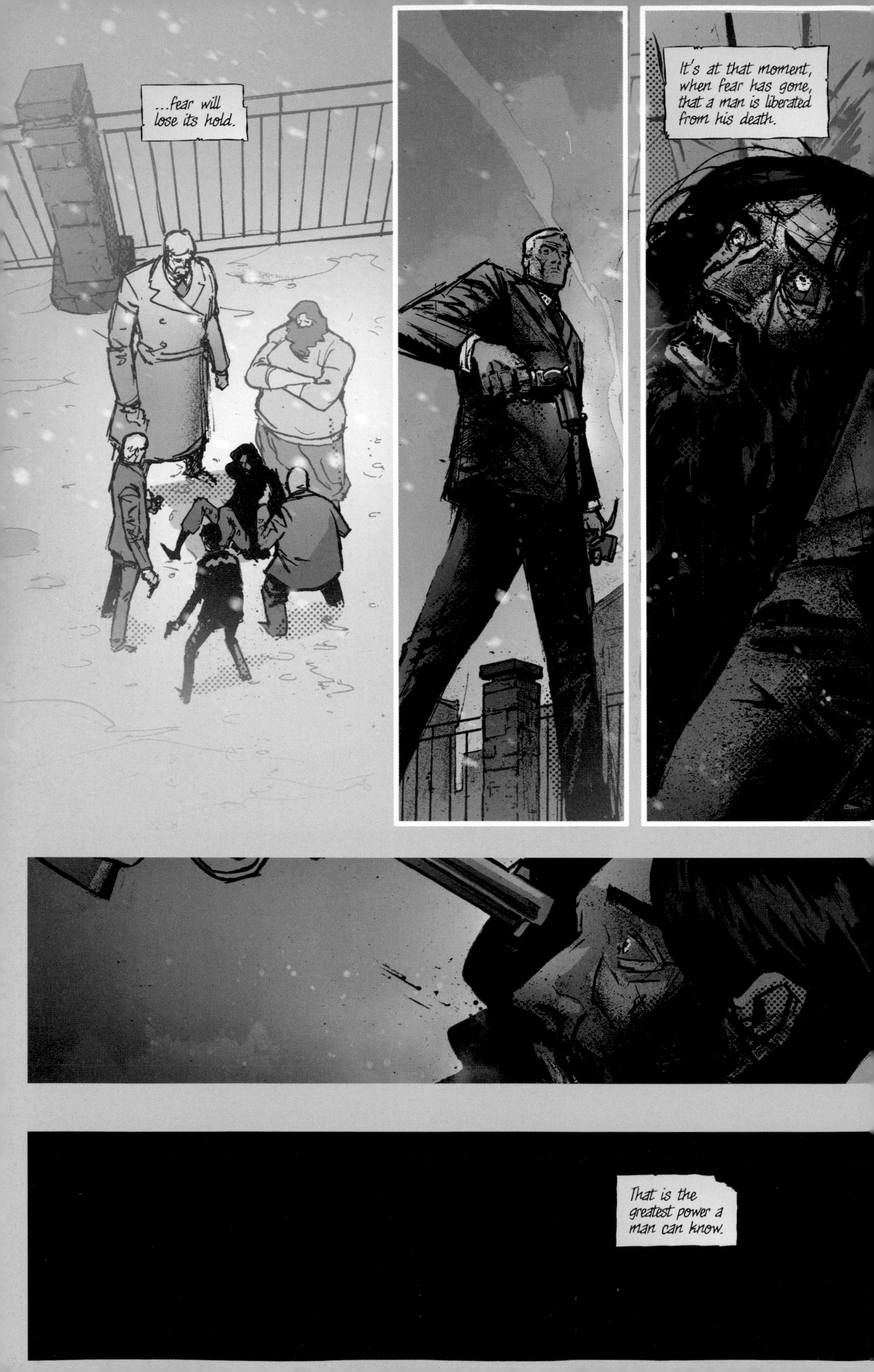
...fear will lose its hold.
It's at that moment, when fear has gone, that a man is liberated from his death.
That is the greatest power a man can know.

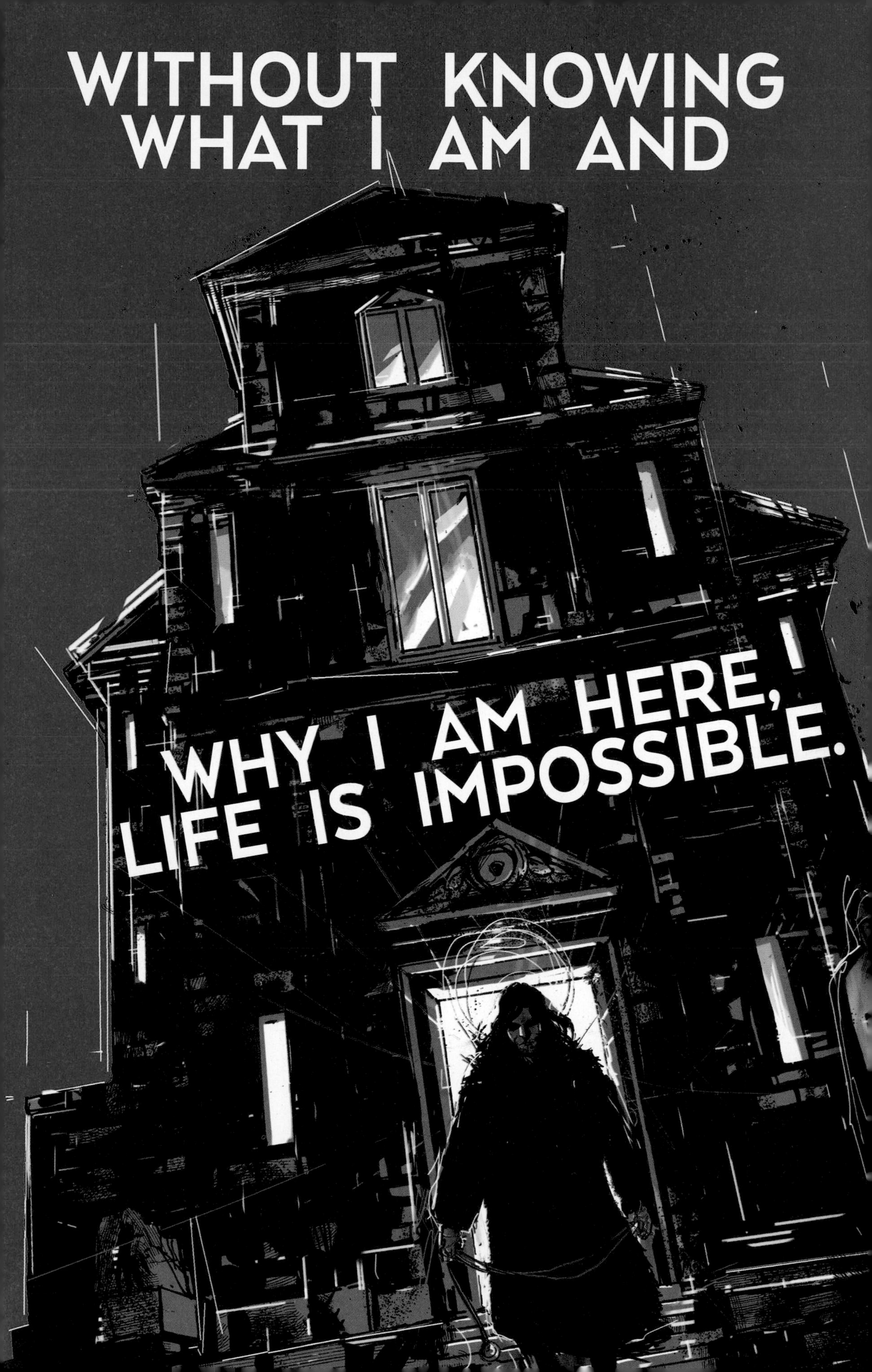
WITHOUT KNOWING
WHAT I AM AND
WHY I AM HERE,
LIFE IS IMPOSSIBLE.

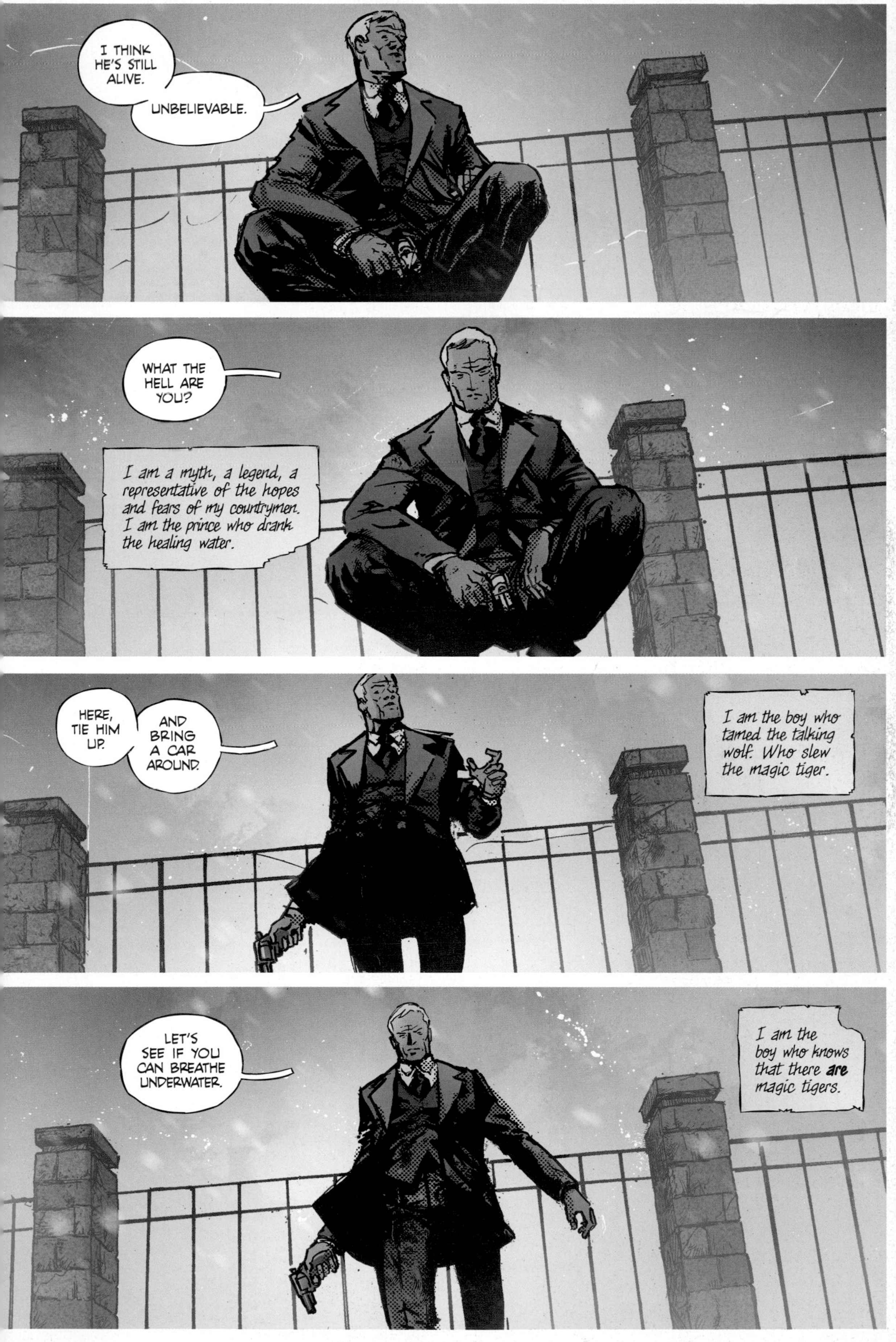
I THINK HE'S STILL ALIVE.
UNBELIEVABLE.
WHAT THE HELL ARE YOU?
I am a myth, a legend, a representative of the hopes and fears of my countrymen. I am the prince who drank the healing water.
HERE, TIE HIM UP.
AND BRING A CAR AROUND.
I am the boy who tamed the talking wolf. Who slew the magic tiger.
LET'S SEE IF YOU CAN BREATHE UNDERWATER.
I am the boy who knows that there **are** magic tigers.

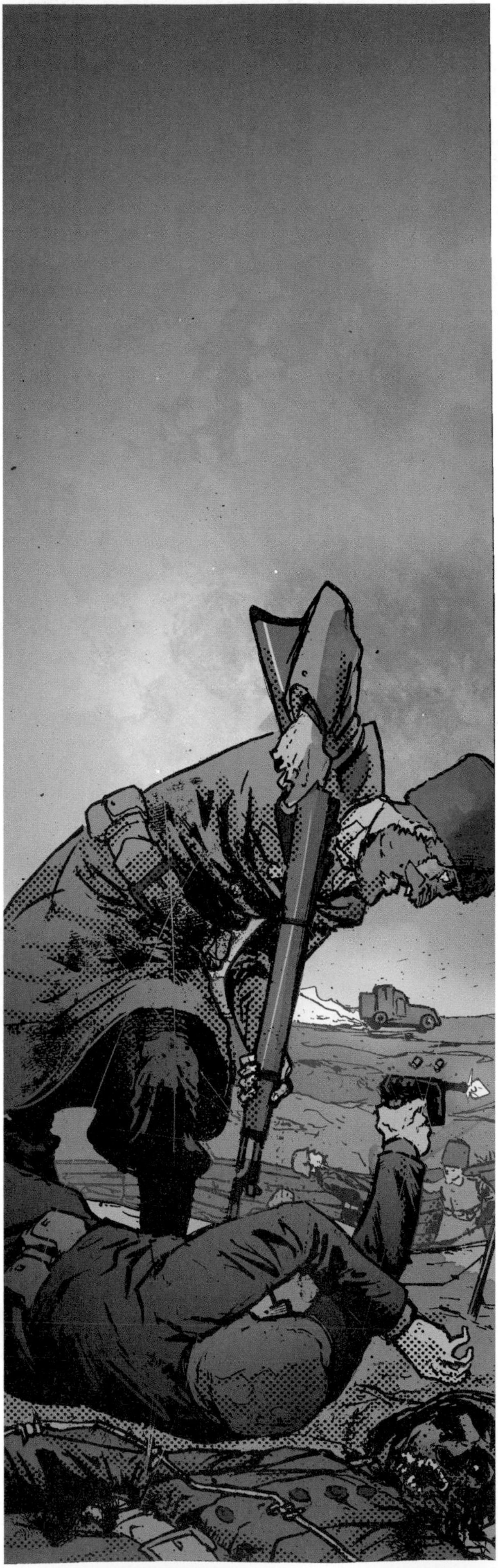
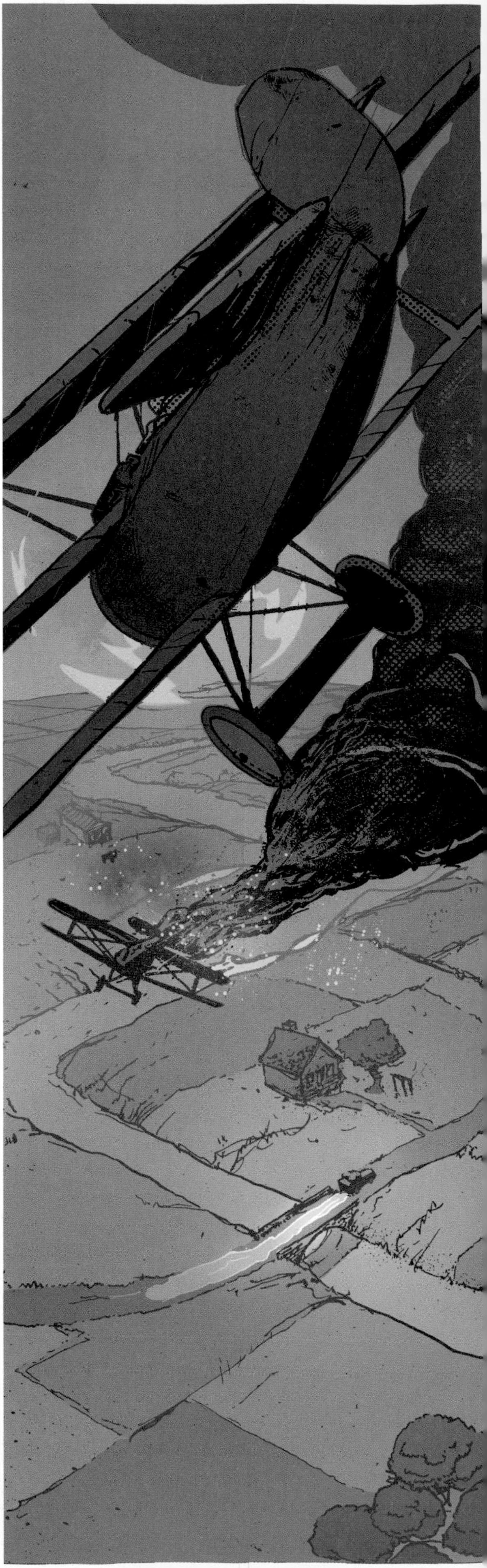

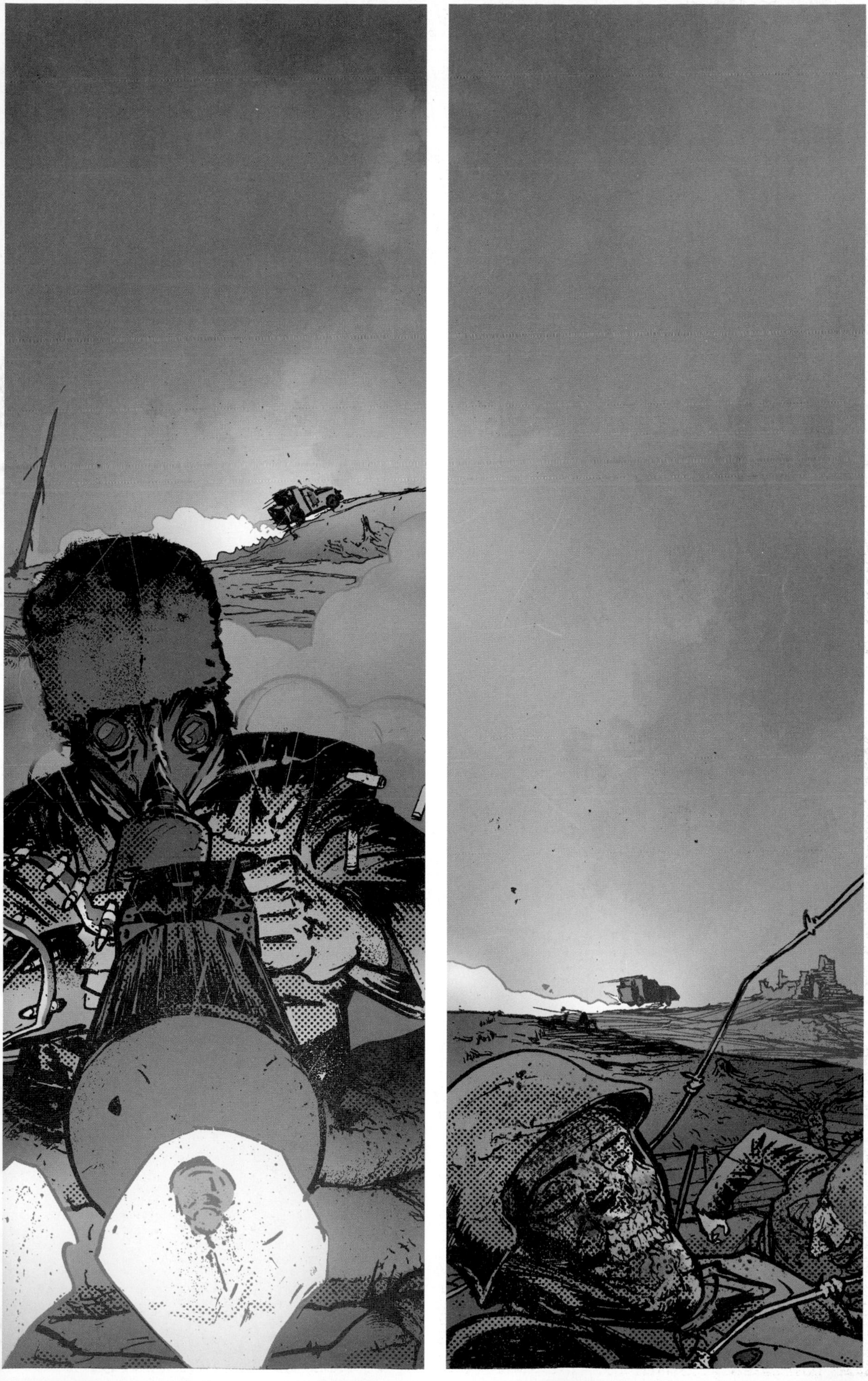

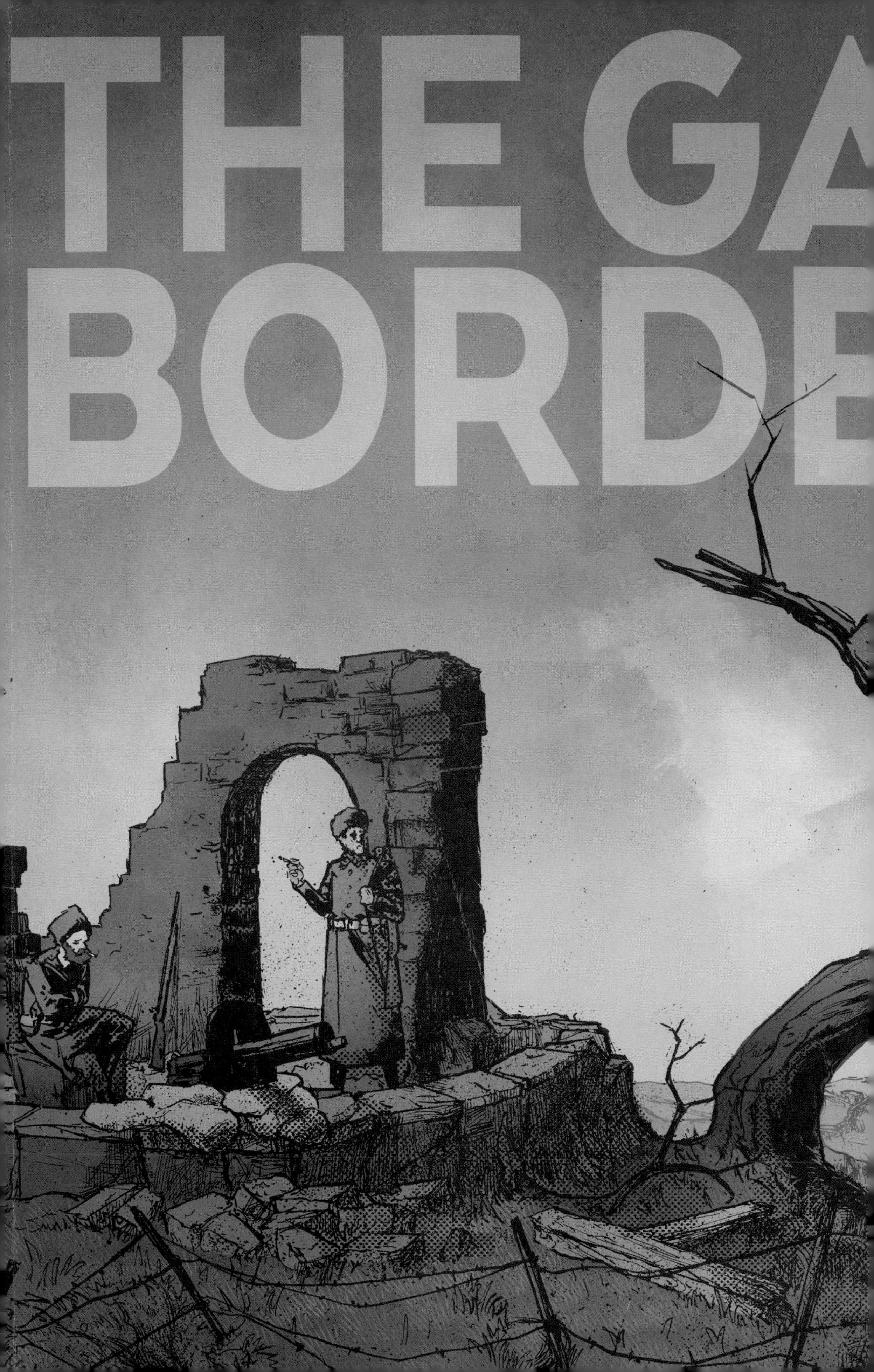
THE GA
BORDE

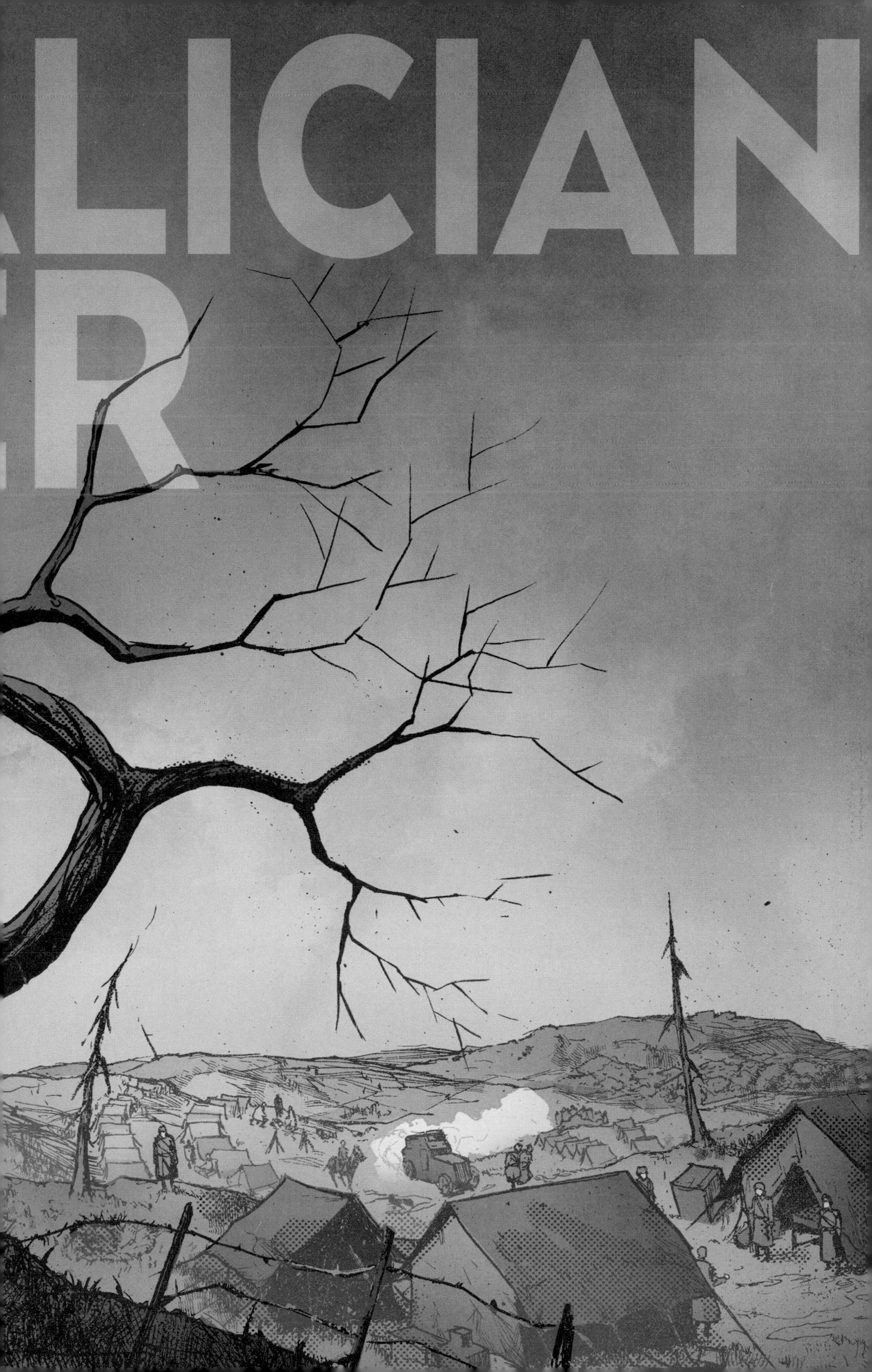
LICIAN
R

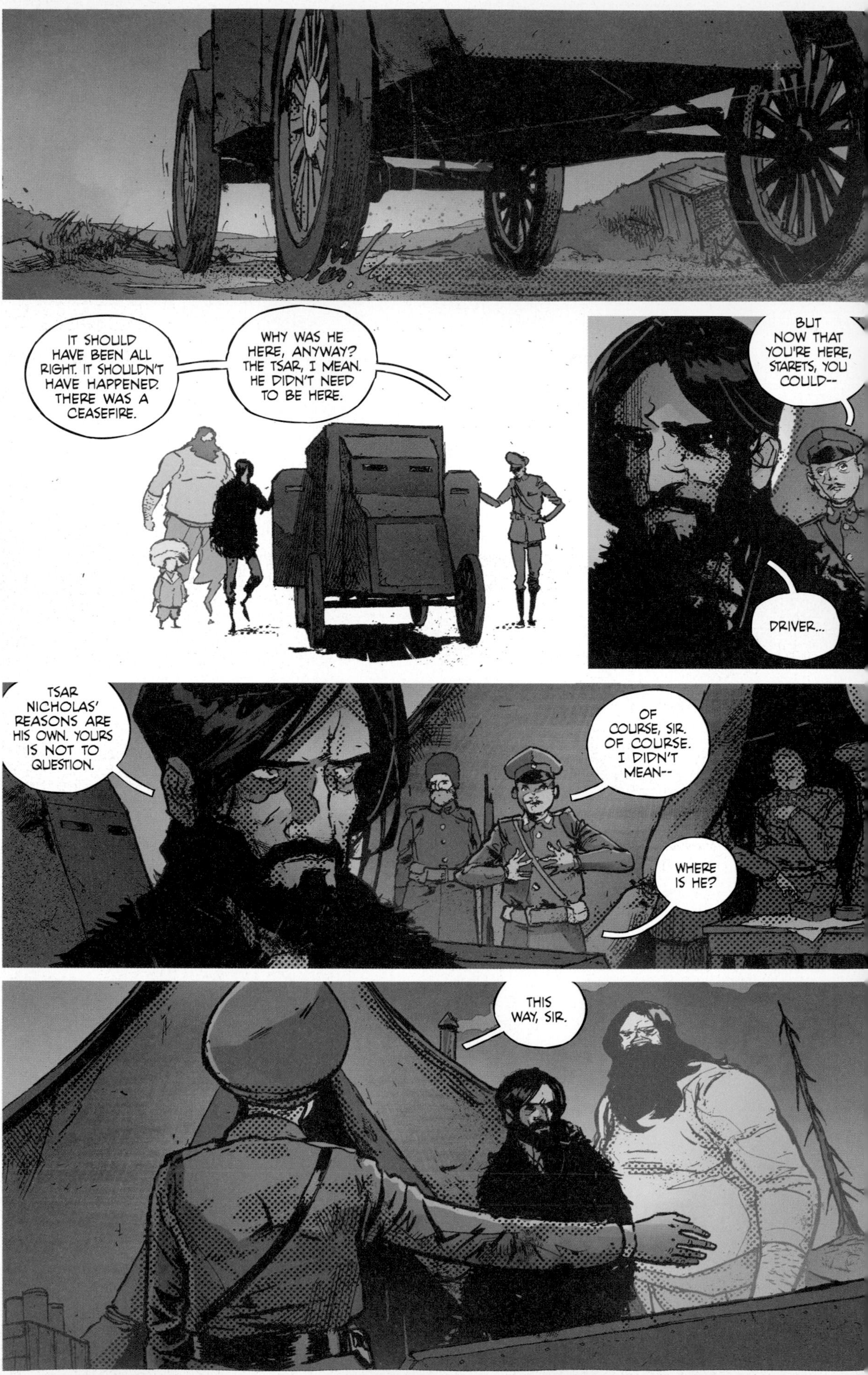
IT SHOULD HAVE BEEN ALL RIGHT. IT SHOULDN'T HAVE HAPPENED. THERE WAS A CEASEFIRE.
WHY WAS HE HERE, ANYWAY? THE TSAR, I MEAN. HE DIDN'T NEED TO BE HERE.
BUT NOW THAT YOU'RE HERE, STARETS, YOU COULD--
DRIVER...
TSAR NICHOLAS' REASONS ARE HIS OWN. YOURS IS NOT TO QUESTION.
OF COURSE, SIR. OF COURSE. I DIDN'T MEAN--
WHERE IS HE?
THIS WAY, SIR.

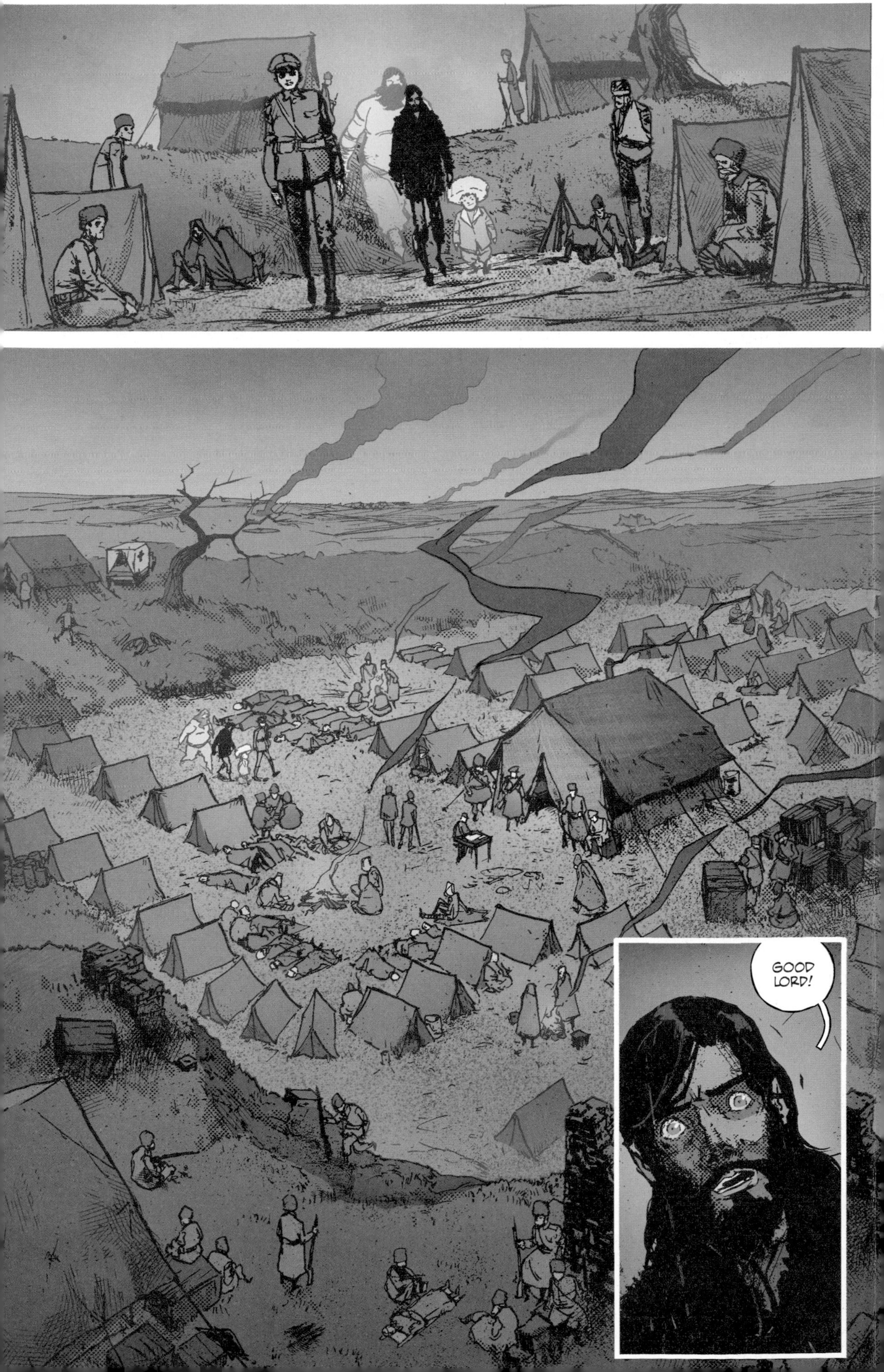
GOOD LORD!

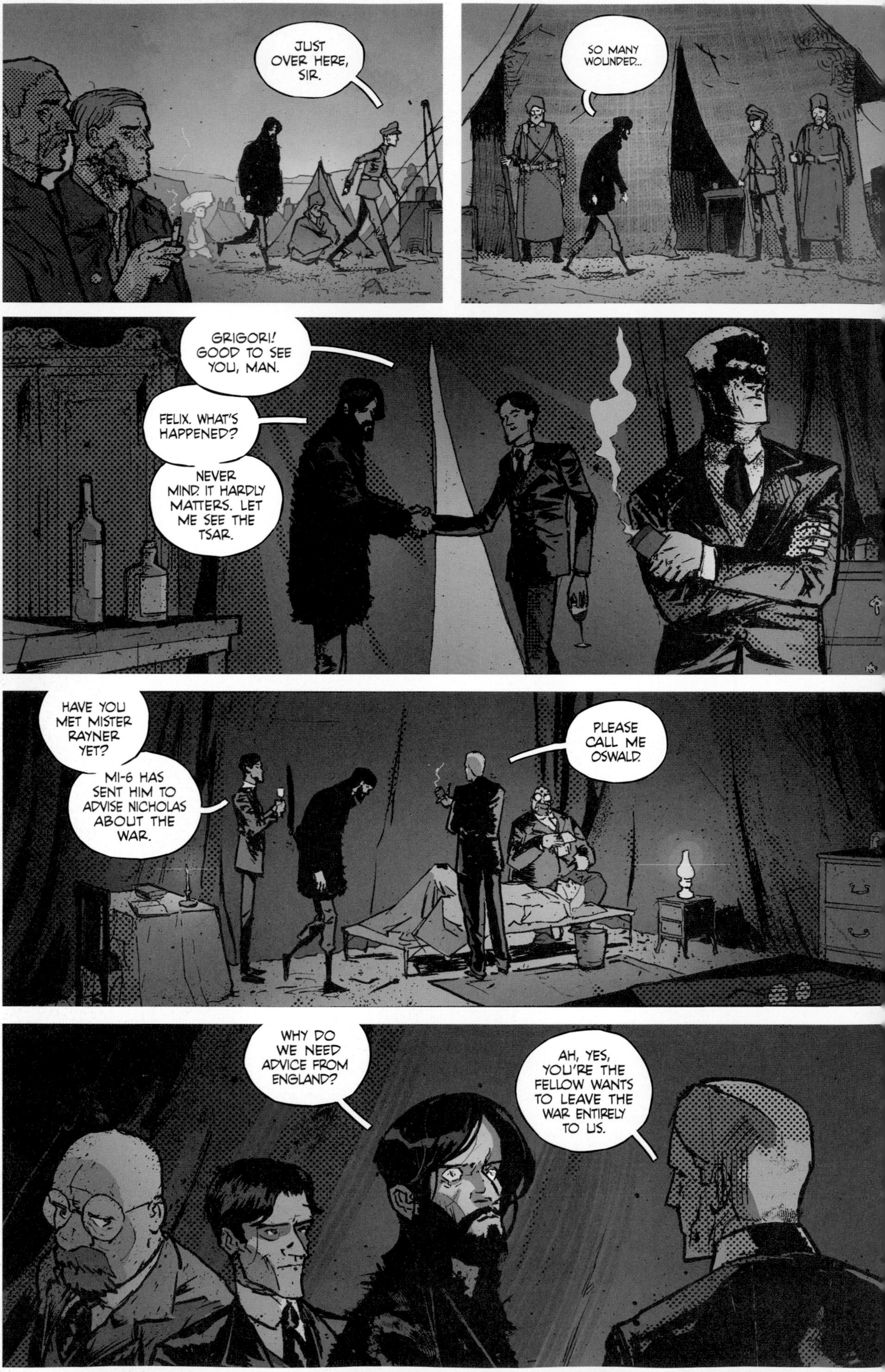
JUST OVER HERE, SIR.
SO MANY WOUNDED...
GRIGORI! GOOD TO SEE YOU, MAN.
FELIX. WHAT'S HAPPENED?
NEVER MIND. IT HARDLY MATTERS. LET ME SEE THE TSAR.
HAVE YOU MET MISTER RAYNER YET?
MI-6 HAS SENT HIM TO ADVISE NICHOLAS ABOUT THE WAR.
PLEASE CALL ME OSWALD.
WHY DO WE NEED ADVICE FROM ENGLAND?
AH, YES, YOU'RE THE FELLOW WANTS TO LEAVE THE WAR ENTIRELY TO US.

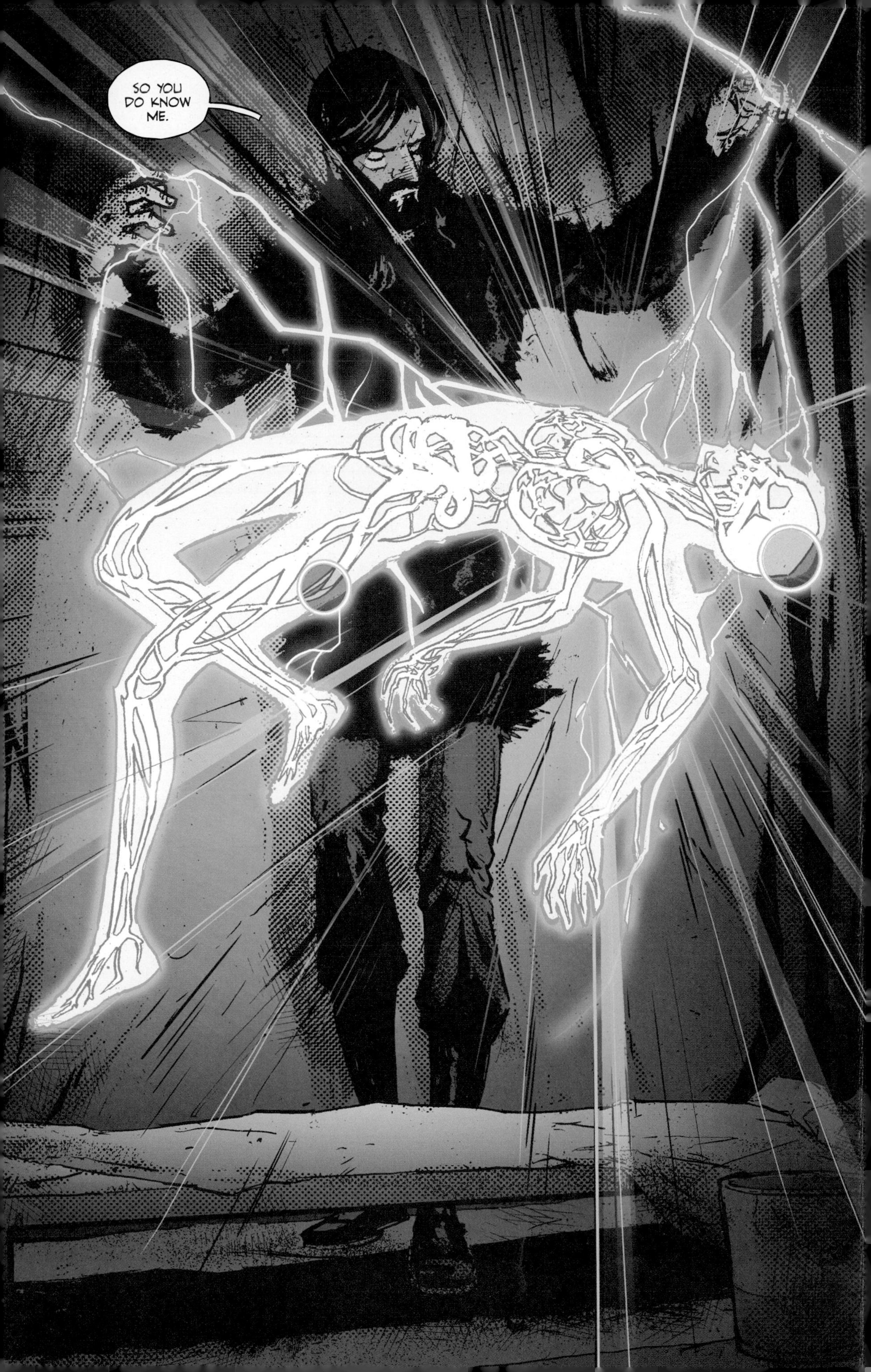
SO YOU DO KNOW ME.

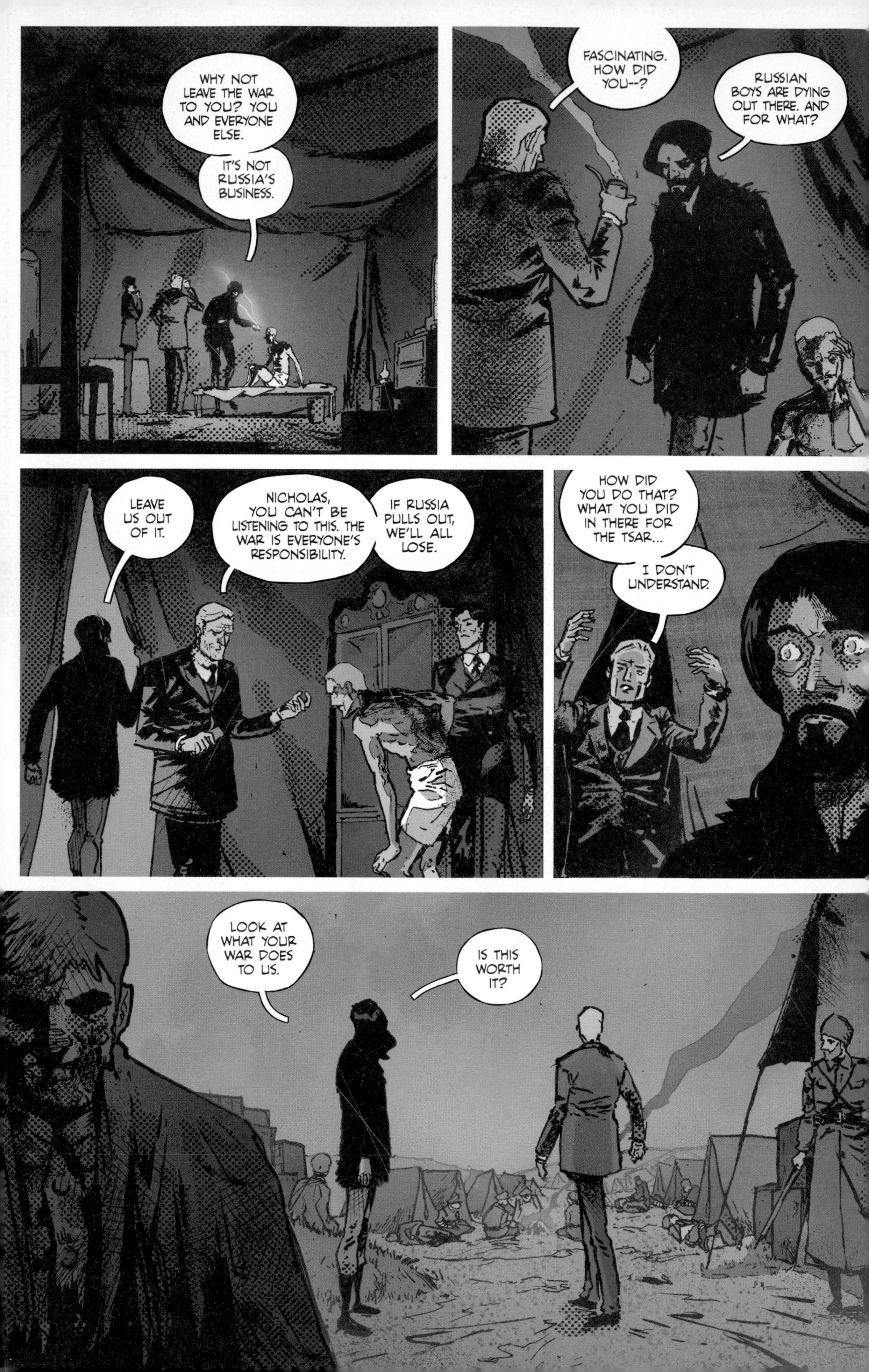
WHY NOT LEAVE THE WAR TO YOU? YOU AND EVERYONE ELSE.
IT'S NOT RUSSIA'S BUSINESS.
FASCINATING. HOW DID YOU--?
RUSSIAN BOYS ARE DYING OUT THERE. AND FOR WHAT?
LEAVE US OUT OF IT.
NICHOLAS, YOU CAN'T BE LISTENING TO THIS. THE WAR IS EVERYONE'S RESPONSIBILITY.
IF RUSSIA PULLS OUT, WE'LL ALL LOSE.
HOW DID YOU DO THAT? WHAT YOU DID IN THERE FOR THE TSAR...
I DON'T UNDERSTAND.
LOOK AT WHAT YOUR WAR DOES TO US.
IS THIS WORTH IT?

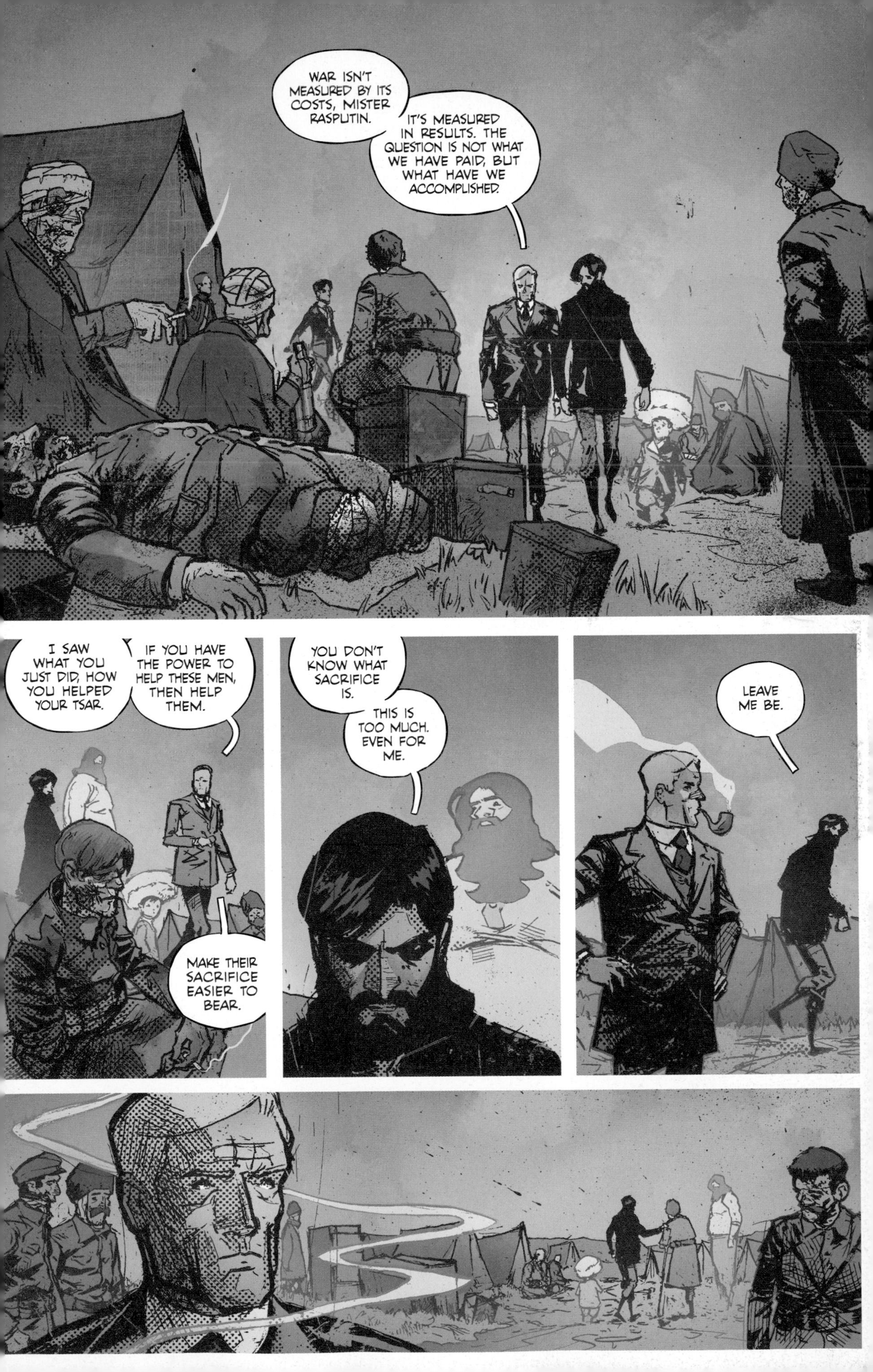
WAR ISN'T MEASURED BY ITS COSTS, MISTER RASPUTIN.
IT'S MEASURED IN RESULTS. THE QUESTION IS NOT WHAT WE HAVE PAID, BUT WHAT HAVE WE ACCOMPLISHED.
I SAW WHAT YOU JUST DID, HOW YOU HELPED YOUR TSAR.
IF YOU HAVE THE POWER TO HELP THESE MEN, THEN HELP THEM.
MAKE THEIR SACRIFICE EASIER TO BEAR.
YOU DON'T KNOW WHAT SACRIFICE IS.
THIS IS TOO MUCH. EVEN FOR ME.
LEAVE ME BE.

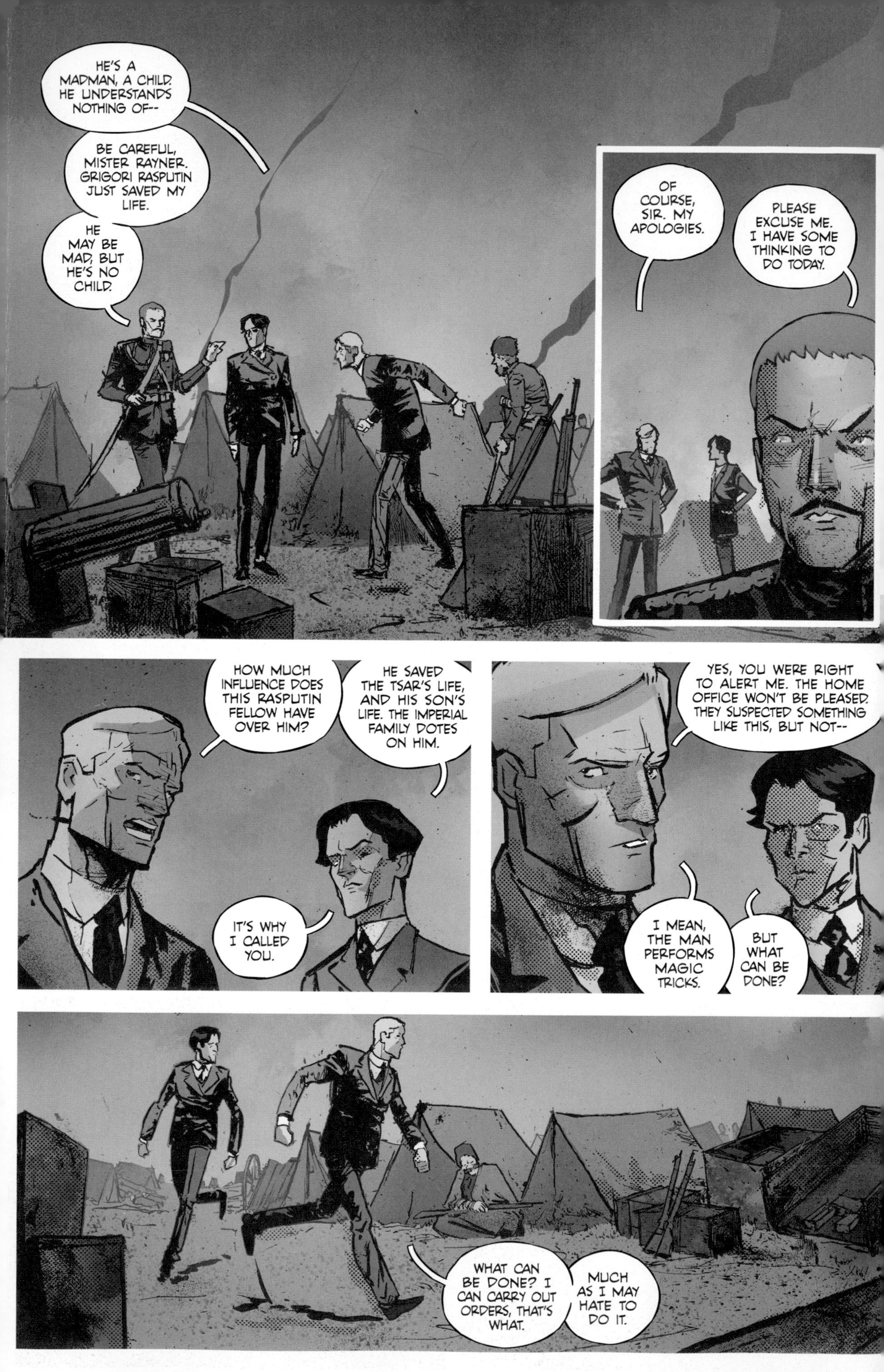
HE'S A MADMAN, A CHILD. HE UNDERSTANDS NOTHING OF--
BE CAREFUL, MISTER RAYNER. GRIGORI RASPUTIN JUST SAVED MY LIFE.
HE MAY BE MAD, BUT HE'S NO CHILD.
OF COURSE, SIR. MY APOLOGIES.
PLEASE EXCUSE ME. I HAVE SOME THINKING TO DO TODAY.
HOW MUCH INFLUENCE DOES THIS RASPUTIN FELLOW HAVE OVER HIM?
HE SAVED THE TSAR'S LIFE, AND HIS SON'S LIFE. THE IMPERIAL FAMILY DOTES ON HIM.
IT'S WHY I CALLED YOU.
YES, YOU WERE RIGHT TO ALERT ME. THE HOME OFFICE WON'T BE PLEASED. THEY SUSPECTED SOMETHING LIKE THIS, BUT NOT--
I MEAN, THE MAN PERFORMS MAGIC TRICKS.
BUT WHAT CAN BE DONE?
WHAT CAN BE DONE? I CAN CARRY OUT ORDERS, THAT'S WHAT.
MUCH AS I MAY HATE TO DO IT.

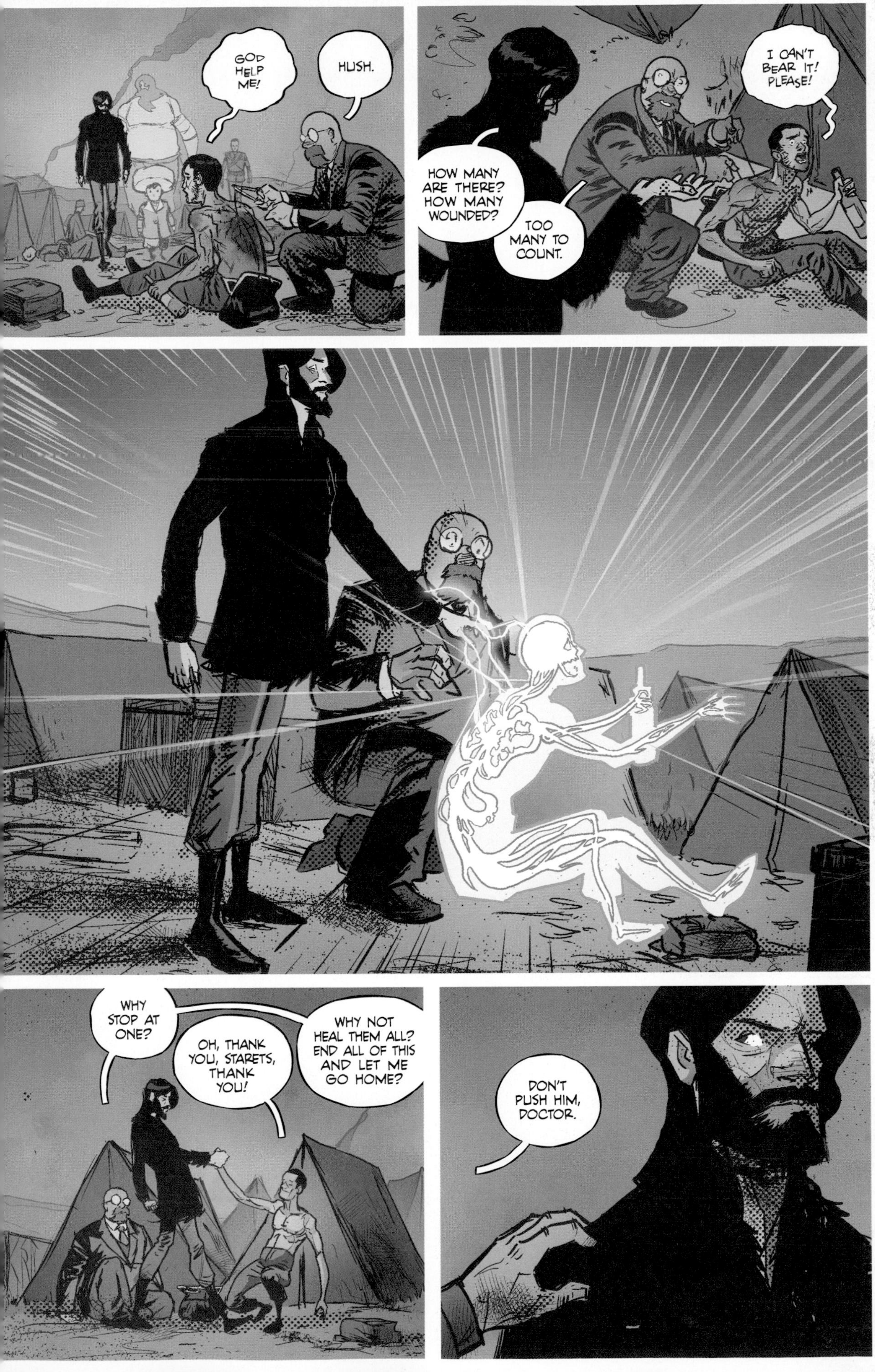
GOD HELP ME!
HUSH.
I CAN'T BEAR IT! PLEASE!
HOW MANY ARE THERE? HOW MANY WOUNDED?
TOO MANY TO COUNT.
WHY STOP AT ONE?
OH, THANK YOU, STARETS, THANK YOU!
WHY NOT HEAL THEM ALL? END ALL OF THIS AND LET ME GO HOME?
DON'T PUSH HIM, DOCTOR.

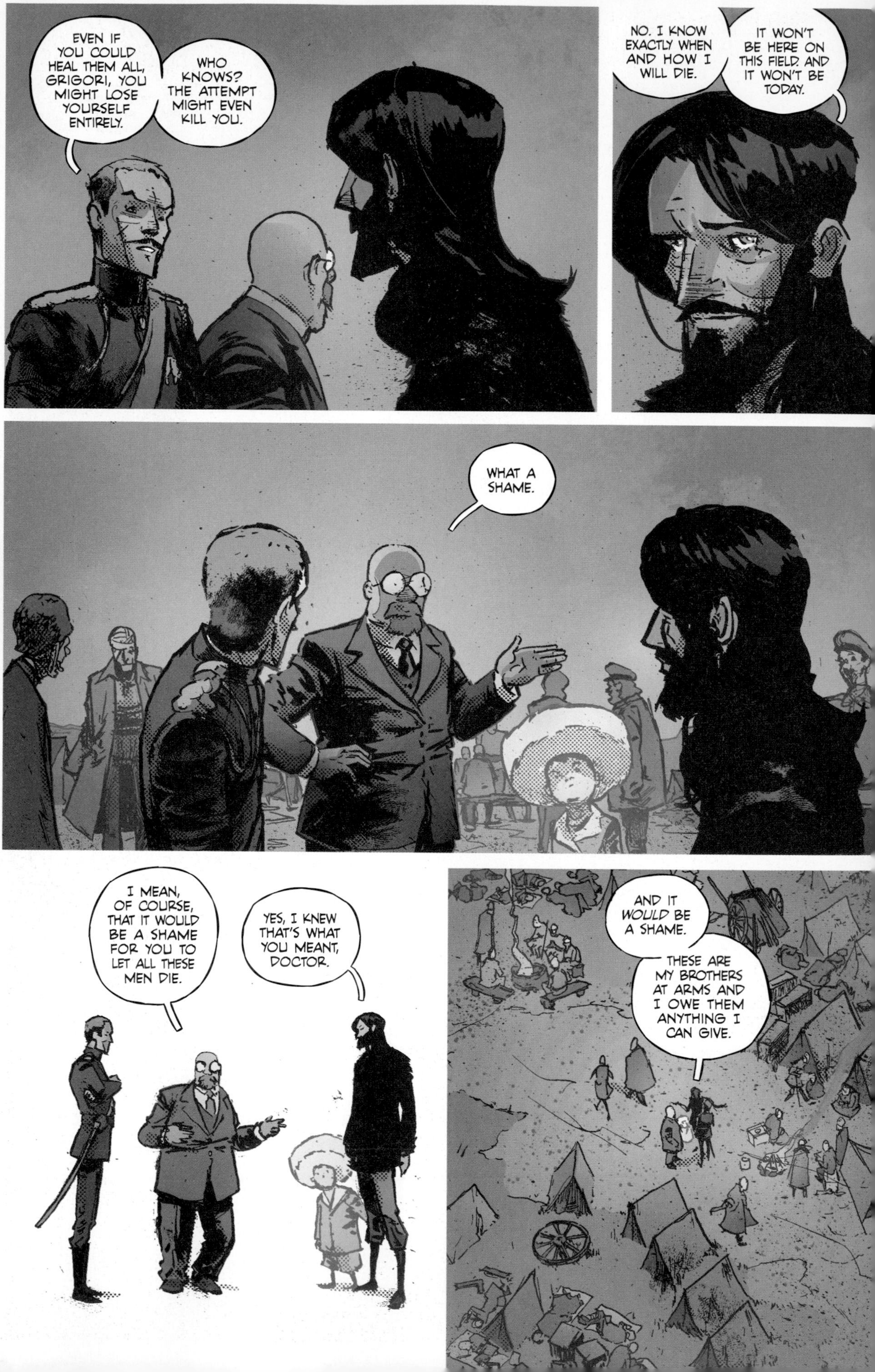
EVEN IF YOU COULD HEAL THEM ALL, GRIGORI, YOU MIGHT LOSE YOURSELF ENTIRELY.
WHO KNOWS? THE ATTEMPT MIGHT EVEN KILL YOU.
NO. I KNOW EXACTLY WHEN AND HOW I WILL DIE.
IT WON'T BE HERE ON THIS FIELD. AND IT WON'T BE TODAY.
WHAT A SHAME.
I MEAN, OF COURSE, THAT IT WOULD BE A SHAME FOR YOU TO LET ALL THESE MEN DIE.
YES, I KNEW THAT'S WHAT YOU MEANT, DOCTOR.
AND IT *WOULD* BE A SHAME.
THESE ARE MY BROTHERS AT ARMS AND I OWE THEM ANYTHING I CAN GIVE.

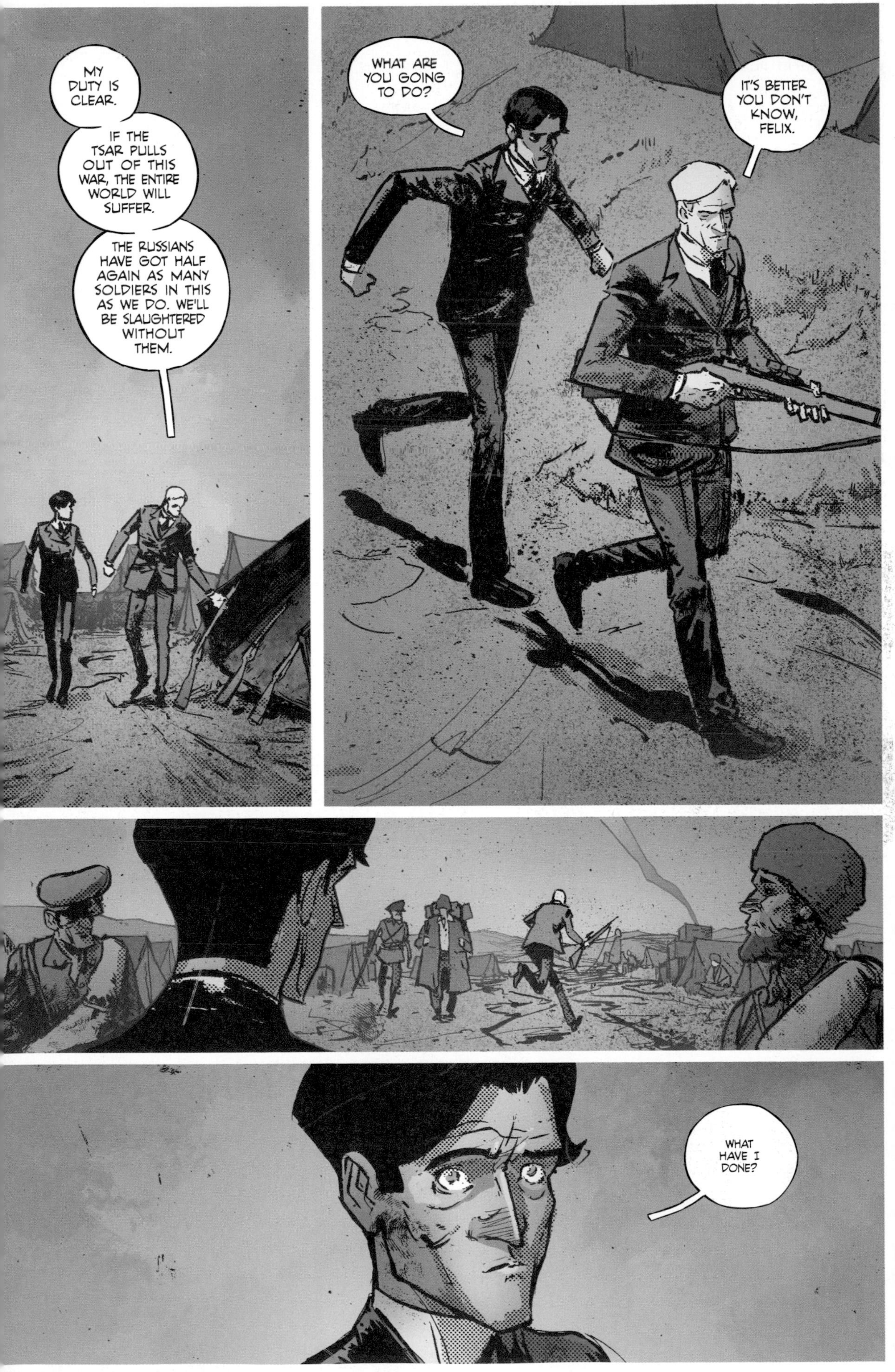
MY DUTY IS CLEAR.
IF THE TSAR PULLS OUT OF THIS WAR, THE ENTIRE WORLD WILL SUFFER.
THE RUSSIANS HAVE GOT HALF AGAIN AS MANY SOLDIERS IN THIS AS WE DO. WE'LL BE SLAUGHTERED WITHOUT THEM.
WHAT ARE YOU GOING TO DO?
IT'S BETTER YOU DON'T KNOW, FELIX.
WHAT HAVE I DONE?

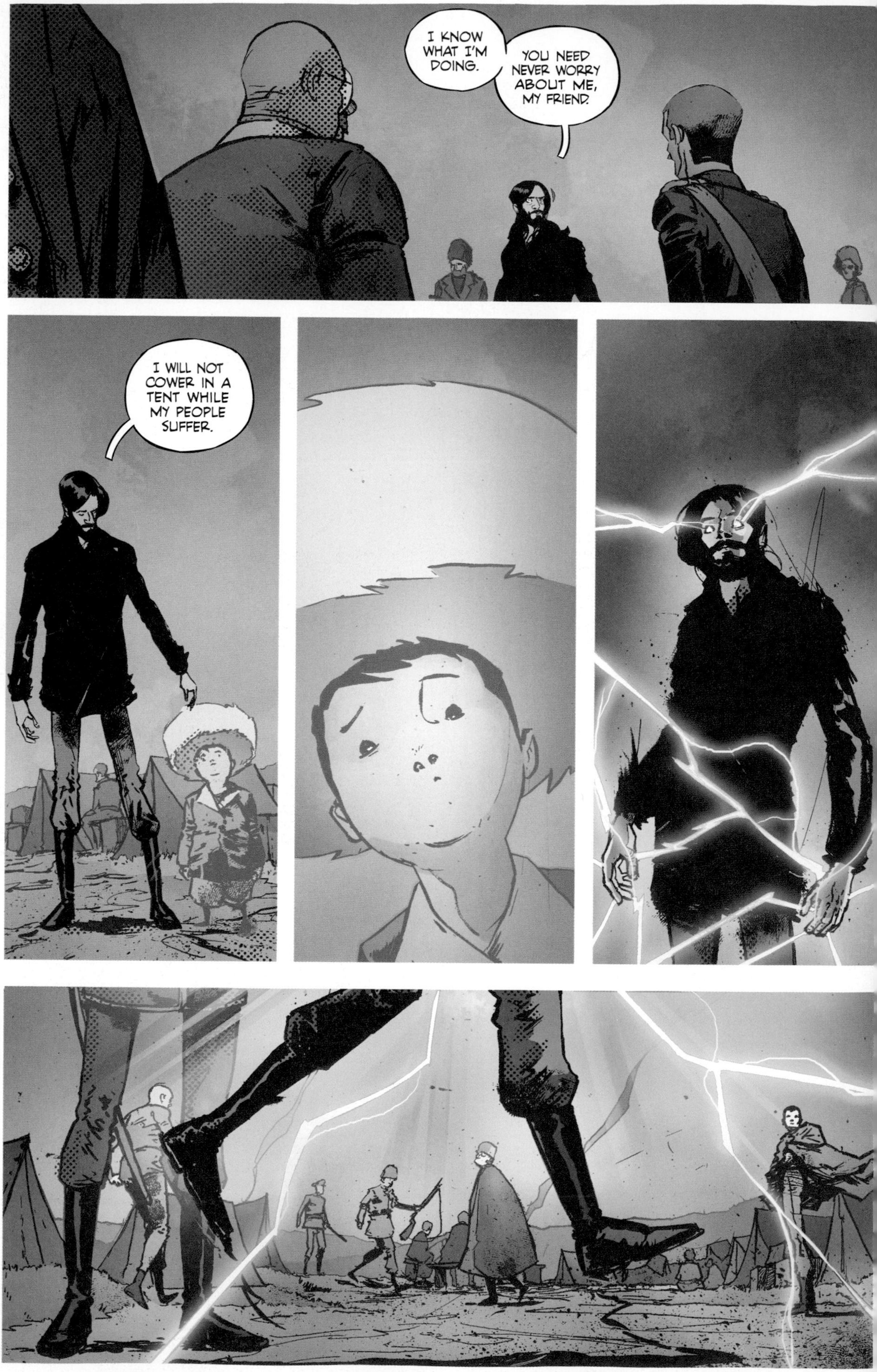
I KNOW WHAT I'M DOING.
YOU NEED NEVER WORRY ABOUT ME, MY FRIEND.
I WILL NOT COWER IN A TENT WHILE MY PEOPLE SUFFER.

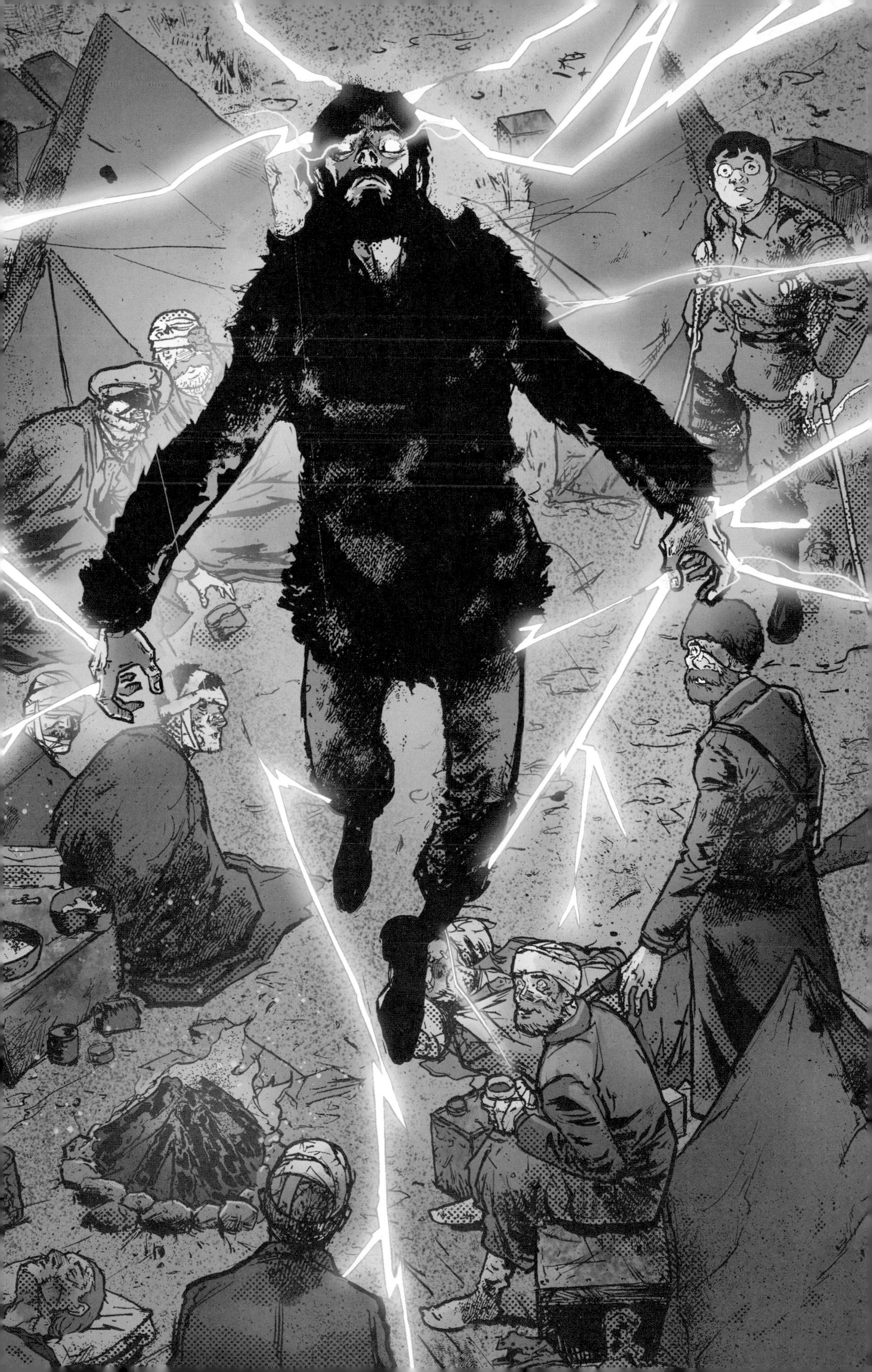

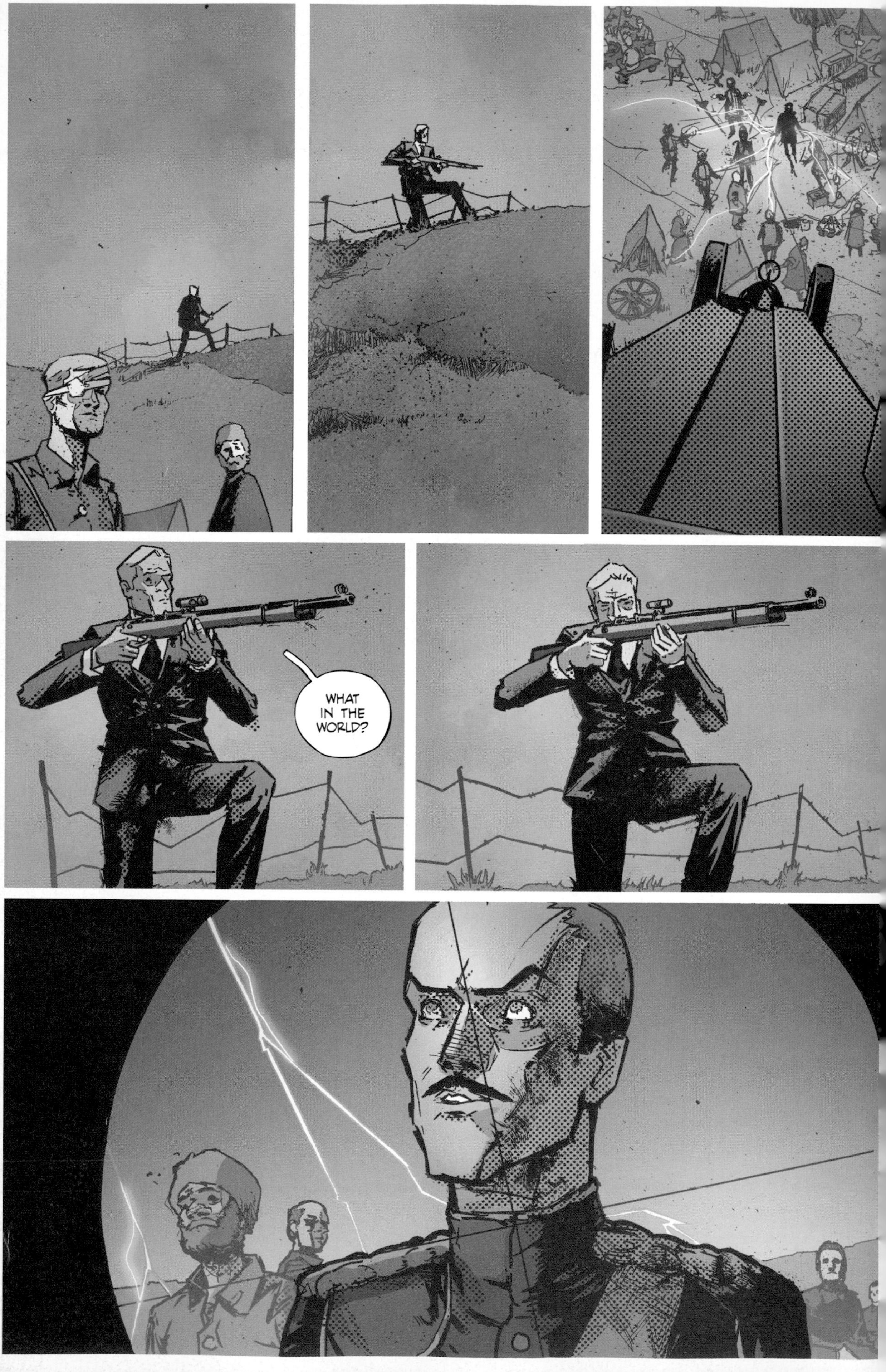
WHAT IN THE WORLD?

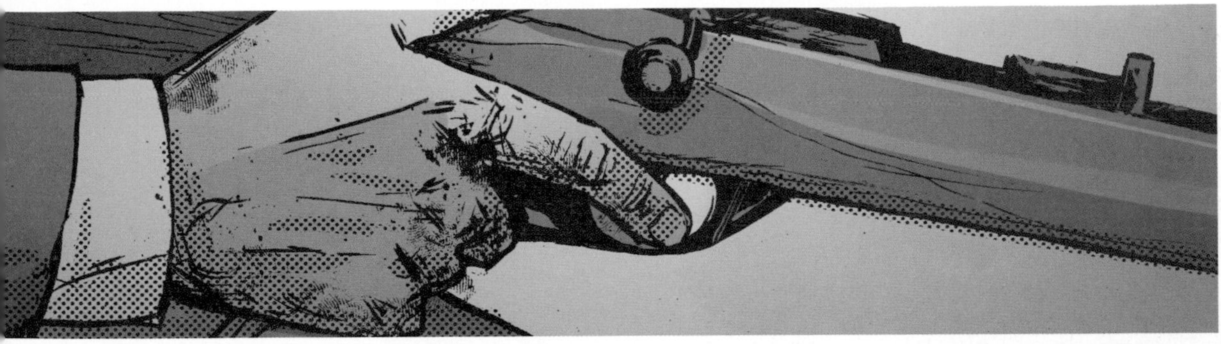

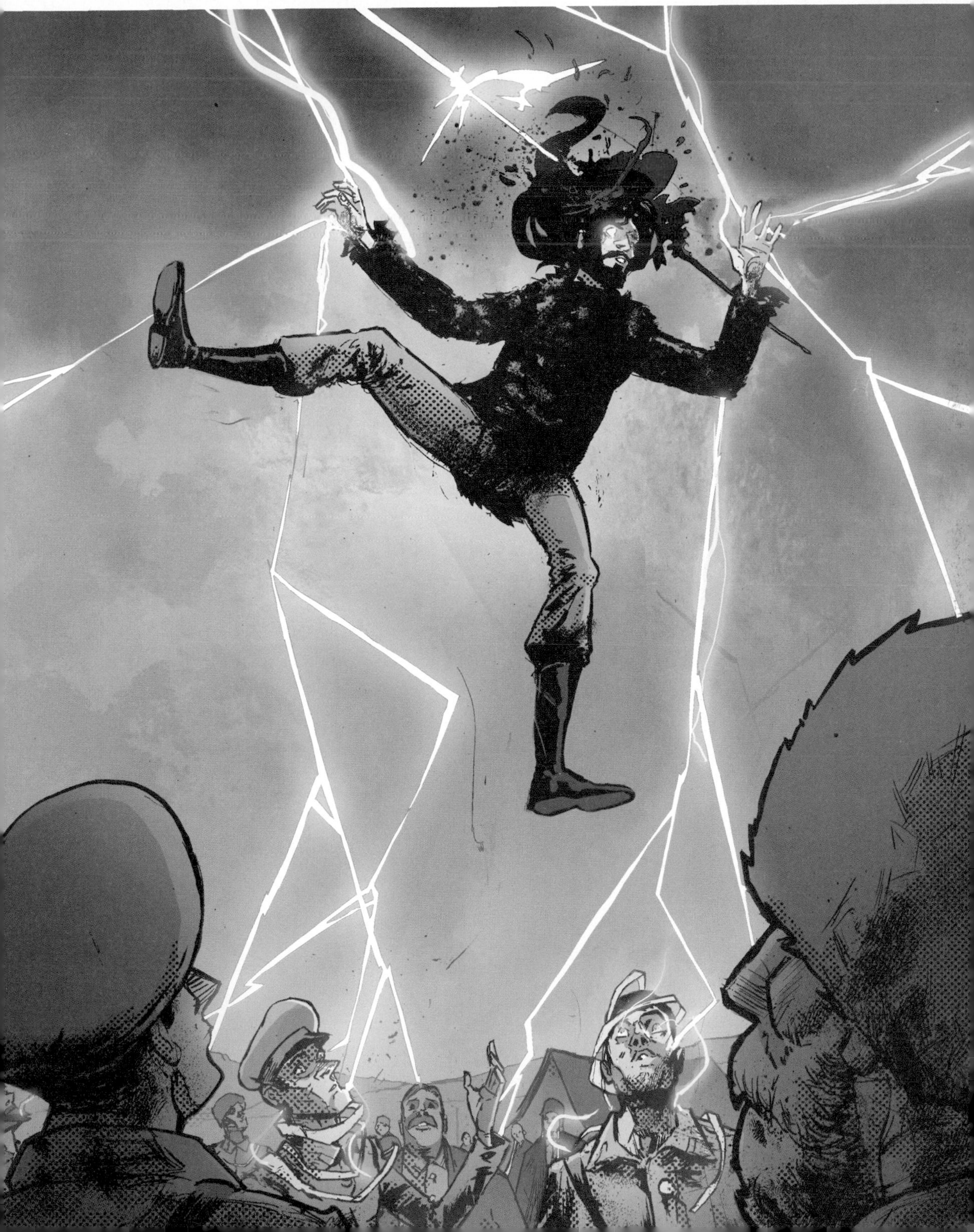

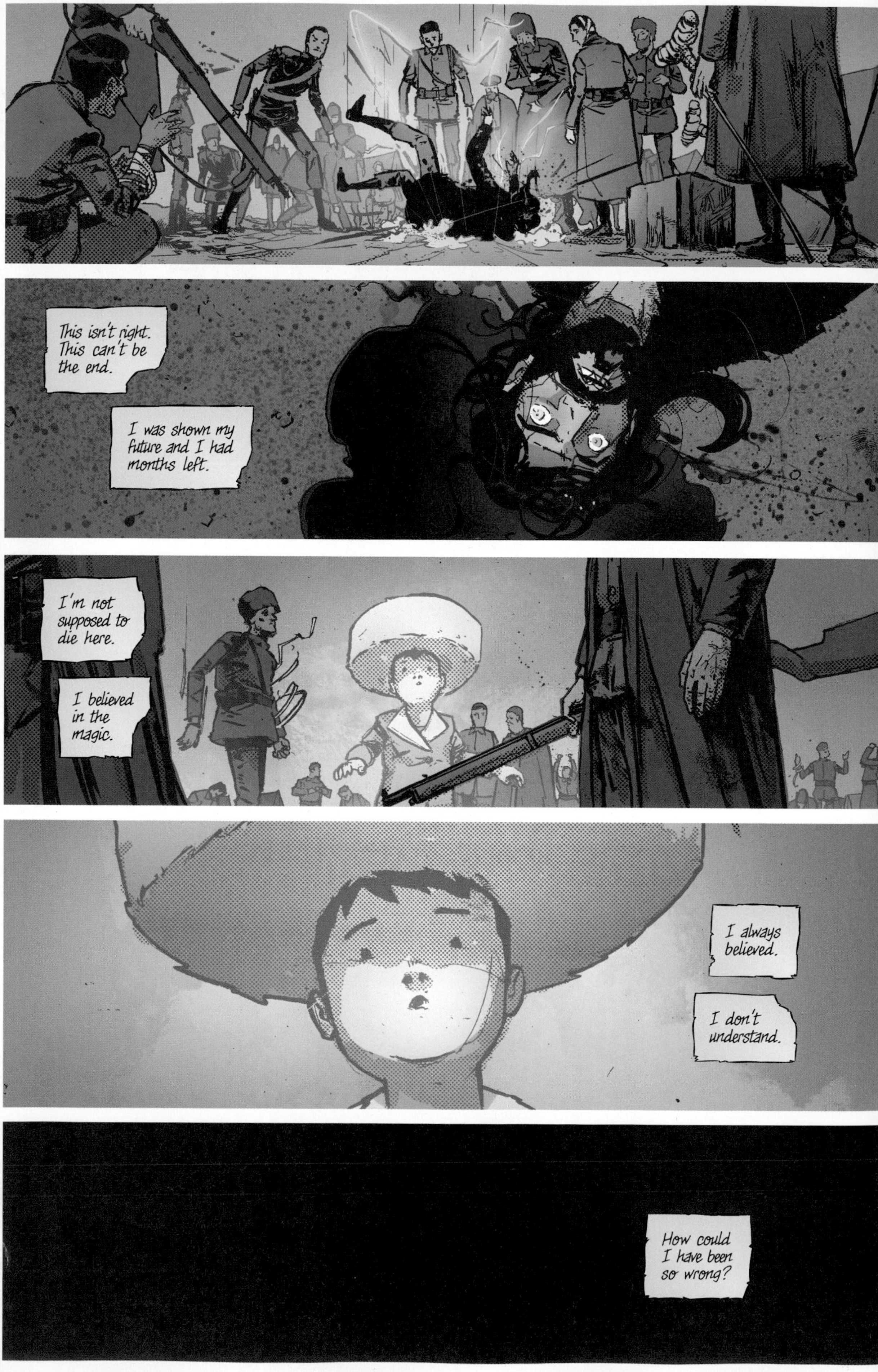
This isn't right. This can't be the end.
I was shown my future and I had months left.
I'm not supposed to die here.
I believed in the magic.
I always believed.
I don't understand.
How could I have been so wrong?

BEHIND THE SCENES
WITH THE STARETS

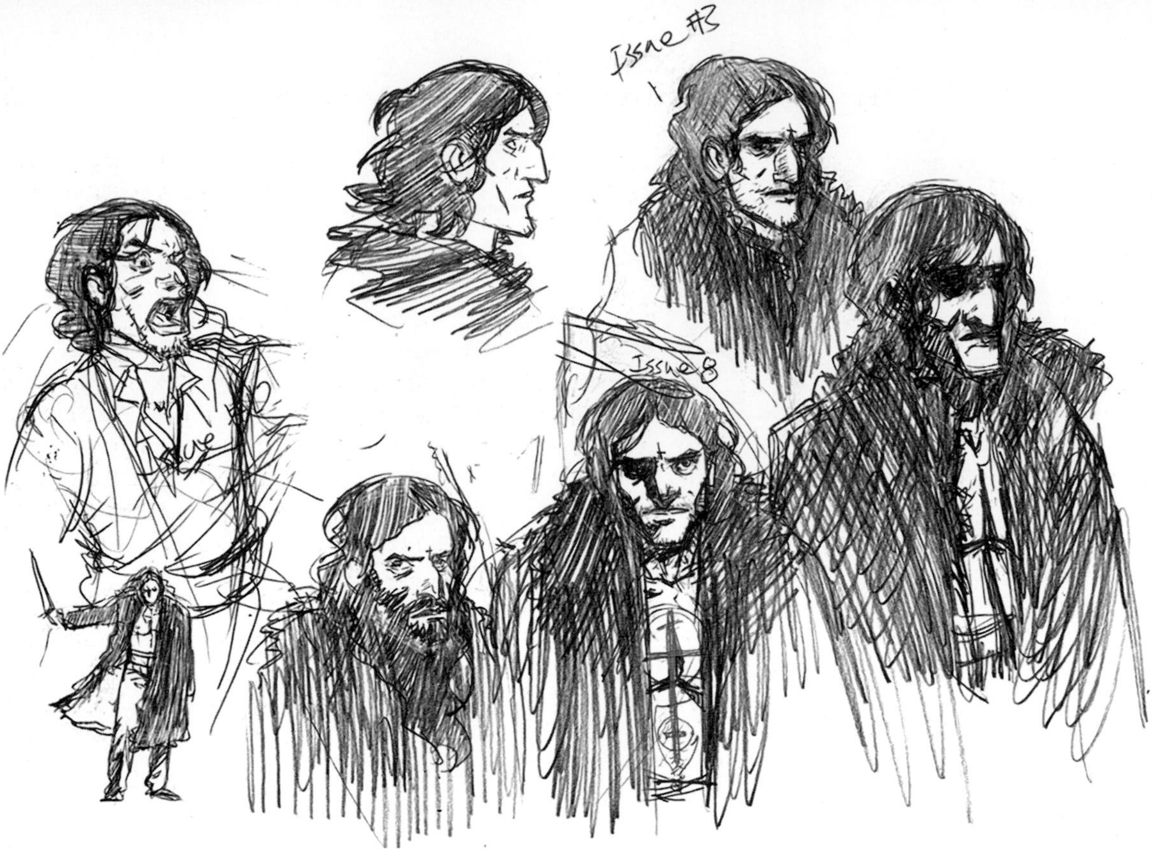
Issue #3
Issue 8

Riley and I decided early in the process of making this book that we wanted to do something different with Rasputin. We didn't want to tell the same "mad monk" story that's already been told dozens of times over. We wanted to pack this with surprises, even for people who were familiar with the actual history of Tsarist Russia.

While I mulled over the structure of the series and wrote the first script, Riley played with the character designs. We wanted Grigori to be younger and handsomer than he really was and Riley spent some time tweaking, making him appear more open and vulnerable. As I recall, the only major change I asked him for was to switch the designs for Rayner and Yusupov.

—Alex Grecian

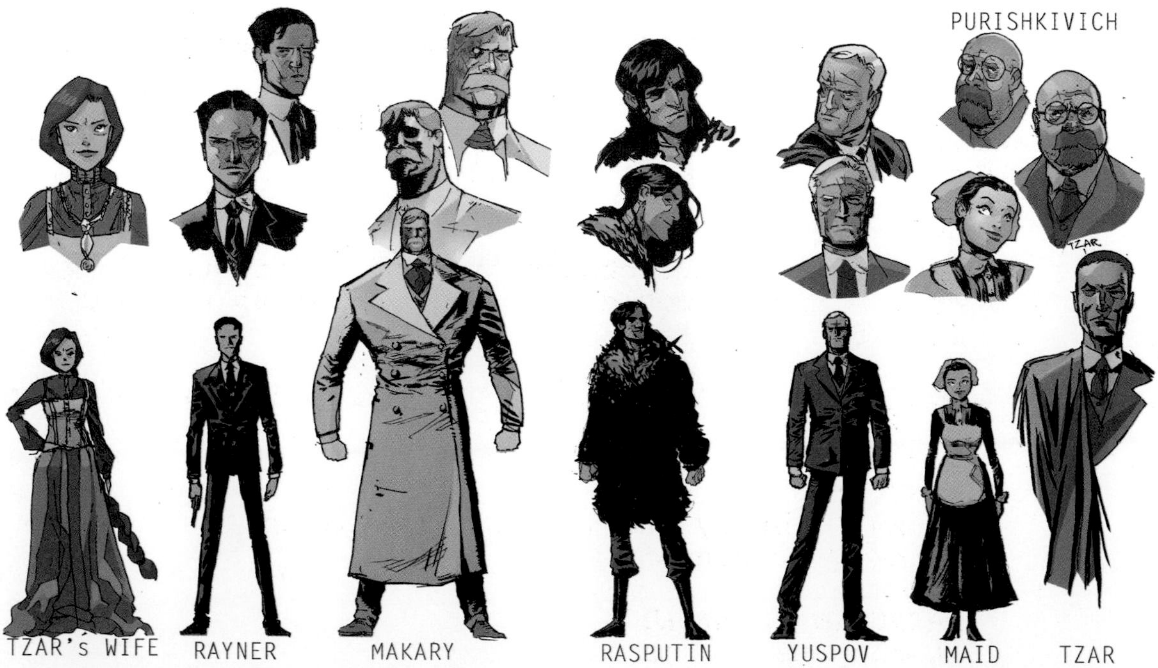
PURISHKIVICH
TZAR's WIFE
RAYNER
MAKARY
RASPUTIN
YUSPOV
MAID
TZAR

RASPUTIN #1
By Alex Grecian for Riley Rossmo

RILEY: I want to treat this a little different than our previous work together, more Mignola-esque atmosphere panels, more freedom for you to draw out the small details that will hopefully bring this thing to life. Anything you're worried about, jump on Skype and we'll talk it out. But as long as the story works, I'll adjust the captions around it.

TOM: The middle portion is largely wordless. I may go in later and add a gasp or SFX, but the majority of lettering, at least for this first issue, will be in the framing sequence. So most of the time when I attribute something to Rasputin, it's actually in a caption box. He's narrating his own story here. I'll indicate when it's a traditional balloon.

IVAN: The middle portion, the flashback, needs to stand out from the framing sequence. I'd like you to color the framing sequence at beginning and end in the vibrant colorful style you used for the Previews story we did. The flashback should be a bit cooler, lots of blues and browns. Don't go sepia, though. Just mute it a little.

Here we go…

PAGE 1 *(6 panels)*

P1: Tight on a glass of wine.

> CAPTION
> *(A different style (maybe borderless?) from the upcoming captions of Rasputin's narration)*
> Petrograd

> RASPUTIN
> Hours after I was born, my mother named me Grigori Efimovich Rasputin.

P2: A tablet drops into the wine from above, splashing against the surface and sinking as it dissolves.

> RASPUTIN
> I would not have chosen that name for myself, but at the time I couldn't hold my head up or feed myself.

P3: Pull back. A maid (KATYA) is picking up the glass on a tray.

> RASPUTIN
> So my identity and my destiny were thrust upon me without my consent.

> RASPUTIN *(cont'd)*
> It happens.

P4: We follow Katya through a kitchen…

        RASPUTIN
        In fact, it happens again and again, to all of
        us. We die according to how we lived and we live
        according to a plan most of us cannot see.

P5: And down a hallway…

        RASPUTIN
        But I can see it. I've always known exactly what
        fate holds in store for me.

P6: And now she's at a door through which we see a banquet
table. Most of the table isn't in view because we're not in
the room yet, but we can see RASPUTIN at the visible head of
the table. Stay tight on him. He's smiling at Katya, at us.
He's haggard-looking. A big bushy beard. We're at the end of
his life.

        RASPUTIN
        For instance, tonight I'm going to be murdered by
        my closest friends in the world.

PAGES 2&3 *(between 1 and 6 panels)*

A double-page-spread. This is tricky to lay out without making it seem static. We talked about it as a Last Supper kinda image, but I think you've got something more dynamic in mind. Katya has entered the room with the wine on a tray. She's heading toward Rasputin, but not there yet. She's sort of off to one side, so she's not in the way. Here, we see the whole table before us, laden with food. Rasputin sits at the head, where we saw him earlier. The other players in our drama are arrayed down the table: Yusupov, Pavlovich, Rayner and Makary. Makary is at the end of the line.

IMPORTANT: RASPUTIN'S DEAD FATHER IS STANDING BEHIND HIM AND WE CAN SEE HIM HERE, BUT HE'S NOT THE FOCUS. It should, in fact, be easy to overlook him.

IVAN: He should be reversed out in the background. I'd like to see a negative effect here.

      RASPUTIN
      These people.

PAGE 4 *(3 panels)*

P1: Katya sets the glass of wine in front of Rasputin. He's touching her arm and smiling.

RASPUTIN *(Not in caption. This is a balloon.)*
Thank, you, Katya.

P2: The wine glass is in the foreground on the table and Rasputin's behind it, looking at it.

RASPUTIN *(Back to captions.)*
I'm quite certain the wine's been poisoned.

P3: He's picked up the glass and is raising it in a toast to his friends around the table.

RASPUTIN *(This one's a balloon too.)*
To your health, my friends.

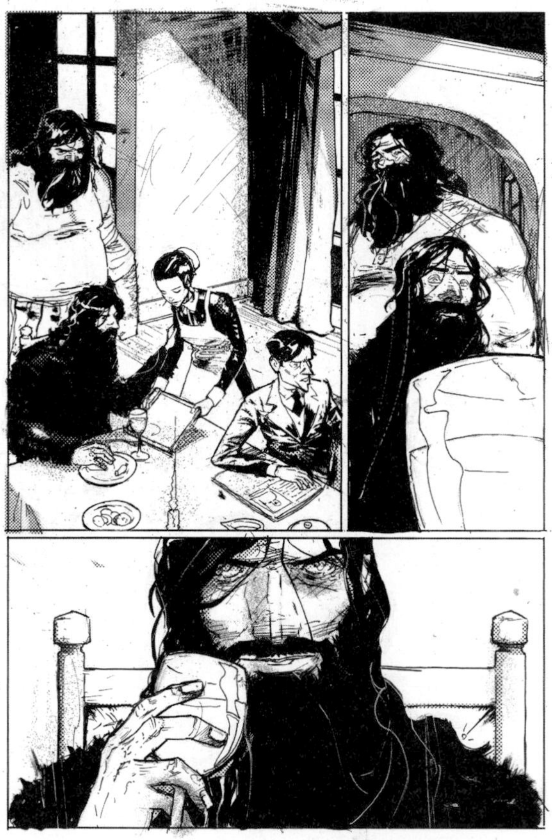

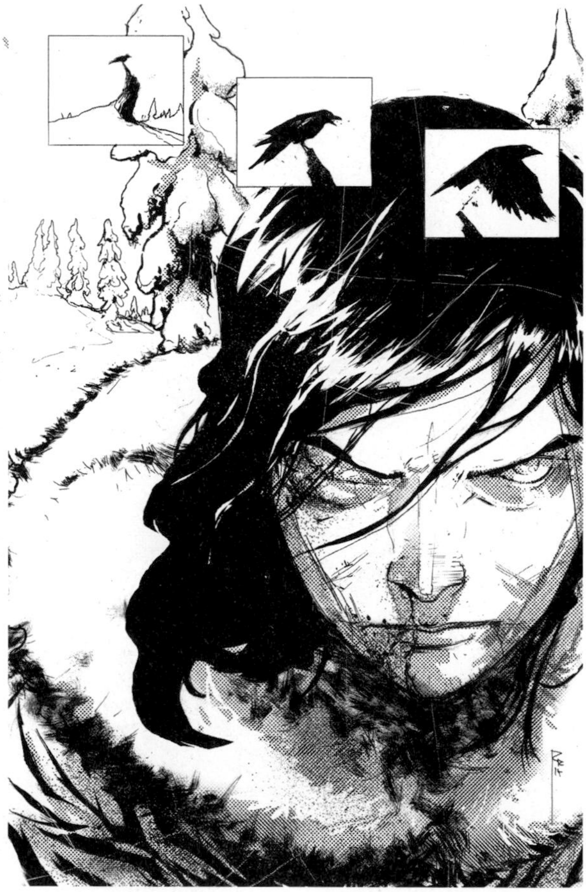

PAGE 5 *(1 panel)*

P1: Tight on Young GRIGORI RASPUTIN's face. He's 12 years old, wearing a parka with a furry hood, looking out at us, his frozen breath visible drifting away from his face. He's got a bruise on his cheek, maybe a black eye, puffy lip, etc. Snow is blowing around him.

RASPUTIN *(Caption)*
And to mine.

PAGES 6&7 *(1 panel)*

Another double splash already?!? Crazy! So this is the first of our establishing spreads. This needs to be designed differently, probably colored differently. The type should be handled differently. We're looking out on a forest, bare trees in a winter landscape. It's snowing, but we don't see any human beings. We're actually behind Little Rasputin, looking out at this environment, but we don't see him here. He's just "off-camera." There's not a living soul in view. It ought to be very painterly.

CAPTION *(no box)*
Siberia

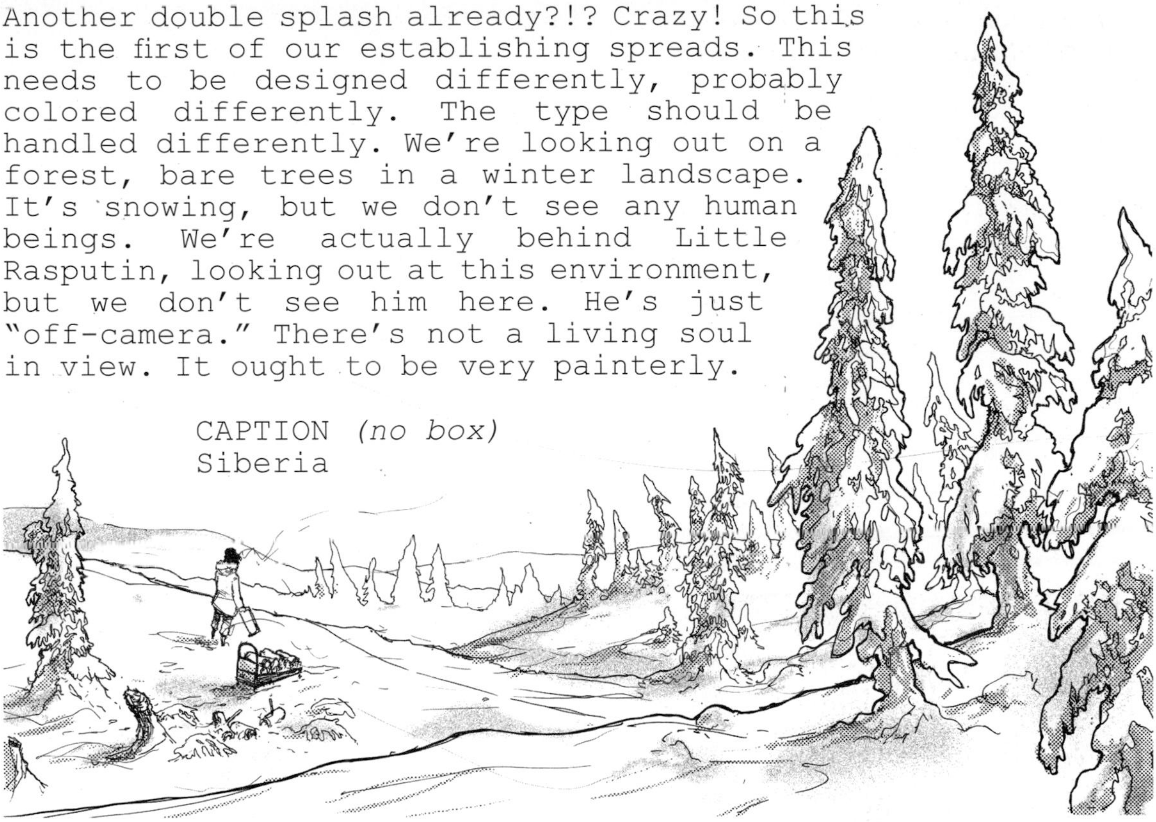

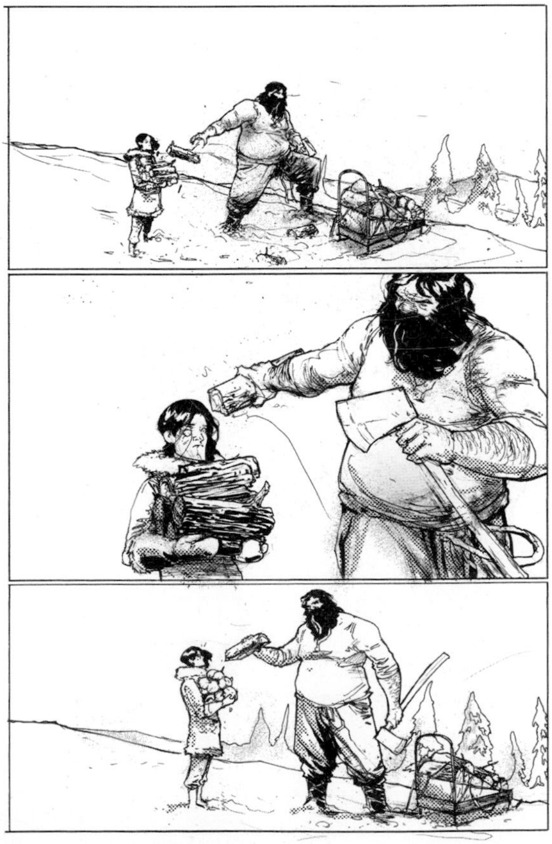

PAGE 8 *(3 panels)*

P1: Young Grigori's arms are out and his father, EFIM RASPUTIN, is stacking firewood on them. Lots of snowy trees in the background.

P2: One log on top of another. Damn. Poor kid.

P3: Pull back a bit. Efim's holding an axe in one hand and using the free hand to keep casually loading his son down. In the background is a sled piled with more wood.

PAGE 9 *(4-6 panels)*

P1: Efim leads the way out of the woods, pulling the sled. Grigori follows behind, staggering under the weight of the firewood.

P2-P6: Let's continue the journey across several panels here, emphasizing how far poor little Grigori has to carry this stuff. Lots of shots of trees, Grigori panting, his breath visible, their footprints in the snow, etc.

PAGE 10 *(6 panels)*

P1: We see a little cabin on the outskirts of a village. Smoke from the chimney. Grigori and Efim are approaching the place, but maybe we don't even see them yet. The village should be in the background, but still a mile or so away.

P2: We're at the cabin. Efim takes a few logs from Grigori and they're leaving the rest in the sled outside the door.

P3: They're entering. Inside, Efim's wife, ANNA is preparing stew at the fireplace.

P4: She looks up, holding out her hand for a log for the fire.

P5: Efim grins, throws it at her.

P6: BAM! It hits her, smack in the shoulder, knocking her back.

PAGE 11 *(4 panels)*

P1: Anna's pissed. She's reaching for the log he threw.

P2: She throws it back...

P3: And it hits him in the face.

P4: Enraged, Efim rushes her.

PAGE 12 *(4 panels)*

P1: Efim takes Anna by the hair. I
see this as very John Buscema, just
reacting savagely.

P2: He hits her. Fist to face.

P3: Grigori rushes at him, tries to
stop him.

P4: Efim throws Grigori easily aside,
barely noticing that he's there.

PAGE 13
(5 panels)

P1: Efim's surveying the room. Anna's
unconscious on the floor and Grigori
crying in the corner. We need to
see, in this and subsequent panels,
that Anna's very badly hurt. Visible
injuries. She might even be dying.

P2: Efim's not happy, but he's resigned
to it. He's gotta keep his family in
order, y'know.

P3: Efim ladles out a bowl of the
stew.

P4: He sits down…

P5: And eats.

PAGE 14 *(4 panels)*

The first three panels should run across
the top of the page, leaving the bulk
of the space for a big fourth panel…

P1: Efim leaves.

P2: Slams the door behind him while
Grigori watches.

P3: Grigori immediately goes to his
mother.

P4: Grigori heals Anna. He's got his
hands on her and there's a big light
display.

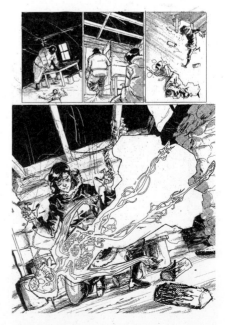

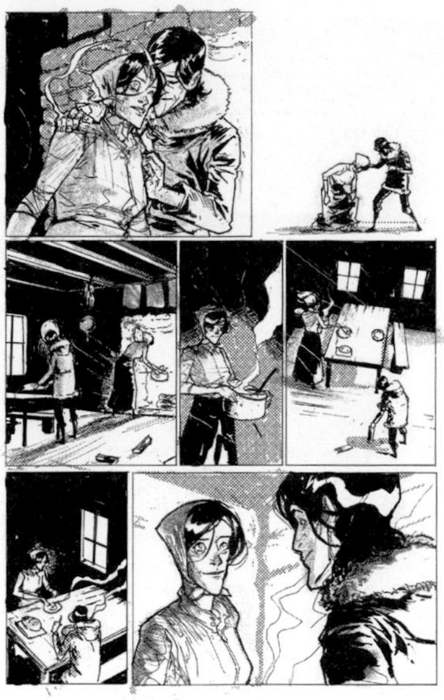

PAGE 15 *(?)*

Spend this page on small panels. Together, Grigori and Anna tidy the place up. She's completely healed, no signs of the injuries Efim dished out. But Grigori hasn't healed himself. He's still messed up. She shows some small act of love, touching his hand or just smiling at him. Whatever you feel works here without it feeling saccharine.

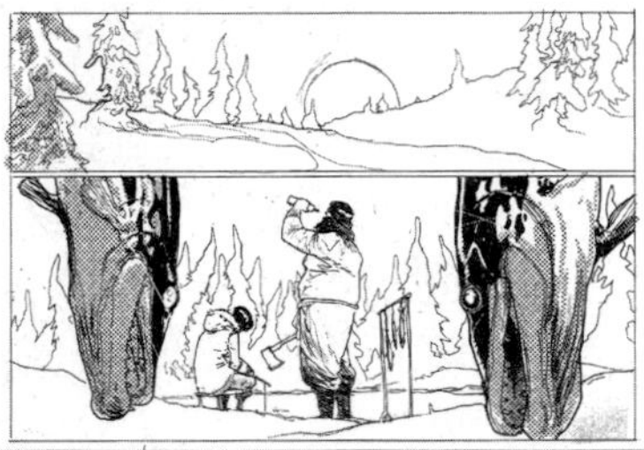

PAGE 16 *(4 panels)*

P1: The sun rises on a new day.

P2: It's still snowy. Grigori and his father are out once more, fishing through a hole in the ice, the deep snowy woods visible on the other side of the river.

P3: The axe is near Efim, ready if he needs it.

P4: And a line of big fish is strung between the trees behind them.

PAGE 17 *(4 panels)*

P1: A bear comes rumbling out of the woods.

P2: It's huge, stands up on its hind legs, challenging the humans.

P3: It swipes at the line of fish…

P4: And Efim reacts, throwing down his pole and grabbing the axe.

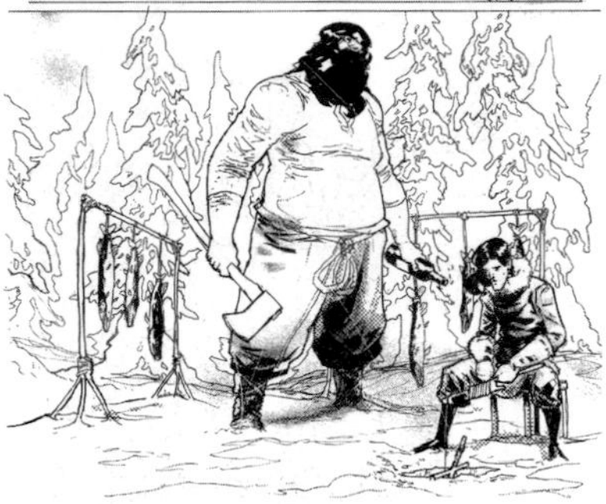

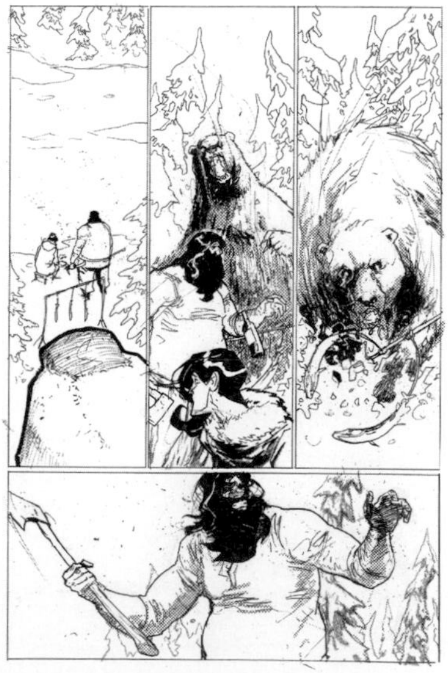

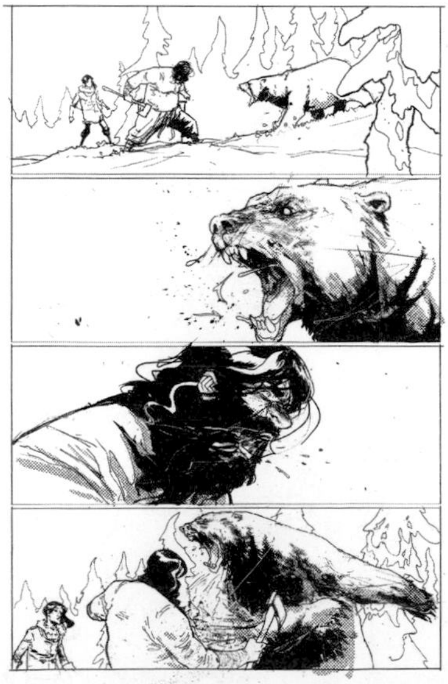

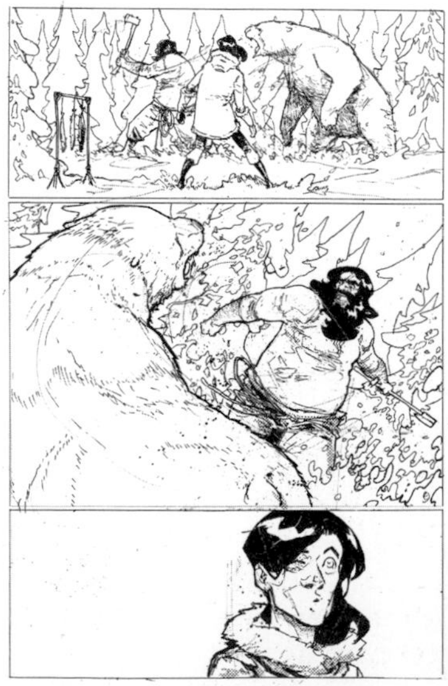

PAGE 18&19 *(spread again)*

P1: Efim rushes at the bear, motioning for Grigori to stay back.

P2: Grigori hides behind a tree, watching.

P3: The bear roars at Efim.

P4: Efim roars back!

P5: And they clash! Just a bare-knuckles fight between an asshole and a bear. Except the bear's got claws and Efim's got an axe.

PAGE 20 *(5 panels)*

P1: The bear claws the crap out of Efim, just rips out his guts.

P2: But Efim buries the axe in the bear's chest…

P3: Pulls it out…

P4: And lodges it in the bear's head.

P5: The bear goes down…

P6: And Efim goes down too. Big flumps of snow as they hit the ground.

PAGE 21 *(5 panels)*

P1: Pull back and show the bear and Efim, lying a few feet from each other in separate pools of blood in the snow.

P2: Grigori finally comes out from behind the tree.

P3: He walks up near his father.

P4: And looks down at Efim's body. (We're looking up from Efim's POV at Grigori.)
P5: Grigori walks around his father. Efim's reaching out to him.

EFIM *(faintly, dying)*
Grigori?

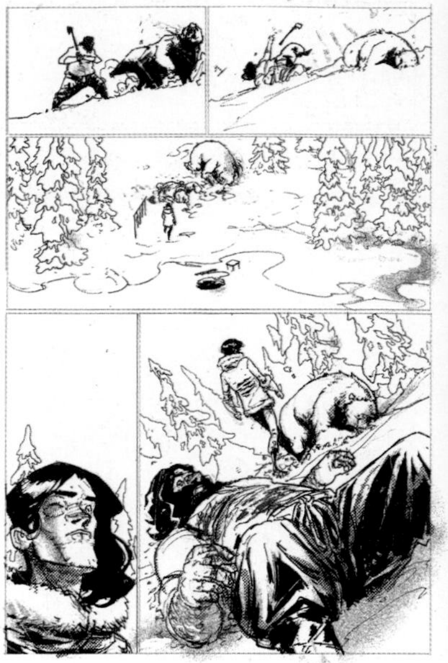

PAGE 22 *(4 panels)*

P1: Grigori kneels beside the bear and puts his hands on it in much the same way he did his mother earlier.

P2: There's the same sort of light display as he heals it.

P3: We're looking past Efim's broken body. Grigori's back is to us, kneeling in the snow looking down at the unmoving bear.

EFIM
(I'd like to use a Stan Sakai-style skull leaving Efim's body as he dies, but if you have a better idea, Tom, I'm all ears.)
{Skull}

P4: The bear wakes up, roaring up and back to life.

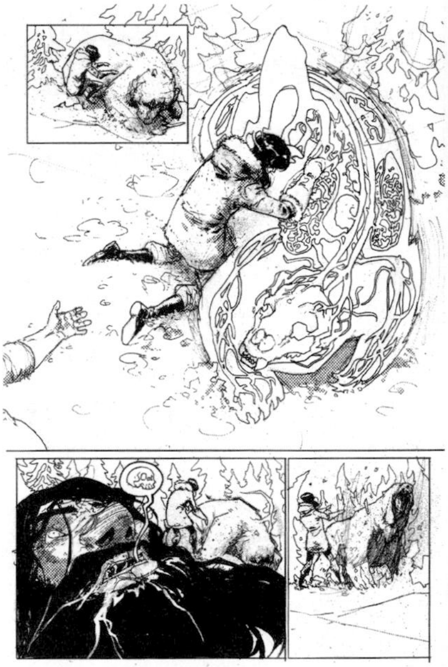

PAGE 23 *(4 panels)*

P1: The bear shakes itself…

P2: It turns its back and rambles back into the woods.

P3: Grigori watches it go.

P4: He looks down at his father's dead body.

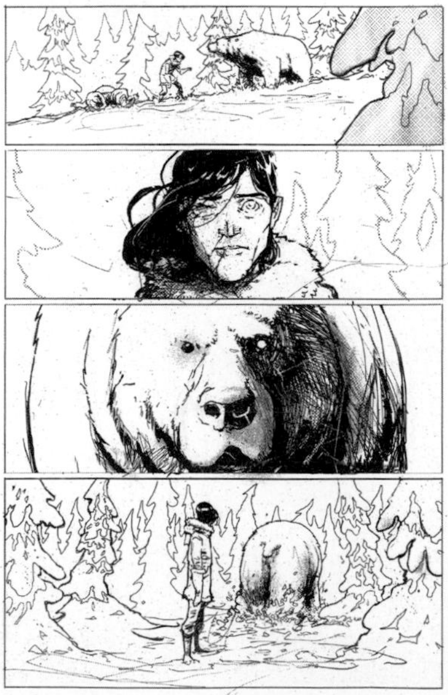

PAGE 24 *(3 panels)*

P1: Grigory picks up the remaining fish that he and Efim caught together.

P2: He walks away into the woods.

P3: Pull back and focus on Efim's corpse.

> RASPUTIN *(Caption)*
> My middle name, Efimovich, means that I am the son of Efim.

> RASPUTIN *(cont'd)*
> Efim Rasputin, my father.

PAGE 25 *(3 panels)*

P1: Back to 1916, back to vibrant color, back to Rasputin, who is still holding that glass of wine up to us. We can clearly see that Efim is now a ghost behind Rasputin.

> RASPUTIN *(Caption)*
> Some people toast to long life or good health.

P2: Grigori sniffs his wine.

> RASPUTIN *(Caption)*
> They pray for spiritual guidance or wish for one last word with lost loved ones…

P3: He hesitates, the others around the table looking at him expectantly. Efim has put his hand on Rasputin's shoulder.

PAGE 26 *(Splash)*

P1: And he takes a big swallow, just downing this glass of poison.

> RASPUTIN *(Caption)*
> Some people have no idea.

BIOGRAPHIES

ALEX GRECIAN is the national bestselling author of THE BLACK COUNTRY, THE DEVIL'S WORKSHOP, THE HARVEST MAN, and THE YARD, the debut novel of Scotland Yard's Murder Squad. He co-created (with Riley Rossmo) the long-running and critically acclaimed graphic novel series PROOF, which NPR named one of the best books of 2009. He lives in the Midwest with his wife and son. Visit his website at alexgrecian.com.

Prolific artist RILEY ROSSMO is responsible for creating or co-creating many critically-acclaimed comic book series including PROOF (with Alex Grecian), BEDLAM, GREEN WAKE, COWBOY NINJA VIKING, and DRUMHELLER. He has worked for Image, Marvel, Valiant, and DC, for which he draws HELLBLAZER. He lives on the Great Canadian Plains with his wife. Visit his website at rileyrossmo.com.

IVAN PLASCENCIA (IVANPLX) has been a professional comic book colorist and graphic designer since 2009. His first work as a color artist was on THE ASTOUNDING WOLF-MAN for Skybound. He has worked for Todd McFarlane Productions, Top Cow, Valiant, Red 5 Comics, and Zenescope, among others. He lives in Mexico City. View his work at ivanplascencia.deviantart.com.

Letterer and designer THOMAS MAUER has worked on a number of Harvey and Eisner Award nominated and winning titles, including the POPGUN anthology series and the webcomic THE GUNS OF SHADOW VALLEY. Among his most recent works are Image Comics' BAD DOG, BANG!TANGO, COPPERHEAD, and UMBRAL, as well as Black Mask Studios' THE D'SCIPLES. He lives in Magdeburg, Germany with his wife and sons. Visit his website at thomasmauer.com.

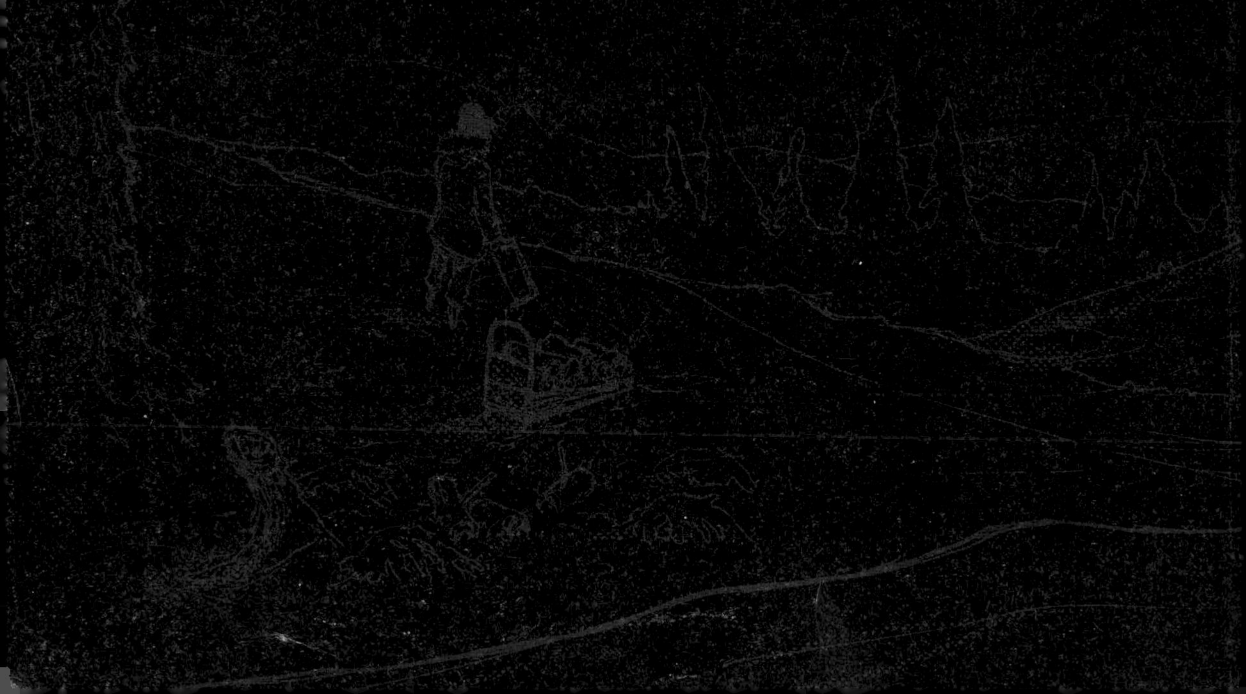